THE
ANAMNESIS

WHITEWASHED BOOK III

ADELAIDE THORNE

For the One who gave me life.

I tried to make this story mine,
but it was Yours all along.

TIMELINE

Year One

Aug. 15 — met EN, Mom + Dad lost memories

Aug. 16 — arrived @ SPO-10

SOCIETY

Year Two

Saecula saeculorum ? ? ?

Feb. 3 — met Chron + Helix @ library

Feb. 10 — left SPO-10, arrived @ academy

Aug. 12 — met Helix @ clubhouse

Oct. 16 — Griffin... watertower w/ ~~Leader~~ Eugene Andrews, brought to lab

Dec. 3 — Left lab, memories wiped, sent back home

Dec. 7 — returned to academy, K Kidnapped

Year Three

May 8 — Goose Swamp mission, arrived @ Durgan's

June 28 — Left Durgan's, arrived at Goose Swamp, found out Chron has EN, got memories back, surrendered to Chron

FREE the Tacemus, save the MTA... but how?

PART I
SAECULA

CHAPTER ONE

THE ECHO JOLTED ME AWAKE.

I hastened upright and received a good-morning pounding in my skull, a headache that doubled as the background clatter continued. Gradually, the noise grew fainter. One last hollow echo before silence resumed. Adrenaline petered out. In the pitch black room, my awareness grew. I understood exactly where I was. And why.

Quickly, I ran my hands over anything I could touch and found four tight walls of stone. Chron's Grifters had stuck me in a cell barely wide enough to stretch in. Damp rock kneaded my feet with every step, until my toes brushed something soft. I knelt to pat the material. The fabric separated into two—a longer piece and something stubbier. I felt along the fabric for several moments before recognition hit. Grifters might've tossed me into a cell wearing only my underwear, but at least they'd thrown some clothes after me.

Dressing in the dark relied solely on instinct and the hope that Grifters designed clothing the same way metas did. I shimmied into what felt like a tunic and pants; then, no longer frigid, continued inspecting the cell. It was longer than wider, and one of the walls leaked a steady trickle that dribbled into a floor crack that spanned the width of the room. Something told me the crack was meant as a makeshift toilet.

I leaned against a dry wall to think. My exhale joined the mist that hung invisible in the air. Each breath in smelled like sour water, and each breath out clouded my nostrils. Pieces of reality dropped like pins.

I'm in Chron's prison.

So are Kara and Ethan.

Freia won't help me.

If I can't figure out how to escape this place, we're all going to die.

The last realization hit like a wallop. It reverberated in my gut and echoed off the walls, a continual clop of misery. *Die. Die. Die.* No—those were footsteps.

Someone was approaching.

I faced the source of the noise—at least I knew where the door was now—and waited, grateful I'd found the clothes before the Grifters arrived. I counted a dozen paces before they halted. Rumbling vibrated in the air and against my feet; it sounded as if someone was driving a drill into my cell. The quake rose in violence, then silenced. Cracks of light framed a rectangular door, enough to spray the tip of my toes with warmth. A series of clicks grated on the door as, presumably, locks unfastened. The door scraped stone and opened.

I stood with fists formed and tried not to squint as light assaulted my unaccustomed eyes. Orange shrouded the silhouette of someone tall, bulky, and dressed in a maroon tunic that reached shin length.

"Do you know where you are?"

I allowed myself a blink. I recognized that voice, and, once my vision adjusted, that gray, pockmarked face. Freia, captain of Chron's guard, consumed the width of the doorway, allowing only snippets of light to glow around her. It was enough for a meta to work with. I saw the tray in her hands, the severity of her expression, and the flame of a wall torch behind her.

"Yes," I said. "Where are my friends?"

"Far. You are alone, Ella Kepler."

How far? I locked gazes with her, finding those black, pitted eyes that used to terrify me. While Durgan's community had fed me scraps, their leader had taught me how to read minds through empathy. Even his own. His lessons remained fresh. After all, I'd seen him just the day before.

Had it really been yesterday? One Grifter lair to the next.

A map of Chron's territory, pieced together from snippets of Freia's memories, unrolled in flashes of scenery. Water led to a boulder, which spread into a hallway. Caverns, a bridge, two guards beside a door, tunnels stacked upon tunnels. I studied the pieces until they made a map.

While I occupied a higher level of the caverns, Chron's other prison for civilians and metas sat below me. Even lower than that was the normal prison for any Grifters who failed in their duties. Classrooms and bedrooms and kitchens and storage closets wove through the caverns, separated by rock and puddles. The Grifters had lived in this national park for a very long time. Civilians suspected nothing. Or maybe they did, and they got cleared. That was why the Tacemus existed. Civilians couldn't report anything if they couldn't remember what they'd witnessed.

A slap against my cheek smarted. Freia stood with one hand raised, like she might strike again. Only seconds had passed since I entered Freia's mind, but she knew what I could do.

"I have endured enough infringement upon my thoughts," she said. "I will not tolerate it from you."

"Freia, why are you here if you have no intention of helping?"

Maybe I should've acted bold, demanded that she keep her word to Helix, but I no longer felt like an angsty teenager, a frustrated adolescent who might spout off sarcasm. I was simply human now, a helpless prisoner who'd just learned to pity the very creatures imprisoning me.

Freia shook the tray she held. "Ledare does not wish you to starve."

"You can help without him knowing. We have a few days before Chron returns from Durgan. We'd be gone—"

"Durgan?" Her twitch rattled the dishes. "What do you know of Durgan?"

I dropped my gaze to the food, which appeared much more appetizing than the meals at my last imprisonment. My stomach gurgled, but I returned to Freia. "Let us go, and I'll tell you whatever you want."

She lifted her chin. "Trickery. I have hid my mind from Ledare for four years. Do not believe I am weak, mind-reader."

"I didn't read you. I know Durgan. I was just with him yesterday."

"The lies of elaks—"

"He lives in stone caves, in a swamp. His wife is Svea, and his oldest son Durgson. His first officer is Jurstin, who betrayed him right before Durgan told me to escape. Chron's headed there now, probably to kill Durgan so Jurstin can rule." The pronouncement soiled my mouth. I wanted Durgan to be alive, but I'd learned the probabilities of battle.

"This is...." Freia caught her falter and shoved strength into her words. "If the harsk is dead, then there is no hope for svags."

Svag—how some Grifters referenced civilians.

"What do civilians have to do with Durgan?" I asked.

"His voice alone defended the weak." She thrust the meal tray into my hands. "Even should you escape with your companions, you cannot succeed. Hela have patiently awaited their dawn. It comes now." She stepped back and flicked a hand. The door stole the light when it shut. Locks refastened and the rumbling resumed as the extra barrier over the door took the last slivers of luminescence.

I wished I could call her back and tell her I'd made it up. *Durgan is fine. Completely alive.* But I couldn't lie. Not to her, and not to myself.

DUSK HAD BEGUN marring the sky when I'd surrendered to Chron's Grifters. Freedom had seemed a short reach away when the captain of the guard presented herself. Freia's name existed on the short list given to me by Helix, Chron's twin sister, who quietly worked against her brother's cruel regime. Helix had assured me the six names would help if Chron ever imprisoned me. Every Grifter on her list was either MIA or dead, all but Freia.

She let Banks escape, argued the inner voice that hoped she'd change her mind. Thoughts of Freia lost to the stronger draw of Banks, Operation Whitewash's agent who'd convinced me to trust him so he could lie to me for more than a year. Despite hating Ethan and hardly knowing Kara, he'd agreed to rescue them in my stead, because Whitewash needed me alive. I still hadn't determined Banks' motives, good or bad, but a liar would always be a liar.

He hasn't lied as much as —

I cut the thought short. As it turned out, very few people in the Metahuman Training Academy had managed to avoid lying to me. Perhaps Banks could hardly be blamed. He'd learned from the best.

Bitterness ground fingers in my skull, but I had no time to sit around dissecting the MTA, Whitewash, Tacemus, and memory loss; Chron would eventually return, and I couldn't be here when he did. The telepathic Grifter had the same ability as me, and though he might not have learned the trick to reading minds, he had two incentives he could use to threaten the answers out of me. Freia refused to help, and this cell had no weaknesses; I was left with nothing but the ability I'd surrendered with. What was the extent of my telepathy?

In the hours after breakfast, I analyzed what I knew about my ability. A few rules seemed constant: mental communication and the potential to see all of a mind—past and present—so long as I made an empathetic connection. Reading Freia had given me the layout of Chron's hideaway, but information wouldn't break me out; only someone else could. Could I try communicating to Freia from here, pester her until she relented? Once, I'd communicated with Ethan through three floors, so it must've been possible to do the same with Freia. Right? Although, no amount of badgering would change her mind. I was better off convincing another guard, though they'd only answer to Freia.

What if I sound like Freia?

As soon as I asked the question, I set to answering it without my usual routine of over-analyzing. I put my fingers to my temples and conjured the sound of Freia's voice.

"There is no hope for svags."

What had that meant?

"Focus, Kepler," I muttered.

Time felt stagnant in my cell. It must've passed as surely as I breathed, but it seemed caught in a black hole that swirled Freia's voice around and sucked out everything else. The faint recollection grew in density until it could be summoned as easily as my own. Freia spoke purposefully, yet a thread of resignation bled through. Maybe she felt as trapped as me.

When footsteps marched in the tunnel outside my cell, I was still mimicking her words. I wouldn't risk attempting this on her; she'd know exactly what I intended. Instead, I'd search her thoughts and figure out which of her guards could be tricked.

The cacophony began as she cleared the obstacles that barred my cell. After the last lock clicked and the door groaned open, I stood ready—but another Grifter had taken Freia's place. This guard levitated the food tray through the entrance, then slammed the door shut without a word. I caught the tray, frozen in surprise. My idea was walking away.

Lunch consisted of fish, berries, and a slice of cheese. Somehow, food tasted worse in the dark. It took several moments of testing the meal with my fingers before I risked nibbling it. While eating, I drafted Plan B.

Freia may have decided it was too risky to deliver my meals; or, she had better things to do. Either way, it wasn't her I needed to fool. Chron wanted me fed, which meant someone would bring me dinner.

When the rumbling began hours later, I assumed a dejected position. Floor bound, with knees to my chest and arms wrapped around them. Light crept on my feet when the door opened.

"Your meal, elak."

Definitely not Freia.

I shrugged. Then, shifting my arms to create a gap, I peeked. The Grifter busied himself with guiding the tray toward the floor. He'd be gone in seconds. I brought Freia's voice to mind and spoke.

You are with the elak?

He paused. The tray hung a foot off the floor.

Bring Ella Kepler to the other elak, I said.

Reading minds required empathy, and it didn't take much to relate to the confused Grifter who heard Freia's voice out of nowhere.

… not until Ledare returns…. He debated with himself.

Your Kapten has spoken, I said. *These are Ledare's orders. He has just given them to me.*

The Grifter wrung his hands, then waved until the tray stilled. "Up, elak," he said.

My heart seemed twenty sizes bigger. "What?"

"Up. Move."

I staggered to my feet and tripped over the tray for good measure. When I edged out of the cell, he moved behind me. Iron fingers gripped my arms, and he pushed.

The cavernous hallway felt like a four-lane street. Freedom distracted me — the change in air and smells. I treasured fresh oxygen as he steered me through the stony passage, guided by bowls of flames that hung from the ceiling, flickering chandeliers as hollow as this lair and with barely enough warmth to pass as a fire.

Holy crap. This is working.

This hall reminded me of the cavern of stalactites and odd rock formations my elementary school had once visited. Only that cavern had colorful spotlights to guide our steps and ropes that kept curious kids from exploring the crevices.

The tunnel ended at an oval door of white stone. Purple and black webbed along the rock like inky stains. The door groaned when the Grifter swept his arm in a motion. He directed me through.

My lips parted. Freia's memories had not done the sight justice.

Beyond the tunnel, Chron's lair forgot it was confined. We stood on a Grifter-made bridge that spanned ahead until the cave swallowed it. The cliffs stretched like a dome, with us like ants passing through. A surge of water gushed continuously from an opening too high into the cavern ceiling for me to spot. It cascaded into the water beneath the bridge. Eroded structures of rock grew out of the pool that glowed orange by the light of the torches set every ten paces.

Five minutes separated my cell from the curve that carried us away from the cavern. The bridge dropped us onto an earthen path that took us to a lower ceiling and tighter walls. The crash of water grew faint. Once the awe dissipated, I felt the tremble of anxiety. What if we ran into Freia? Other Grifters — some in maroon tunics, others in simple linen dresses — passed by. Unlike Durgan's Grifters, who'd jeered and assaulted me, these seemed unmoved by the sight of a meta in transport. Maybe they'd grown used to it.

My guard slowed at a dip in the wall, where more bowl chandeliers dangled. He forced me around the corner, and I nearly rammed into the approaching Grifter.

"Explain yourself, Arvid," came Freia's voice.

I closed my eyes. Despair punched like a cold fist.

Arvid's hold faltered. "This is Ella Kepler, yes?"

"Where are you taking her?"

"The spricka, Kapten. Did you mean otherwise?"

"I have given you no orders to move her."

Arvid fumbled to defend himself, and I tuned him out. My plan had disintegrated as soon as we rounded this corner. Freia was a second away from uncovering my latest ability. Once she marched me back, I'd be under tighter scrutiny than before. This was my one shot; I had to make it count.

As soon as Arvid's grip relinquished, I kicked back—not to hurt, but incapacitate. His legs buckled as I shot past Freia. Grifters were stronger, but metas faster. She reached and touched only the fabric of my shirt, which tore as I bolted past her. The hallway ended, but a gap ran along the side wall. I dashed sideways, into a room illuminated by a claw-like light fixture that hung at eye-level and spread like an angry hand. I blinked past the blaze of fire light and realized I'd met my destination. To my left ran a block of impenetrable cells, with not even a window set in the door. On my other side, standard metal bars formed one cell the length of the room. It contained a single prisoner.

I tore around the light fixture to the huddled figure on the dank, dirty floor. She stared, letting scraps of food fall from her fingers to the clay plate in her lap. When she jerked forward, the plate clattered on the floor. "You can't be here," she whispered.

The words extinguished my frenzy as if someone had snapped and shut me off. I wanted to charge, but I could only stare at the wispy frame of the person who'd once been Kara Watson.

Two navy eyes, sunken in exhaustion, gaped at me. Water pooled around the red rims. Black shadows hung from her eyes and consumed the majority of her sunken cheeks. Her hair fell below her shoulders, tangled and without a trace of curl. Her dress was tattered, covered in layers of dirt and sweat.

I dropped to my knees before her. *Kara,* I mentally said.

A thin wrist slipped between the bars, a hand stretching toward me, as if she didn't care that I was the reason she'd spent the past six months in this miserable condition.

Thunderous footfalls alerted me that this reunion was brief. I zipped back to my feet and spun to the entrance as four Grifters burst through it.

"Stop!" I shouted.

Freia led the charge. Her soldiers carried short spears, though her hands were empty. We faced one another in breathy silence. My pulse couldn't drown out the sound of another heartbeat from behind the barricade of stone that hid him. Rock-steady Ethan, feet away—so close, yet untouchable.

I looked to Freia. *Let me see him, or I'll tell every Grifter here that you work for Durgan.*

Seconds dented the tension. Freia had let Banks escape. She kept me well fed. How much compassion did she have?

Desperation makes us wild, she said, then raised her arm.

I saw the flash of silver before it escaped the barrel. The gun discharged after I ducked and swiveled sideways. Air whistled as another round released. Grifters used guns now, something the MTA had never taught me how to oppose; but dodging these required precision and speed, two things Ethan had ingrained in me. After several shots, Freia emptied her weapon, having hit only stone. I stood near the back now, obscured by the gnarled chandelier.

Freia cocked an arm, and her squadron spread out, after dropping their spears. She wanted to capture, not kill. I eyed the incoming Grifters and knew she finally had me pinned. When their bumpy hands closed in, I leapt against the ceiling like a jumping spider. I landed next to Kara—and before Freia, who had a fist already raised. I reached for Kara and knew I wouldn't make it.

"Ethan! I'm—"

Something hard as a brick met my temple. Vision went foggy just as my legs gave out.

" ...here," I mumbled to the floor as it cradled me. A single word penetrated the haze before unconsciousness reigned.

"Ella!"

It could've been two voices, or one, or none at all.

CHAPTER TWO

CONSCIOUSNESS CAME AS if someone slammed my face into wet concrete. I spluttered, hair streaming, eyes blinking past blurriness.

"You are foolish, Ella Kepler."

That voice belonged to Freia, as did the only heartbeat I heard other than mine. My head and neck throbbed from the blow, and the rest of me felt equally uncomfortable. I lay sprawled in a wooden basin the length of a tub. My armpits ached from how the tub propped me upright. Other than us, the room was empty except for a chair, cushioned and all, most likely stolen from a civilian store.

She stood over me with a dripping bucket and brush, as if she intended to clean the floor with me. Literally. "Helix never informed me of the extent of your power," she said. "You are a weapon."

By "power," she must've meant my ability to mimic her voice. If I hadn't been stuck inside a tub with the knowledge of my failure freshly ingrained, I might've experienced a glimmer of excitement over my potential.

"I don't want to hurt anyone," I said.

"You threatened my life and the lives of my children."

I'd forgotten she had children. The idea stripped away her tough soldier exterior and rebuilt her as an overprotective mother, far more intimidating. Our visual contact lingered enough to creep toward discomfort.

"Yet," she said, and it seemed the grooves in her expression unwound, "I would have done as you have."

Comprehension clogged the otherwise empty room. For the first time, *she* understood *me*.

"Wear this," she said. A scrap of fabric floated over the rim and dropped over my chest.

I inspected the gray dress and frowned. "Why?"

"I cannot wash you through those clothes."

"You're... giving me a bath?"

"No. I am telling you to change your clothing. Then I will bathe you."

For a beat of time, I rejected the idea. Letting someone bathe me—a *Grifter* working for the one imprisoning me—sent a crawl through my stomach. Then I let it go. Maybe this could earn her trust.

After I shimmied into the dress, Freia returned. She spoke little as she scrubbed me with a brush that must've worked great on the stone walls. Raw pain tingled in my nerves, but it felt good, as if she shaved away more than exterior dirt. I closed my eyes and let her attack me like a muddy floor. Awkwardness had extinguished at every forceful stroke. She viewed me as a project, not a body.

"Why are you cleaning me?" I asked.

"None under Ledare's rule can be found unclean. There is a punishment." Her attention moved from my toes to heel, and she scrubbed until she must've sanded down my callouses.

I saw no obvious expression shift across her features, but her thoughts did the speaking.

"You're hoping, if Chron sees that I'm clean, he'll be less inclined to kill me," I said.

"Do not speak his name. Doing so to anyone other than me will ensure he kills you."

"I guess it's our little secret, then."

Her chin lifted. A flicker moved her lips. "You are a strange one." Her voice grew a layer of warmth, a familiarity reserved for a mother reprimanding her children.

"How many children do you have?" I asked.

"We are permitted only two."

"Do you have boys or girls?"

"My sons are Dag and Dahl."

"Good names."

Freia scrubbed a bit softer.

I decided not to speak for a while, afraid I'd prod her into silence. Under the splashes and her distracted concentration, my mind felt the freedom to wander below, where my childhood best friend sat covered in grime while I got spa treatment. A twist started in my gut, and I forced my attention back to Freia.

"My friends could use a bath. Though one of them probably won't let you near him."

She dug the brush; its teeth felt like spikes in my knee. "I will never touch an elak."

"You're touching me."

"You are no elak."

"I can't help how I was raised. Neither can he."

Freia paused. Dribbles of murky water trekked to my calf and slid off. Each plunk made a new ripple. They'd grown into a giant swirl by the time Freia answered.

"I will clean the svag. Not him."

I touched her hand. "Thank you, Freia."

Her gaze rose to mine. My eyes met two mangled holes, but they were hers, and she let them stay on me for a moment.

"Bend your head, little älskling." The room held her voice so it seemed to condense around us.

A quick search of her mind revealed that "älskling" had no formal definition attached to it; just a series of moments with her two sons. I saw their cheeks as she stroked them, their foreheads before she kissed them. An older Hela, his face inches from hers, whispered the word as he drew her close, and she whispered "*My Axel*" in return.

The bath had succeeded in cleaning me but also in gaining her trust. She'd started to care.

Freia, I said, *what do you mean, no hope for svags?*

She scrubbed and scrubbed, though surely my hair was clean enough. *Ledare was not interested in them before*, she said. *Now, he knows he could persecute them with no consequence.*

The MTA will stop him.

Ledare cannot be stopped by one man, Ella Kepler.

One man. She meant Eugene Andrews. *He* had to be stopped first.

But I was just one person, too.

I PULLED MY LEGS tight to my chest and scooted so my back hit the wall. Freia had exchanged my scratchy, burlap clothes for cotton pants, undergarments, and a shirt that fit properly. Fresh clothes and smooth skin felt great, but I would've traded it in a heartbeat for a chance to see Kara again. Since her kidnapping, I'd tortured myself by imagining her in a cell. A few of those images had looked far worse than Kara's actual state, but I'd always told myself *She can't be that bad.* Self-sparing naiveté had encouraged me to believe that Chron had distinguished her from his hated elak enemies. She was only a civilian—surely he would've supplied her with fresh water and three meals a day; a cot to sleep on; blankets for the chill of isolation; access to proper hygiene routines.

No, he'd dumped Kara in a barren cell with only torchlight for company. She'd lost weight, her clothes were filthy, and her complexion fell dangerously close to waxy. Kara needed a way out of this place. Ethan was across the room from her, though blind in his own cell without a window.

Images of them starving, bleeding, and slowly dying harassed my thoughts until they were all I saw. I bolted upright and kicked the wall. There had to be a way out of this cell! A civilian couldn't break free, but a meta could.

The door felt sturdier with every blow, cackling in my face, but I thrashed at the solid stone as if it could wither away to cardboard. Then, when my skin puckered with bruises, I turned to the walls, followed by the floor. The fracture at the back of the cell, the one that ran along the floor, had to go *somewhere.* I could fit both hands in it; my fingers, still crooked from being broken by Jurstin, dangled in cold air, dampened by the constant trickle from the wall above it. I clawed at the hole until my fingernails tore.

"Stupid mountain!" I yelled. Some metas had extra abilities. I was telepathic, Agent Chang could move animate matter; why couldn't—

"Ella?"

My heart received a jolt so fierce, it felt like someone had reached in and pinched it. I kept frozen and replayed the sound. I must've imagined it.

"Can you hear me?"

Okay, that was real. Ghostly and faint, but real.

I stuck my face toward the crack. "Ethan?" I called, hearing his name reverberate all the way down.

"Yes." His voice echoed upward from whatever space lay between us. "Ella, you're... here." It could've been the distortion of the cave walls, but his voice sounded choppy. Strained. "Are you hurt?"

I fought the urge to start cheering and crying simultaneously; my voice cracked as I answered, "I'm fine, I'm fine." I lay on my stomach, as close to the crack as I could get, wishing I could squeeze through it. "Are you?"

"No."

"That's... good." The last word fell out as a whisper.

"Ella?"

"I'm here," I called.

"Don't stop talking."

"Okay." I swallowed. "Can Kara hear me, too?"

"I'll ask." He went quiet. If he asked, I couldn't hear. After a moment, he said, "No, she's out of range."

"Have you been with each other the whole time?"

"Separate cells, but yes."

"And you're able to talk?" I said.

"Hardly anyone monitors this area."

"Good. I'm glad neither of you are alone."

"She's all right, Ella," he said.

I nodded. Pain wrapped around my throat and sealed it tight, but the vice around my heart hurt worse.

"Ella? You need to keep talking. I need to know you're there."

I coughed into my shoulder before moving my mouth back to the gap. "I'm sorry, I'm...."

"This isn't your fault. I've told you. Kara doesn't blame you."

"I had a plan, Ethan, but it didn't work. I don't know how to save you." Anguish scrabbled for escape; I gripped the crack and smooshed my forehead against stone. "I *have* to fix this. I'm trying."

"Stop putting so much pressure on yourself. You...." Though distance and the mountain's structure oscillated his voice, I heard the frustration in it. Ethan was patient, but our situation had a way of robbing us.

He's also frustrated, a little voice nagged, the one I'd come to associate with EN, *because you don't remember him*.

I shut my eyes. Of course I wanted to tell him. More than anything. Ethan had waited long enough for me to regain my memories. Could I tell him here, with my face stuck in what was probably a toilet, with a mountain between us and danger at our heels?

"She knows how sorry you are," he said. "She heard you."

I blinked, forgetting my conflict. "Heard me?"

"You told me about your... internal conversations with Kara."

"Yeah?"

"Somehow, she heard those."

I frowned into the gap until a *Whoa!* shivered through me. Months ago, I'd clued Ethan in to my odd habit of holding imaginary conversations with Kara. From my frustrations with Lydia Burnette to my feelings for Ethan, Kara had sat invisibly on the receiving end. She'd *heard* me? That meant my telepathy could span not just floors, but across state lines, from Georgia to South Carolina.

"I've heard you before," he continued. "I thought I was imagining it. Dozens of times, even last—" He stopped himself.

Last year. Before I forgot him.

"Ethan?"

"Kara and I think you're a telepath. That's why these Grifters want you."

"I—"

Thuds began in the hallway outside my cell. They fell in sync, the clack of multiple footsteps.

"Someone's coming," I called.

He hushed.

These footfalls sounded nothing like Freia's. At least two Grifters neared, then continued past, beyond my cell to the area that Freia's map told me belonged to Chron alone. A chain rattled, and fabric flapped against air. So far, only Freia and one other guard had passed through this corridor. They must've had work to do in Chron's quarters.

The footsteps grew fainter, then stopped. A slam echoed. No noise followed after. The Grifters were likely out of earshot.

"All right, they're gone," I told Ethan.

"We'll discuss this later. What's your layout?" he asked, and I nodded.

We'd spent valuable time reminiscing; we needed to plan our escape.

"From what I've learned," I said, "I'm attached to Chron's private quarters. You and Kara are in the prison reserved for elaks and svags. I mean, metas and civilians. Two guards man the entrance; there's only one way in. Outside, there are scouts. Inside, there are dozens of Grifters, so we can't meet up without being seen."

"So we need low coverage inside and out. But we have no gear, and I'm not in top form."

"I can use my telepathy," I said. "You guys were right, Ethan. I'm still trying to figure it out, but... I'm kind of like the Tacemus."

Ethan had plenty of questions about that. The frustrating part was, he'd already learned this before One wiped his mind at SPO-10. But I'd picked up an extra skill since then.

"Could you mimic the voice again?" he asked after I explained.

"I don't know if it would work twice." I squeezed my eyes shut and waited for an idea to burst into existence. Freia had probably told her guards not to listen if they heard her disembodied voice. Who else would the guards obey?

Chron.

"I could try *his* voice. He's gone, but I think he can communicate long-distance."

"If he's gone, then this is our best window."

"Okay. Let me prac—"

New footsteps sounded, these heavy and fast.

"Hold on. Someone else." I stilled, listening to the Grifter zip past my cell and continue toward Chron's quarters. Something was going on. These might've been servants, preparing his room for his arrival. That meant our window was shrinking while we planned.

The Grifter stopped, footsteps beyond my door. Half a minute passed while Ethan and I kept a silent vigil. When the footsteps reversed in my direction, they'd picked up another pair. The first set whizzed by and kept going. The second paused right outside my cell. Thunder began to grumble as the blockade over my door moved. During the commotion, I called to Ethan.

"Company here. Keep listening."

I stood above the crack and faced the door. Either Freia or another Grifter must've brought a meal. Which one was it now? I'd lost track of time.

Metal finished grinding, and the door groaned open. The Grifter's frame blocked most of the torchlight that washed the stone around my cell, but I saw what the light hit—and didn't hit. A spasm of dread gripped my heart like icy fingers. I would recognize that armless frame in any setting.

I warned you, Chron spoke. *You will watch them bleed, Ella Kepler.*

CHAPTER THREE

AS IF REACTING TO the familiarity, a wire in my brain pulsed. Chron stood, chest heaving, in a black tunic that neared his shins. When our gazes met, time got stuck. A year earlier, our minds had connected like magnets. No way could we look at each other without our brains leaping to join again. Yet, nothing happened. The split-second gaze ended when Chron stepped forward, reached his single arm toward me, and squeezed my face so hard that my cheeks touched inside my mouth.

You were elusive, but no longer. His fingers dug so roughly that talking would've been impossible.

Let them go, Chron. Please.

Misshapen flesh jerked with a smile. *You are pleading? I have extinguished your fire.*

I'm not here to fight. I'll lose. You've captured me, Chron. You don't need them anymore.

No. I do not. But you do. The hope of their safety will keep you pliable until I am finished with you. Then, I will be merciful. You can die in one another's arms.

Looking at Chron, I knew neither fear nor anger. A chunk of me, that anxious bit, had gone somewhere else. My response was purely practical. I jabbed the pressure points on his palm. With effort, I unhinged his hold. Had he been a lesser Grifter, he would've stumbled.

"You're forgetting something, Chron," I said, loud enough for Ethan. "I'm more powerful than you. Isn't that why I'm here? I can read minds consistently. You can't."

Do not lie to me. You suffer the same limitations.

"Yeah, I did, a year ago when we met. But not anymore. I've learned how it works. And I've learned that I can communicate through walls, to every Grifter living here who thinks their Ledare is a fully fledged mind-reader. How do you think they'll treat you once they realize you're a fake?" The idea spilled as it came to me. I had no idea whether it was a bluff, nor what Chron believed. My mental efforts, diverted to blocking Chron from my head, preventing me from reading him. Durgan had taught me how to shield my thoughts; I'd been building that wall since I arrived. There was a chance Chron's telepathy could knock it down, but for now, I clung to hope.

His shoulder twitched. *Any attempted contact with Hela will result in a slow death for Kara Watson.*

"But the damage will have been done. All it takes is a single sentence from me."

They would not trust an elak.

"Some would. You have to know not everyone trusts you. I've realized that even without reading all the minds here."

He swung as the last syllable passed my lips. I ducked, but I had little space to hide. Chron gripped my wrist and wrenched me forward, forcing me into a hunch at the doorway. Pain shimmied along my nerves as he pushed my hand back farther than it should go. He kept it awkwardly angled as he crouched before me to breathe words in my face.

"I do not know pain, but I have often imagined how it might feel." His voice, even murmured, raked the air. "An elak knows to build tolerance, but what does pain do to a svag? A weak svag, fragile, slipping from this world. Kara Watson will feel this pain infinitely more than you. Does this hurt you, Ella Kepler? It will hurt her more. She will weep. She will beg me to relent, but I will not. I will not stop until—"

"Helix," I whispered.

Chron's mouth gaped. His hold lessened.

"We all have our weak points, Chron. Yours is love, just like the rest of us."

What do you know of my sister? he demanded.

"Let my friends go."

He inspected me. Trembling began in his torso and caused my arm to waver. He was trying to read me. Trying and failing.

Chron pulled me upright. I'd hardly registered the relief in my wrist when he grabbed the back of my neck and shoved me through the hallway. I wanted to shout Ethan's name but refused to give Chron any more ammunition.

He forced me along the hallway of cold, dank stone. Eight chandeliers accompanied us. I let Chron maneuver me like a sack, only half present on the trip.

Ethan. I hope you can hear me. Chron is back.

I saw a flash of a richly furnished room, decked out with maroon tapestries and upholstered chairs—and a single, dirty occupant who contrasted the luxury. Chron set me before a Grifter who stood in chains. My eyes glued to his cloak, torn and dirty, but with a mural of colors visible beneath the wear.

Mingled elation and fear scurried my pulse. I knew that cloak. I knew who wore it.

Chron angled me upright, so the Grifter in the multicolored cloak would have a full view. "Tell me, harsk," Chron said, "how your ward knows of my sister."

The Hela king appraised Chron. Durgan had always carried himself with the knowledge of his rank, and he held the same posture now, a wall of composure to contradict the shaking in Chron's fingers. Cuts marred Durgan's skin, and iron bound his wrists close to his chest in a forced prayer; yet, he looked as if he could have flicked his hands to cast his imprisonments free. This could have been his lair and Chron his prisoner.

Durgan's gaze hit mine without flinching.

You're alive, I said.

Keep silent, he answered. His chin lifted, revealing a gash along his throat. "Her mind is a more willing subject," he spoke in the powerful voice I'd heard every day for seven weeks. "Read her yourself, Chron, and leave a prisoner to his prison."

Chron squeezed the base of my head so hard, I worried he would split my neck. "Your commands are empty here, harsk. You lack the authority."

"My authority can only be revoked by a *higher* authority—which you, Chron, are not."

"You suggest that you continue to wield power when your own subjects have denounced you?"

"Yes."

The laugh that twisted in Chron's chest agitated his grip on me. "Your misguided confidence is why you stand before me wearing chains and not your crown."

"My crown remains, Chron, but your power does not."

I respected Durgan's composure, but part of me wanted to beg him to stop antagonizing the Grifter whose fingers were a twitch away from snapping my neck.

Chron shook and lifted me higher before Durgan's sight. "What have you told Ella Kepler about Helix?"

"You can threaten me with nothing else, Chron."

"I can kill this elak!"

"Yes, you can."

Saliva built in the back of my throat. In the Grifters' silence, my pulse stuck out like a patterned knock. Somehow, it didn't jump, as if keeping me steady enough to focus on my sole thought: *I'm about to die.* I stared at Durgan, solid as a statue, then let my eyes close.

Patience, Ella Kepler. Durgan's voice slipped into my thoughts like it had already been there. "You do not need Ella Kepler," he said aloud. "I can answer in her stead. In return, you will release her and any other you have unjustly captured."

You told me it's too dangerous for Chron to learn, I said.

I will ensure he does not.

"You make foolhardy assumptions, harsk," Chron said.

"I have spoken with Helix. It is no assumption."

Chron's hand tightened, then he threw me downward. The floor rose to my face, but I caught myself before smashing stone and rolled out of Chron's footstep. I lay on my back, an unnoticed observer as Chron set his face inches from Durgan's.

"You approached my sister?" he said, close to a whisper.

"Your sister approached *me*. There is much you do not observe in your own flesh, Chron. While you wreak hate, Helix hunts for peace. She informed me of your inability to—"

"Lies!" Chron's palm lashed, catching a fold of Durgan's cloak. The material ripped as Durgan stumbled into the space behind him. He steadied himself before he hit the wall, but the garment had been stripped from him, a mural hanging from Chron's shaking fingers. Chron struck again, whipping the cloak across Durgan's face. Durgan absorbed every whip, uttering nothing, not until Chron relented. The fabric fell to the floor. "*A rainbow disguises ugliness,*" Durgan had told me. Now, he was exposed.

When Durgan straightened, he resumed his former calm as if nothing had occurred. "Read me, and you will find otherwise."

Chron's frame tremored. I thought Durgan had finally spoken his last, that right there I would witness murder—and I knew I would not lay helpless. First came the assessment, because metas did not enter a fight blind. Chron couldn't see me; a heel to the back curves of his knees would topple him. I eased onto my elbows and scooted on the stone.

You will do nothing, Ella Kepler. Durgan's attention had not shifted from Chron, yet somehow he knew. *This fight is not yours.*

I can—

You will do nothing.

I gritted my teeth. Durgan expected me to follow his commands just as any other Grifter had. But this was a matter of life and death, a situation within my potential to fix. I couldn't do nothing.

The thump of footfalls echoed from behind. I whipped my head around. If Chron had summoned another guard....

A slug of anguish ripped me open. A hooded Grifter marched into Chron's quarters, half-dragging a slim body whose head spilled blonde hair no longer curly.

"Kara!" Forgetting that three Grifters monitored me, I rose off the floor and darted to her. The guard made no move to stop me from wrenching Kara free. She felt light enough for wind to carry away.

Kara gripped my upper arms. Her wide eyes portrayed that she knew, same as me, how this scene would end.

"I said both of them," came Chron's voice.

No. Not Ethan too. I knew what Chron intended, and I knew that I'd cave.

The guard raised an arm. I saw the gun right before it discharged. I doubled over Kara, shielding her, but the shot had only one target. The gun made a light *plink*, and a body behind me slumped heavily against the floor.

"For Axel," the guard spoke, voice thick with emotion. She tugged her hood down.

Durgan's soft word filled the room like cotton expanding. "Freia."

She dropped to one knee. "I am yours to command, Onkel," she said, then rose to unclasp his chains.

Uncle?

A sliver of warmth cracked through my tight chest. Freia wouldn't help me, but she'd save her king.

Chron's body sprawled on the earthen floor. Not dead; his chest rose, and his heart still thumped. A dart stuck from his neck. Durgan knelt beside him, a palm over Chron's heart.

"When he awakes, he will suspect who did this," Durgan murmured.

"He will not awaken." Freia marched to Chron, dropped, and wrapped her fingers around his throat.

"Freia." Durgan lay a hand on her arm, which tremored, radiating strength. "This is not the way," he said softly.

"He is a murderer. A tyrant. He deserves death."

"Yes. But you are not his judge. He must be tried, and we must flee." He slid his hand over hers and pulled, firmly. Perhaps he wielded more strength. Perhaps Freia surrendered. Her arm retracted, and she dropped her chin. Durgan rested his head on hers. They probably continued their conversation telepathically.

"Ella."

The scratchy voice pulled me back to Kara. We hunched on the floor, my frame a support for her thin one. Emotion lodged in my throat, and I said nothing.

My hands met hers. She shook, I shook. We held each other in a suspended moment. Finally, Kara. I wished we had another six months right now to make up for stolen time; but, more than relief, I felt the clutch of diminishing seconds. Chron would wake up eventually. Behind us, Freia and Durgan discussed an escape. They couldn't wait for Kara and me to finish reuniting.

I propped Kara straight by her shoulders. "You're going to be okay, Kar, but we need to hurry."

"What about...?" Her arm rose, not in time to block the cough that tore out of her chest. The heaving continued, slick and violent. Mid-gasp, she pushed out, "What about Ethan?"

"I'm going to save him. First, you need to stand." I spoke calmly, keeping every fearful doubt inside. Kara was sick. *Too* sick. She could hardly support herself.

I caught her elbows. I remembered crushing my tin cup by accident, splintering a door, hitting something hard enough to break it. My fingers applied a breath of pressure to Kara when I lifted her.

Fingers squeezed my shoulder. Durgan's hand felt familiar. "Quickly, Ella Kepler," he said.

"There's a way out of here?"

"Few know of this passage." Durgan gestured a section of pitted rock along the wall of Chron's quarters.

"What about the elak?" I said to Freia.

She finished dragging Chron to the chair that scraped stone when she heaved him into it. She exhaled and faced me. "I could only bring one. He remains in his cell."

I tried thinking quickly, aware that Chron could wake at any moment; more guards could discover us; Freia and Durgan wouldn't wait forever.

Thanks to the map in Freia's head, I knew the ins and outs of this lair. I knew exactly where Ethan's cell was and the path that would take us from there to the exit. It stretched a mile of Grifter-strewn territory, but if any meta could outfight a Grifter, it was Ethan.

He's weakened, I thought. *And it won't be just one Grifter.*

I shut my eyes against the doubt. Durgan's fingers pulsed on my shoulder. *Can you take Kara with you?* I asked him. *Keep her safe?*

Who will keep you safe?

Can you do it, Durgan?

His grip faltered. *Look at me, Ella Kepler.*

I shook my head. *I won't leave him here to die alone.*

A scaly pressure met my cheek. I heard Kara's rattled gasp as Durgan tilted my chin toward him. *Yes,* he said. *I will keep her safe.*

I looked into the two gouged pits that concealed Durgan's gaze. A Grifter had never seemed more whole. I clasped his hand. *Thank you.*

Freia, who'd spent the minute loosening a boulder from the wall's bumpy face, settled by Durgan. She had broad shoulders and an unwavering spirit, but her air seemed childlike compared to Durgan's. "You have no more time, my harsk." She gestured toward a dim hole now revealed in the wall. Beyond that, darkness sprawled.

Durgan patted my cheek, then dropped his arm. "Give her your weapon and cloak," he told Freia. "Leave the hood high, Ella Kepler. It is a weak disguise, but it may succeed."

Freia unfastened the gun from her waistband. It weighed about a pound, with a slim, long nose like an old-fashioned revolver.

"Three shots remain," she said. "The serum lasts half an hour. But I fear you will encounter more difficulty with the elak. He knows I took the svag, and he will not willingly leave without her. He is a stubborn one."

She had a point. Ethan would take off running if I told him Kara was in the care of Grifters. It would be easy to lie, say some MTA agents rescued her. He'd believe whatever I said. "I'll just tell him… " I started. Tell him what? I never wanted to deceive Ethan again.

"You must never lie, Ella Kepler," Durgan said. "However, not every fact need be divulged. There is no crime in practicing prudence."

No crime. I couldn't lie to Ethan, but I didn't have to tell him everything, either. Not if telling him the truth would get us all killed.

Kara suddenly tugged at my wrist. Her expression read *Why are you chatting with Grifters?* and the same thought echoed in her mind.

"I have to get Ethan," I told her. "You're going to go with Freia and Durgan. They'll help you. They're not like the other Grifters."

"Durgan." His name seemed stuck to her lips. *I know that name,* she thought.

If she'd been on the receiving end of my imaginary conversations, Kara would recognize more than Durgan. Dozens of MTA secrets lived in this civilian's head.

She coughed, pressed a shaking hand to her temple. "I want to help you rescue Ethan."

I gripped Kara's shoulders. "You can help by escaping, right now. Go with them. Please trust me on this."

"I can't—"

"Kara. Please."

She teetered. When I stabilized her, she wearily nodded. Determined or not, she could recognize her own weakness.

Durgan moved, causing Kara to flinch, but he only extended his palms. "These hands will not harm you."

Her eyes expanded. Doubt fought necessity. Necessity, because she knew we had no time for her to weigh the pros and cons of trusting Durgan.

Freia tossed her garment in my direction. The gun went in my waistband before I maneuvered the heavy cloak over my frame. It smelled of ash and hung loose; inches of extra fabric bunched around my feet.

"You will be unable to take this," Freia said with a motion toward the tunnel behind her. "Chron will be conscious soon. There is another exit—"

"I know it. Thank you, Freia."

She inhaled. *I hope to see you once more.*

Me too, I said. I stepped back from Kara and Durgan. "See you soon, Kar."

In the dim light, beside creatures who blended in with stone, Kara looked wispy as a ghost. She said nothing.

My gaze met Durgan's. *Thank you for saving me again, my harsk.*

He replied something indecipherable; it must've been another language. Durgan had fought his own officers to defend me. Now, he'd watch me leave and wonder, as I had about him, whether I'd survive.

I pulled the hood over my face. Then I ran.

CHAPTER FOUR

THE CHANDELIERS MONITORED MY PROGRESS.

I took the same route I had earlier: along the hallway toward the door cracked with purple stone. Outside the corridor, I hurried along the bridge in the wide cavern without stopping to admire the scenery. This cloak would hide me only from an unobservant Grifter; I needed to walk with purpose. I paid half attention to my path and half to recollecting the voice of a Grifter. That weapon would work better than a stun gun.

Yesterday, I'd gauged the walk from my cell to Ethan's at around fifteen minutes. That had occurred during the day, and Grifters had scurried about their business every few yards. Fortunately, night had fallen; it seemed the Grifters were sleeping. The path leading me into the cavern's mouth had only torchlight for company.

The final paces before the dead end crawled. Was I walking backwards? Tension had knotted my muscles so tightly, I'd probably spring if touched. It took all my willpower not to break into a sprint when I turned into the opening.

The room seemed hotter and quieter than before. What if Ethan wasn't here? I tuned in my hearing and found a pulse behind the third door. I exhaled.

Opening each cell was a matter of grinding the door handle's gears counter-clockwise. My fingers gripped the handle of his door. I would see Ethan. He would see me.

Gears squeaked. Stone scraped against stone. Torchlight from the jagged light fixture behind me fell inward, and I had a glimpse of darkness through the crack before a body lunged from nowhere and yanked my outstretched arms with a force that sent me reeling into the cell. I blocked his attack.

Ethan, stop!

He froze, even before I'd finished speaking. His vice around my wrists loosened, and his hands swept up my arms to rip off the hood. He took my shoulders, holding me a foot from him so he could see me.

Dirt darkened his cheeks, and his hair crept past his ears. I stared into familiar blue eyes, huge with wonderment. Then Ethan pulled me close, smooshing me against his chest. We hugged for hardly two seconds before he stepped back.

"They took Kara."

"She's escaping as we speak. She's safe."

"How? Where is she?"

"She's… sneaking through a side tunnel," I said. "It was too risky to bring her with me. We'll meet her outside. Come on." I wanted to hold him forever, but time allowed us no more than a crammed reunion. "Here. It's got three shots left." I placed the dart gun in his hand and moved toward the foyer's exit. "I know my way around, so I can get us out."

He took my elbow. "Ella." His expression looked hollowed out with a pain that twisted his mouth. "Our chance of survival is slim. I need to tell you—"

"You *will*, once we've escaped."

"No, listen to me. I should've told you, on the roof, but I wanted to wait. Though you still won't understand. I don't know how to express it, Ella, how much I care about you. It's more than—"

I slung my arms around his neck, pressing my face against him. "I remember, Ethan."

His efforts to unwind my arms desisted. "Everything?"

I nodded in his shoulder. "SPO-10. The academy. Everything."

He was so quiet. There was no sound except the torch flames and our pulses. He pushed me off, gently. I trembled when he cupped my face. I thought he'd let go, but his eyes searched mine. Whatever he found made him smile. Like the last embers of a flame giving up the fight, shadows seeped from his expression. They'd haunted him since my return to the academy, shrouding my Ethan with a sadness that hadn't been there before. A reaction to his disagreements with Lydia, I'd thought, but....

His fingers tremored, like they'd forgotten he was always steady. "I missed you," he murmured.

My throat hurt too much to speak. *I know,* I told him.

"I was afraid you'd never remember."

"But I never forgot you completely. You're 'EN.' It's your name. I was trying to remember."

Ethan didn't know how to react to this; he looked so stumped that it would've been funny had we been anywhere else. *Because* of where we were, Ethan gathered himself quickly. He inhaled. By the end of the breath, his jaw was firm and his gaze determined. "Lead the way, Ella. I'm right beside you."

Somehow, I stepped away. In severing the connection, I gained some of Ethan's businesslike composure. The hood, previously held back by Ethan, bunched around my neck. An idea struck. I tugged the cloak upward; it caught at my shoulders. Ethan guided it over my head. I left it in his hands and said, "You can be a guard leading me out."

He slipped it over his frame without asking. It fit his taller, wider build better than mine. He'd look much more like a Grifter once he donned the hood.

"If we come across anyone, let me do the talking," I said. "Worse comes to worse, you have the gun."

He nodded and lifted the hood. It fell over his face, casting shadows over the lower half. "You in front," he said. He took my arms and spun me around, securing my hands behind my waist. "Move out."

IT WAS A LONG, slow walk.

Ethan steered me through the winding cavern. I squeezed his fingers, seeking courage. For minutes, we crept and crept. Our feet occasionally sloshed in puddles. The ceiling hovered hardly a foot above our heads. At some dips in the halls, I could see my breath when I exhaled.

Left, I said.

Ethan guided me left. Noise echoed ahead, and we froze in unison. A slight female Grifter exited a room with a tray of clay dishes in her hands. She stopped short at the sight of us. Ethan's fingers tensed. *Wait,* I told him.

The memory of a Grifter's voice swirled, allowing me to grasp it. *Move along,* I told the Grifter, and she scurried back into the room.

We exhaled. We kept moving. Ethan's hands sweated.

The second Grifter stooped so much that his head neared his chest. He walked toward us, and we met at a high spot in the cavern where the Grifter could fully stand. When he stood straight and looked at me, I knew something was wrong.

"Why do you hide your face?" he asked.

Behind me, Ethan stiffened. His fingers slowly released mine.

Why do you question Ledare's commands? I said. *My business is not yours.* I gripped Ethan's arm and said, *Keep walking like nothing's wrong.*

He pushed me forward. I intentionally stumbled, releasing a cry of pain. This caused Ethan to bend to catch me right as we passed. Once we cleared the Grifter, Ethan lifted me straight and urged me along.

Adrenaline made my limbs shake. Sweat dripped along my jaw. Ethan's pulse beat barely slower than mine.

Quarter of a mile, I said. It curved ahead like an eternity. Uncountable footsteps would get us to the exit that—

Pressure gouged my mind like fingers pressing my eyelids. *You will not escape, Ella Kepler,* Chron's voice erupted. *Not in my home.*

I shoved out the panic. *We need to hurry,* I said. *Chron's awake.*

Ethan's boots trampled my heels.

We heard the exit before we saw it. The distance ahead of us churned with sounds of running water, an open noise not confined to tunnels and ceilings. We rushed toward our escape, forgetting pretense and running side by side until the rock walls squeezed us back to single file. According to Freia's mental map, we'd follow this curve, which ended at an open archway. I visualized the exit as she'd remembered it, saw the haze of rain that rushed behind it—and finally noticed that, in her memory, two guards always lurked with jagged spears.

Two guards! I told Ethan, right as we burst into the territory of Grifters.

The tip of a spear dropped to my chest, but in a moment Ethan had hooked my waist and lifted me out of its path. He brought his other arm high and aimed. The first shot pelted the closest Grifter in the eye.

Where are you, Ella Kepler? Chron whispered into my head, a distraction so jarring that the unconscious Grifter teetered inches from Ethan before I caught him, preventing the spear from plunging into Ethan. A second *pwip!* slugged the remaining Grifter in the throat, but he continued swiping his staff around the small space we'd entered, edging us back. Ethan shot again. The dart sailed into the Grifter's chest and he careened sideways, but not before hurling his weapon at my face. I dropped, and Ethan mentally stopped the spear in its tracks.

He pulled it from the air. "Go!"

I bolted across the damp stone, leaping over the two unconscious Grifters before gravity brought me outside the archway.

IF WE WANTED TO reach the trails of Dewey National Forest, we were going to have to swim.

The entrance to Chron's home wasn't tucked dryly in some tunnel; it hid beneath a torrent of water that splashed at our faces. We stood on a ledge beyond the archway and faced the endless downpour, hardly visible in midnight darkness. It provided just enough room for us both to stand without getting drenched. Above and below us only more stone; before us a veil of water.

Ethan gripped the back of my shirt. "Check the drop." He had to shout. "I'll hold you."

I inched toward the edge until my bare toes clung to slippery rock and water pelted my cheeks. After an inhale, I closed my eyes and leaned forward. Buckets of water crushed the back of my head. I staggered under the weight and felt Ethan shift his hold. A roar of white noise assaulted my eardrums until my head broke free, though the air outside the waterfall still rushed with volume. I quickly smeared my palms against my eyes until the blurriness faded.

Years of wondering what it would feel like to be up close and personal to a waterfall had not prepared me for the thrill of standing in its mouth. Moonlight beamed wavering rainbows in the spray. A blanket of water gushed headlong into the river below, maybe a fifty foot fall. I strained my eyes and found rocks embedded in the rapids, though they jutted farther from the immediate drop point. Around the circle of white foam where the fall met the river, the water appeared dark enough to indicate depth. Waves chopped at the inky stream.

We can make it, I told Ethan.

Tension tugged me back into the onslaught of water for a blip, then to the dark, slimy ledge where Ethan waited. I wiped my eyes again and said, "There are rocks, but stay with the waterfall and we should be fine."

The creep of Chron's voice blocked Ethan's response. *You will not make it.*

"Now!" I said.

Ethan tugged the cloak off. Together we jumped.

Despite near starvation and weeks without our proper training regimen, we barreled down the space that no Olympic athlete would've attempted. Without the echo of Chron's threats, I might have found the leap exhilarating. Water skimmed our backs and pushed us toward the river; I had no time to admire the scenery before we plunged into the quiet vacuum that soothed my ringing ears. My arms flapped upward, though soon the current swept me. I braced myself against a boulder, and the rapids tried shoving me around it, but I found a grip on the stone and pulled myself up. Earthy oxygen filled my nostrils.

I scrambled to the stone's surface and stood like an immobile surfer in a fray of forever gurgling water. Yards away gushed our escape route, which urged the current along the rocky obstacle course. The river continued past a bank of unorganized bramble. I got a strange chill that had nothing to do with the cold. Not ten yards from the waterfall stretched a fenced-in observation deck. Chron's lair hid right under the nose of civilians.

A limb rose from the froth. Ethan heaved himself onto another slab of stone an arm's reach from mine. He pushed the hair from his eyes and scanned the area until he found me.

The three of us alive and out of Chron's prison: check. We hadn't escaped yet, though.

"Bank," Ethan called, pointing, and my heart flipped. Then I saw what Ethan motioned—the dry land instead of Banks and all of Operation Whitewash.

I nodded. "Head for the deck up there," I said, preparing to jump over the divide. *You can hear me, Kara, right?* I thought. *We're in the rapids. We'll head for the lookout deck.*

Knees bent, ankles springy, I pushed myself into space.

Ethan and I hit the ledge of leaves and darted up the craggy incline strewn with moss. From where we'd landed, the only way to reach the deck was by climbing a hill of dirt bulging with roots. We ripped vines from the earth in our effort to clamber upward, creating mud wherever our soggy hold made contact. Finally, the wooden fence bumped our heads. We grabbed the slats. Scaling took another moment. How many moments separated us from discovery? It seemed we'd hiked for hours, but surely only a few minutes had passed since our waterfall leap.

Ethan's boots thudded and my bare feet splatted when we arrived on the deck. Beneath the branches of an oak, Kara crouched over a fallen Durgan.

My stomach lurched. "What happened?" I darted to them. "Where's Freia?"

"She stayed behind. Said she'd hide in plain sight. Durgan collapsed after trying to walk. It's his leg. I don't know if he's...."

"Who's Freia?" Ethan asked her.

Kara looked at me.

I ignored them and rolled Durgan to his back, feeling the sheer mass of him in the burning of my atrophied muscles. A king deserved silk sheets, but he got splinters from wood damp with the waterfall's spray. Durgan breathed shallow gasps and seemed unconscious. Blood stained his thigh. I pressed folds of cloth into the wound, a puckered hole in his bumpy skin. At least Grifters couldn't feel pain.

"Ella." Ethan knelt beside me. "It's just a Grifter. We don't have time for this." He caught the hand frantically dabbing the injury.

"I won't—"

I know where you are, Chron breathed.

My jaw clenched. To convince Ethan, I could drop the name that would always work. If Leader wanted Durgan alive, Ethan would protect him with his life. Lying would be simple—and wrong.

"Just trust me!" I burst. "We need him alive. You carry him. I'll carry Kara."

Ethan deliberated another second before pushing back his hair. He slid his arms beneath Durgan's torso and lifted him.

We heard the splashes simultaneously. Ethan tensed and looked toward the waterfall. He stood, slung Durgan over his shoulder, and peered beyond the railing. I saw his knuckles curl, the shoulder blades beneath his damp shirt tighten. He craned his head over his shoulder.

"Go!"

I scooped Kara up without ceremony and ran before her weight had fully settled.

My bare feet gripped the wooden slats well, despite the algae growth. Ethan's boots thudded right behind. Kara clutched my neck and watched over my shoulder, a sight I had no desire to see. I imagined Grifters crawling up the deck like spiders. Spiders with lethal spears instead of minuscule pincers.

The boardwalk ended at a rocky decline. The trail grew darker there, shadowed under trees that blocked the light of stars and the moon. A few more steps....

Trembling began beneath my feet. The surge of movement, of heavy running on the boardwalk, shot up my legs.

"Ethan, duck!" Kara shouted at my ear.

A tiny projectile whizzed left of us in a jagged trajectory only possible with telekinesis. Ethan had redirected the slim... had that been a bullet? How many guns did Chron's Grifters have?

I gripped Kara, prepared to leap the remaining feet toward freedom. Ethan yelled, "Jump!" right as I did. We scattered particles of midnight dust, soaring alongside another projectile. A shape launched higher above us. My muscles seized, but it was only Ethan leaping overhead. The trail beyond the boardwalk—and the coverage it provided—stretched mere feet below us. When our feet touched earth, gunfire split the night.

I dropped. Kara and I smacked the rocks and tumbled down while the unending discharge of machine gun fire smartly rang. Once our momentum stopped, I dragged Kara to her feet. Ethan, Durgan bunched over his shoulders like an unwieldy scarf, stood waiting. He hurried backward.

Kara and I regained our footing, keeping our necks bent should the guns start shooting for our heads. I scooped her upright once more and caught up to Ethan.

Then, the trees rained.

Dropping from the sky like beetles washed in moonlight came three MTA agents, rappelling on ropes that bounced slightly upward again once their boots touched the ground. They wore helmets but no guns, allowing them to frantically gesture.

"Come on!"

The one closest stood taller than the others, his height and frame familiar even concealed under armor. Banks had safely escaped Chron's forest and returned with Operation Whitewash in tow. I wanted to shout with relief.

He reached for Kara. A wild anxiety flushed her cheeks; she tottered into his arms. He tugged the rope harnessed around his chest, then they shot upward.

Odd emotion kept me frozen. *Kara is safe.* The thought sounded false, yet it repeated as an agent reached for me.

"We're taking the Grifter!" I said to the agent trying to disentangle Durgan from Ethan.

She threw up her arms, then lassoed them around Ethan. With the addition of Durgan, the three of them resembled a crooked monster.

The remaining meta snagged me, and we rose off the earth. The truth wedged reluctantly in my mind, even as I witnessed our escape. We couldn't have found freedom, not yet. Something would go wrong.

We lifted higher than the boardwalk, and I saw that Grifters weren't the only ones using guns. Dressed like members of a SWAT team, four metas unloaded their weapons in the direction of Chron's waterfall. Grifters peppered the rapids, skipping from boulder to boulder as they fled bullets. Cloaked bodies floated face down in the water; the current blended red with gray. Our SWAT team defenders aimed relentlessly, even as the remaining Grifters fired back or flung spears. Bullets rang off spear tips and obliterated them.

The sight soured my stomach. It didn't feel like a victory, not with Freia's warning fresh in my ears and Chron's vengeance in my head.

This is the beginning of your end, he said to me.

I pushed his voice out.

The battle below grew fainter. I moved my attention from the scene in exchange for the equally surreal image of Ethan. His agent ascended faster than mine, meaning I got to glimpse Ethan's boot soles. I didn't even register that the rope pulled us to a plane until Ethan's shoes suddenly vanished inside it. Another moment and our harness sucked us into concave luminescence.

CHAPTER FIVE

THIS PLANE DIFFERED PRIMARILY in size from the previous MTA aircrafts I'd encountered; I felt its expanse as soon as I scooted from my rescuer and found footing in a width still airy enough for several fully clad agents. Only one meta awaited us.

"That's not Chron, is it?" Dr. Saini, white lab jacket contrasting with her tanned skin, gestured us in. The doctor who'd first introduced me to the MTA, who'd worked undercover for Whitewash the entire time, ran a hand through onyx hair, skimming Durgan over with concentrated, tawny eyes. I wasn't surprised to see her; Andrews had mentioned her name, along with a few others from Whitewash, during that fateful water tower conversation with Banks.

"It's Durgan," I said.

Comprehension widened her expression. "Bring him this way, then," she said. "Kara, too."

The angle of Banks' helmet moved an inch toward Kara before he swept her off the floor and darted forward. I'd pegged Banks as unconcerned with any civilian's health, but his careful, swift movements reassured me otherwise.

Ethan, carrying Durgan much less gracefully, trod after through a hallway, this one carpeted and well-lit. A door flew inward. This jet wielded the space for a fully operational clinic. Not as large as the academy's medbay, but it fit a few cots and counters long enough to lay across. A young guy bounded around the room, leaving drawers open and the sink running and syringes scattered over the floor.

Saini motioned to a cot. "Put him here."

Ethan heaved the unconscious Durgan onto a bed that disappeared beneath his wide build. Saini twisted her bottom lip while she scanned him head to toe. Her gaze tightened at the crusted wound on his leg. "Sepsis," she murmured.

That didn't sound good. Neither did his breathing.

Whitewash wouldn't be here if it weren't for him, I told her privately. *Will you make sure he lives?*

She peeled a scrap of bloody fabric from his leg. "I don't care if he's a Grifter, Ella. He's a patient. That's all I see."

I relaxed. She'd always carried warmth, as if being a doctor had stamped the sterile MTA indifference out of her.

"*Doctor*," she said, "get—"

"Yes, yes," the other meta said, darting once again in every direction. "IV and et cetera and I'll be sure to suture—wait." He smacked a hand to his head and tugged at his black hair. "I've never sutured a Grifter."

Saini shot him a look. "Can you stop having a frenzy and remember your training?"

"Will it even bond to his skin?"

Her eyes hardened like toffee. "If you're scared of a Grifter, manage Kara. Presumably, she doesn't bite. Start IV of normal saline at one hundred milliliters per hour for twenty-four hours. Then...." She squinted at Kara's torso. "Fifty milligrams of metamorxophine every six hours times forty-eight hours. And turn off the faucet, will you? It's wasteful."

"Fine!" The young doctor flung a plastic package at Saini and shut off the water with a mental tweak.

"Set her there, Ban—" Saini's mouth pinched tight; she busied herself with cutting away Durgan's pant leg.

My forehead wrinkled. Saini had obviously stopped herself from voicing Banks' name, but what did anonymity matter at this point? Kara probably couldn't care less, and Ethan....

He stood taut, eyes following Banks' movement much like he'd follow the slithering of a Grifter. That calculated scrutiny gave rise to a ping of alarm in my brain. As far as Ethan knew, Banks was a rogue MTA operative who'd abandoned his academy duties last October. Now, he stood on a jet alongside metas who wouldn't say his name.

I wished Saini had said nothing. Then again, if *I'd* recognized Banks, then surely Ethan already had.

Banks laid Kara on a cot with all the caution of one setting glass onto concrete. Forgetting Banks and Ethan, I hurried to her side and took her hand. The unnatural lighting made the shadows and bruising more prominent against her ghastly pallor.

You're safe, Kar, I said, not sure I trusted my throat to unlock.

She tried to stand, coughed, then slumped back to the cot. "Is Dad... is Kyle...?"

"They're okay," I said, then realized I didn't know that for a fact. I checked with Banks. *Right?*

He nodded.

Kara wasn't comforted. "What about Jimmy? He was there. I went inside, but he...." She squeezed my wrist. "Did the Grifters k-kill him?"

For a moment, my mind scrunched to follow the topic. Jimmy? Did we know a....

Comprehension blasted my thoughts apart. Jimmy Daniels, our supposed classmate, fabricated by Whitewash and played by Banks. Kara said he'd been at her house when Jurstin kidnapped her, but that made little sense. He'd been fighting the Grifters at our high school, and would've had no reason to visit her.

"Well...." I scrabbled for a truthful answer, keeping my attention off Banks. "I'm sure he's fine."

"Can the MTA check?"

My brain went blank. After an uncomfortable beat, Banks yanked the helmet free in one swift move. Two gasps hissed in the clinic: Kara's and the young doctor's; he dropped a syringe and said, "You weren't supposed to do that!"

Banks ignored him, gazing at Kara. Unlike Ethan, imprisonment and darkness hadn't marred his features. His skin maintained a healthy glow, his brunette hair kept the chaotic waves that still reminded me of sand dunes.

Kara's grip on my arm faltered. "You're... a meta."

It wasn't a question, and Banks gave no answer.

I couldn't decide whether to offer an explanation or pretend nothing uncomfortable had happened. The other meta severed the tension by marching to Kara and plopping a heap of supplies on the nearest cart.

"Arm," he said, and Kara wriggled her hand free from mine.

"Banks and Kepler. A word in the hallway." Ethan's tone cut sharper than a scalpel. Reading him would've given me unnecessary confirmation—I knew what that expression meant.

Judging by Banks' sidelong scowl, he knew too.

"I'll be right back," I told Kara.

Concentrating on the doctor's work, she nodded.

With a swallow, I moved for the exit.

During our time in the clinic, the agents must've boarded. All was quiet in the hallway, except for the swirl of white noise that muted our footsteps. Ethan pulled the clinic door shut and, before Banks got two strides into the hall, said, "Who's in charge here?"

Banks went rigid. Taller and older than the two of us, he had the same hazel stare that had inspected me from another face. After spending hours resenting those eyes, I couldn't deny the resemblance when it struck.

"You're very much like your mother," Andrews had said to Banks in the water tower last year. Andrews could have been telling the truth. It seemed possible—and it burned my gut to consider—Andrews knew Banks' mother very well.

"An agent," Banks said.

"The same agent who stole this aircraft?" Ethan said.

"No. I'm just a mechanic." Banks crossed his arms, a gesture that added to the thick air of indifference he already emanated, and had emanated their entire partnership. These former partners couldn't have been more different. One would follow rules to the death, and the other would die before a rule defined him.

"Where are we being taken?" Ethan said.

"Why would I tell you?"

"Come on, guys," I said, recognizing the fight instinct stirring in Ethan's form. Whether consciously or not, he'd begun advancing.

Banks scoffed. "Don't, Sheedy. You'll embarrass yourself."

The snub didn't halt Ethan, though it did elicit a muscle spasm along his jaw.

I stepped between them. "Stop," I told Banks. "He has every right to ask these questions. Who's the agent in charge?"

When Banks allowed his attention to unstick from Ethan, I made sure not to blink. The guy who'd deceptively recruited me for Whitewash had intimidated me once upon a time, but those days belonged to the Ella who'd never endured seven weeks imprisoned by Grifters.

Banks rolled his eyes. "Fine." He turned.

I stepped after him, but Ethan pulled me back. He pointed to his temple.

Ella… telepathy… hear me?

He had no idea we used to do this every day at SPO-10.

Yes, I said.

These metas are rogue. Stay with Kara.

The stress in my nerves, still struggling to acknowledge that we'd reached safety, resumed its vicious dance. *I don't think we're in danger*, I said.

We don't know where they're taking us. I'm getting answers. Have you ever used an emergency parachute?

Ethan, no one's going to throw us out of the plane.

"Don't think like that," he murmured. "I need you alive." The typically assured tenor of his voice wavered—not with doubt, but emotion so rarely visible in stoic Ethan. He grazed my cheek, a quick mark with his thumb, then caught up to Banks.

Tension needled my brain. Ethan thought we'd stepped into danger, so he'd follow MTA protocol until he had his answers. Was Ethan going to learn, *now*, every lie his beloved Leader had fed him? Uncovering the truth about Eugene Andrews would rock him to the core; he deserved to hear an explanation from someone who cared about him, not from Banks, who couldn't give two cents about Ethan's feelings. Banks wasn't a villain, but for those he didn't care about, he had no patience. Nothing I said would convince Ethan to wait, but perhaps Banks would listen.

I looked past Ethan, toward Banks' retreating figure.

Don't let the agent tell him about Leader or his parents, I said. *Please. Not yet. Let me do it.* I held my breath. Banks *had* to have some compassion he could muster up; or, maybe disdain would motivate him. Banks wouldn't be keen on enduring an Ethan interrogation.

After a harrowing pause, his head tipped up, then back down.

My muscles unclenched. *Thanks.*

He continued walking as if he'd heard nothing.

Now alone, in a cone of white noise as the jet punctuated clouds, I felt that clamp of relief. Kara was alive, Ethan was safe—we would all be okay. Relief wobbled my legs. It should've picked me off my feet, a joy lighter than air. Instead, my stomach tossed. I pressed my knuckles against my mouth to squelch the nausea. No matter how I reminded myself that we *weren't* about to get thrown overboard, bile burned upward, clogging my mouth with saliva.

I darted for the door across the hall and smacked it open. The neat room had the warmth of a captain's cabin; the twin bed was made, the desk tidy, and a round window gave a view of dark clouds that hid the moon. A foggy door led into a bathroom. I slammed the door behind me and gripped the rim of the toilet. A puddle of water stared back. It rippled in solidarity with my trembling. As tension unclenched its wiry fingers, my body resisted the release. Anxiety had made a comfortable nest in me for more than a year—really, since my first introduction to the MTA. First, the anxiety of evil Tacemus and secrets; then evil Leader and disclosed truths. Kara missing; Ethan missing; Chron out to kill us all—those facts had been my reality, and they had no idea how to vanish.

"Finding Kara has become your fixation," whispered a voice that— deny it all I wanted—had at one point been comfortingly familiar.

I squeezed my eyes and gritted my teeth. He still remained. That Leader's words lingered in my memory wasn't the part I hated. I could ignore words but not their effect. He'd done what he'd set out to do and made me trust him. Day after day he'd trained me, consoled me, advised me, all the while knowing I was a telepath. I'd believed he cared about me, but those afternoon lessons were simply his way of monitoring me.

Out of everyone I'd met within the MTA, no one had delivered more false information than Leader. He'd denied recognition of the symbol; he'd pretended my lack of telekinesis was nothing unusual; he'd played ignorant of which Grifter might've kidnapped Kara; and, worst of all... he'd manipulated me into confiding in him over my own parents.

An alarm triggered an automatic deflection. I couldn't go there, not to the painful reality I'd forced myself to forget. Not to Joe and Sue Smith.

"Two innocuous names for two innocuous people."

I pushed them back and back, but they persisted and finally burst into existence. Whitewash had sent my parents to Texas with no recollection of their former selves or daughter. Once again, they had no clue who I was. Even after One had given them fabricated memories of me during my brief return to Briarwood, Mom and Dad had never fully returned. Those fabricated memories were gone and replaced now. Our last genuine interaction had been the day Ethan first appeared in my life, whisking me away from the danger at my high school fair.

During my second time at the academy, every phone call home had actually been with Agents Walker and Chang, Leader's first officers. They'd nagged me about the symbol, about Kara, causing me to dread our conversations. Meanwhile, Leader assuaged my guilt by dismissing it. Per his encouragement, cadets didn't seek out relationships with their parents because the separation was "too difficult." In reality, the parents of cadets didn't even know their children were still alive.

I leaned back, shoving the pain away like a stranger who had crept too close. These lies — they were my battle, the reason Operation Whitewash had pulled a telepath onto their side. Here I was, tricked and manipulated and snatched from every familiarity, a mind-reader destined to infiltrate the cruelest mind of all. Eugene Andrews had trained the cadet assigned to crack him open. Whitewash wanted to uncover how he controlled the Tacemus, and I was the only known telepath with the ability to sift that information out of him.

That's not the only ability you have.

A tighter, colder dread churned in my gut. I hadn't let myself ponder the other aspect to my telepathy. The Tacemus weren't Andrews' puppets alone. They were mine, too. Something in me could force the Tacemus to obey. Andrews had realized that when his Tacemus listened to me instead of him.

Realizing what Andrews could do had filled me with disgust. To consider that same power applying to me... I felt tainted. I could do the exact thing Operation Whitewash hated Andrews for, the very thing we fought to undermine. I wanted to pretend that ability had no part in me, but I couldn't. That potential might've been the key to freeing the Tacemus.

A light knock disrupted my efforts to regurgitate this anxiety. Dr. Saini entered after a beat. Instead of sticking to the safety zone, she squatted right beside me, where any moment she might regret coming close. I couldn't summon the strength to warn her that I was about to puke.

"It's going to be all right," she said softly.

"Saini, I...." I stared at her. I wanted to spit the truth out and get it over with. The nausea might disperse then, but it would be temporary. I'd have to voice the truth all over when One joined us. I'd wait until I could say it once and never again. That seemed fair. He was, after all, running Whitewash.

Saini gripped my shoulder and gently shook it. "I came to see about your fingers. Let's get you up."

Fingers. Okay. I could do this. Not only the Tacemus depended upon me; the clueless metas did, and even the Grifters. Before leaving Durgan's, I'd promised to find out why the MTA warred with Grifters and if peace could exist. Tacemus, metas, Grifters—I had to carry them all.

Good thing metas were built for heavy lifting.

I stood, finding my legs steady. "How's Durgan? And Kara?"

"You don't know when to stop worrying, do you?" she said, shaking her head. "They'll mend. Now, let me see your hands."

I waved my swollen hands before her. Jurstin had broken them days ago, and they'd mended poorly. She turned my wrists, not squeamish over the crooked, discolored digits extending from them.

"Do you want permanently disjointed fingers?" she asked.

"Not really."

"Good. I'll have to re-break them." Her gaze shifted; a syringe and some vials floated from her lab coat. Saini jabbed the needle into a cylinder of clear liquid, then punctured my hand without warning.

"What, now?" I said. "Don't you need to x-ray them or something?"

"Could you trust that I know what I'm doing?"

"Okay. Sorry."

Saini gave the medicine two minutes to kick in, two minutes I spent preparing myself to have my bones broken. Then, she attacked each finger by bending it or crushing it underneath her palm. I bit my tongue and forced myself to watch. Metas didn't flinch.

After I was left with eight even uglier fingers, Saini began delicately wrapping them. "Once at base, I can give you hand guards instead of these splints," she said.

"Understood." I blinked toward the wall. "Whitewash's base, right?"

"Yes. Speaking of, where's Ethan?"

"Talking with Banks and the agent."

She took her time securing my pinkie, which would only escape its binding by some miracle. "Ella, you need to prepare yourself for the possibility that Ethan might react poorly to the truth about Whitewash."

"I know. He loves Andrews."

"Exactly my point. He'd rather believe Andrews than a team of rogue metas."

"No, he cares about truth more than his feelings."

"Above both, he values obedience. Loyalty. Those traits can tend to make one... blind." Though she tiptoed, meaning weighed down every word.

"You've been listening to Banks too much," I said. "I know Ethan. He'll be on our side."

A moment passed before she conjured a smile. "I'm sure you're right."

I knew so, but I wasn't smart-alecky enough to say it.

She probably caught my gist, anyway.

OUTSIDE THE WINDOW, clouds chased us, visible in flits of time when the moon struck them just right. We'd been airborne roughly an hour when the intercom chimed with a five-minute ETA.

I slid off the clinic counter, grateful for the interruption. Dr. Lee—who'd finally spilled his name—had spent the past twenty minutes reciting gruesome medical procedures in an effort to quell his anxious nature.

Saini had allowed my return once Kara and Durgan were cleaned up and changed. Both lay asleep on their cots, plugged into machinery, Durgan looking out of place in a white hospital gown. Ethan and Banks had yet to return from their conversation.

"You know how exhaustive briefings are," Saini had said, "and Ethan seems the thorough type."

Yes. *Too* thorough. Banks and the agent had their work cut out for them in the avoidance department.

Saini assigned me IV-holding duty. She and Lee collapsed the cots' legs, using telekinesis to keep the beds afloat. Saini managed Durgan, Lee handled Kara. My job was to trail between them with the two IV poles.

Once the departure signal flashed, Saini started forward. I felt as anxious as Lee while she steered Durgan toward the doorway, but the gap was wide enough for the cot to fit through. I followed after with the poles, which rolled across the floor, dragging like gimp legs.

The passenger hold lacked the agents who'd filled it before; the seatbelt sign flashed at no one.

"Where's everyone else?" I asked Saini.

"Packing."

I frowned toward the cockpit, though who knew where Banks and Ethan had settled. For an innocent conversation, it wound up being pretty long.

Saini glided Durgan down the ramp, into a wide hangar of concrete. Its roof was missing, replaced by a starlit night. The breadth of the jet filled the hangar; other than that, it contained a few shelves and a floor absent of oil stains.

Lee concentrated on Kara, mouth puckered with the effort of steering her smoothly offboard. Once he cleared the ramp, Saini picked up the pace until we reached the exit.

A breeze gusted, one so familiar that comfort danced along my skin. The acrid pinch of saltwater hit my nose, and I breathed deeply. Whitewash operated near the ocean, something I hadn't enjoyed since joining the MTA. The Florida blood in my veins felt right at home.

A jungle of palm trees and salt brush neighbored our path down a curve of dunes. We were forced to walk slower on the uneven ground. Waves sighed somewhere out of sight.

We followed the dune's turn, leaving the jungle behind just as the cloud coverage passed the moon. The dunes had deposited us near the water's edge. A giant building, not unlike the hangar, took shape, standing first in a long row of warehouses that shouldered a dock. It seemed an industrial marina, square warehouse after square warehouse. A few boats lapped on the low tide, strung to the dock with ropes.

Did Whitewash own the entire marina? It stretched a quarter mile; beyond that, a pier and the beginnings of a neighborhood of beach houses. This base shared land with civilians, which seemed risky. Or was it smart? Whatever it was felt foreign, as if aiming for as non-MTA a vibe as possible. The MTA worked in seclusion, between forests, yet this base bumped against an ocean any civilian could swim through.

A trail of dead grass carried us from the dunes to the door of the first building, which looked corroded and smelled of minerals.

After lowering Durgan, Saini gripped the knob; blue light glowed beneath her skin.

Ah, there it is. MTA's signature electric blue.

A rectangular outline appeared above the knob. Saini pressed a keycard flat against it, and the glow hummed and shimmered while debating whether she was ally or foe. After a chirp, the door clicked open.

CHAPTER SIX

GOING FROM NIGHT TO artificial day was never easy on the eyes, especially meta vision. I squinted at the overload until instinct took over and adjusted the intake.

I steered the IVs into a foyer that began with a low ceiling, then inclined ahead. My bare feet scuffed on a thin, brown carpet beginning to unthread. The narrow foyer muted our steps until we reached the open ceiling.

The warehouse seemed uncertain about its purpose. Was it a meeting hall or fitness center? Near the far wall, squishy desk chairs surrounded an oval table that could easily sit twenty. Exercise pads, a boxing ring, weight-lifting gear, and storage closets consumed everything else — because, secret headquarters or not, every meta needed a gym. The open floor plan made for an odd feel. Everything at the academy was quartered off, but Operation Whitewash didn't mind mingling.

A spiral of stairs climbed to a second floor whose rooms were visible from below. We could've been standing in the courtyard of an apartment complex, though these boxy rooms had fogged glass instead of brick to keep them private.

Once we'd all situated beneath the landing, Saini and Lee contorted their arms about. The IVs and two cots rose, somewhat eerily; telekinesis would always be foreign to me. They drifted, creepy as coffins, over the railing, until they rested on the next level. Then, up we circled.

On the second-floor landing, I couldn't make out any shapes through the obscured, glass walls that divided the rooms. In the center of the second floor, like a square, sat a clinic much more open than the academy's. There, Lee and Saini set to arranging Kara and Durgan. The cot legs came back down, and I navigated the IV poles so that each stood warden-like by the designated patients. Both slept on. Durgan's breaths came rapid and sharp; Kara's sounded weak and slick.

I sat near her elbow and took her damp fingers. Under the clinic's lighting, she looked like a zombie. "When can she go back to Briarwood?" I asked.

Saini inhaled. "Here's the situation. We are currently operating a thread away from scrutiny, and we can't afford to... to be any more visible than we already are. Returning Kara will require paperwork and publicity, none of which we're keen on. The good news is, we're very, very close to our end goal. Once we've reached it, we'll have the ability to orchestrate a smooth return home. I don't foresee anything longer than, say, two weeks. And that's being generous. Are you following?"

I got it. Whitewash couldn't come into the limelight and risk getting caught by Andrews. "But her dad and brother probably think she's dead," I said.

"Yes, and I'm sorry for that. I wish we could tell them otherwise, but this is extremely delicate. Perhaps we can anonymously nudge the civilian police in the right direction, but I can't guarantee."

In the grand scheme of things, another two weeks seemed like the blink of an eye. To the Watsons, it would drag like two years. Did Kyle miss the sister he'd bullied? Months ago, I would've declared otherwise. I *had* declared otherwise. My feelings toward Kyle had changed. I hoped he missed her and regretted every unkind word.

"While we're on this topic," Saini said in a tone firmer than before, "I'd like to remind you that the MTA is classified. You have full access to this facility, but Kara does not. Can I trust you not to tell her anything about our operation? The more she knows, the more dangerous for her. You know what happens when you learn too much."

Her meaning slugged deep, to that spot in my memories where I'd shoved tanks and memory-wiping and the breathless words of Eugene Andrews. I'd learned too much, but he'd learned more—about me.

"I won't say anything," I said. "But there are things she already knows. Ethan was with her for seven weeks. They must've talked about the MTA."

"We're aware of that, and we'll mitigate the damage as much as possible. Now, to matters of health."

Saini was adamant about fixing my hands. A drawer beneath the sink counter opened. Out floated a pair of restrictive gloves that I traded with the finger splints. They fit over each hand like wrist guards, but longer. Next, she had Lee concoct a drink chock-full of "replenishments." She ordered me to chug one liter, all the while bemoaning my weight loss as if I'd grown skinny just to offend her.

"Banks said Durgan didn't feed you," Lee said, rocking on his heels.

I eyed the sleeping Grifter. "It wasn't his fault. His first officers disobeyed orders without him knowing."

"Sounds familiar." Lee's grin made him appear twelve.

"All right, Ella." Saini gestured the exit. "It's three-hundred hours. Go to sleep."

"Where would the agent have taken Ethan?" I asked.

"You're prohibited from worrying about anyone else. *Bed.* Doctor's orders."

"I don't think I'll be able to sleep."

"Well...." Saini tousled her hair and glanced to Lee.

"What?" he said.

"Ping the others. Let's do the debrief."

"Now? It's early morning!"

"You napped on the flight over. You'll be fine."

Lee grumbled and groaned but shuffled toward the doorway. He pressed a call button embedded in the wall and said, "Kepler's here. Debrief." The announcement echoed in the clinic.

Debrief. Within the hour, Whitewash would know I shared equal power with Andrews.

I followed them to the landing, realizing as I padded along that I was still barefoot, wearing damp clothes given to me by Freia. With my gloved hands and unevenly cut hair, it'd be a miracle if Whitewash took me seriously.

"Can I change first?" I asked Saini.

After pointing me to a room in the far corner of the second floor, she excused herself, adding that I should come downstairs once finished.

The room reminded me of mine at SPO-10, compact and sparse. The bed filled a rectangular nook in the wall, just a mattress and pillow with no blanket. A closet sat wedged in the wall. Inside I found neat stacks of clothing, a few hanging jackets, and one pair of boots. Saini must've directed me to the room meant for me; the cargo pants stayed on my waist, and the shirt fit. The boots moved with that stiff resistance of new shoes, but at least they seemed the right size.

I was the only one on the first floor. Everyone else had gone either outside, upstairs, or behind the door near the head of the conference table. I found a spot where I could eye the foyer, stairs, and door simultaneously. Several silent minutes passed before the door opened and a familiar figure emerged.

I swallowed the instinctive tensing. He and I were on the same page now. Lies or no lies, we both worked for Whitewash.

Banks did a quick scan of the room—hoping someone else could be a buffer between us? After recognizing defeat, he took a seat with enough distance to keep us comfortable. In the silence, our breaths began to sync. We must have realized it at the same time; I slowed, and he sped up.

I could hold a grudge against Banks forever. Tempting, but the empathetic part of me that Durgan had awoken fought my stubbornness. He'd warned me that telepathy presented as much a gift as a curse. If I wanted to read people, I had to understand them. *"It is very hard to hate one with whom you empathize,"* he'd said. That meant, when the time came, I couldn't even dislike Andrews. My ability wouldn't let me.

Analyzing Banks alongside these uncomfortable truths, another layer of him peeled off. Banks had lied to me, yes. He'd behaved as an aloof, seemingly indifferent undercover agent, not caring to mince words when it came to giving me assignments. Yet, despite every reason to find him irritating, I began to see another aspect to him. He cared about things enough to fight for them. Banks had joined Whitewash to help the Tacemus, which meant he wasn't indifferent. Not at all. He was the product of the MTA's corruption and lies— someone never properly cared for but still fighting to care for someone else.

"Where's Ethan?" I asked, pleased at how conversational I sounded.

"In his room until we've figured out how much to tell him."

"What *did* you tell him?"

"Nothing." Banks absently touched the checkmark scar near his temple, a defining feature that set him apart from Andrews.

I pushed past the hunch. I'd never tell him my suspicions, not unless he admitted it first. Knowing Banks, he'd rather get an arm lopped off than consider any relation to Andrews.

"Thanks," I told him. "And thanks for organizing our rescue. I'm assuming that was you."

He nodded, ran a hand through his wavy hair. "How's Kara?"

"Still asleep. Why... why were you at her house?"

"You went there. I had to monitor you." He scratched at a crack in the table.

A part of me had wondered whether Kara had mixed up details. Banks' confirmation meant he'd been there when she was kidnapped...

and failed to prevent it from happening. "And you saw the Grifters?" I asked, trying not to sound accusatory. All the same, how could a trained meta have let the Grifters escape?

He looked straight ahead, but I doubted he registered the wall. If he did, I would've hated to be in its place.

"I was by the curb. By the time I realized she wasn't coming out, they'd already left." His fingers got stuck in a half curl. "I tracked them. They'd gone too far. They had a truck."

Suddenly, I had an inkling why he'd volunteered to rescue Kara in my stead. I wouldn't have thought a guilty conscience could plague Banks, but it must've followed him from Briarwood. Another billow of pity for him wafted by, and this time I didn't argue with it.

"She's alive, Banks. That's what matters."

He sought my eyes. "I'm—" Banks pulled his reply short and faced another direction, right before the door swung forward.

Three older strangers, identically dressed in the leisure pants and t-shirt of the MTA, cut their chatter off when they spotted me. The woman lifted a hand to wave, while one of the men stayed attentive to the grid screen he held a foot below his eyes. The other man bounded forward.

"Ella Kepler. We meet at last." He was mid-thirties, fair, with thick, wavy brown hair. "Dominic Bist, procurement. Please call me 'Dom,' because it's a nickname, and no one ever calls me by one. I'll introduce my MTA partner because he never speaks. This is Arthur Finch, civilian studies." Dom groped blindly behind him, found Arthur's shoulder, and tugged the latter forward; Arthur let himself be dragged without lifting his eyes from his grid. A pair of headphones trailed from his ears.

"Arthur *is* his real name, but Finch is not," Dom continued. "Though we know our true surnames, we keep to the ones the MTA gave us. It's less confusing that way. The rather formidable woman beside me is Hina Akamu, construction. What size clothing are you, Ella? A small?"

I opened my mouth, wondering what to address first.

The woman stuck out her hand. "Just call me Akamu." She had a round face and dark eyes nearly obscured by her thick sheen of bangs.

"But 'Hina'—" Dom started.

"Is my name, yes," Akamu said. "We don't all follow your rules, Bist."

Dom clasped his hands matter-of-factly and inclined his head. "Hina has, as the civilians say, a stick up her gut."

"That's not how it goes," Banks said.

"What would an engineer know?" Dom demanded of him.

"Probably the same as a procurer." Akamu prodded Dom's side. "Sit *down*, Bist. You're looming like a cloud."

"How very poetic, Hina."

"Thank you."

The three of them took the seats between Banks and me and proceeded to stare, except Arthur, who likely wouldn't have noticed if the table erupted in flames. Arthur seemed almost grayish. His hair blended between ashy and brown, his skin equally dusty.

The door swung open again, and a woman in her late twenties scuttled out. Her eyes bugged when she saw me; color flushed her fair, freckled cheeks.

"This is Amy Lane, my fellow procurer," Dom said with a sweep of his hand.

Amy took stilted steps toward me. "Hi! It's such an honor to meet you, Kepler. I can't wait to work you. *With!* Work *with!*" She smacked her fingers over her mouth, then sunk in the chair beside Dom with an expression that seemed halfway tearful.

I tried giving her a smile around Dom, feeling odd that anyone was honored to meet me, but she gave the tabletop her full attention. "Thank you," I said. "What's a procurer?"

Dom's neck did a slow pendulum. For once, he had no answer but an affronted gape.

"It's an innocent question," Akamu said, picking at her fingernails. A smirk tugged at her mouth. "No one is suggesting your job could be handled more efficiently by a computer."

"Of course not, Hina, because that would be absurd," Dom said calmly. To me, he replied, "You've noticed you're in a building, yes? With furniture and clothing and wonderful air conditioning? These commodities don't simply appear like on trees. Amy and I take meticulous effort to—"

"Yes, and we're all very grateful, but who *designed* the building?" Akamu said.

"Who ordered the supplies?" Dom returned.

"Holt did. By pressing a button. On the computer."

"He only knew what to purchase after we streamlined the entire process! Really, Hina. You're beginning to sound like Agent Cassidy."

"Unfair," she said. "My insult wasn't remotely near that caliber."

Another trio entered the room then, wearing the outfits of agents, which made sense; evidently, everyone in Whitewash had different duties. Some people had to be the muscle.

"Speak of devils," Dom said. "Here are three of our four agents." He pointed to each as he spoke their last names. "Keswick, Porter, and Cassidy."

The agents clearly believed their jobs prohibited pleasantries. I'd never met an MTA agent who smiled, and these three offered no exception. Keswick, early forties, had a flattened nose and sharp eyes cast my way, like he was envisioning the various ways that he could break my bones. Porter, warmly tanned and barely younger than Keswick, messed with his watch as he took a seat near his companions. The female, Cassidy, reminded me of Ethan: straight dark hair cropped above her ears, and blue eyes that observed all.

"I don't believe you'll have the pleasure of meeting Luke Bender, Dr. Marie Webb, or Zachary Holt today," Dom said, "although, in a manner of speaking, you've already been acquainted. Zachary's computing genius ensured —"

"Holt has done more than Bist can detail," Hina interrupted. "All Webb did was create the nosebleed serum. Bender's in procurement, so we know he's done as much as a worm in a cocoon."

"Nosebleed serum?" I said.

"Sheedy's nosebleed." Across the table, the female agent — Cassidy? — scrutinized me. "After Integer wiped him."

Apprehension wrung my gut. That nosebleed had discouraged me from telling Ethan the truth again — which had surely been Whitewash's aim. "So clearing people isn't dangerous," I said.

"Unless you're a Tacemus and the object is Andrews," Dom said airily. "Then it's all rather Russian Roulette, to quote Arthur."

"Stop talking, Bist," said Cassidy. "Look at Kepler. She'll keel over."

Dom and Hina peered at me. If they were hoping for a soldier of the same stock as Ethan, they'd be rolling their eyes before the hour was up.

What Webb's creations had done made my stomach toss, but these metas, products of the MTA no matter how fiercely they rejected that, had grown used to cold strategies. I swallowed, brought my hands to my lap, and began a steady tap against my thigh.

Drs. Saini and Lee entered next. I remembered then that One had mentioned fifteen total members. Ten people sat around me and three were absent, which meant two more—One and someone else—would come marching out of that door. The idea of being introduced to just two more people made Whitewash seem minuscule. What could fifteen people do against all of the MTA?

The door opened, and out came the last unknown member of Operation Whitewash. When a pair of steely eyes inspected me from over an equally iron mustache, my first reaction was to shout that we'd been discovered. This man first met me in a Briarwood safe house a year ago, and after arguing with Dr. Saini and rebuking Ethan, he'd dropped me off at SPO-10 with advice as gruff as his personality. After my memory loss, he'd caught up to me a second time and whisked me straight from Briarwood to Andrews. Because he was, after all, Andrews' first officer, member of the Society—and the man who'd impersonated my dad.

Agent Walker, graying but still broad as a bear, betrayed none of my surprise as he purposefully strode to the head of the table.

I found my muscles tensing with the effort of staying bolted to my seat. "You're part of Whitewash?" I said; because, although already obvious, I needed to hear him confirm it.

Agent Walker, clad to match his three fellow agents, took his seat. He was easily the oldest in the room and carried himself with the same air as any meta, proving that age had failed to mellow him out. "Commander in chief."

"I thought One was."

"A Tacemus can only do so much."

All this time, I'd pegged One as the mastermind behind every Whitewash plan, but it seemed One had been following yet another meta's orders.

"But he's coming." I looked at the door as if the Tacemus would spill out any moment. "Right?"

"Not until later," Walker said.

Though One wasn't Whitewash's head, admitting my power without him there didn't sit right, not when this ability affected him more than anyone else. When he arrived, I'd tell him first. Then, I'd take it to Whitewash.

Walker drew a grid screen from his pocket. His wrinkles grew tight around the mouth, but he had the air of one refocusing. He laid the grid flat on the table, tapped the screen, then looked to me. "All right, Kepler. Was your time with Durgan fruitful?"

No one in Whitewash cared if working with Walker made me uncomfortable. I'd have to borrow that indifference. Or fake it.

Taking a breath, I redirected my focus to his question. It seemed odd how little Whitewash knew of something that had dogged my wonderings for weeks.

"Yes," I said. As the word released, I knew an interrogation would follow, probably a demand for proof. My own questions would be tossed aside, questions about the fundamentals of Operation Whitewash. I still wasn't clear on who I worked for. Rather, who I *didn't* work for. And so, before Walker could bark out orders, I quickly said, "I have questions first. How are Whitewash and the Society related?"

Walker didn't flinch, his mustache calm though his lips pursed.

"They're not," Banks spoke. He'd always been the one to answer questions when no one else would. "The Society is under the MTA umbrella."

"But *you're* in the Society," I said to Walker.

"I'm also one of Andrews' first officers," he said, obviously certain that cleared everything up.

I returned to Banks. "What does the Society actually do?"

"Guards information," Banks said. "It's a tiered system. New members know less. Veteran members know more. First, we learn the truth about Grifters. If we can handle that, we learn that the MTA operates outside of civilian laws. Last comes the fact that our parents never gave us to the MTA. We think there might be an even higher level, but we have no proof."

I'd stumbled upon one Society meeting at which Andrews himself had been absent—probably intentionally. He had already earned my trust and denied any recognition of the symbol. Had I found him directing the secret club that the symbol belonged to, that trust would've shattered.

Who *had* I seen in that meeting? McFarland, Vires, and Koleman. Lydia Burnette, too. Did she know she'd been kidnapped from her parents? I couldn't believe it. She'd been Ethan's partner for too many years. They didn't get along now, but I knew she still cared. Lydia had to know Ethan believed his own parents had abandoned him.

"Why would the MTA want anyone to have this information?" I said.

Walker crossed his arms. "Some metas have to know the truth. The MTA has existed since the seventeen-hundreds, and we're still invisible. That is entirely because of the Society. Back to your telepathy. Are you confident you can read any mind?"

The remainder of my questions vanished into Walker's steel expression. "Yes," I said.

A wave passed through the table occupants. It threw up an immediate barrier between the metas and myself, because they must've known—same as me—what would come next.

"I want a demonstration," Walker said. "What number am I thinking?"

Conscious of the attentive silence in the room, I looked directly at him, then wished I hadn't. Facial hair had never been a cause for discomfort, but something about his made me edgy. Walker, his voice disguised as my dad's, had listened to my woes and told me he loved me. Why on earth would I want to go anywhere near his mind?

"Focus on what unites us," Durgan had instructed me. Even Walker—with his burly shoulders and ironed-on mustache—was human. And every human had something relatable. Right?

I considered my every interaction with Walker, reliving them, breaking them down. He'd first met me at the safe house near Briarwood, where he'd bickered with Saini over what to do with me. An act? But for whose benefit?

As I considered his behavior toward Saini, a tunnel opened in the mental airwaves between us, like light streaming through a hole. From that tunnel crawled a trail of words. *... eight... nine-hundred... seventy-eight... nine-hundred...*

I blinked. "Nine-hundred and seventy-eight."

He kept his reaction in check, but a spark lit his eyes. "And Cassidy?"

"Nine-hundred seventy-eight?" Dom called. *"I* could have told him that. It's his favorite number. Hardly impressive."

As Hina Akamu told him to hush, I looked to Cassidy, whose bright eyes reminded me of Ethan's. Her mind opened like a spring.

Negative-one... Stupid Kepler in my head... No, twelve. No, negative-one. Negative-one....

"Negative one," I said.

Great, she thought. She rolled her eyes.

"Again," Dom said, "Cassidy *is* a negative one, so—"

"And Porter?" Walker said.

I chewed on my smile from Dom's remarks and glanced around. "Which one...?"

A guy rapped on the table. He was one of the agents, tan, with eyes like a coalmine. I knew nothing about him, and now I had to break into his head. However, his didn't prove much of an obstacle.

A challenge... could be, no... pi. Three and one-four-one-five-nine-two-six-five —

"Pi," I said.

Dom let loose a dramatic sigh. "Of course. Porter's *always* thinking of food."

"She means the numerical value," Porter said.

"Good," Walker said, nodding. "What else can you do?"

"Speak telepathically. Sometimes I can overhear Grifters when they're in groups. Not sure why."

"How far is your range?"

"With Kara and Sheedy, I think my range is unlimited. They heard me when we were in different states."

To see the interest opening Walker's expression reminded me that my ability *was* pretty impressive.

"You can read more than current thoughts, right?" Agent Cassidy asked. I would've mentally referred to her as *Ethan-agent*, except I didn't want to compare him to someone who looked carved from ice. "You can read old thoughts?" she said.

"Yes," I said.

Her mouth twisted with discomfort. She looked like she'd prefer to say more, but Saini spoke up.

"Is this something you see, or hear?"

"Both," I said.

"You can *see* the memories of others?"

"Yes."

Saini, unlike Cassidy, leaned forward with palpable interest. I may as well have been a science experiment. "You don't steal the memories, do you?" she asked.

"Not that I'm aware of."

"Can we set some ground rules here?" Cassidy waved her hand for attention. "One telepath was bad enough. We all have a right to privacy."

"Except Andrews," one of her fellow agents said. A laugh moved around the table.

"Kepler doesn't seem the type to pry," Walker said.

I nodded. "If I had it my way, I'd be telekinetic instead. Trust me, I won't go around reading your thoughts left and right."

"You did with Sheedy," Cassidy said. "At SPO-10."

I'd forgotten these metas knew all about my time with Ethan at SPO-10. They'd likely monitored us the entire six months. Realizing that made *me* feel like the one under the telepathic microscope.

"He gave me permission," I said.

"Does anyone give Kepler permission to read their thoughts at her whim?" Cassidy asked the room.

"I do," Dom said. "That is, I give her permission to read *yours*, Keswick. You see, I've worried for years the only thing you think of is how to kill us in our sleep."

"Only you, Dom." Keswick, the broad-shouldered agent with the squashed nose, never glanced up from the knife he cleaned. "You snore."

A series of chuckles bounced from member to member, leaving me with a strange realization. These weren't the bland, stiff metas I'd expected. They were familiar with one another and traded inside jokes as easily as jabs. The members of Operation Whitewash… they were *friends*.

Walker, however, refrained from cracking a smile, as if he viewed the jokes as an interruption. I had a brief mental image of Ethan frowning as Vires and McFarland pretended they weren't flirting with each other, then disregarded it. Ethan and Walker were nothing alike.

"So," Walker said, "we've established the only person Kepler will be reading is Andrews and anyone else who might stand between us and him."

I reflected on Andrews' allies and remembered his most powerful, another first officer. "There are more metas who can do extra things," I said. "Banks told you about Agent Chang?"

"Andrews calls them 'proteans,'" Banks said. "They're classified. One's had trouble uncovering info."

"Has —"

Walker cut me off with a flip of his hand. "We need to know what happened in novum after Banks left."

I swallowed my question. Later, I'd come back to this. Maybe these "proteans" made up the extra level in the Society?

"Novum?" I asked Walker.

"The water tower," Banks said.

Just three words sent my heart speeding. Finally, I'd have to dredge up the event I'd yet to understand.

"Andrews tested a sample of my DNA in his grid. Whatever he saw…."

"*All this time…* " he'd murmured.

All this time *what*? I was a protean?

"It shocked him," I told Walker.

His lips grew thinner, and his mustache, in contrast, resembled a dust broom.

"So he *does* know how to identify the protean gene." Dr. Saini spoke softly, as if in understanding to herself. Then, she seemed to realize we all watched her. She shook free of her stupor and turned to me. "We were never sure if he understood how to detect it. We knew, when we allowed the MTA to first discover you, that something in your DNA might alert Andrews to your ability. So we forged a quintex strand, and that's what's in your MTA file. Fake DNA. But if he tested a sample of your *real* DNA… that means, the entire time you were back at the academy again, he knew you're a protean."

"This also proves there is more to this protean project," Cassidy said. "Why is Andrews randomly testing his students' DNA?"

Walker shook his head. "The protean project has never been a priority, and it isn't now. Where did he take you next, Kepler?"

"Why did he think to test your DNA in the first place, Ella?" Saini, ignoring Walker's obvious attempt to redirect the subject, plopped her chin on her hand. "You must've given him an indication."

My fingers, hidden under the table, played with their gloves. "A Tacemus was there, reading me. I don't think Andrews knows everything I can do. He just suspects some things."

"Suspects some things?" Cassidy cast her hands wide with incredulity. "For all we know, Andrews knows she's a full-blown telepath!"

"Why does it matter?" Banks said. "She's not even at the academy anymore. He has no idea where she is."

"What happened next, Kepler?" Walker spoke loudly over Cassidy's exclamations.

"I woke up in a tank, in some lab in the middle of nowhere. He said…." I felt suddenly as if the breathing tube was shoved back down my throat, stealing all the moisture in my mouth. "It would keep my muscles in shape."

Dr. Saini nodded. "Stasis chamber. Those are meant for Grifters." A disgusted sigh rolled in her throat. "You were in the chamber from the night of the novum incident until December third?"

"Yeah, until Chang took me from there to the jet where One cleared me."

"So Chang knows where this lab is," Agent Cassidy said.

"Not anymore," I said. "Andrews said he'd clear her."

Cassidy twisted toward Walker. "It must've been Integer. He probably wasn't prepared, which is why he doesn't remember. That means the lab's location is in Integer's head. Kepler can—"

"We stay on task," Walker barked. "The protean project doesn't tell us anything we need to know in order to read Andrews."

"We need eyes on this, Walker. You've been putting us off for years, and the project's just gotten bigger. Now's not the time to ignore it. Imagine how many Changs there might be? If we find them before Andrews, we might finally have less depressing numbers."

"Speaking of numbers," I interrupted, "Banks told you that Andrews listed a bunch of names in novum, right? He knows about Whitewash."

"We've known that," Walker said. "Andrews has slowly pieced intel together. We didn't realize he'd learned Whitewash's name, or so many members, but...." Walker shrugged, his eyes alighting on Dr. Saini for a spell before he returned to me. "At this time, it's too dangerous to use Integer. Each time he clears Andrews, he risks death. So we operate knowing that our moves are monitored. Some of us have avoided detection, but Andrews suspects even me. We have Sheedy to thank for that bit of intel. He and I had a little chat before Chron invaded Goose Swamp."

"What?" I said.

"Andrews sent Sheedy to confront me. The Grifter attack interrupted us. Sheedy never got the chance to report back—meaning Andrews doesn't know we had that conversation."

"So Andrews doesn't know that *you* know he suspects you."

"Correct. Gives us an advantage, but means I will have to move carefully when I bring him in."

"And when will that be?" I asked.

Focus reined in, shaking loose the wisps of distraction. *This* was the reason we sat at this table, in this base. I prepped myself for Walker's answer.

"Integer's with him now," Walker said, "so he's been unable to report in. Until we have word, we won't know where to rendezvous. But, if all passes without a hitch, we'll have Andrews by the end of the day."

I refused to let my expression budge a centimeter. *Today.* Today I'd look him in the eye and somehow find the empathy to peek past that deceptive persona.

"What happens next?" I said.

"Operation Whitewash exists to wipe out corruption in the MTA, starting at its head," Walker said. "We do this slowly, because it's blasted hard to expose the truth when the Tacemus follow after to erase our work.

That's why eliminating Andrews' power over them is our first priority. Once we're certain we won't be read or have our allies forget our conversations, we can work faster. Our end goal is maneuvering a change of leadership. The MTA commander always elects his successor, but if we can overturn that custom and appoint someone we trust, we'll have succeeded."

"Who do you intend to take charge after Andrews?"

"Amy's got some ideas." Walker nodded at the sandy haired Amy Lane, who ducked her head at the attention. "She's our strongest recruiter and has the ear of not a few leaders. Though the Tacemus prevent us from going public, those we *have* convinced have stayed true. Our immediate operation remains small, but our reach grows."

"And this new commander will fix the other issues?" I said.

"There are dozens, Kepler. To which are you referring?"

"Metas are stolen from their parents, and Grifters aren't actually stupid animals on an endless killing spree. Durgan wants peace with the MTA. I promised him I'd make that happen."

"Those issues can't be fixed through a simple change of command. Two-hundred years of rhetoric will take time to cut through. But eventually, when the situation has stabilized, we will implement phase two." Walker crossed his arms; a pair of giant biceps boxed in his chest. "Speaking of Durgan, he stays put for now. We're not risking anything. No one comes or leaves who doesn't need to."

An argument grew in my throat like a bubble of oxygen. Durgan wasn't some cadet; he was a Grifter king, with a family probably worried sick about his safety. But, knowing by now how metas operated, I decided to discuss this with Walker later.

"Kara isn't allowed to know anything about Whitewash," I said, "but I'm assuming the same doesn't apply to Sheedy, since he's in the MTA. Right?"

"Sheedy can have full access to whatever information he wants. What he can't do is leave his room until we complete this operation."

"Can't leave his room?"

"Correct," Walker said.

"Why not?"

"He's a loose cannon."

"*Sheedy*? He's the most responsible cadet at the academy."

"And the most loyal. To Andrews."

"Because no one's told him the truth yet," I said.

"Go talk to him and see what he says, Kepler. He's heard the truth."

A cold whoosh punched me in the chest, causing my heart to flop like it was seasick. I looked at Banks, who busied himself with staring across the table as if monitoring Agent Keswick's knife-cleaning took top priority. "I thought no one told him anything," I said to Banks, trying my hardest to keep my voice level.

Walker waved his grid, which told me nothing, until he dropped his explanation. "He's listening now. I let him hear this entire briefing. Two birds, one stone."

Ethan was currently listening? Judging by the general lack of reaction, I realized I was the only one unaware.

This entire briefing.

A replay, uncomfortably slow, unraveled in my recollection. We'd incriminated Andrews with a dozen different crimes. Did he know Andrews was Leader? I hoped he'd never heard the name. We'd discussed my telepathy—okay, he already knew that much. Durgan as an ally we could easily explain. Anything else? Hopefully we hadn't—

Metas were stolen from their parents. I'd been the one to say it. Those were the words that couldn't be unsaid.

I stared at Walker. For that beat of time, he was the only Whitewash member who existed. He was, after all, the head. What kind of tactless person would lock someone in a room, then force a painful truth on them via an audio broadcast? Unplanned, unfiltered, unforgiving?

He was just being pragmatic, tried that cautious voice of empathy.

It doesn't matter! I would've liked to shout outside my head, too. Instead, I drew enough breath to bring the ache back in my lungs. "Where is he?" Though I kept the anger from my tone, it wobbled anyway.

After returning my stare, Walker nodded to Saini.

The doctor stood, all politeness around her mouth. "Follow me, Ella."

I beat Saini to the door through which everyone had earlier emerged. In waiting for her to catch up, I caught Banks' profile. He'd known. He could've warned me.

Let it go.

I twisted the knob and stepped through the opening. Before the door closed after Saini, I caught Hina Akamu's voice.

"Face-off: Kepler versus Walker. Who wins?"

A swell of voices called "Walker," but a few said "Kepler."

I didn't want to face off. I'd be happy to never see Walker's face again.

Saini directed me through a galley, where silver kitchen appliances bedecked the walls.

"I don't get how Whitewash's methods are all that different from the MTA's," I said.

She swiveled to face me, stuck halfway between a dining area and a hallway beyond it. Saini, one of the kindest metas I'd encountered, currently resembled a mother bear who wanted nothing more than to swat me flat. "Agent Walker did you a favor. Ethan responds best to authority. Had you told him your own way, he would've doubted you."

"Every bit of information you have on Ethan comes from Banks, who can't stand him."

"You and Banks aren't the only people who've interacted with Ethan. I knew him when he was in primary. Integer can read him. Walker was the one—" She cut her sentence short. Her protective countenance disintegrated as quickly as it'd come.

"The one who what?" I said.

She pressed her lips together, eyes on the ceiling. After visibly battling her resolve, she sighed and folded her arms. "You'll probably read me if I don't tell you. Walker retrieved him when he was born. Brought him to the MTA. Before you lash out, it wasn't personal. That's the job of an agent. We've all done our share of evils for the MTA. We had to learn it was wrong somehow."

I imagined Walker racing from a hospital with a baby carelessly tucked in the crook of his elbow. The mental image set my jaw.

"Ethan wouldn't have done it," I said.

"Don't be so sure. He's an obedient little lackey." Saini grimaced, then continued through the hallway. The green shag carpet looked odd beneath our military boots. Ceiling-to-ceiling wall paneling made the space dim and cramped. Nothing screamed "covert operation," and maybe that was the point.

The hallway reached a dead end at a single door, though not before it forked right, a shorter hallway that fit a room barred by windows and double doors. It could've been some CEO's office, its windows decorated by mini blinds.

"He's in there," Saini said, indicating the double doors. They were standard business style, with impenetrably fogged glass.

"Will we have privacy?" I asked.

"The room is soundproof, but there is a camera. And a listening device for audio."

"Why?"

"This room's meant for Andrews, and we want him under twenty-four-seven supervision."

"You put Ethan in Andrews' room?"

"It's not a Grifter cell," Saini said calmly. "Besides, he'll be relocated soon enough." She palmed the glass above the door handle. Blue light chased around her hand until it formed a square. Several buttons appeared in the flat console. Saini stabbed one, and the window blinds — evidently digitized — fizzled out of existence.

Ethan stood in the center of the room, his arms crossed, his eyes square on me. He didn't look angry or hurt; his gaze was focused and his jaw locked. This was battle-ready Ethan, prepping for... what, exactly?

"He's malnourished. I'll bring him food." Dr. Saini turned from the sight. Trouble creased between her brows. "You probably won't believe me, but I'll be unhappy to see you get hurt."

"He's not going to attack me."

"Your heart, Ella. That hurts worse." After another grimace, she jabbed a second icon. "Fifteen minutes. Then we're getting you. It'll do no good to drag this out." She yanked the door open, and I stepped quickly through.

CHAPTER SEVEN

THE ROOM CAME FURNISHED with a bed, wardrobe, and desk. Its style matched the hallway: outdated, as if Whitewash had designed it years ago and hadn't touched it since.

Behind me, a *zing* chimed; the blind overlay dropped over the windows.

I crossed the room and stood before Ethan. He'd nearly dried from our waterfall plunge, which had washed the grime from his tactical outfit and skin. His hair, straight as ever, looked strange so close to his ears, giving him an appearance that bordered on unruly.

"Ethan, I'm sorry. I didn't know they were broadcasting that to you."

He put a finger to his lips. His attention had drifted upward, not absently but with purpose. After a beat, he moved around me, one arm extended. The desk chair skidded along the floor before lifting. Ethan caught it from the air, set it before him, then stepped onto the seat in one swift progression. In another deft motion, he elbowed a ceiling tile. Plaster spat over his face and caked his arm. He fisted through the hole he'd formed, feeling around before yanking loose a black device strapped inside the ceiling by a colorful spray of wires. The frayed ends sizzled when Ethan wrenched them entirely from their perch. He tossed the box to the floor; it clattered in protest, right before Ethan landed on it. He stomped the device into slivers.

Well, at least he'd eliminated some supervision.

Ethan gestured me toward the bathroom. I followed, feeling tension creep into my muscles. Instinct guided them, a warning reminder: *You're a meta. Get ready.*

I settled by the tub. Ethan slid the door shut. Then we were alone, finally, after weeks of physical separation and months of memory loss. But this was not our happy reunion. Ethan stood close with his head bent toward mine, driven by determination instead of longing.

"This room is clean," he murmured, "but keep your voice low, just in case."

"Are you okay?"

"What happened after I left with Banks?"

"We landed at base. Why? What happened to you?"

"Banks injected me with some sedative. I woke up here."

"Oh." Of course Banks did. He'd told Ethan nothing only because Ethan wouldn't have been awake for any of it. "I can see why that would make you concerned. Um —"

"Do you know where they've put Kara?"

"She's in the clinic. She's fine. We're all fine." I rubbed my forehead. Whitewash's great plan, meant to eliminate drama, had only set Ethan on high alert. Why would he trust anything from the people who'd knocked him out and tossed him inside a locked room?

I held his arms, wishing gloves didn't separate my hands from his. "I know this looks bad, and I don't agree with how they treated you, but Whitewash isn't the enemy."

"Ella, they've done something to your memories again, but I will get us out of here. What's the headcount?"

"We can't leave, Ethan. We have nowhere to go, and Kara's on an IV."

"We'll take her to a civilian clinic. Then we'll notify Leader. He'll send someone to pick us up."

I couldn't help cringing as his exclamation of unfailing trust reverberated along the tiled walls. That was his first reaction, had always been his first reaction: contact Leader. Ethan's father figure never failed to provide whatever Ethan requested, the very man whose MTA agent knew Grifters were in the Dewey Forest and that Ethan could've been there — and failed to coordinate an extraction. Even Leader's most loyal commanding officer was expendable.

I gripped his hands now, disregarding the discomfort. "Listen to me. I know it's the last thing you want to believe, I know it hurts, but Leader is not the man you think he is. If we contact him, that'll make things worse."

He stepped back. Shook his head. "Whitewash is manipulating you."

"No they aren't. It's true, my memory's been wiped before, but by *Leader*. When I got my memory back, I saw how he ordered the Tacemus to clear me. He's the reason people lose their memories, Ethan."

"Operation Whitewash is using you for their own gain. You're letting their lies influence you."

"I was there, Ethan! I remember what Leader did to me."

"Memory can be faulty, as you know better than most. And I've been wiped by Whitewash, haven't I? The agents mentioned incidents from SPO-10 that I don't remember. How can you guarantee that what you know is the truth if Whitewash regularly employs memory-wiping?"

Much as it frustrated me, I forced myself to consider his perspective. Yes, memory fabrication existed, and my mind *and* Ethan's had already been manipulated by One. He could have done it again; but, after bouncing back from memory loss and replacement, I could recognize false ideas.

"I've had memories implanted. Some vague part of my mind believes I was homeschooled for a year, though it's hazy, without much detail. But what happened with Andrews? I remember how cold I felt after the tank, how tight my limbs were because Chang was controlling them. There was a family crest in the lab. *Saecula Saeculorum.* I can smell the car that he transported me in. Those are details Whitewash wouldn't know. You heard them—they didn't know that lab existed, much less that it's surrounded by trees. How do I know something they don't?"

"Perhaps Leader did take you to a lab, and Agent Chang was there, but Whitewash could easily conflate those details into a memory they want."

Ethan could logic his way out of anything. Worse, he had a welt on his temple as hard evidence that Whitewash didn't hesitate to use extreme measures. It stung to admit, but Saini had gotten it right: Ethan refused to believe me. Maybe it was a defense mechanism. Rather than accept the painful truth, he'd argue until he exhausted his defenses. Then, who knew what would be left to support his self-assurance?

"Stop, Ethan," I whispered. "I cared about him, too. But he's not who you think he is."

"You have no proof for any of these accusations. Stealing metas from their parents? That—" His sentence caught, strained by a hesitance that—finally—allowed doubt to pain his eyes. Ethan shook his head. "He would never allow that."

"What if I get you proof?"

"There *is* no proof. These are the baseless words of a rogue group of metas who have no jurisdiction. The fact that you blindly trust them indicates, to me, that they've tampered with your reasoning. You would never support this, Ella. I know you. Trust me. You and Kara are in danger." He looked desperate now, not for anyone's assurance but mine.

I wished his logic could win. Of all Andrews' crimes, this burned the worst. Acceptance meant Ethan's entire life was a lie. He'd been serving neither his nation nor his parents' wishes but the commands of a psychopath.

"I heard him admit to it, Ethan. He doesn't think metas belong with civilian parents. I know these memories are mine, and they're true. Can't you trust me?"

"I trust you. But I don't trust your memory. Not when memories can be manipulated."

I dug my palms in my eyes, at once noticing the pressure that had been creeping toward the surface this entire conversation. It should've been easier than this. I'd known Ethan would be reluctant, but I had no tools to combat utter denial.

"I don't know what to do. You heard Walker. He won't let you out."

"Agent Walker is smart," Ethan said, some bite deepening his voice. "He knows exactly what I would do."

"But you don't have to do that, Ethan. Prove them wrong! Work with us! All we're doing is reading Andrews and electing a new commander. No one will get hurt."

"As far as they've told you. What happens after?"

"We patch up what he destroyed," I said.

"Metas will resist. There will be bloodshed."

"We'll worry about that if it comes."

"Please don't do this, Ella." Now he whispered, once again moved by the raw emotion that sometimes found him. He caught my face and leaned close. Earnest resolve brightened his eyes. "We can escape. We'll take Kara home, then we'll find someone in charge and deal with this through the proper channels. Rogue organizations are bound to fail. Whitewash *can't* succeed."

The temptation to let Ethan be right pulled my heart. It would be easy to give in, fight side by side in a battle out of these walls.

Ethan picked up on my hesitance; his voice grew more confident. "If the idea of Leader makes you uneasy, we don't have to turn to him yet. We'll go to your parents. They'll help us."

I ducked my head. The reality of Mom and Dad couldn't be suppressed, not with Walker around, or even Ethan and Kara. Durgan instructed me on how to hide thoughts, but it seemed the more I buried them, the more they sought the light above.

"My parents... don't remember me again."

His hands, tangled in my hair, tightened. "Who ensured that, Grifters or Whitewash?"

I wanted so badly to blame Chron, but this jab had come from my allies in the other room. My answer wouldn't come. Ethan already knew it anyway.

He tilted my chin up. All his intensity had given way to compassion. "I know you're confused. It's not your fault, Ella. Whitewash has lied to you. But you can fight back. You're more powerful than they are. Read them. Find a weakness in their base. You and I can communicate long-distance, right? We'll make a plan, and we'll go somewhere safe."

He made it seem simple, but Ethan didn't understand what Whitewash fought against. We might've operated outside the MTA's jurisdiction, but, if not Whitewash, who else would unveil the truth?

I met Ethan's gaze. "Eugene Andrews controls the Tacemus like slaves. He tells little girls, like Bridget Avary, that Grifters are evil monsters. He ordered someone to steal you from your family. He manipulated me into trusting him over my own parents. He needs to be stopped, and I'm going to work with Whitewash to make that happen."

With every word, his expression had grown tauter. When I finished, Ethan stepped back. His earnest fire had disintegrated entirely. Instead, a weak flame of resignation wavered. "You're going to get killed," he said.

"I could've died on the missions we went on together, but you didn't try stopping me then."

"Because your death would've been honorable and not the result of stupidity."

A slap would've hurt only slightly more. Anger spiked, foreign from anything I'd ever felt toward Ethan. Yes, he was confused. Betrayed. Tired. Probably starving. But he'd molded his opinions on something he understood nothing about. "You think I'm being stupid?" I said.

"That's not the right word." He prodded the divot between his brows, then said, not at all gently, "Foolish, and naïve. You're putting your life and your abilities into the hands of—"

"People I can't trust because they've manipulated me? By your logic, I'd also be an idiot to go back to the MTA. So what should I do, run off and start my own one-man operation?"

"You should obey the legitimate authority."

"The MTA is not legitimate, Ethan. If *you* would stop being foolish and naïve, you'd see that."

"I—" His lips pressed together, and he drew in air that he expelled in one spurt. "Are you reading my mind?"

"*No*," I said, bothered by the assumption. "I know you think you're right ninety-eight percent of the time, but this is that two percent, Ethan."

Compassion had deserted Ethan's features. He'd never glared at me before. Until now.

A knock came from the room beyond. "Time's up, Kepler," called a scratchy voice I thought might've belonged to Agent Keswick.

Neither of us reacted, though inwardly I felt relief. This conversation had rattled us. Saini had been right about that, too.

"I'll bring you evidence." I moved toward the bathroom door, but Ethan blocked the threshold. Reluctance clicked across his expression. In his thoughts, dozens of strategies mounted. None of them ended with me leaving this room.

I stepped back. "You can't lock me in here."

"You're their weapon. They can't do anything without you."

"So you're going to hold me hostage in your bathroom? It's not going to work, Ethan. You're outnumbered."

"How many?"

I sighed. "Fourteen."

His focus drifted. Calculations stacked, various Macto techniques for fighting multiple enemies.

Something thumped on the bathroom door. "You kids have had enough alone time in there," Keswick said. "Back up, unless you want splinters."

"Hold on," I called.

Ethan wouldn't budge. I knew that as definitively as I knew the ocean outside was wet. He'd bar the door until it collapsed onto him, and he'd go down thinking he'd done the right thing.

My frustration trickled out. He cared to a fault I couldn't criticize, because at least he always meant his mettle.

When I moved, Ethan tensed. I squeezed beside him and squared my shoulders against the door. *I disagree with you*, I said, *but I don't want you to get hurt.* I braced my palms. "Okay, Keswick. Knock the door down."

"So… you both *want* to be injured?"

"Yes," I answered.

"Teenagers," Keswick muttered.

Confusion won out the battle-ready glint in Ethan's expression. He stared at me almost helplessly. "Wait," he called. Ethan pondered a moment more, then shut his eyes and swallowed. "I surrender." He stepped away from the door.

"Pity. I was amped for a fight." Keswick snagged the handle; I moved before the swinging door hit me.

"I'll bring you proof," I told Ethan.

He stared back, saying nothing. It seemed we'd both lost.

I followed Keswick and left Ethan to his thoughts.

CHAPTER EIGHT

AGENT KESWICK, ABOUT WHOM I knew nothing other than the fact that he'd probably punched a lot of Grifters, stuck to me like tape. He gave me space to breathe only when we exited off the galley. Cassidy, the female agent who'd argued with Walker over the protean project, circled the other male agent—Porter?—in the boxing ring. They were the only ones around.

"Where'd everyone go?" I asked Keswick.

"We've got duties other than babysitting you, Kepler."

I shrugged off his remark. The qualifications for life as an agent must've read, *Needed: impatient metas with gruff personalities.* Ethan would make the only kind agent in the MTA, probably because he'd never trained in agent studies. Despite Ethan's vocational schooling as a primary school "traditor," Andrews had assigned him the post-grad duties of an agent, and Ethan had accepted his fate.

Another reason to fight against the MTA. I wouldn't let them squash the goodness out of Ethan.

McFarland trained in agent studies, I remembered, *and she's nice.*

Maybe so, but, as a member of the Society, she'd kept the truth about Grifters from her MTA partner, James Reynolds. Nice or not, she'd chosen MTA duties over the bonds of friendship.

Did everyone pick and choose what to believe?

No. Not Ethan. He's one hundred percent textbook MTA soldier.

Surely Whitewash had evidence incriminating the MTA. Dr. Saini would know. I wanted to check on Kara and Durgan, anyway.

In the clinic, Kara lay closest to the door. The IV dripped, and a machine blinked her vitals. Her breathing fell smoother than it did earlier, which gave me some relief. Before I could move closer, Saini's murmuring drew my attention toward Durgan.

He sat upright on a throne of pillows. The hem of his hospital gown had been bunched high, above his knee, giving a full visual of one bumpy and one discolored leg. Gauze wrapped his right kneecap, below which revealed skin tinged with black blistering. He seemed uninterested in Saini's diagnosis but gazed toward the wall. Had his fingers not twitched every other word, he could've passed for sleeping.

"... reevaluate you every hour to see how you're responding." Saini paid no attention to my entrance. She seemed intent on provoking a reply from Durgan, but only Dr. Lee gave her any acknowledgement. The young, anxious meta bobbed his head and took notes on his grid.

"My belief is the antibiotic will prove effective." Dr. Saini waited, mouth slightly open with hopeful expectation.

"Thank you. You may leave." He waved her out. Durgan, a Grifter, shooing the MTA doctor out of her own clinic.

Saini's eyebrows settled halfway on their journey toward the ceiling. I would've grinned, but worry for Durgan nagged me. Yes, he was a king, familiar with ordering his subjects. He did not, however, ignore them.

After taking a moment to readjust her shock, Saini spoke. "If you have any questions, Dr. Lee can answer them." She was a professional; she'd maintain proper etiquette.

Lee, not so much. "Did you hear—"

"It's fine," she muttered, dragging Lee by his coat.

Durgan took no notice of their exit, nor my approach. I inched toward his feet. "May I sit here?"

He still spoke toward the wall. "You may."

The flimsy bedsheets crinkled like static when I sat. "Thank you for getting Kara out, Durgan."

"You are welcome."

"Once you're healed, we'll take you back to your family. Are they at your home?"

His finger twitching desisted. "They are not."

Trepidation tingled, a spark waiting to ignite. "Do you... know where they are?"

If the wall had begun shifting colors, I doubt he would have reacted. When he spoke, his gravelly tone dropped to a tremor. "You mean kindness, but your questions... cause a pain I cannot bear." Durgan finally looked at me. He had a face dried of tears. Grifters couldn't cry. I didn't think he'd have the will to, anyway.

"Chron was not merciful. My family sleeps now."

The center of my chest coiled. "Durgan." My voice sounded strangled. "I am so sorry. I didn't know. I...." Nothing came after that.

"Do not ask me to speak of it. I cannot. Read me if you must."

Some memories held too much pain to share, let alone witness. Instead, I reached for his hands. When words failed, touch helped, though I couldn't fathom what comfort such a tiny gesture could give. The contact supplied an unexpected connection, a microscope directly into his memories. Scenes interrupted my vision of Durgan and the clinic.

"You will not have your peace, harsk." Chron, *his only hand tight around a female Grifter's throat, jerked his arm. Her struggle went limp.* "Your wife was a traitor to her kind. Your children will share her fate. Your heir already has. Durgson soiled his name with cowardice when I killed him before classmates who did not defend him." *Chron turned to a small Grifter forced to kneel. She cried out, then was silenced. He and a companion moved to the next, one by one, all dead in under a minute. Durgan could do nothing but watch.*

I longed to recoil, sparing myself the pain, but willed myself to accept these memories as a way of uniting with Durgan. One had instructed me to control my attachments as a method of sealing off the thoughts of others, but too often I'd *over* attached, even when it hurt. To reject Durgan's memories—even though he hadn't deliberately sent them to me—would seem like a denial of everything he'd endured.

"My friends betrayed me, betrayed my beloved, my children...." His present-day words swiped through the memory, relieving me of its burden. Durgan's fist clenched, crushing my already distorted bones with sharp pain, but I couldn't move.

"Durgan... " I whispered. I couldn't suppress my shaking, even as I directed every effort to maintaining a solid, dependable frame for Durgan to lean on.

He gripped my elbows. "Do not weep for me," he said hoarsely. "Soon, I will see them. I feel my end, rushing—" Durgan's grip grew so intense, I bit back a groan. Then, suddenly, his hands went limp. He collapsed backward onto the heap of pillows, stone-still for a moment of horror. With a rattled gasp, he writhed, limbs bucking so violently they smacked the bedside cart and sent it flying toward the wall.

I shot off the bed. "Saini!"

She raced into the clinic, Lee tripping after her. Saini took a wide-eyed glimpse at Durgan and said, "We need to cut it, now! Tie it."

Lee skittered from drawer to drawer, tossing supplies airborne in his hunt for the spool of floss-like string he eventually found. Meanwhile, Saini caught a syringe mid-flight from the shelves, then jabbed it into Durgan's chest.

"Wait outside, Kepler," she barked.

Jamming my arm against my mouth, I rushed to the exit and pulled the door shut behind me. I blinked and blinked. Durgan writhed on. Chron was still murdering his children.

How could Chron, who'd nearly let me free when Helix rebuked him at the library, have lost enough humanity to murder innocent children? Maybe she'd been the one keeping his humanity intact. Helix was MIA, and this was how he'd succumbed without her.

I squeezed my temples but couldn't release the regret. Durgan had asked me to warn his son, Durgson. I'd told him to take his mother and siblings to safety. He....

My thinking faltered. Chron had told Durgan he'd killed Durgson in his classroom, but Durgson had already left. I'd seen him disappear down the crowded hallway. Durgan's thoughts mourned all six of his children—but, before him, Chron had killed only three, and mentioned the other deaths in passing.

An odd swoop fluttered inside. Moments passed before I recognized it as hope. Some of Durgan's children might've escaped. Chron hadn't wanted him to know that.

I spun back inside the clinic. If Durgson still lived, Durgan likely knew where he would've escaped to. When he awoke from surgery, he wouldn't have a leg, but maybe he'd have some family. I could fix this, help someone, after having done a terrible job helping Ethan.

I peeled the curtain back just enough to spot Durgan's head. Lee and Saini ignored me. I'd never searched an unconscious mind; would it even work? Sleep formed a blanket over Durgan's thoughts—no, a sheet. Fully covered but thin enough to see through.

Following curves of rough stone, Durgan thought to the young Grifter who bobbed alongside him. *"Come with me, son. Today you will learn what a king must know."*

The scene flashed to a narrow, low tunnel whose ceiling dripped water. Durgan and his son crept along until they reached an exit hatch. *"Follow the water until it ends,"* Durgan said. *"There will be help for you and your siblings. It is your duty to protect them should I fall, Durgson."*

"Yes, Papa."

I caught sight of a familiar swamp, a highway, a tiny convenience store whose sign flashed "MPV Grocer." With an inhale, I brought myself out of his head. The doctors didn't even notice me leave.

Downstairs, a few more Whitewash members had come to life. The agents boxed. At the conference table, Banks, wearing dirty coveralls, scrubbed his fingers with an oil-stained rag while a few others ate breakfast—Walker included.

I marched to the head of the table. "Can we talk?"

Walker glanced up from his bowl of oatmeal.

"Chron killed Durgan's family, but some of them might still be alive. There's a grocery store that his family uses as a refuge—the place Helix told me about last year. MPV Grocer. Durgan's remaining children might be there."

Walker put up a hand. "After we've secured Andrews, we'll look into it. Not today. Integer has waited eighteen years for this moment. We can't afford to jeopardize it."

"Durgan might be dying! Please. He's the reason I know how to use my telepathy. Don't we owe him?"

"We will help him. *After* Andrews is secure."

"We don't know when that will be or if Durgan will last that long. His kids could relocate in the meantime."

Walker shook his head. Whitewash didn't like interruptions—I got that, so much so that I'd agreed to temporarily abandon Kara and Ethan in favor of helping Whitewash first. Couldn't Walker see that this was a matter of life and death, though?

I kept my stance, adjusting only the intensity of my gaze. "Please, Walker," I said. "These are young Grifters. His *children*."

As Walker appraised me, something stirred him enough to shake out a few wrinkles. If I'd guessed Walker could come across as anything other than a bristly bear, I would've pegged his expression for... normal? After blowing air through pursed lips, Walker called, "Cassidy." He waved the boxing agents over. "You three. Gear up. Plainclothes."

Relief had never felt so light. Somewhere, behind that chest of steel, Walker had a heart.

"Finally." Cassidy slung her towel at Agent Keswick. "I'm sick of beating these two."

"I'll come." Banks rose, dropping his dirty rag.

"You have obligations here," Walker said.

"I've checked the aircraft. Nothing left to do."

Walker's mouth thinned, but he said nothing.

Though I feared pushing my luck, I wanted to ensure this mission succeeded. "Durgson will recognize me," I said, "but he's not going to listen to a group of metas. I won't get in the way."

"Correct," Walker said, "and you'll follow orders and refrain from doing anything rash."

"Okay. Sir," I added, and Walker lifted a brow.

"If you don't want someone rash," Cassidy called, squeezing a water bottle over her head, "why send Banks?"

I gauged Banks' reaction. He looked indifferent.

"This way I know where he is," Walker said. "Try not to lose him again, Miranda."

Miranda Cassidy's blue eyes popped. "You *Miranda'd* me? When has that ever worked?"

"It works today, CG." Walker returned to his oatmeal with all the air of having just sent us off to buy groceries.

Miranda, who appeared slightly mollified at having been assigned commanding general, barked for us to follow her. Three agents, one mechanic clad in coveralls, and I tromped through the galley. Smells of syrup and bacon caused my stomach to gurgle. Recognizing breakfast made me realize I'd been awake since yesterday morning.

I'd sleep and eat when this was over.

Maybe.

The hallway passed Ethan's room and concluded at another door. It led to a garage the size of a small backyard. Four black SUVs formed one neat row, behind that a dozen motorcycles. A white transport van, parked perpendicular to the rest, took up the rear. Hanging on slat boards in place of hammers and saws, guns of varying sizes gave the garage the distinct feeling of danger. Gear, from bike helmets to cartons of explosive "bursts," took residence on every counter, yet nothing appeared cluttered or disorderly.

"What do civilians wear in grocers?" asked Miranda—no, "Cassidy" had already stuck and would stay.

"Normal clothes," I said; then, registering the impending *Duh, you idiot* about to erupt from her, added, "It's summer, so t-shirts and flip-flops."

"'*Flip-flops?*' Am I supposed to know what that means?"

"Sandals," Banks said. He pointed to a shelf.

For a minute, the garage disappeared to a swirl of clothes and accessories. Cassidy ran every article of fabric by me, though Banks' frequent interruptions revealed he had a decent grasp of acceptable civilian attire.

"He did spend all of three days in a civilian school," Agent Keswick said dryly.

Banks ignored this, elbow-deep in a box of hats.

Keswick had a point. Banks had lived as Jimmy Daniels less than a week; a cadet studying civilians would know more about fashion styles than Banks.

Once laden with armfuls of gear, the guys set to changing. Cassidy directed me to the white van and disappeared into an SUV. In the privacy of the van, I slipped on a yellow shirt and jean shorts. Tennis shoes replaced my boots, and a baseball cap went over my short hair.

When I exited the van, I tried not to laugh. Having exchanged his coveralls for plaid shorts and a polo, Banks currently looked like a golfer, especially when he added a visor. Agents Keswick and Porter were equally non-threatening in jeans and t-shirts. Cassidy emerged from the SUV in capris and a purple top that showed her defined biceps.

"Color makes your scowls less apparent." Agent Keswick winked at her.

Cassidy glowered.

The agents planned to arrive onsite first, allowing them to sniff out danger. Keswick and Cassidy filled their backpacks, completing the vibe of mature college students. Porter, the only animo of the agents, packed a dismantled rifle into a violin case; animos fought ranged. After slinging the case over his chest, he settled on a motorcycle. Cassidy gave the order, and three bikes rumbled away.

I climbed into the passenger seat of the van, expecting an interior that resembled some futuristic cockpit, but it showed nothing out of the ordinary. Behind me, there was no divider from the cab—spacious enough to fit three Grifters.

Outside, morning sun overwhelmed the fluorescent glow of bulbs, trading sterile white for soft yellow. The garage faced heaps of brush that blew in the summer breeze. Following tire indentions that faded into the sand, Banks left the base behind. He steered clear of the ocean, trekking alongside the industrial buildings of the marina. It continued to strike me as odd how close Whitewash had planted itself to civilians. They strolled fifty yards away, clad so brightly it looked staged. This entire setting screamed artificial, but they were the real ones, weren't they? People suntanned and tossed beach balls. They didn't read minds or go on secret missions.

The lull of passing wind was barely loud enough to mask the awkward silence between Banks and me. The last time he and I had been alone, we'd been on our way to Chron's. That conversation could've ended... better.

"So," I said, "why'd you want to help Durgan?"

"Can't you just be grateful?"

I frowned, too tired to restrain a rebuttal. "Can't you be pleasant for once in your life? What's your deal, Banks? You do nice things, and then you act annoyed about it."

"Back to analyzing me, then. Are you going to ask about my childhood next?"

My toes, wedged into shoes slightly too small, and fingers, constricted by gloves, couldn't even curl. Banks could be as infuriating as my old partner, Vires. With Vires, though, one could banter back. Banks seemed to lack the patience.

He left the wharf behind in pursuit of a highway. It felt odd, seeing civilian passersby and knowing how separated we were from them. Separated from each other, too. Side by side, we traveled, though not in sync. For all our secret moments together back at SPO-10 and the academy, not once had Banks and I existed in solidarity. He was aloof, a disconnected figure, bending rules as long as he'd understood them. Within this rogue operation, he still charted his own path. Every cadet, from Lydia to McFarland, disliked him. Even Vires, who should've bonded with Banks over disregarding the rules, couldn't stand him.

I scratched at the door handle, trying to ignore the surging pity — no doubt the side effect of my telepathy. Outside of One, Banks had no friends. He'd excluded himself from the cadets and chosen a fight none of them knew anything about. Why had he joined Whitewash?

Maybe because we fought the people we feared the most.

I'd already decided never to bring it up, but that resolve passed by like the cars on the highway. "We can talk about it," I said softly. "I won't think of you any differently."

He sighed. "What now?"

"I was there in the water tower. I heard what he said about your mom. And I'm not blind, Banks. I've always thought you two looked alike."

His hands tightened around the steering wheel. Banks glowered at the road. Even now, with that contorted profile, he resembled Andrews. Where had Banks' personality come from, though? Andrews came across as calm and paternal. Furthermore, he was Leader. Banks refused to lead anyone.

"Look," I said. "Maybe you're his son, maybe you're not. If so, all it means is you have some of his DNA. It doesn't mean you're anything like him."

"We both chose mechanical engineering as our vocation." He spat the words out so quickly, I knew he'd said them before, even if only to himself.

"So? Reynolds and I studied civilians, and we both have reddish hair and freckles and ask too many questions."

"You and Reynolds aren't related." His fingers slipped down the wheel. "We're both impatient," he muttered.

"Everyone in the world is impatient."

"We're both liars."

"I'm beginning to think everyone's a liar, too. But at least you admit it. Andrews wouldn't. You're very different from him. But if you notice a similarity you don't like, fight it. No one is forcing you to be like him. You can choose. Keep the good, and fight the rest."

By the furrow of his brows, it seemed he'd never considered his options—or knew he had any to begin with. Banks slouched in the seat with all the air of a defiant teen. "Are you going to tell anyone... about this?"

"No," I said. "Promise."

At the oath, his confusion thickened. Perhaps Banks had no idea how to accept a promise.

A car horn blared, causing Banks to jump. I swiveled my attention forward in time to see the traffic signal zoom over us. "Red light!" I yelled.

Banks swerved into the opposite lane, which only added additional cars to avoid.

"What are you doing!"

"Shut up, El!" Banks skidded back to our lane. The van teetered toward the shoulder, but Banks jerked the wheel in the opposite direction, and the tires came thumping down. We bumped along, until Banks eased up on the gas, and the van eventually steadied.

I released the armrests; the cushy rubber was pulverized.

A dribble of sweat escaped Banks' visor. As he tried sneaking out a heavy exhale, his hands relaxed. The steering wheel, squeezed and contorted, resembled burnt plastic.

"Maybe I should take over," I said.

"I know how to drive. Stop distracting me."

"This isn't my fault!" I rubbed my forehead and let out a shaky laugh. "Can you imagine Walker's reaction if we died in a car crash, of all things?"

His mouth twitched. "He'd refuse to come to the funeral."

I grinned. After a moment, Banks almost did, too. I didn't know whether it was our conversation or nearly crashing, but somewhere along the path, we'd breached the great divide.

"Did you ever learn anything about your mom?" I asked.

"I'm not in the MTA's files. Andrews must've deleted all the loose ends. I have nothing to find her with."

"DNA tests?"

"I've never had one done."

"The worst it could do is tell you something you already suspect. The best? Finding your mom."

He let out something between a scoff and a sigh. "Maybe one day, Kepler. My lineage is low priority."

"Now you sound like Walker."

This time, Banks released an actual snicker. It had a short life, dying quickly to a noncommittal throat-clearing, but it made me smile. He inhaled a deep breath, and it kept him buoyant. Somehow, he looked less like Andrews than five minutes earlier.

"So," he said, "how has Sheedy adapted to Whitewash?"

"You mean, what does he think of the people who knocked him out and imprisoned him? He thinks you guys are great."

"It doesn't matter what we've done. He'll distrust anything that's not the MTA."

I rolled my eyes. "Let's change the subject."

"So it's fair to pick around my brain but not yours?"

"Correct."

"Well," Banks said after a moment, "at least we'll always have something to disagree on."

"And at least I'll always be right."

He smirked. "You're nothing if not loyal, Ella."

My name came to his lips too easily. It wasn't the first time. He was inconsistent with what he called me, unlike other metas with their strict observance of the last-name-only rule.

A memory's echo sounded in my ear. "You called me 'El' earlier," I said. "Did you pick that up from Kara at Whale's?"

A deadpan mask swallowed his smirk right up. "What do you want me to call you?"

Though he'd diverted the question, I let it be for the sake of not imploding our friendship within the first minutes of existence. "It doesn't matter," I said. "Just stick with one."

"I'll stick with Ella, then."

"Cool. And I guess I'll stick with Banks."

"I guess you will."

So much for hoping he'd share his first name. *William,* Andrews had called him — to which Banks had protested. If not William, then what?

"What about Jimmy?" I said.

He trailed a finger down the mottled steering wheel. "Jimmy isn't real."

"Neither is Banks."

He stayed sealed as a clam.

"Fine," I said. "Banks it is."

CHAPTER NINE

FOUR HOURS LATER — because Banks sped — brought us to Capitol, South Carolina. It turned out Whitewash's base was in Virginia Beach, a crown to the body of Grifter-infested states of the Carolinas. The MTA had training academies in Virginia and West Virginia; but, in the six years Whitewash had operated out of their base, their closest calls had come with civilians.

Outside, an afternoon drizzle plinked on the asphalt. MPV Grocer sat off a highway in the dip of a hill. Metal railing bordered the road, protecting pedestrians from the drop to the river below. The river that led to Durgan's home.

Banks and I made directly for the store. Our job entailed the least danger: interview civilians. A place this small and isolated must've had regular patrons. If any of them had seen a Grifter, they'd remember.

Agent Porter had an aerial lookout in a tree, while Cassidy and Keswick trekked up the riverbank, hunting for Grifter tracks.

"And no one's going to assault Durgan's children, right?" I said, inching hair out of the way to adjust my earpiece; I'd clipped the mic to my shirt.

"Not unless they assault us first," Cassidy answered.

"They won't."

"Anyone ever tell you you're naïve, Kepler?" piped Agent Keswick.

I thought of Ethan and said nothing.

A bell tingled at our entrance. MPV sold what its name boasted: meat, produce, and veggies. The smells stoked my hunger.

A few late morning shoppers strolled through the store, which could've fit inside the first floor of our warehouse. We wouldn't have many places to hide, but neither would the Grifters.

Behind the checkout counter, a middle-aged woman scanned items, chatting with customers by name.

"We'll ask her first," I told Banks. "Let me do the talking."

"Copy that, Sheedy."

I paused to raise a brow at him.

"What?" Banks said. "Did I misspeak?"

"Yes, *Jimmy.*"

A glimmer of reaction, one I had no idea how to read, showed before Banks went neutral again.

We slipped into the checkout line. I decided upon the same tactic I'd tried on the MTA's forest ranger near Chron's territory. He'd hid the truth, which I'd found only by reading him, but this civilian woman would have no reason to lie. If anything, she'd be chatty. Who wouldn't want to talk about strange-looking people with gray skin?

Once our turn came, I plastered on a smile and rested my arms on the counter. The woman — *Eileen,* her tag read — glanced from my gloved hands to Banks beside me.

"Hi," I said. "Random question. Have you, by any chance, seen anyone odd around here lately? Someone with — and I know this sounds weird — gray, bumpy skin?"

Eileen's finger drumming paused. Her pinched lips worked side to side, multiplying the wrinkles in her chin. "No," she said. "Nothing like it." She turned her attention to a customer behind us. "Next."

Her tone of dismissal scraped like stone, far rougher than the friendly mood she'd carried with her previous customers. That departure from the sociable Eileen of a minute earlier convinced me to try again.

"It's just, my friend said she—"

"I told you no." Eileen, gripping her side of the counter, leaned in. "If you don't skedaddle," she said quietly, "you'll be lookin' at my Mossberg. I don't serve your kind here."

My lips parted. Nothing emerged. Discomfort bulldozed my thoughts into smithereens.

"Did that civilian just say *your kind*?" came Cassidy in my ear.

"What's she doing with a Mossberg?" Porter added.

"Get," Eileen said. Her hand dropped beneath the counter.

I stepped back, bumping Banks. Why didn't he say anything? Eileen had flattened us both. In unison, we skirted the patrons behind us and darted down an aisle of canned food. Once certain Eileen couldn't see us, we slowed.

"She's hiding something," Banks said, rattled as me, though his bright polo diminished the intensity of his cross-armed stance.

"But what?"

"Your ridiculous clothing offended her, didn't it?" Cassidy said. "You had one job, Kepler!"

"The Mossberg—"

"No one cares about the gun, Porter," she interrupted.

"You're overlooking something crucial here," Porter said. "A civilian woman keeps a pump-action shotgun in her business. That powerful of a weapon, close range—it's not for common thieves. She's expecting a durable enemy."

"Grifters," Agent Keswick said.

"Good job, Kes."

"Think they're threatening her?" Banks said.

"No," I said. "Durgan wouldn't threaten a civilian."

"Read her, then," Cassidy said.

I chewed my cheek. I should've expected that next. Well, I'd practiced my telepathy on civilians before, back at SPO-10. This didn't have to be any different.

Mae Keane, I remembered as I edged around Banks. At the convenience store Ethan and I used to frequent, I'd conversed with a civilian woman as warm as Eileen was icy. She'd given me a wooden trinket, round and painted with colors of the sun, as a good-luck token against my fears.

Eileen would give me a hole in the stomach instead.

I kept to the outskirts, coming at Eileen from the opposite side of the store. The freezer shelves snaked until they reached a break in the wall. A restroom arrow hung above a narrow hallway. In the alcove, I might be able to spot Eileen without sticking out.

Banks crept after me. He slipped into the hallway, wholly out of sight, while I peeked my head into the danger of Eileen's vision.

She was staring right at me.

I scurried back until the hallway swallowed me from view. "She's watching," I said.

A drawn-out sigh whooshed in my earpiece. "Do you know nothing of discretion, Kepler?" Cassidy said.

"Unlikely," Keswick said. "Kepler was hard at work in civilian studies."

Banks pointed toward the exit. "We can—"

"I am hungry," someone spoke.

"—move back into the aisles and try from there," Banks continued over the interruption.

"Quiet, Tam," spoke another.

"Do not yell at him!" said a third voice, higher-pitched and gravelly—and completely ignored by Banks.

"I was not yelling," the second voice said, while Cassidy asked why we hadn't moved yet.

I put my finger to my lips, waving at Banks when he opened his mouth. *Can you not hear that?*

"Hear what?" he said.

"You spoke harshly," the girlish voice said. "Papa says we must be kind, even when we are impatient."

"Stop mentioning Father," said the second voice. "I am in charge now. You will both be quiet, unless you wish to join the elaks."

"Eileen will not let that happen, Durgson!"

My heart pounded; Durgson wasn't the one who needed to worry about being overheard. They were here… and Eileen knew. With that shotgun, she was protecting Grifters. From *our kind*. It was supposed to be the other way around. The idea seemed so strange, so unfathomable, that my head protested while my gut found it true. Somehow, this civilian woman knew about Grifters, about the MTA, and had sided with the creatures most people would mistake for aliens.

Don't make a sound, I told Banks. *The Grifters are here. I can hear them.*

He scanned the hallway in obvious confusion, a pointless pursuit. Only I could hear them, though I'd done nothing to initiate the contact. Sometimes, when groups of Grifters telepathically communicated near me, I intercepted their conversations.

Durgson made another terse remark to the Grifter who must've been his sister; then, they silenced.

"Afternoon, folks," rang Eileen's voice through an intercom. "Store's closin' early today. Sorry 'bout that. If y'all could bring your items to checkout, much appreciated."

Banks checked his watch. "Not supposed to close until eight," he said.

"What do you mean?" Cassidy asked.

"The store is closing. We have to leave." He flipped his shirt collar up and murmured, "Kepler says she can hear the Grifters."

"And you can't? What kind of meta are you, Banks?"

"I'm not a protean. It's a telepath thing."

"Well, where are they?" she asked.

Banks and I surveyed the hallway. The first door, closest to us, read *Employees only*. The remaining doors indicated bathrooms, the last one blocked by yellow caution tape. An "Out of Order" sign hung taped above the knob.

I pointed. *There?*

Banks shrugged.

Very helpful. I'll go see. Make sure Eileen doesn't realize.

"Whatever you say, Sheedy."

Banks moved from the alcove while I tiptoed toward the barricaded restroom. Grifters had poorer hearing than metas, but I was unwilling to risk anything. By closing the store early, it seemed Eileen had already gotten wind of the quiet circumstances unfolding. No need to alert the Grifters too soon.

Outside the restroom, I listened. Pulsing beneath the doorframe came three distinctive heartbeats. Durgan had witnessed the murders of three of his children; the remaining three were hiding in a civilian bathroom.

I rapped the door. "Durgson?" I murmured. "It's Ella Kepler. I know where your father is. He's safe. I can take you to him."

Ella Kepler? said the girl. *She is —*

Be quiet, Ly! answered Durgson.

The chatter ceased. I pressed an ear to the door. Grifters and metas automatically disliked one another, and likely Durgson was no exception to that rule. However, he must've remembered I'd been the one to warn him to flee. I figured that counted for something.

Then again, according to Agent Keswick, I was naïve.

"Grifter sighting, east window," Agent Porter spoke.

I held my communicator button so hard I probably broke it. "Don't shoot! It's them!" I planted my boot on the handle. My foot went clean through, and the whole thing tumbled inward. Above the sink, the crank window let in a flurry of wet wind.

I clambered over the sink and through the opening, which squeezed so narrowly around me, I wondered how the Grifters fit. When I dropped outside, a puddle squelched under my boots. I glimpsed only the metal railing and the river that churned beyond, before a shape barreled from my perimeter. I squeezed against the building, and a Grifter charged past.

"Durgson? It's—"

He let out a cry and sprinted at me like a linebacker.

"I have a shot," Porter said. "Do I take it?"

"Porter, no!" I jumped onto Durgson's back. He bucked so forcefully, my stomach churned. Riding a bull would've been easier. "I'm. Trying. To. Help. You!"

Durgson twisted; the movement succeeded in launching me toward the river. I grabbed for the railing. My fingers hated me, but I slung myself over. "Stop, stop, stop!" I dropped to my knees and raised my hands. "Please. Just listen."

He froze. The heaving of his chest sounded like a bear panting.

"Kepler is now surrendering to the Grifter," said Porter.

Cassidy gave no reply. She and Keswick had gone inconveniently mute.

The Grifter, eldest son of Durgan, the one Lydia Burnette had risked her life to help, stared at me for so long, a line of sweat had the time to build, dribble, then fall. He'd been around six years old when Lydia met him, but time had brought him closer to thirteen, though he carried himself with as much assurance as Ethan.

Finally, he said, "What do you want, elak?"

"It's your father. Durgan's sick."

"My father is dead."

"He's not," I said, starting to rise.

Durgson growled and stepped closer, so I crouched again.

"Okay, okay. Look, we're not here to hurt you. We're here to take you to him. Chron had us both, but Freia helped us escape. We brought Durgan to our base and we're nursing him back to health, but he needs you. You and your siblings can come live with us, where you'll be safe."

"My family is dead because my father trusted elaks. Chron is right."

"Incoming—" Porter started.

"You shameful åsna!" A shorter Grifter pulled herself over the railing, where she must've been dangling.

I steeled myself, but she swept past me and smacked Durgson square in the cheek.

What in the world was happening?

Durgson turned his face, growling again, but he didn't raise an arm to defend himself. The young girl huffed before spinning to me.

"My brother is mean," she said. "I trust you, Ella Kepler. Where is our Papa?"

Durgson glared at her, most likely pelting her with telepathic arguments, but she ignored him.

"We'll take you there," I said. "I promise."

Durgson dragged his sister closer to the window. I could've eavesdropped, but I gave them their privacy, all the while kneeling in case sudden movement made Durgson warier. Their other sibling likely hung somewhere behind me. When I listened, I detected a rapid pulse.

"Cassidy, Keswick, check in," Porter said in my ear.

No answer.

"The civilians are leaving," Banks said. "Make sure the Grifters stay out of sight."

"They...." I paused, noting a sound, quick and rough like a branch scratching metal. More attuned listening revealed that someone nearby grunted. After checking that Durgson and his sister were still inaudibly arguing, I leaned backward.

From the railing, a small Grifter hung, legs anxiously pumping in the air. The river carried itself along the rocks thirty feet below. His fingers scrabbled for purchase, especially when he noticed that *I'd* noticed.

Do you need help? I asked.

The Grifter shook a vigorous "no." Then, instantly, his head bobbed up and down.

I smiled. *Take my hand.* I reached over the railing and cupped his wrist. He scooted his other hand an inch and continued a painfully slow progress before all ten fingers clutched me. I got a grip on his arm and lifted.

"Do not touch him!"

I didn't see Durgson react, but I felt his fury a second after, when something struck my forehead. I staggered and lost my grip. The little Grifter squealed. Beneath my mental disorientation, panic grew. He was going to plummet straight into the river.

I forced my eyes open, then wondered how hard Durgson had hit me. The little Grifter appeared to be levitating. He trembled, hovering in the sunlight, too scared to remove his hands from over his eyes. As he rose, a wooden packing crate came into view beneath his feet— probably, I guessed, the same crate Durgson had thrown at me. The crate carried the Grifter away from the river. Except for Agent Chang, no one could telekinetically control animate matter, but someone *could* control the crate.

"This might gain the older one's trust." Porter, from wherever he was, guided the Grifter and his crate over the railing and safely to the asphalt. Durgson's sister scooped the little one right up, all the while shouting endless insults at Durgson for nearly killing Tam and being, generally speaking, the dumbest brother in existence.

"Banks, are—" Porter started.

"Enemy sighting!" came Cassidy, finally. "Six metas headed your direction. Take cover, now, or those Grifters are good as dead."

CHAPTER TEN

I FROZE.

"What?" Banks' voice lashed at my ear.

"We had to go radio silent until they passed upriver," Cassidy said. "Two deadeyes, two ferios, and two civ liaisons. They're cadets. Look like Js." Each detail she spat was a nail in our coffin. "Get out of there, Porter. If any of them are Society members...."

"Roger," Porter said. Andrews had mentioned Porter's name in the water tower, along with Saini, Lee, Dom Bist, Arthur Finch, and Amy Lane. Nearly half our team made the watch list. Did Society members know about Whitewash, or was Cassidy being paranoid? Better safe than sorry. Porter wasn't the only one in danger, either. *Where Grifters go, there we must also go,* Andrews had told me once. If any of these cadets caught sight of Durgson, Ly, or Tam....

I cut through the bickering between Durgson and his younger sister. "We have to go. Right now." Then, predicting his indecision, I added, "The people I work with want peace with Hela, but the rest of the MTA don't. There are soldiers headed here as we speak. We need to get to safety immediately."

As if intent on proving my prediction correct, Durgson steered his siblings farther from me. "We will not go with you, elak."

"Please, Durgson! You're in danger."

"I will protect my family. Leave."

Currently, I was hungry as Tam and exhausted as a zombie. But I refused to let the MTA tear another family apart. I'd set out to reunite Durgan with his children, and I'd see that responsibility through.

Ignoring the back-and-forth blaring in my earpiece, I said, "You're either coming with me, or we're going back inside that window. Five seconds, Durgson."

He looked ready to chuck another crate. Tam's tiny voice, rising around Ly's clutches, gave him pause.

"Please, broder, can we go inside? I am scared of the elaks."

I wished I could hide myself in a Grifter's skin. Everything about me felt unnatural.

Durgson stomped his heel, causing a dozen fractures in the asphalt. That didn't seem like a yes, but he shielded his siblings and guided them back toward MPV's bathroom window.

I exhaled. "I'll stay with them until the cadets leave," I said into my mic. "Where is everyone?"

"Porter and I are in the van," Banks said.

"Copy," Cassidy said. "ETA of thirty seconds for the cadets. The deadeyes are taking the perimeter, ferios are scouting along the river, and the two civs are going inside. Kes and I will rendezvous if we can sneak past."

I glanced over my shoulder. A drizzle tapped the river, and mist drifted along its flow. In thirty seconds, MTA cadets would breach the fog.

"So only two cadets are coming inside?" I asked.

"Correct," she said.

That eliminated some tension. Ferios, whose MTA training centered on hand-to-hand combat, would make a more dangerous match than two cadets who studied civilians. If the ferios continued upriver, past MPV, and the civilian liaisons were unable to enter a closed store, maybe we stood a chance at avoiding detection. Two deadeyes would be monitoring the perimeter, but so long as we stayed inside, we'd be safe.

I shimmied through the window and cranked it shut. Durgson tried to wedge the fallen door back into its frame. A busted door would be a blazing red flag to any cadet—but, with luck, none of them would have the opportunity to see it.

Something rapped the door. "Durgson?" called Eileen.

He shifted the door aside. When Eileen glimpsed me near the window, up came the shotgun formerly propped like a staff. She tucked it against her shoulder and aimed.

I raised my arms. Fatigued or not, I could probably dodge a blast. Right?

"She does not intend harm," Durgson said. Nice of him, considering the crate incident.

"She and her friend were asking questions," Eileen muttered. Gray, wiry hairs obscured the scope; she blew air from the corner of her mouth, and the flyaways danced up her wrinkled forehead. She wore a flannel shirt and jeans and, by expression alone, would've been intimidating even without the pointed shotgun.

"Because we want to help," I said. "But listen, there are soldiers almost here who wouldn't hesitate to…."

Tam, the youngest, clung to his sister's leg with a whimper. I cleared my throat and said, "Is this the safest place for us to hide? We're exposed with the window."

Eileen's scowl turned her face into a mass of wrinkled skin. All this distrust, just because she pegged me as the "other" guy.

She jerked her head, then the gun. "This way."

Durgson followed first. Ly took Tam's hand and pulled him along. I leaned the door against the frame to keep anyone peeping through the window from seeing the hallway. Then, I caught up.

"The civilian woman is hiding us," I murmured to the team. "We'll stay put until you give the all clear."

"Hiding you *and* Grifters?" Cassidy replied. "Is she blind?"

Eileen led us out of the hallway and continued toward the checkout counter, beyond which stood another door for employees. "Another window back there," she called. "Could sneak y'all out."

I stepped from the alcove, relaying Eileen's message to the team. Banks and Porter agreed to meet the Grifters at the window as soon as the coast was clear.

Across the store, the entrance doors seemed a beacon, shouting for the attention of every cadet. The counter wall was my primary goal. Once the Grifters passed it, they could crouch and turn invisible.

"Incoming, front door," Banks chimed.

I darted ahead and bumped into Ly and Tam. "Hurry," I said.

Tam, with nervous energy, hopped forward and tripped. Ly teetered sideways. I caught her shoulders, pulled Tam upright, and shoved them toward the safety of the counter, where Eileen and Durgson were secure. So close, a few more steps….

Ly scuttled through the opening. I lifted Tam and tossed him toward the ready arms of his sister. The front door jangled with a knock, and an unmistakable voice called from the other side of the glass.

"Ella?"

From my toes upward, everything lurched. Recognition called, more tempting than the sound of my name. I turned my head.

Framed in the outline of the door, the neon *CLOSED* sign flashing on his ruddy cheeks, James Reynolds cradled his eyes and peeked indoors. The shorter girl beside him, honey hair in a ponytail, splatter of freckles stretching across her tanned skin as she gaped with cocoa eyes—sweet, timid Bridget Avary couldn't have offered a more unwelcome sight.

All three of us had gone buggy. Banks shouted in my ear, Durgson telepathically urged me to move, and I wished time could pause and allow me a calm beat to think. James and Bridget probably hadn't seen the Grifters. Otherwise, they'd have smashed in the door already.

"What are you doing here?" James called.

His question reminded me why we'd come. I knew what to prioritize. Banks and Porter were in the van, Cassidy and Keswick strolling the river, but the Grifters hadn't found safety yet. Not if James and Bridget decided to search inside. Yeah, the store was closed, but my presence told them breaking and entering was a viable option.

I held up a hand and forced a smile. "Just a sec." I turned to hide my moving mouth. "I've been made. Taking out my earpiece and mic. Stay put, especially Banks. I think I can convince them not to come inside."

"Who put you in—"

Cassidy's voice dissipated when I tugged the marble from my ear. In the pretense of scratching my neck, I unclipped the mic. Then, I stretched, tossing the devices beyond the counter as I moved my limbs around. Durgson hovered in the employee's room doorway, out of James' and Bridget's view.

Get inside, Durgson. I'll keep them away. My team will meet you by the window when it's safe.

He stepped back and shut the door, obedient for once.

Drawing in air like it'd otherwise vanish, I walked something uncomfortably reminiscent of a death march. There had to be a silver lining in this. Of the cadets, my old roommate and old classroom companion were the nicest and certainly the two I'd prefer to run into over Lydia, McFarland, or Vires. Those three were undoubtedly here. Earlier, Cassidy's warning had called to mind vague, random MTA cadets. Academies were all over; I hadn't considered that I might know any of the newcomers.

Naïveté worked against me today.

I flipped the lock and pushed open the door.

"I can't believe you're alive!" Redheaded James, freckled from face to toes, beamed. Cadets weren't affectionate, but this studier of civilians had never fit the MTA bill. He gave a quick hug. We were the same build, though I'd lost my muscle. Our heads bumped, and the rainwater dusting his hair smeared on my cheek.

Bridget took his gesture as a cue to follow suit. She and I shared an embrace, the effect of which had me all the sudden elated. I bounced in my shoes, not sure where the giddy energy stemmed from. It felt foreign, an invasion of my emotions, and I didn't like how it sought to undermine the panic.

"Yeah, I'm alive," I said. "Long story. What are you guys doing here?"

"Tracking," James said. "What about you? Where have you been, Ella? We all assumed you were dead. You and...." Slowly, his happiness muted. "Do—do you know Sheedy's MIA?"

"I've... I'm...."

The cadets appeared to take my garbled words as a reaction to the news about Ethan. The mood shifted from joyful to mournful.

"I'm sorry," Bridget whispered.

James clapped my shoulder. "We'll find him. You turned up, didn't you? That's a good sign! And—" He paused.

I'd heard it too. Footsteps. My stomach plummeted when two more cadets appeared around the corner of the building.

"So you weren't lying, Reynolds," Vires said. Beside him, McFarland stared. Unlike James and Bridget, who wore white shirts and black jeans, these two donned full gear—complete with weapons.

This mission couldn't have gone worse.

Vires had grown taller, tanner, his olive eyes simmering in distrust. Though I hadn't understood his dislike for me my second time at the academy, I'd since remembered he was holding the world's longest grudge over the clubhouse fire incident. He'd risked his life for mine— and, probably of higher priority for him, his looks. Vires needn't have fretted. MTA technology had prevented any scarring from third-degree burns. His skin maintained its flawless warmth, and not a single brown curl had been lost to the flames.

Unlike Vires, McFarland hovered far below six-feet, of a similar height and build as her MTA partner and me. Where James was ruddy and Vires a golden brown, McFarland had a darker coloring that passed through her eyes and into her smooth bun.

"What are you doing here?" Vires demanded.

"Right. We haven't gotten to the bottom of that." James awaited my reply with friendly intrigue.

Quick. Think. I could give an answer that wasn't quite a lie. "Same thing you are," I said. "I followed a Grifter this way."

Vires folded his arms. "You tracked a Grifter on your own?"

"Is that where you've been the past two months—tracking this Grifter?" James asked. "Why'd you go alone? Why'd you leave the academy?"

"Still curious as ever," I said, making myself smile. I had to act normal. Pleasant, as if sweat didn't tickle my neck and panic didn't squeeze my gut. "It's something I had to do by myself."

"Which direction did the Grifter go?" McFarland asked. For her part, she had the same quiet, calculating look she always wore.

"It might've gone upriver," I said. *Please, just go,* I inwardly begged.

"Where's Sheedy?" Vires' question, abrupt and loud, sounded accusatory more than curious.

"Why are you asking me?" I said slowly.

"So you're aware he's missing. How did you discover that while you were *tracking*?"

"I mentioned it," James said.

Vires lifted his chin. I read danger in his expression. "You've been—allegedly—tracking a Grifter for seven weeks," he said. "Surely you intercepted some intel as to Sheedy's whereabouts." Even without the addition of *allegedly*, it would've been obvious to anyone that Vires considered me full of it.

"We'll discuss this later," McFarland said. "We need to pick up the trail."

"Why," Vires said, "when we all know the trail ends at this location? The trail of *three* Grifters. Not one, as Kepler claims."

"What's your point, Vires?" she said.

"She's lying."

"Why would she be lying?" James said.

"Because she's protecting Banks," Vires said.

I dared not swallow. Vires probably scrutinized the length of my exhales.

"Banks?" James repeated. Beside him, Bridget peered at Vires, a tiny crinkle between her brows. McFarland, on the other hand, sought an explanation from me. Something close to doubt awoke in her previously calm manner.

"Who will we encounter when we enter this building, Kepler?" Vires asked.

"Banks isn't in there, Vires," I said.

"Then you needn't be concerned if we investigate." Vires clunked his staff on the sidewalk; a *zing* of energy hummed from the tip. He took one step forward.

In the millisecond before moving, I knew my ruse had reached its end. The cadets *could not* enter this store. If they did, the Grifters were good as dead.

I blocked the doorway and looked Vires and his triumphant smirk dead-on. "Fine. You want to know the truth?" I said, though my question wasn't for him. I turned to James and Bridget. "Ask Vires and McFarland about the Society."

McFarland blanched.

"I knew it." Vires tipped his "pulser" staff forward. Its point hummed a foot from my face. He was a clavio—our academy's *only* clavio, as he'd frequently reminded me—and had mastered staff-fighting to an unnerving degree that he'd never shied from boasting about.

A tiny inhale came from Bridget's direction.

"Why are you aiming that at her?" James asked. "What on earth is this about?"

"It's about Banks and his petty plan to dismantle the MTA," Vires said. "He's been indoctrinating Kepler since she first arrived."

"I don't need Banks to see the truth," I said. Vires had released his weapon; perhaps the time had come to reveal mine. Andrews already knew, anyway. "Perks of being a mind-reader," I added.

Even James struggled to breach the silence. United by speechlessness, the cadets appeared otherwise divided. James gawked, his nose twitchy with a seeming almost-sneeze. Bridget's eyes had expanded to maximum circumference. Uncertainty kept McFarland's dark brows arched, but Vires' skepticism seemed forced, failing to conceal the pulse of distinct discomfort.

"You expect us to believe you can read minds?" he said.

"Leader already knows. When he found out, he had me cleared. By the Tacemus. But I have my memories back now."

This proclamation, trailing after the news of my telepathy, made little impact.

"You remember everything?" James said. "Because the—Tacemus? That's Latin, but not a noun...." Bewilderment caught up to him; he palmed his forehead and looked to his MTA partner.

McFarland offered no answers.

"That's the name for the MTA servants," I said. "Leader makes them steal memories, and the MTA blames Grifters because it's easy. Grifters aren't the enemies you think they are."

"They're human, aren't they?" James spoke breathlessly, gripping the back of his neck. "I've always thought, since passing J...." He looked to McFarland. "Did you know?"

Her mouth stayed frozen with spooled secrets. James continued staring, but she refused to answer, bound by the silence that had conducted their conversations for most of their partnership. It took several seconds for the painful realization to tighten his eyes. When it did, James turned his head and didn't look at her again.

"This is exactly why Banks should've been quarantined," Vires said. "He's far too persuasive, especially to an impressionable Fallow." He brought his pulser beneath my chin. "You're coming with us."

I swallowed, eyes on the pulser, keeping my neck taut. "If I'm a Fallow, I'm not part of the MTA. You can't force me to do anything. So you guys can leave me here, and none of you will have done anything wrong."

"I'm CG," McFarland said. Guarded confusion worked across her dark features. "*I* decide what happens to Kepler."

Registering the halt in her voice, I remembered the moment I'd caught her slipping from a Society meeting, at which she'd finally heard the real story of Grifters. She'd come close to crying. That meant, in her core, she struggled.

You know there's something off with the MTA, I said, plowing forward despite her shock at my voice in her head. *You can help us. There's an organized team of metas trying to do what's right.*

"Operation Whitewash," she breathed.

Vires' arm jerked. His suspicion vanished. He wore concentrated alarm now. "They're enemies of the MTA, McFarland."

"Why? We've never been given a definitive reason."

Vires knows more than he's admitting, I told her. *Ask him about your parents.*

It was a leap. I hadn't read him; perhaps he knew nothing about how the MTA acquired its cadets.

"My parents?" McFarland stared up at Vires. "What do you know about them?"

He tensed his jaw, stone-faced. "You know I can't answer."

That was all I needed. Vires knew—and he went along with it.

"Why not?" McFarland asked him.

"The same reason you never told Reynolds."

At that, McFarland turned her cheek and went mute.

"Told me what?" James asked her, though this didn't sound like his usual curiosity. An edge of distress darkened his voice. "What's the Society? What's Operation Whitewash?" When James realized his partner was lock-lipped, he redirected to me. "Kepler?" Desperation cracked the word.

It sickened me to witness the MTA's strategies unfold. Even now, with half the truth exposed, McFarland and Vires stuck to protocol. Bridget and James deserved better.

"The Society is—"

Two thumps cut through my speech. Approaching up the sidewalk, long-necked rifles slung across their chests, Lydia Burnette and Koleman walked in the mist. Lydia stared, much as she had once done from a picnic bench on my school's campus. Months ago, this girl had been my fighting partner and enemy. Then Durgan told me his story, I regained my memories, and now—now I only pitied her.

"You should've knocked her out by now," Koleman yelled. Lydia's partner after Ethan was his opposite in every way. Stocky where Ethan was lean, careless where Ethan was measured. Even from this distance, the jagged scar along his face protruded. "Your job is to protect this information."

"You're part of this too?" James called. "Does everyone know... but me?"

"I don't know either, Reynolds," Bridget said softly.

The two cadets halted next to Vires. It was now six versus one. If Banks, Porter, Keswick, or Cassidy intended to swoop in, now would've been a great time.

"You're a telepath?" Lydia's voice was a low dent in the fog of moisture and tension. She'd turned wan over the months, looking almost sickly pale, giving her hair a whiter sheen rather than buttery yellow. I might've grown scrawny and pasty in Durgan's caves, but Lydia hadn't fared much better. I had an inkling why.

"Yes," I said.

"Lying again," Vires said. "You can't convince me of that any more than you can convince me to join your illicit little group. This effort's not even laudable."

Evidently, Vires' head could swell indefinitely. "I can prove—" I began.

"What's the truth about my parents, Kepler?" McFarland interrupted.

"If you don't know," Koleman said, "it means your handler thinks you're too weak."

She spared him a ferocious glare that lingered when she returned to me.

"I don't know that I should be the one to say it," I said.

"Tell me," she said.

"It's not only *your* parents, McFarland," Vires spat. "The MTA owns all of us. Our families believe we're dead."

I closed my eyes and swallowed. I would've said it gentler, but it mattered little how we divulged it. Some things couldn't be spun into a fairy tale.

"Wh-what?" James said faintly.

"You can't seriously be this naïve," Koleman said. "No one knows the MTA exists. Why would a government let powerful metas operate? And why should we obey authorities weaker than us?"

"But... " James said, "I don't understand. How could our parents think we're dead?"

"The Tacemus," I said. "They fabricate memories, and the MTA fabricates the rest."

Silence hit. These seemingly robotic cadets carried layers that wouldn't easily molt. Practiced decorum kept them from crying or yelling; they bore their heads high and kept emotions in check. Bridget, probably the most sensitive of them, was the only one trembling at this discovery. When our eyes locked, a jolt of anguish knocked me breathless. It slammed out of nowhere, along with the realization that Bridget believed everything we'd said—and couldn't bear it. She was only thirteen, too fragile for this harsh reality.

McFarland, after inspecting Lydia's and Koleman's detached mannerisms, switched her attention to Vires. "You lied to me," she said, so quiet civilian ears would've missed it.

He held his chin high. "I don't owe you anything."

"But, I thought—"

"You thought incorrectly."

She flinched, and Koleman sniggered. The rest of us pretended nothing had happened, though James watched McFarland with the same betrayed expression she wore.

... said there was nothing between them... another lie....

Most days, telepathy had more perks than benefits. I didn't want a closer glimpse at anyone's pains. At least James could feel, though. The only thing motivating Koleman was derision for the cadets he'd grown up with. And Lydia... she didn't appear part of the conversation. Her gaze rested on me and Ethan's name on her thoughts.

Koleman suddenly snapped. He swept his rifle up and took aim down the sidewalk, where Agents Cassidy, Porter, and Keswick casually strode in all their plainclothes glory.

"Koleman, stand down!" McFarland yelled.

He shouldered his gun; a finger played with the trigger. "They're with Whitewashed."

"White*wash*, you runt," Cassidy called.

Her words carried an effective punch. Lydia pointed her gun and Vires his bracer, but McFarland went shell-shocked. Little movement came from James or Bridget.

The three agents joined our circle, so obviously unconcerned by the tension and aimed weapons that, though outnumbered, they took the lead.

"Now," Cassidy said. "Step away from Kepler."

"No chance," Koleman said.

Agent Keswick chuckled. "Feisty."

"Pipe down. I'm speaking to your commanding general," Cassidy told Koleman.

Whatever confusion she might've felt, McFarland turned it off. "Kepler is under suspicion. So are you."

"Yes, but we don't care what the MTA thinks." I half expected Cassidy to fake a yawn, but she managed not to overplay the detachment. "I'll make it easy," she added. "Back off Kepler, or my team moves in."

"What team?" Vires said.

"I'm glad you asked."

Some searched left, others ahead. Cassidy's army swarmed from the right. Three people, dressed in the attack gear we'd stowed in the van, rounded upon the cadets with rifles bigger than the deadeyes'. They wore helmets, concealed from head to toe, but I could guess that Banks was the tallest and Durgson the bulkiest. As to the third figure, slender yet firm, I had a weird inkling she was Eileen.

Cassidy could hardly hide her satisfaction as the cadets took stock of the new numbers. Whitewash now outmatched by one. "You have ten seconds," she said. "Don't forget we're in civilian territory."

That last bit impacted McFarland the most. She scanned the highway ahead. If the cadets caused a scene, she'd be held responsible. Worse, a gunfight increased the chances that some civilian would show up and get killed in the crossfire. After inhaling and setting her shoulders straight, she called, "All cadets, stand down. Kepler goes with them."

From my peripheral, I saw Koleman's barrel swing. The shot fired as I ducked—an automatic reflex, and pointless, because animos never missed.

I dropped flat. When glass shattered, I flinched, expecting a volley of bullet spray. Was my adrenaline keeping me from feeling the pain of a hole in my side?

People were shouting, scuffing up the sidewalk. I peeked. My vision still worked—a positive sign. Keswick and Banks had Koleman by the arms, while Agent Porter fought a battle of telekinesis for control over Koleman's gun. It hovered vertically between them, blurry as it jerked between the two metas. Koleman seemed to have the upper hand, until the gun pulled away and smacked into Porter. Koleman glared at Lydia, as if she'd interfered, but she wasn't even looking.

"Did he hit you?" A wide-eyed James crouched next to me, hand extended.

I stretched my limbs and craned my head. No blood. Porter must've redirected the shot. "I'm fine," I said, gripping James' hand.

Koleman had actually tried to kill me. I'd known he was a jerk, but this went beyond obnoxious.

Writhing against his captors, nose bloody, Koleman refused to return my stare. He wore a distracted gaze, so much more unnerving with blood staining his leer. "Wipe them of everything," he said.

Only meta vision, fine-tuned and capable of drawing meaning out of watery details, enabled me to comprehend Koleman's words. My eyes were on his, and his on someone else—a figure behind me, reflection slightly warped in Koleman's pupils. Even warped, that bald crown was undeniable, though not as concerning as its owner's open mouth.

I made the connection, and instinct followed.

Stop, I said.

Mirrored in Koleman's eyes, the Tacemus shut his mouth. *Yes, Mistress,* he answered.

My heart hammered. I wasn't concerned with how the Tacemus had come to be here—I wanted to know why Koleman could control him.

"Do it!" Koleman screamed. "You pathetic—"

The insult cut out when Banks clunked Koleman's temple with the butt of his gun. Concealed by the helmet, Banks still radiated loathing.

Everybody reacted in various stages of distress once they noticed the Tacemus on the sidewalk. Vires, closest to him, seized the opportunity to attack the memory-wiper.

Duck left! I told the Tacemus.

By a miracle, he avoided Vires' swing. Before the cadet could try again, I leaped in front of the Tacemus, ramming into Banks, who'd evidently had the same idea.

"Don't touch him!" Banks shoved Vires, launching him backward. He rammed into the building; chunks of red-and-brown brick broke off.

McFarland directed her bracer at Banks in an instant, which prompted Porter to take aim. In the commotion, I tugged the Tacemus away from the tousle.

"What are you doing, Kepler?" Cassidy called.

"Taking him somewhere he can't wipe us."

"I'll do it." Banks swiveled around from Vires. His hands were shaking—though, when he set a palm on the Tacemus' back, the movement stilled.

I accompanied them down the sidewalk, leaving the arguing behind as Koleman's commands replayed again and again.

Can Koleman control you? I asked the Tacemus.

We do not understand the question, Mistress.

I peered over his head. "How did Koleman do that?"

Stomping down the sidewalk a pace ahead of us, Banks' helmet only magnified his heavy breaths. "Andrews can force them to obey someone else. It's a short leash, and limited."

"Why?"

"So someone can make them clean up his messes for him. There's usually a Tacemus on missions involving civilians. Koleman must've gotten the control for today." He balled his fists. "Sick that anyone would...." Banks faltered, then walked faster.

I swallowed. It felt as if bits of the broken brick had landed in my throat. As we continued uphill, my conscience pushed harder than gravity, and the reason for it walked smackdab between us. The truth might cause Banks to hate me, but I would've rather destroyed our semi-friendship than carry this mud any longer. He'd find out soon enough, anyway, once One returned and I let the secret out.

I moved around the Tacemus and caught up to Banks' strides. "Banks, I—"

"You don't have to say it. I already know."

I halted. After a moment, so did Banks. He turned his helmeted head toward me and gently stopped the Tacemus from proceeding further.

"How?" I said.

When he answered, his words seemed stuck to the visor. "One's known since you were young. He used to bring Tacemus to Briarwood to see if your presence would spark their freedom."

I grew acutely aware of the rain. It felt colder, drawing out goosebumps. I wanted to shrink, or swipe Banks' helmet and hide behind it. "I... controlled them?"

"By accident."

"Oh." I couldn't voice anything else. Neither did Banks. I feared showing too much with my expression, so I hurriedly said, "Then Whitewash already knows."

"No. We haven't told them."

"Why not?"

"Because it's not their business." Clipping the conversation, Banks continued uphill.

The Tacemus and I trailed after. A corner of me wished to see Banks' face, but gratitude for his mask conquered. If he was disgusted, at least I wouldn't have concrete proof.

The sidewalk ran out. Obscured by the untamed forest that bordered this road, several motorcycles sat damp with rain beneath straggly boughs.

Tentatively, Banks prodded the Tacemus into the trees. He obeyed without question, without complaint. He didn't even turn around to see us off but stood there, a lonely figure by the bikes, rain misting his bald head. Maybe he couldn't wipe the water away unless someone told him to.

"Did you control him?" Banks asked quietly.

This admission took time to surface, probably enough to give Banks his answer. "He—he was going to wipe us," I whispered.

Banks lingered a moment, watching the Tacemus. Then he walked away.

I squeezed my eyes shut until they watered. *I'm so sorry,* I told the Tacemus. *I'll make sure you're freed. I promise.*

We do not understand, Mistress.

Don't call me that. Please. Call me Ella.

Yes, Ella.

I dragged myself after Banks, toward the thin sprawl of buildings and our team, whose arguments lashed. Not as loudly as my guilt. Banks' long legs loped faster than mine; intentionally so, I figured. Until he slowed.

"It's not your fault," he said. "What you can do. Keep the good, fight the rest."

Confusion overrode my discomfort. He'd quoted my speech from earlier, which meant he'd been listening to me. *Me*: the Tacemus-controlling Fallow who was just like Andrews.

Suddenly, I followed his meaning. No one could understand the burden of that similarity better than Banks.

I stared up at him, tried to express my gratitude, and couldn't get a word out.

"Why is your mouth hanging open?" he said.

I clammed it shut and said, *It's not.*

"Right."

The drizzle lessened, lighter than fingertips. Banks' visor carried a layer of mist and fog, all the more screening his reaction. Then, the mask vanished as Banks tugged the helmet off and said, "I'm looking forward to Vires' expression when he realizes who pushed him." He resumed walking, features neutral, and spoke as if picking up the threads of a different conversation.

"You're terrible at keeping your helmet on," I said, chewing back a relieved smile.

"And you're obsessed with rules, Sheedy."

"No I'm not, Jimmy."

Though he rolled his eyes, I was fairly certain I saw humor somewhere in that face.

Banks was the most confusing person I'd ever met, but I didn't mind.

We hadn't made it halfway downhill when Vires jutted his staff toward Banks and called, "I *knew* it."

"I'm sure you did," Banks said.

After Cassidy yelled at us for taking so long, I hurried back to MPV, while Banks ducked toward the side window. Koleman lay in an undignified crumble, stickily breathing, and Durgson and Eileen must've gone inside.

"Let's go." Cassidy motioned her hand.

"Wait," Bridget murmured. She passed a volley-like inspection between McFarland and me. She looked timid as a mouse. Then, determination furrowed her brows. She tiptoed around James and headed... for Cassidy. There, she stood, dwarfed by the agent but clearly on her side. Bridget was joining Whitewash.

When our eyes met, a sheen of solidarity, warm as a desert breeze, overcame me. I'd forgotten how potent Bridget's emotions felt, as if her tiny frame couldn't contain them, so they had to find a home in someone else. If I hadn't joined already, I would've signed up in two seconds.

"Me too," James said. The word was a whisper, but it was his, and he claimed it. Not one to make much noise, he might as well have been a giant stomping those five steps from his position to Bridget. He twisted around and faced the cadets, flushed and shaky but unwavering.

"You're... leaving the MTA." McFarland's leg twitched, as if she ached to follow that path and fought the magnetism.

James looked at her long enough for tears to glisten. Sucking in deep, he turned away.

Cassidy skimmed the two cadets up and down. Rather than the usual sarcasm, her blue eyes shone with intrigue. "Take off anything trackable."

"That includes your bracers." McFarland exhaled. When she breathed again, the oxygen restored her composure, filling up the spaces left behind by uncertainty. She squared her jaw and yanked the bracers off her arms. "I'm joining Operation Whitewash, Burnette. You should do the same." She didn't address Vires; and he, brooding, ignored the comment.

If I'd had to stake a bet on which cadets would join, McFarland would've been lowest on my list. She was a rule-follower through and through, even amid emotional confusion. Though her decision didn't make sense, I gladly accepted it. They were coming back with us. Allies. *Friends*. With a jolt, I realized I didn't have too many.

"You can't win," Lydia said. "The MTA will crush you."

"No one asked for your opinion, animo," Cassidy said.

"A powerful animo." Porter, rubbing his neck, regarded Lydia. "You're wasting your talent on your partner."

Lydia kneeled beside Koleman as if Porter hadn't spoken.

Agent Cassidy waved the cadets toward our bikes. Before following, McFarland spoke quietly to Vires. "Griffin would have joined."

His gaze moved, but she was gone.

In the horrible quiet, I inspected my other former partner. Lydia wasn't going to come and made no effort to explain why. Unfiltered words longed to gush. We had too much unsaid between us.

"Could I have a word with you in private?" I asked her.

After a poorly controlled eye roll, she strolled around me. I headed toward the side of the building opposite Eileen's employee room and didn't stop until Vires was twenty seconds behind us.

Lydia faced me with her arms crossed. "What, Kepler?"

"Ethan's alive. We rescued him. He's fine. Skinnier, but still Ethan."

Her inhale hitched. Spasms had broken along her face as soon as I said his name. They waged a battle, shifting between anger and hurt. With a rigid swallow, she erased her features of any emotion. "Is that all?" she said.

"I know I was rude and difficult when we were partners, so I'm sorry. I'm also sorry for lying about the whole clubhouse incident and never saying anything when you got in trouble. That was wrong. I wish things had turned out differently."

"I don't think I believe you."

"Well, I meant it," I said. Her snippy remark didn't carry the punch it used to. Durgan's memory had rewritten my perception of her. I wanted to explain what her act of kindness toward his son had instigated. Because of Lydia, Durgan had chosen peace over war. Might that convince her to join Whitewash?

It didn't matter. The story wasn't mine to share, and Lydia seemed too stubborn to listen. After a nod, I left, hoping I'd softened her dislike.

Who was I kidding? She probably loathed me more.

Coming around the building, I came face-to-face with Vires, who reeled back as if I carried some disease.

"I refuse to be sequestered with Burnette and that inept," he said, jerking a thumb over his shoulder.

"So, that means you're coming?"

"You're evidently a proficient mind-reader." He shoved past me.

Vires was a liar. His decision to come had nothing to do with who he'd be stuck with but who he would miss. Either way, I was glad to have another ally, someone who'd been halfway toward my friend at one point.

"It'll be good to have you," I said, hurrying after his lengthy strides.

"I know."

"Right. I mean, you *are* the academy's only clavio."

"Don't blather, unless it's to tell me something I don't know."

These attempts were going nowhere. I let him escape me.

Even with Vires haughtier than ever and Lydia still convinced I was the scum of the earth, I couldn't shake the feeling of victory. Durgan's three remaining children were safe, we'd picked up four additional allies, and Banks had reminded me that sharing similarities with Andrews didn't make us like him.

As I headed for the van, Lydia's expression, branded like a stamp, overlaid that tiny flicker of triumph. It didn't take much to squash it. I'd grown used to despair—and, I suspected, so had she. Despite understanding the truth, she couldn't bring herself to change it.

Well, once we had Andrews, *everything* would change. Even Lydia Burnette the animo couldn't redirect that.

CHAPTER ELEVEN

LY WAS THE MOST talkative Grifter I'd encountered. And, unlike Grifters, she cared little for the giant division between Hela and the MTA.

While Durgson sulked and pretended he heard nothing of our conversation, Ly talked nonstop, acclimating to the van with more ease than her siblings. Tam sat in his sister's lap and stared at Agent Porter.

Cassidy's questions centered around Eileen. No one with the MTA had met a civilian who knew anything about Grifters, much less wanted to help them.

"Papa once protected Eileen and her husband from a thief," Ly told us. While the shop owners had initially feared Durgan's unusual appearance, they eventually accepted him and returned his kindness by offering their store as a shelter. Their relationship spanned over a decade.

Porter and Cassidy—Keswick and Banks sat in the cab—took Ly's story with amazement. Knowing the truth about Grifters' humanity was one thing; having a civilian reach the same conclusion was stranger.

Ly talked us through the Grifter uprising. "Mama warned Papa not to trust Jurstin, but he would not listen to gossip." Ly held her head high, squeezing Tam like a stuffed animal yet somehow oozing spunk.

Jurstin's name sent a spike of pain to my fingers. "Where's Jurstin now?" I asked.

"He rules. But no one will love him like Papa. That is not true," she said, turning to Durgson. "They *did* love him."

No doubt annoyed at having his private conversation displayed for all to hear, Durgson gave up on feigning deafness—and secrecy. "You see from the eyes of a child," he told her, which was strange, considering his own young age. "Speak no more. The elaks do not care."

"Do you?" Ly demanded of us.

I didn't want to prod Durgson into further frustration, but I also didn't want Ly believing we were indifferent.

Cassidy surprised me by speaking first. "We care," she said.

"You see?" Ly said to Durgson.

He shook his head. "Then say nothing for Tam's sake."

Ly started to argue, then rested her chin on Tam's head and kept quiet for the rest of the drive.

We arrived in Virginia close to dinnertime. Cassidy, Keswick, and Porter decided who got "cadet duty" through an MTA-themed version of Rock, Paper, Scissors, clearly biased because each agent thought *their* choice—animo, clavio, or ferio—should win. In the end, Porter was humble enough to switch to ferio's rock if it meant beating Cassidy's clavio, so she grumpily agreed to meet the cadets at the hangar.

"Before you do that," Banks shut down the van and twisted in his seat, "don't tell them Sheedy's here."

"Why not?" I said.

"Because they'll listen to him, and he's in denial."

"That's not—"

"He's still opposed, even after hearing Walker's speech?" Porter asked.

"*No*," I said, "he's just confused because no one's given him evidence."

"Talk to Amy Lane, then. She's our... " Porter paused, warily eyeing Tam. The little Grifter was leaning toward him as if slurping up his words. "Evidence person," Porter muttered, then bounded from the van.

Though it bothered me how little Banks trusted Ethan, he might've had a point. I knew Ethan would come around once he had proof, but it was true that the cadets would be more inclined to listen to him than anyone else.

Keswick sauntered indoors to warn everyone else not to mention Ethan, though Banks hung around the van while the Grifters unloaded. Ly and Tam ogled the vehicles, but Durgson stalked forward without turning his head.

I could understand his distrust. His community had turned against him and killed half his family. The reason? Durgan had been too lenient with elaks. With *us*. I feared that Durgan's decision to house me for seven weeks—without killing me in the end—had sent his Hela over the edge.

And to think, we were all here now because Lydia had taken pity on the Grifter currently singeing me with his glare.

"Are you going to open the door?" Durgson waited by it with all the air of a prince—which, in a manner of speaking, I supposed he was.

Banks and I shared a look before he made a motion and the door swung forward.

During the walk through the empty first floor, the younger Grifters gawked at everything from the boxing ring to the spiral stairs.

Outside the clinic, I motioned for the Grifters to hang back, then edged inside. It'd be better to get an idea of Durgan's state before three desperate kids crowded him.

"Ella?"

Mid-glance, I switched trajectories. In her cot, Kara sat upright and leaned on the wall. The IV tubes trailed from her bandaged arm, still pumping. Whatever metamorxophine was, it worked fast. Her pallor bore a slight flush, and the shadows swallowing up her cheekbones had subsided.

I bounded over. "You're awake!"

"Yeah, I—" Something behind me caught her attention. Her lips parted. Surprise energized her eyes.

I prepped an explanation for the presence of three Grifters.

Then, Kara said, "Hey, Jimmy."

Oh. Right.

He straddled the doorway, having not yet committed to entering. Banks uncomfortably shifted under her gaze. He braced a hand against the doorframe, like any second he'd shove off and bolt. "Durgan's not here," he said to me, determinedly avoiding Kara now.

"Dr. Saini moved him to a bedroom a couple hours ago," Kara said.

"All right," I said. "I'll go find him. Be back in a minute."

She nodded.

Banks sidestepped back onto the landing when I passed. Ly and Tam clung to each other, giving Durgson a yard of space. "He's been moved into a different room," I told Durgson.

"Where?" he demanded.

"Um." I checked Banks. *Any ideas?*

"Last room on the right," he said, indicating the hallway.

If you knew that, why'd we even come up here? I said, but Banks, staring toward Kara, didn't appear to hear me.

Durgson swept past us, and his siblings dashed after.

"Hold up," I called.

We fought a battle of speed that I won, much to Durgson's outrage. I rapped the door and, hearing no answer, cracked it open.

In a compact bedroom identical to mine, Durgan lay unconscious in the nook that formed his bed. Still in a hospital gown, he looked even more ridiculous shoved into a cranny too small for sturdy Grifters. But his chest evenly rose and fell, and that was all that mattered.

When Tam saw Durgan, he squealed and ripped free of Ly's leg. She raced after him. Durgson hovered in the doorway. The acid had wilted from him. He looked on his father as if in a stupor.

"What is his illness?" he asked.

"An infection in his leg. They had to amputate it."

"You dismembered my father?" Durgson's rage returned, and he vented it by shoving me out of his way. Ly and Tam had to make room for him, yet once at Durgan's bedside, Durgson froze again.

I shut the door and smiled. "Well," I told Banks, "at least—"

I blinked. He was nowhere in sight.

"Too tired," I mumbled, shuffling back to the clinic.

When I pushed the clinic door open, I blinked again. Banks had crossed the threshold but hadn't made it much farther. It was hard to tell *where* he wanted to stand—next to Kara? By the sink? Before he shoved his hands beneath his armpits, I noticed their clenching. He moved closer to Kara, then back, then closer again.

"Mission accomplished," I called.

Banks spun around. Wordlessly, he strode from the room.

I regretted interrupting. Maybe he'd been close to finding closure.

Then, setting Banks aside, I moved to Kara's cot, not sure how to start conversation. Every day since December had passed with me wishing for a reunion with my best friend. Now that we had nothing separating us, words vanished.

I tapped the skin near the bandaging. "Does that hurt?"

"No. Has anyone talked to Dad or Kyle?"

"I—I don't know. But I'll make sure you get safely home soon."

"Okay." She spoke casually, either for my sake or hers, but I heard the crack in her demeanor.

"Kara, I'm... so sorry." I looked at her with two burning eyes until I felt close to bursting. With an anguished surge, I wrapped my arms around her, almost forgetting not to squeeze. Seeing Kara ached, when it should've filled me with joy.

She dropped her head onto my shoulder. I couldn't tell which of us did the shaking.

"Your voice kept me going," she whispered. "Hearing you... it was like a book, distracting me. And then—" She straightened, swiping her wrist across her cheeks. "Ethan got there, and he verified that I wasn't crazy." Kara tried a watery smile. "Where is he?"

Nothing budged when I swallowed, so I silently said, *Downstairs.*

A nagging within me needed to rupture. Forget Banks—*my* actions had led to her kidnapping, and she had to hear it, lest she mistake me for some hero. Everyone had shoved the opposite down my throat, because none of them had known the truth: Ethan had told me not to approach the Grifters at the library near SPO-10, but I did anyway. That moment with Chron had started the domino effect to today. Kara needed to understand that I was no random third-party to this scenario but the primary instigator.

"It's my fault Chron kidnapped you," I said.

She reached forward, jarring as a Jack-in-the-Box, and locked her fingers around my wrist. "Don't say that. Please." Kara shut her eyes. "Whatever happened in the past, it doesn't matter anymore. Let's just... move on."

I would've rather tossed out a few more condemning remarks. Did Kara understand? How could I make her see?

I opened my mouth. Her eyelids had stayed fast. Without the royal blue as a distraction, I noticed how her facial bones ran as if her skin clung to them.

Chron had already done enough harm. I refused to add more.

"All right," I said.

We sat, uncomfortably quiet, and listened to the IV drip. I didn't know how to proceed. I'd be the first to admit that circumstances could define us for better or worse—and, lately, "worse" conquered. Every horrible incident of the past two years existed in overwhelming clarity, while the good memories made as much a dent as a drop of mud in a pool. I couldn't blame Kara for being who she was now instead of the cheery girl of my memories. The problem was, I'd changed too. We might've survived imprisonment and Grifters, but what remained of us could disintegrate. Watching the cadets fall apart had reminded me how delicate friendships were.

A tinkle of glass punctuated the silence. I shrieked, launching off the bed so fast I tugged the blanket with me. All appeared ordinary in the clinic, but I continued my swivel, coming thirty degrees before I saw the syringe that had fallen off the counter.

A new noise interrupted, this one stranger. Confused, I completed my rotation. Hands pressed to her stomach, Kara tilted her head and laughed. The chuckles came jumbled at first, but when she caught my quizzical stare, the chortles picked up. "I thought... " she wheezed, "metas were... supposed to be... serene."

I watched this for a moment. Then, feeling my lips quirk, I plopped beside her and joined in. Soon, we were laughing way beyond what the situation called for, but neither of us could resist. Tears mixed in, and I didn't pause to question whether they came from sadness or mirth. I couldn't have pointed to the last time I'd laughed like this—doubled over, sometimes emitting nothing at all. It felt better than the coldest glass of water on the hottest summer day.

Eventually, Kara pushed her hair back and rubbed her cheeks. "I've never heard you shriek like that," she said.

"I make a horrible meta."

"Clearly."

"Speaking of horrible metas, did Ethan ever tell you about the time he shoved me off a pine tree to prove that I'd survive?"

Kara giggled. "Somehow, I'm not surprised. You definitely know how to pick them. Remember Bradley?"

"Not cool. You're breaking the code."

"Some things are too good for codes. Remember when he wrote you—"

I squashed her mouth, and she swatted my hand away.

We settled on the cot, both aware of the tension we'd fractured, and how dangerously close we'd come to letting the darkness win.

"Did the MTA make us believe Jimmy went to Whale's for four years?" she said.

"Not the MTA exactly, but metas, yeah."

"So, he was only there to be your bodyguard?"

"Kind of."

"I thought...." After fiddling with her IV bandage, she lifted a shoulder. "I guess it was part of his act."

"What was?"

Faint color stained her cheeks. "Are you reading my thoughts?"

"Ugh, no. Everyone thinks all I do is pick through their minds."

"They *think* that?"

"Yeah, they...." Noting her quivering lips, I paused, replaying her emphasis. Then I grinned. "Very funny, Watson."

"You walked right into—"

Someone's shouting was thrown through the open doorway like a shockwave. "You shouldn't have left him alone!"

That inflamed passion had to belong to Banks. Walker shot a rebuttal, and chatter broke out.

Kara's brows drew, and I pinched my lips. I'd predicted a spat once the cadets entered base, but this argument had a weightier feel to it.

Footsteps pounded on the landing. Figures dashed past the clinic and jumped, foregoing the stairs. The conversation below grew thicker.

I stood but didn't make my exit. Whitewash could handle its own disagreements. Kara needed company.

"It's okay," she said. "You don't have to babysit me."

I recalled Agent Keswick's remark and hoped I hadn't given off the same vibe. "I'm not babysitting you, Kara." I situated once more by her feet. "I want to be here."

"Really, it's fine. I'm feeling tired again, anyway."

"Nice try."

She exaggerated a yawn and leaned on her pillow with shut eyes. Fake snores came next.

"You're ridiculous," I said. When the feigned sleep continued, I shook my head. "Fine. See you in a bit."

Downstairs, everyone in Whitewash appeared present, a crowded jumble near the conference table. The cadets were interspersed too. In the gaps between bystanders, I spotted a familiar bald head. My pulse ticked, and I raced the remainder, squeezing by Bridget. Sweat and soot patching up his white turtleneck, a Tacemus—and I could guess which one—stood there bleary eyed and woozy. Banks clutched One's shoulder, every bit intent as One was faint.

"One?" I moved to his side and touched his other shoulder. "What happened?"

He stirred. Storm cloud eyes, too big for his wan face, searched me. The presumed head of Operation Whitewash, the man who'd shielded me from the MTA for sixteen years, had the strength to rip away limitless memories; today, he looked close to falling over.

Read me, he said. *Goose Swamp. After you left.*

He meant the day I'd regained my memories, then learned of my backstory with him. During our last interaction, he'd admitted that he'd monitored me my whole life. He'd cared about me. At some forgotten point, I'd cared in return. *Finny,* I'd nicknamed my lost childhood friend. I'd accused him of manipulating my life, then left him by the side of the road. He'd begged for my forgiveness. I'd essentially given him a "maybe."

With this guilty introspection fresh as the welt on One's forehead, I lightly touched his temple and tried shutting our observers out. Porter began a question, Cassidy shushed him, and the onlookers quieted. Reading One was entirely possible; I'd done it a few days ago. In the presence of Whitewash and the cadets, my efforts faltered.

Focus, One said. Naturally, he was in my head, though it was meant to be the other way around. *I am here to help you,* he added. *Once you have succeeded, I will leave your head and not return unless you ask me.*

Why would I ever ask him?

The question came unbidden, and I knew One heard it. Telepathy was unkind. I had to exert myself to read minds, but the Tacemus could dissect us without trying, and that had its drawbacks. His entire life, One had been privy to every variety of unpleasant, knee-jerk reactions, including those aimed at himself.

You will experience the same, he said. *We are not so gifted as everyone assumes. But read me now, Ella. Tell the others what happened. I am too weary to tell my story.*

Weary—suddenly, I wanted to keep my eyes shut for the next eight hours. My telepathy didn't allow for that. Gritting my teeth, I did what Durgan had taught me and focused on what united One and me. I clung to that ribbon of unity, then fell into One's head.

THE MOMENT HAD COME in which One could no longer control her. Today, she knew the truth: he was a master as cruel as his own.

He hiked the sandy median along the highway until Agent Walker arrived. The man skidded across the asphalt. His tires pointed back toward Goose Swamp. "Tell me everything," he said.

On the drive toward the Navy base, One relayed his interaction with Ella. The agent wondered why One had not removed the kidnappings of Ethan Sheedy and Kara Watson from Ella's memories. Without her friends in danger, she would have accompanied One to Virginia. One had considered the idea until he'd found the same in Ella's mind. She'd expected him to do so—to delete as he had always done, even at the cost of lives. Knowing how ruthless Ella believed him to be, One had found himself suddenly powerless.

Agent Walker and One used the spare time before Master's arrival to ensure One's clearing could not be easily identified. It would not do to raise Master's suspicion at this juncture. When Master arrived, they skirted the curious military personnel and met him near the security box.

"… she's still detained." Agent Kearney, disguised in military fatigues, gestured to the row of buildings beyond the gate.

Master followed the agent's pointing. He appeared harried, impatient, as he behaved in most matters concerning Ella. "Take me to her, Walker." Master marched forward in long strides, though they stopped when he noticed One. "Has this Tacemus interacted with Kepler?" Master asked Kearney.

The agent shrugged. "Don't know, sir."

"Was he here when Kepler arrived?"

"Yes, sir."

Master's features narrowed to a shrewd point. He ordered Agent Kearney aside and entered the security box. The two agents and One waited outside as Master configured the surveillance feeds displayed on various monitors.

One refrained from glancing at his ally, lest they appear suspicious. Both knew what the surveillance footage would reveal.

Ella had disappeared.

One could tell the exact moment Master discovered this. Master swore, leaning heavily forward.

"What is it?" Agent Walker asked.

"Her cell is empty."

Kearney started. "That's not—"

"It's entirely possible. She had help."

"From who?" Walker said.

Master cast his attention sideways, inspecting through the glass window—inspecting One. "Come with me."

Yes, Master.

One did not dare risk eyeing Agent Walker as Master and servant strode from the other two men.

"Andrews," Walker called.

Master waved a hand, Walker's only answer.

One barely noticed the path they trod. Surely he'd miscalculated, and today his strenuous planning had met its demise. Master suspected him. One could clear Master of this realization, but clearing carried both risk and sorrow.

They reached a parking lot of vehicles both military and MTA. Master told him to take the passenger side.

Once seated before the steering wheel, Master turned to him. "Did Ella speak to you?"

Not certain what the security footage may have showed, One opted for the truth. *Yes.*

"Did she order you to help her?"

One hesitated. It did not matter what Ella commanded—One was free to disobey. Master could never learn this, yet One could not bring himself to lie and claim she had controlled him.

He had paused too long. This gave Master another answer.

"I see." Master nodded. "She's commanded you not to tell me. She knows. Likely her full memories are restored."

The chirp of a ringing phone sounded from Master's pocket. "Andrews," he answered. After a pause, he straightened, alert and fervid. "What did she look like?... You fool. Find her!" Master tossed the phone toward the passenger floor mat and jabbed the vehicle's ignition button. The reverse mechanism engaged, the SUV spun backward. After a lurch, the vehicle sped from the lot.

One caught a name on the call screen before the phone turned dark. *Phillip Lane.*

Neither passenger spoke on the drive, except when Phillip Lane called with quarterly updates, all of them unpromising. When Master turned down a road whose entrance bore a wooden sign spelling *Dewey National Forest*, One's worries mounted. This had been Ella's destination.

Master parked outside a small cabin, worn with cobwebs and dirt. After ordering One to follow him—an order he could refuse, though he chose not to—Master ignored the blissful civilians and wrenched open the cabin door. He marched passed a reception desk and small gift shop, eventually thrusting open another door, this one affixed with a nameplate of one Ranger Phil.

Phillip Lane, then, pretended to be a ranger, just as Agent Kearney pretended he was a Navy officer.

Master searched the office as if quite familiar with it. A surveillance camera had been installed in this room, too; Master watched the footage through Ranger Phil's desktop computer. Ella had borrowed the MTA's habits and faked an identity. She hadn't fooled the ranger, and One could see why. Despite the yellow sweatshirt, evidently lifted from the gift shop, her questions were too pointed and her manner too controlled for a civilian. However, she'd escaped before the summoned Tacemus could pin her down.

One had not realized a Tacemus lived in this very forest, alongside Ranger Phil, a man who, contrary to what he'd told Ella, knew Grifters resided here. This was unsettling. Certain members of the MTA *did* know of the existence of Grifters in Dewey National Forest. Banks had wasted months before uncovering this information, and it had only been an educated guess.

Toward nightfall, Phil's phone calls stopped. When Master began initiating the calls and received no answers, he picked up a pace around the cluttered office, dialing repeatedly and never achieving a response.

Midnight passed before One asked permission to use the restroom. He locked himself in and retrieved the phone hidden in his waistband. *Dewey National Forest,* he messaged to Agent Walker. *Phillip Lane.*

He waited five minutes for an answer. Having received none, and not wishing to be gone long, he deleted his message and returned to Ranger Phil's office. Master, leaning over the desk with his head bowed, did not glance up when he said, "Go to sleep, One."

One had no choice but to feign instant slumber. In a moment, Master lifted One and carried him to another room. Master lowered One gingerly to the carpet and laid his suit jacket over One's short torso. Then he exited.

Banks often queried why One called Eugene Andrews "Master" when the man had lost use of that title eighteen years ago. One had never found the words to explain that the title did not bother him so much as Eugene Andrews' abuse of it. In events such as these, One regretted the fatal passing of time that had turned Eugene Andrews from a quiet man to the man cold enough to let Ethan Sheedy die. One had served the older Eugene Andrews before his death, and he'd served the current commander his entire reign. He'd seen what such enormous power had cost: Eugene Andrews' humanity. That, One thought, was worth saving almost as much as every Tacemus.

Eventually, he slept, and was awoken by Master.

"I'm going out, One. Don't leave this cabin." Master looked weary. He guided One to the breakfast laid in Ranger Phil's office, then departed.

Agent Walker relayed the news that Banks had not found Ella, though the tracker embedded in her bracelet gave Whitewash an indication as to her location. She had not moved since last night, which meant either the Grifters had chained her in place, or they'd found the tracker and removed it. The latter was unlikely. Grifters did not carry the same technology as the MTA.

Twilight darkened the windows when Master at length returned. He headed directly to Ranger Phil's desk chair, slumped into it, and shielded his face. He sat like this for many moments, until his phone rang. One expected Master to be invigorated by the noise, but he took his time in answering. However, when he saw the caller's identification, his eyes widened. Even so, he let the rings continue, readjusting his posture as he did so. Clearing his throat and wiping the fatigue from his expression, he tersely answered, "Yes?"

One did not think the caller was Ranger Phil; Master spoke too detachedly.

"It was a matter of business... I will meet you to discu... Really? Have you?" Master's fingers curled, though his tone indicated no such anger. "Certainly, then... I am at the welcome center... That won't be necessary, Chron... I said, that won't be—" After a pause, he removed the phone from his ear and dropped it. Master took in deep mouthfuls of air.

One had years of practice maintaining a neutral expression. The news that the MTA commander was dialoguing with Chron tested One's strength.

Master swiveled around. One blinked through his surprise, though Master seemed unaware of much outside his own mind.

"Need to hide you," he muttered and moved to One's side. He steered One from room to room, searching, never satisfied. After minutes, Master stowed him in the cubby of the receptionist's desk. Master pushed the chair in and draped his coat over it.

Less than ten minutes after Chron's call, a fist hammered the door off the porch. Master gave One the order to stay put. From his cramped position, One strained to hear the proceeding events.

A squeal of hinges. Master's voice. "Get to it, Chron. I'm busy."

"Your time has come, elak." The throaty words were followed by scuffling—the sounds of rushed footfalls, a thud, and a grunt.

"Don't be a fool." Master panted. "My soldiers—"

"Your soldiers do not know you are here. That *I* am here. You cannot deceive me, Andrews. Phillip Lane had a weak mind. You should have chosen one of stronger constitution as the keeper of your secrets."

One curled tighter in his hole. Then Chron had read Ranger Phil's mind, and likely murdered him afterward. By what Chron had revealed, it appeared none in the MTA, outside the now-deceased Ranger Phil, knew of Chron's presence in this forest.

"If you want to waste the most powerful bargaining chip you will ever have license of," Master said, "by all means: waste me."

"No," Chron said, "I will not kill you yet. That would be, as you said, a waste."

Master scoffed. "I know you're powerless to read me, but I do admire your perseverance. It's your only useful quality."

"You speak truly, Andrews. My skill evades me when I desire it most. But I am counting on another to rent the barricade that keeps you from me. *She* is one of useful qualities."

Same as One, Master knew of whom Chron spoke. She had accomplished her objective, and now her life rested in Chron's unforgiving hand.

"You underestimate Ella's loyalty," Master said. "She will never aid the Grifter who kidnapped her friends."

"I have seen her mind. That loyalty will be your ruin, Andrews."

Another grunt accompanied the dull drone of something being dragged. Footsteps and sound receded. The door slammed shut.

One trembled for several moments. He must call Agent Walker. Why could he not bring himself to move? Fear was spoken of as numbing. One had not comprehended that truth until now.

It seemed with excruciating effort that his hand felt along the waistband for that portable aid. One typed the appropriate letters. The words that didn't blur before his vision were stark and gray, like a Grifter's face. One's vision had grown cloudy, and his nostrils choked with fumes. He noticed he'd begun to sweat. The air beneath the reception desk had thickened.

He twisted about and smashed his forehead against the desk. At this pain, One dropped the phone with its incomplete message. When he opened his eyes to search, he saw only smoke.

Oxygen had vanished, as if One drew in air from a furnace. He crawled forward. The floor warmed his hands. *Chron set the building aflame,* he realized.

One closed his eyes and ordered his shaking to cease. But for eighteen years, One's body had rebelled against commands. Today was no different.

Heat seemed melded to his skin before he found the courage to move. He recalled a window in the room he'd earlier slept in. That frame stuck in his mind like a map. One pushed into the wave of heat whose intensity made him gag. He could not say how many minutes evaporated until he felt the window. The latches worked, and he lifted it. At the rush of wind and heat, he gasped.

Outside, he staggered and could not move quickly enough. One hurried toward the main road, intent on setting distance between the Grifters and himself. He'd lost his phone in the burning building; he would have to find another. Perhaps, then, he might stop shaking.

I STEPPED FROM ONE'S head. The shock mirrored in his features did justice to the coil in my gut. Dread inching up my throat, I faced the group.

"Andrews has been captured by Chron."

CHAPTER TWELVE

THE TEAM MERGED TO the table, drawn like magnets. As each member took a spot and it became apparent the cadets didn't know where to sit, Walker finally noticed them. Like his seat had stabbed him, he clambered upright and pointed to the group. "Where did they come from?"

"That," Cassidy said, stretching her knuckles, "is a long story."

The cadets, differing from Whitewash in both age and attire, lost some of the grit that had driven them to abandon the MTA—except Vires, who looked cockier than ever, peering over the table in haughty observation. James flushed from hairline to neck, half obscuring Bridget, who'd ducked behind him. Surprisingly, even McFarland showed uncertainty. The usually collected cadet seemed dazed, as if she couldn't figure out how she'd gotten there. After scanning her teammates and finding them mute, she must've realized the explanation fell to her. McFarland set her shoulders and said, "We were on an assignment and intercepted Kepler. She explained Operation Whitewash's purpose, and...." Her strength faded, and she added, without much conviction, "We thought it our duty to join."

She now seemed to second guess that decision. Joining Whitewash had been out of character for her. Maybe she'd gotten swept up, though that also seemed uncharacteristic.

"Have they been vetted?" Walker asked Cassidy.

"You do realize I have a brain."

He glowered, though the irritation lived briefly. Walker motioned for the cadets to stand along the wall. Then, he swiveled to me. "What did Integer tell you?"

The air of tension spread, vicious as a cloud with lightning claws, until an unclean hush settled. I glanced at One, cornered between Walker and Banks. The Tacemus had calmed, though memories shadowed his face. Though Saini had given One water and declared him free of serious injury, Banks bounced his leg and seemed ready to cart One to the clinic at the remotest hint of illness.

"They were in Ranger Phil's office," I began. The story took less than a minute to tell. I focused on the primary plot, skipping over One's internalizing. His sidelong gazes expressed appreciation for that.

Whitewash and the cadets shared a different string of concern. For Walker's team, this presented a massive wrench wedged in an eighteen-year-long plan. For the cadets, Andrews was akin to their principal, a figure they'd known their whole academy careers. But he'd lied to them, and that changed things. Vires, naturally, looked as if he couldn't care less. I was surprised to find similar unconcern in James. His features puckered with frustration more than regret. Bridget was appropriately downcast, but McFarland's composed mask cracked the widest, letting disquiet slither through.

Cassidy ended the lapse following my speech. "Let's be clear here," she said. "Other than the dead ranger, the MTA *doesn't* know Chron's in that forest?"

"Right," I said, checking One for verification. He nodded.

"Why does Andrews have a relationship with Chron?" Dr. Saini tousled her inky hair.

"I don't know," I said, "but I did notice MTA weapons while I was in there. I figured Chron stole them."

Walker rapped the table. "How advanced is Chron's telepathy?" he asked me.

"He doesn't understand how to use it. Durgan never taught him, and he didn't get the answer out of me."

Chron had intended for *me* to read Andrews, which meant we'd been imprisoned at the same time. How close, in strolling Chron's territory, had I come to Andrews—and how angry was Chron that he'd lost not only the tool to reading Andrews but two prisoner incentives *and* the Grifter he had just overthrown?

"There's a telepathic Grifter?" McFarland, with alarm clear across her dark features, reminded me of Ethan in how she treated every situation as dire.

I was going to have to tell him about Andrews—and give him evidence that Whitewash wasn't evil. Well, at least Ethan's seriousness would be appropriate.

"Yeah," I said to McFarland, "but his ability is inconsistent."

"Inconsistent or not, he now has the MTA commander." Elbow on the table, Walker cradled his forehead and sighed. "We need to organize an immediate extraction."

"With what numbers?" Agent Cassidy asked.

Everyone tallied up individually. Excluding One and including the cadets and Whitewash's remaining three members operating outside base, we made a team of nineteen. Unimpressive when considering the length of Chron's territory and the probable army of Grifters inside.

"Didn't you say Amy has MTA allies?" I asked Walker.

The light-haired Amy Lane had to be in her thirties, but her ducking mannerisms pinned her closer to Bridget's age. "Some, yes," she said, "but they're too intimidated to go public right now."

"Why don't we just let Chron kill Andrews?" Cassidy crossed her arms. "Problem solved."

"Great idea, Miranda dear," Hina Akamu, round face bright with mirth, called. "Not sure why that didn't occur to us."

Cassidy's fist thudded the table. "Do *not* call me—"

"Chron won't kill Andrews until he's extracted information," Walker said. "We can't let that happen."

"Plus, Andrews' death won't free the Tacemus," Banks said. "He can't die until we know how to help them."

"And the Grifters," I added.

Along the wall, Vires rolled his eyes.

Picturing our infiltration, I remembered the waterfall hideout had more than one exit.

"Did he see them use the tunnel?" Walker asked after I explained.

"He was unconscious. But... it's possible he figured it out."

"He's not going to leave that exposed for long," Agent Porter said. "We need to act soon."

For an hour, the members of Whitewash spitballed ideas. Divert our current efforts to recruiting more bodies, or come at Chron with a small team that could potentially sneak in and out undetected? Alert the MTA and let a well-stocked army of metas rescue Andrews for us? That idea was McFarland's, and Walker cleaved it in two. If we enlisted the help of the MTA, Whitewash couldn't control the outcome.

We'd come no closer to a plan when Walker mentioned the time. After announcing that he and Amy would visit our sparse allies first thing in the morning, he ordered us to bed. The word alone made me yawn, but my focus, ever alert now, jumped to the next problem. Or problems.

Should I visit Durgan? No, it was late, and he'd want alone time with his family.

Kara? She was likely sleeping.

Do the cadets need someone to show them around? I checked; Dom Bist was grandly gesturing them toward the stairs.

Is One okay? I might not have been the person for that job. Banks and Saini already crowded him, anyway.

What about Ethan? Even if asleep, he'd want to wake up for this news of Andrews. Maybe I could show him evidence too. Though he and I hadn't worked through our spat, I couldn't rest while Ethan still believed we were villains out to destroy all he held dear. The sooner he knew the truth, the sooner he could leave confinement and see his friends.

"Hey, Amy," I called amid the bustle. Feeling the cadets' eyes on me, I motioned her toward the kitchen. Once in the still of the galley, with Amy nervously shifting from foot to foot, I said, "I was told to ask you for evidence against the MTA? Something I should show Sh... someone?"

She exhaled, and her shoulders relaxed. "Oh! I see. Yes, I do have something like that. Could you—would it be all right—I could get you a grid, but those are in the supply closet...." Amy wrung her hands.

I smiled. "I can wait."

In another minute, Amy returned to the galley with a black, electronic grid screen and a digital watch, the latter for access to Ethan's room—she'd evidently caught the gist. After showing me the basics of the watch and making sure I knew how to play the video footage displayed on the grid, she left.

The screen displayed a pixelated doorknob. I tapped play, and the door swung inward.

Seated behind his desk, emanating—even in video—the air of a busy principal he'd worn so many times, Andrews glanced up. His ever-present Tacemus shadow eyed the camera and bobbed a tiny nod. He kept flickering in and out of view, until I understood that I was viewing him through a lens hidden in someone's eye.

"We need to talk." The gruff voice belonged to Walker.

Tossing a pen to his desk, Andrews stood. One of the bookshelves boxing in Andrews' office slid aside, and Walker followed him through the opening into a small, dim area resembling an interrogation room. Andrews took one of the two chairs, and the Tacemus leaned against the sliver of wall that had shifted to conceal the meeting.

"We missed one." Walker threw a manila folder to the table, forcing Andrews to move his hands. Andrews lifted the flap and scanned the first sheet of paper as Walker continued. "She's sixteen. Lives in Florida. I know that's Maher's territory, but you need to know the system's faulty. She was scheduled for a birth retrieval that no one filled. We only found her because the girl's DNA flagged Dr. Saini's tracking algorithm." He paused. "I took the liberty of visiting Florida."

Andrews, who'd splayed the folder's contents across the table, looked up from his reading. "And?"

"She's living a normal life. Nothing indicates she's a meta. Doesn't even participate in athletics."

"But you're obviously convinced otherwise, else you wouldn't be here."

"I walked past her yesterday and nicked her with this." A pocket knife waved in the camera's peripheral. "The cut's gone today."

I rubbed my arm, even though he hadn't specified where.

"Did you run the DNA from your blade?" Andrews asked.

"That's not my job. Send Chang." The video jerked as Walker leaned over the table to tap the papers. "This is the first true Fallow, Andrews—and no one noticed. Not her family, her school. Not us. That's disquieting."

Andrews dragged a sheet closer. I saw a candid, sideways image of me before he took up the page in his hands and studied it for a minute.

"If the data's conclusive and she's a meta?" Walker said.

"Metahumans do not belong with civilians," Andrews said flatly.

"You can't rip her out of that life. It's ingrained in her. Even the Tacemus can't fabricate away an existence."

"No, clearing her would be a waste, and potentially dangerous." The sheet returned to the table. "I see this as an advantage. We can observe Eleanor Kepler in an isolated setting and monitor her performance. She'll answer the question of whether an untrained metahuman loses all potential."

"How will we bring her in?"

"It must be organic. She has to believe in the MTA." Andrews brought his hands together in front of his mouth and drummed his fingers. Not an evil villain gesture but the movement of a man simply thinking. "We'll stage hostile activity and rescue her from it, gaining her faith. Her family will be cleared, the Grifters blamed, and she'll have no option but to give her life over to the MTA."

Walker's eye camera panned to One. It must've been him; no other Tacemus could look so distressed, as if, even after all this time, One had forgotten the type of man he worked for.

"Sounds risky," Walker said.

Andrews stood and buttoned his suit. "Risks are the MTA's prerogative, Agent Walker." He set a hand on the file. "Was there anything else?"

"No, sir."

"Speak of this to no one. Enjoy your drive back to Huntsville."

I stabbed the pause button. Saliva and bile pooled in my mouth, burnt as it went down, then stung as it came up again. Minutes after hearing my name, Eugene Andrews had begun his plan to destroy my complacent existence. The commotion at the "Welcome Back, Whale's!" festival before junior year—that had been *staged*?

The image of Andrews burned my eyes. More than his image. Every event since August of two years ago picked up weight and collapsed on my shoulders. I covered my face and slid against the cabinets, until I sat on the tile and shook. A scream boiled in my throat, but I had to keep it in. The super hearing of metas confined me, as if I were the one stuck in the square frame of a grid screen.

What had I been thinking? I couldn't wake Ethan and shove this down his throat. Ethan, the faithful cadet unaware that he'd been handpicked to spy on me.

The door clicked. I quickly brushed my cheeks and moved upright in time to appear somewhat presentable as someone stepped into the galley. My features froze. There he stood, the man in black and white who'd done more controlling than Eugene Andrews.

One looked as tired as me. He shut the door but came no closer, sagging beneath a forlorn shroud that made his eyes heavy. I'd cleared my thoughts, but even a Tacemus could notice crying.

You must know, he said, *that I am sorry.*

I turned my head. "Who cares about one person's life compared to the fate of thousands?"

I do.

The tiny words bristled my defensiveness, especially because they were true. One *did* care. Yet he'd acted as he had for the greater good. "But sometimes, controlling people is necessary," I said. "It's effective, at least."

That was hardest to admit. I was in Virginia, wasn't I? Safe, trained in telepathy, and willing to read Andrews? Whitewash's plan had succeeded. Controlling people had some advantages.

You cannot believe what we have done was good. One took a feverish step forward. *Effective, yes. But good? We have lied to you. Controlled you. We are guilty. Do you understand that it was wrong? That you did not deserve this?*

My jaw ached as I tried not to bite too hard. Tears mercilessly clogged the corners of my eyes. "Then—" The word cracked. *Then why did you do it?* I asked. *Why couldn't Whitewash have found a better way?*

Because we know nothing else.

One's unabashed confession struck a memory. Helix had said something similar about metas. Whitewash fought the corrupt upbringing that still impacted them.

Bitterness stung my eyes, and every sour thought welled. Kara was far from home. Ethan was in denial. The cadets were hurting. I wanted to fix them, add their problems to my growing to-fix list. One's problem, too. He carried sorrow because of Whitewash's actions. I saw it in his eyes and felt it in my chest. The curse of a telepath who worked better as an empath.

"Let's just move on, One."

I will do what you ask.

"No," I said sharply. "Don't obey me. You—" I caught my words and the heaviness of One's expression. "Why didn't you tell me what I can do?" I whispered.

His eyes contracted. *I did not want you to bear that burden. I see how it tortures Banks. He speaks carefully around them, afraid that one day he might give an unintentional command.*

By telling me this, One addressed what neither of us had mentioned. Banks must have told him that we'd broached the subject of his potential relationship with Andrews.

"So he can control them too?" I said.

He does not know. And would rather never find out.

I could understand that. I wished I didn't know.

"I've been waiting for you to get here," I said. "I'll tell everyone tomorrow."

I would urge you not to. But. I have lied enough. No more. I wish to right my wrongs. I will not lie again. And I will never read another thought nor wipe another memory. That mellow voice carried the conviction of an army. Reading him would've been unnecessary. One had meant it. The ability that had powered Whitewash for years—he was discarding it. Just like that.

Maybe it was dumb, trusting the man who'd lied all my life, but I believed him.

"Why don't you think I should tell Whitewash?" I said.

Because we are all weak, he said, *and power is tempting. They would mean well, but there are some in Operation Whitewash who would want you to use that power.*

An image of Agent Cassidy rose as confirmation to One's belief. Whitewash wanted to stop Andrews; what better way than by pointing his own weapon at him?

Same as One, I wanted to forge a new path. I'd done my share of hiding truths. At the same time, there *was* a difference between a deliberate lie and withholding information.

"Durgan told me it's not wrong to conceal information," I said. "He says some stuff's better left unsaid. So, if we don't tell Whitewash, it's not the same thing as lying."

I couldn't believe I'd landed on this side of the conversation, with One of all people. He absorbed it with a thoughtful air.

Durgan is one of the few I trust, he said. *If he believes a truth can be concealed, then....*

"Then we say nothing. Unless we have to?"

One slowly nodded.

If events didn't pan out and Whitewash ran out of options, I could reveal my trump card. For now, Operation Whitewash could chug along without this intel.

In the quiet, exhaustion roiled, a roller coaster that unsteadied my legs. I played it off by curling into a perch on the floor. After a pause, One settled beside me. I got the feeling we could've maintained our spots until morning, neither speaking, and it wouldn't have felt awkward.

"How did Banks get involved with Whitewash?" I asked.

Cadets do not pay attention to their forgettable servants. He did. He followed me. When I discovered him, I could not read his intentions. It was nearly a disaster. One smiled, so rare a sight I performed a double-take. *He had to do much to prove he was trustworthy,* One added.

"I'm surprised Walker let a cadet join."

You are mistaken. Banks let Walker join.

"But Walker's in charge."

Because Banks does not like the responsibility. One's sidelong glance conveyed what he'd left out of his answer.

"Oh," I said. Then, suspicious that fatigue had muted my comprehension, I eyed One again. Meaning still lingered in his expression. I'd understood correctly. Walker was in charge of *Banks'* operation. He'd started Whitewash, then passed along the reins. It fit: I couldn't picture Banks doling out orders. But he was also terrible at following them, which made him a continued mystery.

Had I been wide awake, I would've tossed out some questions. Curiosity faded as my forehead dipped onto my knees.

You are tired, One said.

"Yeah," I mumbled. "Sorry."

Never apologize to me. It is I who must apologize to you. Whitewash must as well. But they are too stubborn to admit their wrongs. I will do so for them.

Noting his renewed vigor, I peeked over. One, leaning close, didn't blink as he said, *On behalf of Operation Whitewash, I apologize for every pain we have caused you.*

He offered something I'd never expected. *Did* Whitewash regret their actions? I hoped so. I managed a nod. My head felt heavy. So weary. The tension in my throat loosened, but it came out as a cough that turned into a sob. I cried into my knees and didn't flinch when One found the courage to pat my shoulder.

I forgive you, I said. *Okay?*

You do not have to.

I know. That's the point. I tilted my face toward him, trying a smile, and felt the physical follow-up to my statement.

Thank you. His small smile finished erasing my former wariness of One. Suddenly, he looked less like a mind-reading clone and more like an old, exhausted man. For the first time, I saw One as he could be, something he'd never truly been.

Free.

CHAPTER THIRTEEN

VAGUE CHATTER WOKE ME. Light stirred through the far window of the clinic. A digital projection on the wall gave the time and date. 0704, August first. On the twenty-eighth of June, I'd left Durgan. Three days later and we'd found ourselves under the same roof.

A bed over, Kara breathed easily, sounding much less congested. The dark circles had finally dissipated, and a hint of rose had settled in her cheeks. Dr. Saini's concoctions worked fast.

Opposite the cots, a group hung near the line of counters and cabinets. Banks hunched over a small table that hadn't been there yesterday, while Saini stood cross-armed, observing him. Behind Banks, only One paid me any mind.

You should have slept longer, he said.

And miss all the fun? I gave a slight smile that he returned.

Seeing Banks, I remembered One's revelation from last night. Here was Whitewash's co-founder, a role he wanted nothing to do with. He really *was* Andrews' opposite.

I swallowed. That was probably intentional.

Saini noticed me and shook her head. "Lee should've given you a sedative," she called, then cast a glance toward her young assistant. He lay atop the counter, slumped against the wall with an open book in his lap. His drooping chin poked his collar bone. Dr. Saini sighed and said, "Evidently, he gave it to himself."

"I've never seen a meta nap," I said.

"Sometimes I wonder if he's a meta." She pushed out a small frown, but her affectionate tone failed to match the expression.

Screws and wire parts cluttered the table, shoved in a U around whatever Banks tinkered with. Though only half complete, I could tell the sheaths of metal, about the length of Banks' arm, would form the shape of a leg when put together. A silver-and-black foot, complete with toes, waited on the counter.

"Is that for Durgan?" I asked Saini.

"Yes. Banks kindly agreed to build it."

"Any update on Andrews?"

"Agent Walker and Amy are currently discussing the matter with our allies. News of Andrews' disappearance has reached the MTA. We're the primary suspects."

That complicated things. McFarland had suggested we contact the MTA for aid in rescuing Andrews, but they'd never help if they suspected us.

I massaged my jaw and felt a gap through my cheek. Remembering my missing tooth made me think of food, and my stomach gurgled.

"Stop moving for a moment, Ella." Saini's eyes had narrowed. A cylindrical device, similar to a laser pointer, floated off the counter, and she aimed it at my face.

I automatically winced, but it emitted zero light. Before I could inquire, Saini nodded to herself, then turned to the counter.

"Your stomach's obnoxiously loud," Banks said.

"I'm fine," I said, distracted by Saini, who squeezed white paste into a mold suspiciously shaped like a tooth.

Breakfast is in the galley, came One.

"I'll be—"

"Open your mouth, Ella," Dr. Saini interrupted.

Confused, I did as she requested, skirting back when she thrust something toward my face. "It's a replacement," she said, waving the tiny white molar.

"But, how did you—shouldn't you measure first?"

"I already did. Mouth open, please."

Banks paused his work to watch Saini maneuver the fake tooth toward the back of my mouth. I hadn't thought the gap was that obvious, but Saini evidently noticed everything.

"Jaw firmly locked for two minutes," she said, gluing my mouth shut with her fingers until she was certain I'd follow directions.

I couldn't have disobeyed anyway; a numbing tingle had begun in my gum, gaining traction and spreading icy pricks along the left side of my face.

"Two minutes without questions from Ella," Banks said. "You should lose teeth more often."

I can still talk, I said.

"Not as loudly."

I can yell, too.

"Obviously." Banks rubbed an ear.

"Good morning, Kara," Dr. Saini called.

Banks sucked in a hiss and dropped a black torch. Wires began smoking.

Kara, shifting her IV pole along, padded across the clinic in wool socks and a hospital gown.

I offered her my arm. *How are you feeling?*

"Like I don't have pneumonia anymore."

You had pneumonia? I stared at Saini and branded her with the same question.

"She's fine, Ella." Saini checked Kara's IV bags, frowned, then summoned full ones.

"Hi, Jimmy." Kara had stopped near the work table. Her voice was friendly, her smile genuine, but Banks stared as if waiting for her to hurl a rocket at his face. He still assumed she blamed him for the kidnapping. Meanwhile, Kara grew fidgety under his watch.

"Please stop bleeding on my sterile equipment, Jimmy." Saini put a slight emphasis on the name, perhaps reminding him to stick to the role.

I followed his gaze down. He'd stuck a spiky prod into his fingertip; beads of red wetted the metal piece below his hand.

Banks jerked the object out of his skin, snatched up the bloody equipment, and turned to the sink. Kara fiddled with her hands, a flush creeping up her neck. Telling her the reason for Banks' behavior seemed a breach of confidence, but I didn't want Kara feeling snubbed.

He's a meta, I said. *Metas are weird.*

Her smile looked forced.

"Jimmy is right, Ella," Saini said lightly. "Your stomach is loud. Go eat."

"I'll still be here when you're done," Kara spoke over my automatic protest.

After promising Saini I'd steer clear of chewy foods, I left, intent on returning to my to-do list. Check in with Durgan, verify that Vires hadn't begun an argument with someone, tell Ethan about Andrews....

My stomach flopped at the prospect.

From the boxing ring came constant clacking, so sharp I winced. Cassidy and Vires staffed amid a cheering cluster. With the exception of Keswick, they rooted for Vires.

Cornered between Dom Bist and Hina Akamu, McFarland leaped from the table as soon as she saw me. "I see, thank you," she said to them before politely nodding, then not-so-politely rushing from Dom's response. She blocked my path. "Have you heard an update?"

"Only that Walker and Amy are trying to get allies," I said.

"There's no other plan?"

"There is," Cassidy called. With a swivel and strike, she flicked Vires' practice staff out of his hands. As it sailed toward Keswick, she thrust her staff into Vires' chest and said, "*I'm* the only clavio in Whitewash. But," she reached, and his staff flew into her grip, "you're not terrible." She tossed him the stick.

Vires turned, scowling. When he caught McFarland's cool gaze, he lifted his chin and feigned nonchalance. If McFarland and I had been better friends, I would've told her to shrug him off. Well, maybe doing just that would make a closer friendship possible.

Ignore him, I said. *He's being rude.*

Her forehead furrowed. Guarded with her own emotions, McFarland seemed unsure how to read anyone else's.

Cassidy danced around Vires and sailed over the ropes. "Get Integer," she called to me.

"Why? And do we have to call him 'Integer'?"

She sighed so loudly it echoed up the walls. "Filling in for Banks?"

"Why do you want him?" I repeated.

"So we can toss him in the ring. Why else, Kepler?"

I stood firm. I wasn't One's master.

Not his. Just the rest.

I gritted my teeth and felt a twinge.

"I'll get him." McFarland marched toward the stairs.

"She's very austere, isn't she?" At the table, Dom stroked his nose.

Whatever Cassidy wanted with One, surely a meeting would follow. James and Bridget would want to join. They weren't around, which left the galley. That worked out. Galley meant food.

I peeked my head through the doorway. A wave of salty, meaty bacon nearly knocked me flat. My stomach sang.

"Oh, good morning." James waved. He and Bridget, empty plates pushed aside, sat near Dom's mute MTA partner. Arthur Finch, earplugs trailing from his grid, paid them no mind.

"We were trying to talk to Arthur because we were told he studied civilians, but," James eyed Finch and whispered, "I don't think he's listening."

"It's not just you. I've never seen him without headphones. Anyway, I think we're about to have a meeting out here."

The cadets scurried from the table. I snatched a handful of bacon off the counter before joining them.

The gathering circle separated at our approach. McFarland scooted sideways to make room, but James avoided her; and, since Bridget had taken to following him, she skirted McFarland too.

"... according to Kepler, you should have the memory." Cassidy gestured me over. "Read Integer and see if he's got the location of the protean lab."

She was still assuming One had wiped Chang's memory and retained the lab's location. No surprise that Cassidy chose to pursue this during Walker's absence. "Doesn't Walker—"

"Walker has no excuse putting this off," Cassidy said. "If we can't get to Andrews, the protean lab is our only option."

"I stand by my theory that Walker is a protean and wants to prohibit us from taking advantage of his ability," Dom said.

"What's his ability?" Hina asked him.

"He can count backwards without ever growing weary."

"That does sound useful."

"What's the protean lab?" James asked.

I tuned out the conversation and checked One. Something else might've lived in that lab. I'd never given much thought to the Tacemus' identical appearance, but there could only be one explanation. Cloning was the stuff of science fiction, but so was telekinesis and telepathy. If the Tacemus were clones, someone had to be creating them.

It's possible the protean lab is where the Tacemus are... created, I said.

He surveyed the wall. *Yes.*

I waited for the proper words of comfort to arrive, but what could be said to subdue the chill of knowing your existence had been engineered in a lab? He lived because a trick of science, but that didn't make *him* a trick.

We don't have to look for it, I said. *Walker doesn't want us to, anyway.*

If we do not search, we ignore their existence. One faced me. *They deserve to be found, Ella.*

Pity stirred. Remembering that lonesome Tacemus, motionless in the rain, I found myself nodding. *Okay. Give me a moment.*

But finding Chang's memory took less than that.

THE WALL BEHIND WALKER'S vacant chair at the head of the table lay covered by a projection screen and that screen by a map. Red marker made a squiggle connecting northern Georgia to southern Tennessee. From the tip of the squiggle, new lines fanned—because, though Chang had paid enough attention to notice that the lab hid somewhere around Montvale, Tennessee, she'd never uncovered its exact location. Not for lack of trying, but Andrews knew how to keep secrets.

We had to narrow down the location based on the duration of Chang's flight from the Georgia academy to the lab, calculating for wind and aircraft speed. Everyone scrutinized their grids in silence, which they only broke to affirm or rule out a possibility.

"Too industrial."

"It'd have to be inside a mountain."

"There's certainly enough trees."

"Here?" Dom turned his grid. It showed a dog park, where Labradors chased balls and one lady walked with a puppy strapped to her chest.

I wanted to laugh, then felt restricted by the presence of superiors. A weary chuckle rumbled in my throat anyway.

McFarland had suggested scouring satellite images in the potential areas, earning a stark reminder of how much the MTA controlled. Satellite feeds were doctored, bird's-eye views of academies replaced with images of uncut land. That knowledge gave us some advantage, though. If Andrews did control map searches of the protean lab, he'd have to replace the image with something believable. He wouldn't insert an image of a supermarket over an otherwise rural area.

Cassidy erased marker lines over the minutes, ordering me to dip back into One's head any time Whitewash needed more specificity. I hated returning to Chang's memory, watching the replay of how she and Andrews had brought me to the lab, hooked me to the stasis chamber—and left me there for months. Only one thing in her memory struck my interest: the name *Colette*, Andrews' access code for his building and computer. Chang had found it stupidly sentimental to use a name as a password. I couldn't figure it out, either. Did Andrews actually care enough about anyone to type their names over and over? I wondered if Colette was Banks' mother.

It wasn't *stupidly* sentimental; it was just sentimental, and that made zero sense.

Eventually, we narrowed our search. She circled three lines and wiped away the remainders. The protean lab was in one of three places spread out around Montvale, Tennessee.

"We'll recon," Agent Cassidy said. "I'll contact Holt so he—"

"What is this?"

The table silenced as all heads turned toward the foot. Dr. Saini stared at the projection. I briefly wondered how Kara and Banks were faring alone in the clinic, a question that got sucked away as understanding dawned on Saini, turning her expression sharp.

"Agent Walker gave express orders—"

"Don't tell me you agree with him," Cassidy said. "You're a scientist, Saini. Your curiosity isn't piqued?"

"My curiosity is irrelevant. Agent Walker has asked us not to pursue the protean project."

"Yes, because he forgets we're not cadets. He might do some planning, but Whitewash isn't his operation."

"Is it yours, Cassidy?" Saini's tone encroached upon icy.

"Technically," Dom interrupted, with all the mildness of one asking about the time, "Operation Whitewash belongs to Banks. Shall we seek his opinion?"

"Agent Walker is in charge," Saini said, "which Agent Cassidy has clearly forgotten."

Cassidy smacked the wall, denting the projection display. "Enough with the judgment, Saini. I didn't hear anyone else complain about this plan. Thanks to me, we've narrowed down the location."

"And I suppose we sat here trimming our nails while you did all the work, Miranda?" Hina Akamu called.

"For the last time—"

The galley door creaked open, and Walker and Amy strode through. Chairs scraped the floor as everyone shifted.

"We had a blasted hard time getting Rodriguez to listen to us," Walker said, entering uncomfortable proximity to the blinking screen. "We're under fire, and no one trusts a thing we say." He rested his hands on his hips and absently glanced toward the source of light. His eyes focused. "Tennessee? What's this?"

Dr. Saini cleared her throat. "Yes, Miranda, tell Agent Walker your brilliant plan."

Cassidy looked ready to punch another wall—or, better yet, Dr. Saini's nose. When it became apparent Walker awaited an answer, she set her fiery glower upon him. "You said it yourself, Walker. No one's going to help us, and unless we can recruit five-dozen additional troopers, we don't stand a chance against Chron. The lab is our only option."

By everyone else's expressions, I wasn't the only one holding my breath. Bridget gaped at Walker with such obvious trepidation that it affected my own pulse and turned my neck sweaty. It might've been more bearable had Walker yelled; his quiet seething increased the tension.

"I've done nothing wrong," Cassidy said. "If you'd been honest with us, I wouldn't have pushed this so hard."

"Honest about what, Cassidy?"

She chewed the words before launching them. "You're a protean."

We all went mute as Arthur Finch.

If a snake had entered a staring contest with Walker, Walker would've won. Cassidy deserved a medal for enduring the length of his silent, narrowing scrutiny. I could've read the answer instead of waiting for Walker to speak, but the current contents of his mind were probably lethal. *Was* he a protean? Dom's joke had seemed just that.

Amy Lane released a relieved sigh when Walker opened his mouth. "Fine," he said. "We'll do it your way. I'm a protean."

Saini made a protesting noise; Walker jerked a hand without addressing her. "No. She's made up her mind. Let's hear the rest of your plan, Cassidy. What next?"

Her arms folded, though she didn't appear victorious. "What's your ability?"

"Does it involve counting?" Dom said. No one laughed, not even Hina.

"I'm certainly not a mind-reader," Walker said to Cassidy. "You wouldn't be here if that were the case."

She glared. Within those bright blue eyes rested the dimmer spark of shame.

Confession or not, something rubbed the wrong way. Walker, a protean? I couldn't see it. However, he didn't seem a liar.

Noise sounded from the second floor. A dozen heads swiveled. Durgan, leaning heavily on Durgson, limped along the landing. Tam clung to Ly's hand and followed behind. Durgson guided his father toward the stairs. Something reflective caught the light. His leg—Saini had already fitted it.

Once Durgan stumbled on the first step, I knew the rest would be a nightmare. I hurried to help.

Durgan, somehow majestic in a crinkled hospital gown, smiled when I stopped on the step below them. Poking from the hem, the metal prosthetic could've been a boot of armor, though sleeker than a knight's.

I thank you, he said. *Dr. Saini said the idea was yours. You have returned my family to me, something I did not believe possible.*

You're welcome, Durgan. A lump turned baseball-sized in my throat, though it cleared when I caught the intensity of Durgson's glare, as if he believed my presence might infect his father's other leg.

"Let me help you," I said.

"My father does not need—"

"Quiet your pride, son," Durgan said.

Durgson fumed. None of his family members felt guilty about publicly reprimanding him. I'd be annoyed, too.

Selfish elak… how dare she approach him… if she were dead, they would be alive….

I turned my head. Empathy had its downsides.

Despite an unspoken tug-of-war between Durgson and me, we managed to steer Durgan around the staircase without anyone face-planting over the edge. Once we touched the first floor, Durgson encircled his father's waist and lifted him away from me, stalking all the way to the table until Durgan touched his son's shoulder. Durgson situated his father so that the latter's good foot touched down. Durgan tested the prosthetic's weight and relaxed. Though Durgan stood crookedly, he emanated strength, the air of regality shimmering around his frame like a gold cloak instead of a paper one. All of Whitewash gazed upon him as if they couldn't resist—though that might've been gratitude for the distraction from Walker and Cassidy.

"You have saved my family," Durgan said. "You tend my wounds and shelter us. May we return the favor in kind." He spoke a foreign phrase and held his hand high.

Durgson stiffened at the gesture.

"*Talar du svenska?*" James leaned eagerly forward; but, upon receiving no answer from either Grifter or Whitewash, he flushed and settled back.

"Which one of you saved Tam from the river?" Durgan asked. The Grifters must have told him how Agent Porter's telekinesis scooped Tam up.

"Agent Porter," I said, pointing.

When Durgan glanced his way, Porter dropped his hands beneath the table. I imagined they were struggling to unclench. It wasn't every day an MTA agent stared into the face of his enemy.

"I thank you," Durgan said.

Porter cleared his throat.

Durgan gently pushed Tam. The little Grifter inched toward Porter, wringing his hands. The top of his head barely cleared the table. He stopped a foot from Porter, who warily inspected Tam as if waiting to be assaulted. Then, attention cast downward, Tam mumbled, "*Annans skada glömmes snart.*" Then he scuttled back to his father and hid behind his leg, though he peeked around it to solemnly watch.

Porter nodded, eyes wide with the expression of someone who's fairly certain the other person is crazy. "All right. Affirmative."

"I see that I have disrupted your discussion." Durgan clasped Durgson's arm. "I will leave you."

The four Grifters turned. At the mention of "discussion," I remembered the reason Cassidy had gone against Walker's wishes in the first place. "Maybe you can help us," I called.

He waited. All of Whitewash did, too, and I detected more than curiosity in their stares. Once before, Durgan had provided the aid Whitewash needed.

"Chron kidnapped Andrews," I said, "commander of the MTA."

At Chron's name, Durgson hissed, and Ly smooshed Tam's face into her hip. Their father's chest heaved; he gripped Durgson's wrist and spent a moment with his head bowed. "There is only one," he said slowly, "who can convince Chron to release your commander."

Walker, not recovered from his ire, barked out, "We're not giving him Kepler."

"No. Certainly not. I speak of Helix, Chron's sister."

"She's missing," I said. "Do you know where she is?"

"I do not. I am sorry."

"Any idea how to find her?"

"I have tried this already and failed. She is our greatest ally. It is her voice alone to which Chron will listen."

I'd seen evidence of that a year ago, when Chron and I first met and he attempted to drag me off. Helix had kept Chron in check. Without her voice, he'd helped Jurstin overthrow Durgan and kill half his family.

Her *voice*.

Helix wasn't here, but *I* was, and I remembered what she sounded like.

Anticipation ticked in my chest. I lifted my head to Durgan. "What if Chron *thought* it was Helix?"

CHAPTER FOURTEEN

IN THE SOUNDPROOF BEDROOM, I couldn't hear the scenes that raged below. I imagined them instead, picturing Walker's veins bursting as he unleashed his frustration on Cassidy. Would he reveal his supposed protean ability?

Durgan and I faced each other in the room Saini had assigned to our Grifter allies. It lay farthest from everyone else, tucked in the corner of the second floor. Though Durgan had told Durgson to stay by the conference table and befriend Whitewash, he instead sulked nearby. His siblings, on the contrary, watched with fascination.

For the past thirty minutes, I'd sat cross-legged and blindfolded on the floor, allowed strictly telepathic conversation. My instructor lacked the ability he currently trained me in; Helix had taught him all he'd needed.

Durgan had finally answered the question I'd carried for more than a year. My ability to hear Grifters in groups depended on the Grifters themselves, not me. They could speak collectively, sending their telepathic communications out like a radio broadcast, audible to any listener within range. As a telepath, I automatically tuned in.

Range was the question we currently sought to answer. Chron and Helix could speak to each other across any distance. Since I'd already communicated to Ethan and Kara over hundreds of miles, Durgan believed I could attempt the same with Chron. The ability, same as mind-reading, merely required an understanding of the target.

I dwelled on each member of Whitewash, sewing invisible stitches between us. Once I could breezily communicate to them, Durgan believed I could apply the same technique with Chron. The harder part would be making sure he heard Helix and not Ella Kepler.

By manipulating my voice projection, relying on memory, I started wondering what else I could project. It took willpower, controlling my anticipation when I asked Durgan. I craved his answer but feared it, too.

"If I can project a voice," I said, "could I project a memory?"

The blindfold helped; it prevented me from seeing whether he looked affirmative or doubtful.

"Let us find your answer," he said.

I had a memory gathered before he asked. Treating the random scene—eating breakfast at the academy—like a thought I wanted to share, I tried passing it along. In the silence, my anxious heart seemed like another person in the room.

"Memory, academy, breakfast," Durgan said, and my nerves tingled with hope. "Your voice repeats it. That is all I hear. I see nothing."

"Oh," I managed. Hope vanished like a visitor rejected at the door. At least the blindfold hid my disappointment, though Durgan still noticed.

"You are not expected to be omnipotent, Ella Kepler," he said softly.

I nodded, realigning all my efforts toward not crying. Durgan didn't know the root of this pain. I shouldn't have, either. They were supposed to be blocked out. Forgotten, like they'd forgotten me.

Durgan meant to train me for the next twenty-four hours, but Dr. Saini interrupted our session in the evening to remind us of our physical health. She delivered a stack of meals to the Grifters, then ordered me away for a proper night's rest. Though I had my own room, I hated abandoning Kara to solitude, so I headed for the clinic.

Kara sat on the counter, casual as if this were her house instead of an MTA facility. Leaning against the adjacent counter, Banks spun a pair of pliers around, giving the tool his attention and, at the same time, appearing not to notice it. I felt grateful he'd kept her company, though who knew what they'd talked about. Then, remembering Banks' earlier discomfort around her, I understood. He must've gotten the issue off his chest; otherwise, he wouldn't have stood so close.

"... because of the heat," Kara was saying; then, she saw me and smiled. Despite the sallow cheeks, she seemed normal as ever. "Hi!" she called. "Look. Jimmy found some spare yarn." She swiveled her wrist, showing off the red string bracelet. Another one dangled from her fingertips.

Whitewash's inventory happened to include red yarn? Kara bought it, but I knew the yarn wasn't random. Banks had needed it to replace the one burned away during the clubhouse fire, a replacement he'd installed with a tracker, so Whitewash could keep an eye on me.

He rotated the pliers faster, keeping his profile aimed downward. Banks could guess what I was remembering, but I'd let go of irritation with him.

"Thanks, Banks," I said, and I meant it.

"Good rhyming," Kara said. "How was your telepathy session?"

I stopped in my tracks. "Didn't Saini give you the whole 'tell Kara nothing' spiel?"

"Calm down, Sheedy," Banks said, though relief softened his scowl.

"Sheedy?" Kara glanced between us. "Did you and Ethan get married without telling me?"

"No," I said, "Banks just likes to call me that any time he thinks I'm remotely bossy."

"Remotely?" he said.

"Oh. Well, you *can* be bossy, El," Kara said, grinning.

Honestly, Kara could've teased me all she wanted. Hearing her talk, seeing her smile — it left little room for my pride.

The IV pole took up space on her left, so I squeezed between her and Banks. He pocketed the pliers and budged over.

"Where is Ethan, by the way?" Kara said, knotting the yarn around my wrist. "I haven't properly met him. Or thanked him."

"*Thank* him?" Banks said, as if he'd much rather say, *You mean, punch him in the face?*

"Yeah. I owe Ethan a lot. My life, probably. He talked me through everything. It's much scarier when you're in the dark. Then, we did some training. Nothing intense, but he got me moving. Before that, I was a slug."

Mixed in with regret over Kara's situation and an influx of gratitude for Ethan, guilt poked through. Ethan was isolated, still without proof and unaware of Chron's latest move. The day had proven too hectic for that chat.

"He's... " I started and couldn't finish.

"Sheedy's always busy, no matter where he is," Banks said.

I peeked at him. Had McFarland replaced Banks? No, there he leaned, the sourness gone and replaced by something less hostile. He'd pointed out Ethan's stubbornness to the rest of Whitewash, but something currently held his tongue. Taken generously, one could say Banks had *defended* Ethan.

But that was absurd.

Dr. Saini entered then, full of rebukes for Banks at having lingered so long. Under her vigilant watch, Kara and I hurried to bed. The lights soon clicked off.

"Night, Kar," I said, then promptly passed out.

I AWOKE TO A tap on my shoulder.

"You're needed downstairs," Dr. Saini whispered.

The digital display read 0419. It shed the only light on the clinic walls.

Kara kept sleeping as Saini led me down the empty stairs. 0430 was standard wake-up time; base lay in a lull.

"What's going on?" I asked Saini.

"Agent Walker has an assignment for you."

I straightened my shoulders and wished I'd changed out of my leisure clothes. At least I'd put shoes on.

An assignment—from one protean to another?

He waited in the galley. After a nod to Saini, he turned.

I caught up in the hallway sectioning off Ethan's room. "Where—"

"To test your range. I want you learning how to fly, too."

That made sense. The first part, at least. Who knew why he wanted me to fly.

When Walker veered off the hallway and stopped before Ethan's door, I wondered whether Ethan had been relocated. Walker rapped four times before unlocking the handle. The door eased open; Walker stuck his head through and called, "Up, Sheedy."

Did Walker have the strong desire to get assaulted?

Ethan, also in loungewear, stood by his bed, wincing at the sudden light. A pillow crease indented his cheek. That didn't grab my interest so much as his hair—or lack thereof. Gone was the disorderly length of black in favor of the clean-shaven cut of when we'd first met. I'd forgotten about the scar etched up the side of his head.

He frowned at Walker, then me.

"I'm taking Kepler on assignment," Walker said. "Could be dangerous. Your skills would be useful. Two minutes." He backed out, butting me in the process. With a grumble, Walker steered me into the hallway.

"What's going on?" I said after he closed the door.

"It's as I said. Sheedy's a good soldier, particularly when properly motivated. But you'll put these on him." Walker tugged metal wrist cuffs from a pocket. "I don't trust him to walk to the aircraft without incident."

I eyed the cuffs, a prisoner's accessory. "You're going about this the wrong way. He *is* a good soldier, but he's not going to help Whitewash until he trusts you."

"He'll help if it means protecting you."

"I don't know about that."

Walker folded his arms.

"He needs evidence," I said. "Let me talk—"

"Evidence?" Walker scrounged in a jacket pocket and found his grid.

"I can show him," I said.

"No, you stay put." He tucked the grid under his armpit.

"I'm his friend. I should be the one to talk to him."

"You're too involved. I'll handle this."

I stood there, testing arguments, staring into Walker's set expression and knowing none would work. The two minutes vanished, and so did Walker, into Ethan's room for a conversation I was excluded from.

This seemed a bad way of showing Ethan the truth: by Agent Walker and some cold data. *I* wanted to tell him, to manage the conversation so Ethan came out of it as unscathed as possible. He'd already been blasted by that first Whitewash briefing. Walker wouldn't be any less matter-of-fact in person.

Something else wrapped around this emotional tangle. I'd already had a talk with Ethan, and it had convinced him of nothing. Proof would do what my words hadn't. Walker had taken that role from me.

I counted a slow five hundred before the door opened. Ethan exited first. He wore tactical gear now, but I zeroed in on his face. I'd never seen that expression, nor the red veins in his eyes. His met mine and tightened further. When Walker stepped behind him and clapped his shoulder, Ethan looked away.

"Forward and right, son," Walker said.

They passed by. I tried to ignore Ethan's thoughts, but snippets leapt at me like sparks from a fire.

My parents... Agent Walker... Leader knows.

I remembered what Saini had said. Twenty years ago, Walker stole Ethan from his parents. Evidence—Walker had it firsthand.

I wanted to run to Ethan, but Walker blocked the way.

We moved into the garage. Three packed duffel bags rested on a workbench. Walker tossed one to me and two to Ethan; he caught them robotically and slung one over each shoulder.

"Describe the weather when you left the protean lab—December third, correct?" Walker scanned his grid, then glanced up at my continued silence.

"We're going to the lab?" I said.

"Yes, Kepler. The weather?"

The protean lab, after yesterday's fiasco? I checked Ethan. He didn't share my shock. Walker had briefed him already.

I felt as if I'd missed something more substantial than breakfast. "Uh," I said, rubbing my forehead, "it was chilly. Not freezing, but cold."

Walker typed away. "Any rain?"

"No."

"On the drive from the lab to the hangar, did you see mountains?"

"No."

"Buildings?"

"Don't think so. Just a lot of trees."

This satisfied Walker. He typed a moment more, then nodded. "Move out."

The garage door ascended. Walker forewent the vehicles and walked into the dark outdoors.

On the trek through the sandy bluff dividing base from the hangar, we fell into a line. Walker moved to the front, not bothering to monitor Ethan. I took my chance to sidle next to him.

I'm sorry, Ethan.

He nodded, staring ahead and slightly down. Unfocused, without his usual *I'm on a mission and alert* intensity.

I touched his fingers, once again hating my gloves. He didn't flinch, but his face registered no comfort, either.

We reached the hangar after a silent walk.

Walker palmed the locking mechanism a second after my foot crossed the jet's threshold. He weaved around the table in the cabin and stopped near the cockpit. "Five minutes." He didn't have to explain the time gap: Walker was giving us a moment to chat—oddly kindhearted of him.

A snap of another door, and we were alone.

Ethan pulled the straps over his head and placed the duffel bags in a seat. Clean-cut and shaven, he looked thinner and paler. The cabin lighting didn't help.

A dozen statements fell short of my lips. Finally, I set my bag down and moved in front of him. "You can talk to me," I murmured.

Even when the floor began to rumble with engine power, Ethan kept still, other than the trembles induced by the jet. No—Ethan was shaking. His eyes shone glassy, his mouth a pinched line, and he shook with the effort of controlling that expression, maintaining its hardness so the tear wouldn't release. MTA soldiers refused to cry. He'd never come close to it, not even when my old J instructor, Griffin, had died.

"I failed." His words came out sharp. "It's my responsibility to lead, to have answers. Everything I gave was inadequate."

Ethan's concern skipped past the fact that Andrews had lied to him, because those lies had personal consequences. By following Leader for about a decade, Ethan believed he shared in that guilt. Ever the faithful cadet, he'd led the toughest missions, made excruciating calls, and had earned the position of commanding officer at a younger age than typical—but all those badges had come with a price.

"Listen to me," I said. "You did everything in your power to lead cadets well. *He* is at fault. He lied to all of you. Don't blame yourself for his mistakes."

"I don't. I blame myself for mine."

"You didn't know, Ethan."

"What does that say about my character? My peers knew. *You* knew. I was blind." Veins raised blue and angry in his knuckles. "I don't understand how a cadet could realize the truth about his origin and do nothing to prevent it from happening again. Our parents never had a choice, and... and some take no issue with that."

The person behind *some* hovered in Ethan's thoughts, just one cadet. Lydia was in the Society, and now Ethan knew.

"We take issue with it, Sheedy." Agent Walker crowded the cockpit doorway, studying him.

If it had been me, I would've concealed my sorrow and pretended all was well, but Ethan treated Walker's presence no differently than mine. Ethan *was* blind, in a way, baring himself without fretting about people's opinions.

"Your friends made the right call," Walker added.

Ethan turned his head and quietly said, "Not all of them."

Walker must've told him that the cadets had joined—excluding Lydia.

"I've dealt with my share of dissenters," Walker said. "You have to let them go. People have their reasons. Most times they don't make sense, but they'll see when they're ready."

"How can you justify that when Operation Whitewash is founded on dissension?" Ethan said.

Walker let out something of a weary sigh. "Our goal isn't anarchy, Sheedy. This situation's as hierarchical as you like. It's your priorities that are unbalanced. Yes, we are disobedient to the MTA. Better that than disobedient to truth. Now," he waved me to a seat, "Sheedy's been briefed. It's your turn. Sit down."

Disobedient to truth. The phrase ran through Ethan's head like a clip on repeat. It stuttered when he wondered whether Andrews had ever cared about truth.

I wished Walker had waited two extra minutes before emerging. Ethan had finally come around to Whitewash, and it had ripped him up. I wanted to stamp out his doubts before they multiplied; but, as always, metas stuck to a timetable and didn't care much for delays.

"Andrews got in with a handprint and voice prompt," Walker said. "We can mimic those, but we have to assume security will be tighter inside. You'll stay with the aircraft."

"Why didn't you bring more backup?" I said.

"Plenty of backup." Walker motioned the duffel bags. "While we're gone, I want you communicating to everyone on the team. As far as Whitewash is concerned, we are testing your telepathy and teaching you to fly. Nothing else. Understood, Kepler?" Walker's gaze was steel.

"So," I said, "you want me to lie to Whitewash."

"I want you to be conservative in what you disclose."

Saini had woken me before anyone else for this secretive mission, so cagey that Walker had recruited Ethan out of confinement. Hiding things from the MTA made sense, but Whitewash was meant to work on the same side.

"Why are we here?" I said.

Walker plucked at his mustache a long moment, carefully regarding me. "It's possible we won't succeed against Chron. In that case, this lab is the logical next step." He lowered his arm. "Cassidy wants a protean army. That'll never happen. We can't expect their allegiance, and we don't know what they're capable of. So I'm going to make sure Cassidy never finds the name of any protean. If Andrews is storing the data here, I'll destroy it."

"Destroy it? What if we need another protean to help free the Tacemus?"

"Then you can ask me where I've hidden the backup file."

Clandestine or not, it sat easier in my gut knowing that Walker's motivations seemed decent. Cassidy acted boldly enough to investigate the lab behind Walker's back; she'd have no qualms unearthing protean intel the first chance she got. None of us knew what the proteans could do. Chang's telekinetic control over people promised enough danger. How could we safely convince an unknown number of potentially powerful proteans to fight on our side and not the MTA's?

"So then," I said, "are you a protean?"

His eyes rolled. "No, Kepler. I am not."

Sure, Walker could've been lying, but somehow that didn't fit.

I nodded. I understood, more than Walker thought, that some intel was better left undisclosed. "Okay. We were never here."

"To the cockpit, then."

I hesitated, eyeing Ethan, but Walker was impatient.

A distressing amount of screens and joysticks consumed nearly every inch of the narrow cockpit, but Walker told me I only needed to memorize the controls for take-off and hover; everything else operated on autopilot.

"Provided Chron believes you're Helix, I have a plan for rescuing Andrews," he said. "You'll need to man the aircraft."

Walker stayed put on the other side of the center console. Our squishy chairs sat low to the ground; my knees threatened to bump the dashboard. I would've rather joined Ethan, but Walker wanted me to grow comfortable in the cockpit. The same didn't apply to him, yet he lingered. I wondered if he wanted to avoid Ethan.

Did you tell him you were the one who stole him? I said, not nearly surprised by my question as I was by Walker's decision *not* to immediately hurl me overboard.

He let a severe ten seconds pass. Walker's face kept getting tighter, like it could scrunch into nothingness. He darkened the dashboard with his frown before sending out his low answer. "That's between Sheedy and myself." Walker tipped back and grunted. "But I can tell you this, Kepler. I regret many things I've done, for both the MTA and Whitewash. I don't like lying or manipulating."

"But it's effective."

"Doesn't matter if it's effective if it's wrong."

I skimmed past him, finding the clouds an easier source of contemplation than his words.

"While we are on the topic of effective but wrong...." A sticky noise, the sound of a jaw rotation, preceded Walker's next words. "The choice for the role was between me and Agent Rand. I volunteered. Hope you never meet Rand. Nasty fellow."

Out of context, his words meant nothing. Neither of us had mentioned my parents, but they were always there in my heart, whether or not I acknowledged them. And so, though Walker's speech would've made little sense to anyone else, it meant everything to me.

I shook my head, but his attempt at an apology stuck, finding its home easily in my heart. Without realizing it, I'd craved this moment. One had already apologized on his behalf, but now Walker finally owned it. He'd impersonated Dad, following Andrews' sick plan to discourage me from trusting my parents. And he'd done it to spare me from dealing with someone far worse.

"Then... thanks, I guess," I mumbled. It seemed, having embraced the empathy that allowed my telepathy to operate, I'd become someone quick to forgive—because I was much quicker to understand.

He turned his head, dubiety apparent in the tilt of his brows. Then our eyes met. Emotion jerked his expression, setting wrinkles along his face. Walker curtly nodded before resuming an unnecessary observation of the sky.

CHAPTER FIFTEEN

WE REACHED MONTVALE CLOSE to 0800. Once we flew above a promising stretch of land, Walker sent a drone below to scan the scenery. When the drone's camera faced a dirt road marked by "No Trespassing" signs, I nodded. I recognized that line of trees.

My stomach began to twist and not from hunger. I imagined rows of containment tanks, with hundreds of lifeless Tacemus preserved in goo. How could the MTA do it—create and enslave a group of people?

Walker rallied Ethan, then returned to oversee our landing. We would avoid the landing pad atop the building, in case that triggered an alarm. He had to guide the plane to the private road leading up to the lab.

I ducked out of the cockpit, since Walker didn't need me for this. Ethan stood near the exit hatch, adjusting bracers over his wrists. I'd seen this Ethan so many times: the serious cadet prepping for his newest mission. Less frequently, I'd seen him smile.

"Hey," I said. "You okay?"

He shifted a bag over his shoulder, seemingly preoccupied with mission prep and nothing else. He checked his bracers again, tested the stability of the mic clipped to his jacket lapel. His fidgeting stopped; and, freed from distraction, his eyes lifted to mine as he finally said, "You knew about this at SPO-10?"

"Some of it. I told you what I knew, and then... One wiped your mind. That's why you don't remember my telepathy. I only found out the stuff about cadets and their parents when I went off with Andrews the day Griffin died."

Griffin's death had triggered everything that followed. I'd admitted to lying about what Lydia saw between Helix and me at the clubhouse; I'd decided to stay with the MTA and put home on hold; and, perhaps less important but still momentous, Ethan and I had finally voiced our feelings for each other. He'd agreed to wait on the academy roof until I returned from my meeting with Andrews. That return came far later than anticipated.

"I'm sorry I didn't come back," I said softly. "I hope you didn't wait long."

Ethan braced his knuckles against the wall. "I waited eight months." His head dropped, and he sighed. "I regret ever defending the man who did this to you. I'm so sorry, Ella. I understand now, and...." Unfamiliar emotion darkened his gaze. "Leader will know the consequences."

Walker emerged from the cockpit then. Before turning, my eyes lingered on the four indents in the wall where Ethan's knuckles had rested. That answered my question.

No, Ethan was not okay.

Walker tossed me a small zipper bag and told me to wear the mic and earpiece, tuning me in to their communication. He reminded me to practice my telepathy, then popped his elbow against the button along the wall. The exit hatch fell into a ramp, scuffing asphalt. Sunshine and a clean breeze, thinner than the beachy air at base, brushed my cheeks.

"Shouldn't take longer than an hour." Walker summoned his duffel bag, grabbed hold by the strap, and stepped down.

Ethan followed onto the ramp. "See you soon."

I nodded and opened my mouth, but a cheery farewell came too slowly. Within seconds, he and Walker were two figures stomping through the grass.

I plopped onto a window bench and leaned back. Anger toward Andrews grew like a stain. Something about this place, where he had kept me in a stasis chamber for months, and potential Tacemus floated like specimens....

My leg ached; I'd pinched my thigh too hard. *Focus*, I thought, breathing out. It did no good to stew.

To ensure my telepathy was working, I'd need someone to tell me. I doubted my ability to *read* long-distance; although, I'd done so with Ethan. Could I with Kara?

I mentally reached, imagining her on the seat over. *Kara?*

At first, a barricade of silence answered. I eased back on the straining. Her voice came as a sputter.

Ella... somewhere... can you hear me?

"No way!" I said aloud. My elation evaporated when I realized this ability could've prevented her time of imprisonment. If only I'd known.

Yes, I said, treating that realization like an intrusive guest. *Apparently I can read you long-distance, too.* After saying it, I understood the implication. *Sorry. I know it's invasive. Agent Walker* – wait, did Kara know who that was? —*uh, the guy in charge wants me to practice my long-range telepathy. I want to try communicating to everyone in the building, but I won't know if it worked unless someone tells me.*

They tell me… and I tell you?

Yeah.

Okay. How do I… I'll ask Jimmy.

Is he with you? I asked.

Yes… with me….

Cool. I'll try him first.

I figured it'd be good to start off simpler and work my way up. Funny—a few days ago, I never would've said that correspondence with Banks would come easily. I rested my chin on my palms and brought to mind Banks, his fear that he was Andrews' son, and the tiny buds of friendship we'd finally watered.

Testing one… Testing two… Testing thr –

Tell her I heard the first time.

I blinked. *Banks? I can hear you.*

What? No… get out of my head.

I withdrew the connection, bewildered. Reading Kara had an explanation, considering the length of our friendship, but *Banks?* In proximity, I'd ducked into his thoughts once or twice. Perhaps I could read everyone long-distance. That seemed unlikely.

I moved to the cadets next. Bridget, my former roommate, had the closest connection with me. If I *could* read anyone's thoughts from this distance, hers would be first. However, I got nothing, and I had to return to Kara to see whether Bridget had heard me. That took another couple minutes, as Banks had to find Bridget for the answer. In the process, he dragged all the members of Whitewash into the clinic.

They're all here, Kara said. *You can start.*

In this fashion, I traveled without budging a step. I worked first through the cadets, finding conversation easiest with James and toughest with McFarland. She heard nothing of my voice for five minutes.

After cycling through nearly everyone present and reading no one else, I considered the conclusion that, for whatever reason, Banks had made it onto my tiny list of long-range transmitters. While the others had eventually heard my voice, none of their thoughts had unveiled.

Finally, I sought One. *Testing one… testing two –*

I hear her.

One? Are you communicating to me?

No. I am thinking.

I prodded my temples. Unexpected, but reading One made sense. Even though I couldn't remember his presence during my childhood, that link evidently remained. It could've been a telepath thing, too.

Okay, I said. *Moving on.*

Has Banks told you yet? One thought.

Told me what?

I see. He will not tell you. He is embarrassed. You must read me.

Well, this had taken a strange turn. *What's this about, One?* I asked.

You have seen his worst. But you have also seen his best. That is worth remembering. For his sake, if not yours.

No doubt One was referring to something in the endless list of events he'd stolen from me. The reminder of my missing memories didn't unnerve me; I was more concerned about what they had to do with Banks.

Are you still here? One wondered.

Had Saini not replaced my tooth so recently, I would've clenched harder. I pinched my forehead. *Where do I look?*

CHAPTER SIXTEEN

SHE WAS A BALL, as tightly wound as she could be without disappearing, though she wanted to. Maybe if she squeezed harder, she'd squeeze herself into the past, before noon, before cars were invented.

"How long are you going to stay here?"

Ella turned her head at the voice. From her curled position inside the tunnel on the playground, the boy seemed crooked in his crouch, though he'd tilted his head at the same angle as hers. Though he was a stranger, he was staring as if he not only knew her, but knew exactly why she was hiding inside the tunnel on a Saturday evening.

"What?" Ella said. Her voice echoed.

"You've been here for fifty-eight minutes."

"You've been watching me? That's weird. Leave me alone." And she turned her head again to face the slanted blue plastic that enclosed her. She wasn't normally rude to complete strangers, but today, Ella felt like a different sort of person altogether. The sort who froze and didn't do the right thing at the right time.

"I know why you're here," the boy said.

"No, you don't."

"Yes I do. There was a vehicle accident. A woman died."

Ella tugged on the thighs of her jeans, tugging his words away from her. She gave the boy a second glance. He had wavy hair like dirt, with eyes a mix of his hair color and her own green eyes. The boy looked a few years older than her, maybe twelve.

"How'd you know that?" Ella whispered.

"I heard about it. Your parents are looking for you. You shouldn't be out here alone. Civilians can be dangerous."

As if she didn't know *exactly* how dangerous people were, and how delicate, alive one moment, and the next bleeding blood that didn't stop.

Ella wanted to throw up.

"Are you going to talk about it?" the boy asked.

Ella shook her head, finally wondering the questions she should've wondered when he plopped beside her hiding spot: Who was this oddly formal boy? Why had he been counting minutes? Was he dangerous? All at once, she felt uncomfortable.

"I should go," she said. Her legs stayed crossed.

"You don't have to be afraid of me," the boy said. After that, he gripped the tunnel and maneuvered himself inside, until he was curled beside Ella. With legs longer than hers, he looked completely uncomfortable attempting to make himself smaller.

Despite everything, Ella wanted to laugh at how silly he looked. And despite his unexpected appearance, she decided she trusted him. There was just something about him.

"What's your name?" she asked.

"Banks."

"Banks?"

"It's my surname."

"Sir name?" Ella repeated, wondering if Banks were wealthy.

"Correct," he answered and offered no further explanation.

"I'm Ella Kepler," she said, "but you can just call me Ella."

And they sat in the tunnel until the sun had taken its light, and the moon had replaced it with shadows. They didn't speak, but to Ella, it felt natural. For the first time since 12:13, Ella was calm.

"I really should go now," she said finally, shocked by how the tunnel made her voice boom.

"All right," Banks said. He scooted toward the exit.

Ella began to follow. She'd managed to dull most of her pain and fear—that is, until she saw it. A tiny spider, hardly threatening, crawled the curl of the tunnel. Ella had never feared spiders, but at the sight of it, an unexpected clamminess overtook her. She couldn't move. Instead, she watched it in numb horror. Its pointy legs, bristling body, eyes that magnified the harder she stared.

Outside, Banks had noticed her frozenness. He reached a finger inside, let the spider take hold—Ella shivered at that—and lowered it to safety on the dirt.

Ella could breathe again. She brought a shaking hand to her forehead and felt cold sweat.

"Are you ill?" Banks asked.

"I—I...."

"It's all right," he said when she continued her muteness. "You can be afraid of spiders if you need to be." He stuck a hand in the tunnel, outstretched for her to take it. So she did. Hers was damp and trembling, but his felt dry and firm. He helped her out of the tunnel and into the vastness of the night, where he steadied her, hand in hers, until the cramped feeling left her legs.

Suddenly, Ella was crying, the first tear she'd shed that day. "I was supposed to call an ambulance," she whispered, "but I fainted, and then she... she—"

"It isn't your fault," Banks said. She caught a hint of impatience in his pointed lips. "Sometimes, situations are outside your control." He spoke a bit like a robot, forced and technical. "It's not your fault."

Ella wiped her eyes on her wrist. She didn't really believe him, but he was trying to be nice. "Thanks," she said.

He nodded. "I'll walk you home. You shouldn't—you shouldn't have to be alone." He stepped into pace beside her, letting her lead. Ella and Banks walked the half mile back to Blossom Lane, and Ella didn't feel alone anymore. Not at all.

SHE SQUEEZED HER THIGHS together so they would stop bumping his. The two of them were getting too big to both fit on the metal slide, but a hot, cramped seat was better than the splintery mulch that decorated the ground. Plus, the slide offered privacy, and Ella knew Banks would only talk to her if they were alone.

"I should get back to Kara. It's been a year since the accident, and...." Ella swallowed, looking at that blonde head hardly visible over the bushes that separated the picnic bench from the abandoned playground at her elementary school. Kara needed Ella, who had made a promise to always take care of her. "Wanna come with?"

"No."

"You're so weird." She poked his arm. She'd learned that he could block these sorts of attacks—but she'd also learned that he allowed her to bug him.

"*Weird*," he said, crinkling his nose. "That word is stupid."

"No it's not. Why won't you meet Kara? She thinks I'm making you up."

"Because I'm not here to make friends."

"Why do you say stuff like that? Do you mean... *I'm* your friend, right?" She peeked at him, nervous to see his reaction. They sat so close that she could see brown and green swirls in his eyes.

His forehead grew wrinkled. Without much emotion, he said, "Yes. You're my friend."

Quickly, Ella looked down to hide her watering eyes. He had maintained his odd comings and goings for a year, but Ella knew, in a tiny corner of her heart, that he did it out of some sense of duty. She'd never understood *what* duty, but clearly he felt obligated to visit her. Maybe he thought he had to be nice because of the car crash.

"I'm gonna go." She stood, her thighs sticking to the slide in the heat. "See you later, I guess." He'd notice her crying if she lingered, so Ella hurried over the mulch.

"Ella."

She stopped. He rarely called her that. After wiping the tears away, she turned.

Banks held an arm up. He nudged his watch, exposing his wrist. A peep of red showed. Ella's heart pattered as the yarn bracelet came fully into view. "We're friends," he said.

Twisting her own red bracelet, she bounded closer to him, tears long forgotten. "You kept it!"

"It's against dress code, so I have to hide it."

"So it's a *secret* bracelet," she said solemnly.

He nodded, smiling. "Yes."

"That's so cool. Wow. Maybe Kara and me will hide ours, too."

"If you want." Banks stretched his arm and let it hover above her head. Ella waited, squinting upward and feeling as if she shouldn't move just yet. He rewarded her patience with an awkward ruffle of her hair, a gesture neither of them knew how to respond to.

She giggled. "Why'd you just pet me?"

"I wasn't *petting* you." He scowled and crossed his arms. "You're so immature."

"Ooooh, 'cause you're *so* old."

He rolled his eyes.

"Oh," she said. "I forgot. I figured out your first name."

"What is it?"

"Charlie. Charlie Banks."

He shook his head. "I don't have a first name. I don't have a last name, either."

"How can you not have a name? Everyone has a name."

"Not me. All the students at my school have files with their full names and birth records, except me. I don't exist."

Her heart felt small. He'd just said what she'd already suspected: Banks lived in an orphanage. He must have been left on the doorstep, like in a movie she'd seen. His parents might have even been dead.

"I'm sorry," she whispered.

"It isn't your fault."

"I know. Well, I mean...." She felt flustered, too uncomfortable at the serious topic to think of anything smart to say. Then she brightened, struck with an idea. "You don't need records to have a name. Here, I'll give you one so you don't have to worry about it."

He stepped closer, obviously curious. "All right," he said.

"Um." She concentrated on the names that she knew, suddenly worried that he might not like what she came up with. "Not Charlie, I guess. How about... Steve? Jake? No, James. It's my grandpa's name. It's a good name. James Banks. James... James Daniel Banks, 'cause you have to have a middle name. Does that... " she wrung her hands, feeling shy, "does that work, James?"

"Almost," he said. His face was unguarded, and emotion swirled like the colors in his eyes, giving him the look of a young boy instead of a reserved teen. "Forget Banks. It's not my name. I'll be James Daniels."

"Okay," she said, smiling. "James Daniels it is. See you around, James." She waved again and skipped off to Kara, hoping she'd cheered him up like he always cheered her.

THE BOOTH TABLE VIBRATED as Kara's phone buzzed. Ella didn't bother checking the time; she knew that alarm meant eight-thirty.

"Okay," Kara said, scooping up her pencils and calculator. "You understand it now, right?"

"Uh-huh," Ella said. "And, if not, we all know Jimmy loves helping me with math. Right?"

The two girls peered at their friend. Seated on the opposite booth, he showed the same glassy stare, vacantly trained on his portable screen, which he'd continued the whole two hours at Kevin's Koffee.

"Your eyeballs are going to dry up and fall out," Ella called.

He ignored her.

Kara squeezed Ella's arm, which meant *Leave him alone.* Ella sighed and helped Kara pack up. When they finished, Kara scooted off the seat and lingered by the edge, waiting for the routine that followed every eight-thirty exit. But Jimmy didn't notice.

Sneakily, so Kara wouldn't realize, Ella prodded Jimmy's foot until his head snapped up.

"What?" he said.

"Do you *want* Kara to get mugged in the parking lot?"

His gaze flicked Kara's way, then focused. Abruptly, he snatched his screen up and slid out of the booth. After easing—*more like* yanking, Ella thought— Kara's backpack off her shoulders, Jimmy sped toward the exit, leaving Kara behind.

"He's so—"

"Be nice," Kara said, and Ella swallowed her complaint. "Pick me up at four-thirty?" Kara added.

"Mmm. Let's make it nine-thirty."

"AM? Perfect." Kara grinned. "You're not getting out of this, El, even if I have to drag you."

"Yes, yes, we can't miss the most important event of the year. What would Whale's do if we didn't show?"

"Exactly. See you tomorrow." Kara bent down for a hug, then skipped off after Jimmy.

He returned to the booth after a few minutes, and though he immediately hid himself behind the electronic screen he carried non-stop, Ella could tell something bothered him.

"Did she say no?" she asked.

"To what?"

"Your marriage proposal."

Jimmy kicked her foot, a lot harder than she'd bumped his. "Don't be annoying."

"Why am I the only honest person in this trio?"

"Honest? Or meddlesome?"

"I'm sorry, I'd rather not watch you guys pine over each other until we all die."

"Kara's better off with someone else."

"Yes. So I've heard. A million times. You're so dramatic." Ella spun her protractor in circles. Considering how long it had taken Jimmy to meet Kara, it was dumb that he was taking even longer to admit his feelings. "If it were me, I'd want a guy who just says what he's feeling without being all weirdly secretive."

"Like Bradley?"

"I hate you." She stretched across the booth and yanked at Jimmy's screen. Though he quickly jerked it out of her sight, she'd caught a glimpse of a familiar headshot image. "Are you stalking Sheedy *again*?"

He ignored her, so she threw her pencil at him, which of course he caught without looking.

Jimmy had complained about the infamous Sheedy the past couple years, though lately his irritation with his goody two-shoes co-worker had filled Jimmy with the obsessive need to learn everything about him. He was always reading the guy's file.

After a sigh, Ella plopped her chin on the middle of her textbook. Why her high school insisted upon summer math projects, she would never understand.

"Why are you so grumpy?" she asked. "Is it work stuff?"

"Yes."

"Want to talk about it?"

"No. Stop fidgeting. It's distracting."

Ella stilled. Jimmy had acknowledged her maybe five times during the last two hours. "You know what?" she said, slamming her textbooks into her backpack and gathering her pencil bag. "You're obviously in a bad mood, and I don't feel like dealing with it. Hope you have a nice time stalking Sheedy, or whatever it is you're doing." She grabbed her phone and edged out of the booth, waiting to see if Jimmy would notice she was leaving. He said nothing, eyes glued to the screen. Huffing in disgust, she stalked out of the coffee shop and headed for her car.

She didn't know why Jimmy had been so impatient lately. Not that he'd ever been patient, but at least he hadn't taken every little thing out on her. Why did she even put up with Jimmy's antics? His mysterious appearances and disappearances, the obvious lies. She knew so little about him, other than the fact that he'd grown up in an orphanage where kids beat each other up on a daily basis, and now he worked in some police station in a different city.

If she peeked past her frustration, though, she knew why she put up with him. She'd known him since she was nine, had shared hundreds of memories with him, and she cared about him. She owed her friendship with Kara entirely to him, since he'd prodded Ella into going to Mrs. Watson's funeral. Kara constantly reminded her that Jimmy needed help, and Ella wanted to offer that help. Only, how could she help someone who didn't want it?

She threw her backpack onto the passenger seat and slammed the door. Jimmy was standing a foot away. She didn't even flinch. "You're doing the thing again. You said you'd stop."

"I know." He focused on a spot below her eye.

Ella scrutinized his somber expression, and some of her frustration melted. "What's going on with you?" she asked, leaning against her car.

"Work."

"You're lying." Then she rolled her eyes, annoyed all over again that he refused to tell the truth just once. "I'm going home," she said, walking around to the driver's side. "Next time you want to pop up, try being honest." She shoved the key into her car door, but Jimmy's hand was suddenly on hers. He spun her around, then quickly stepped back.

"I'm not going to 'pop up' anymore," he said. "This is the last time we're going to see each other. At least, like this."

"What does that mean?"

"It doesn't matter."

"Jimmy, you're—"

"Listen to me, Ella." He put his hands on her shoulders and stared into her eyes, so intensely that Ella's heart stammered with panic. "You have to do it right. If you can't help them, no one can."

Ella gaped at him, wondering how in the world their conversation had turned into yet another cryptic Jimmy moment. "You're freaking me out," she whispered.

"You have to be selfless. You have to trust me, even if it seems illogical. I know telling you this is pointless—you'll forget everything." He hung his head, still clutching her shoulders. Then, something gave him renewed strength. Jimmy straightened and peered down at Ella. "I know you didn't ask to be born with this ability, and that you'll despise me, one day, when you understand that I knew the whole time. But you *have* to get over that, El. This isn't about you or me. We fight for those who can't fight for themselves."

None of the responses bouncing in her mind came close to expressing her confusion. And, if she was honest, her trepidation. She hated when Jimmy said things like this. They reminded her how little she knew of him and made her feel like a mouse who'd befriended a giant.

After watching her inaudible panic a moment longer, Jimmy stepped away with a disappointed air that made her shrink further. "This was stupid," he said. "You have no idea what I'm saying." A car whooshed past, headlights illuminating the impatience in his eyes. Then he sighed. "Goodbye, El. I'll see you tomorrow. Try to hate Sheedy as much as I do. And don't let him influence you. I won't be able to stand you if you're anything like him." He shook his head and muttered, "It should've been me instead."

"What—"

Jimmy stepped aside, revealing a tiny man who stood behind him. Ella jumped back, banging her elbows against her car.

The man stood much shorter than her and had no hair. His features conveyed nothing particularly menacing, but Ella felt scared of him.

"Do you know him?" she asked.

"I've said goodbye," Jimmy said to the short man. "Yes," he added, and then, "No... *No,* I'm not going to... Because she's not a child, One."

Watching Jimmy talk to himself, Ella couldn't decide whether to laugh or run.

"Fine," Jimmy said, sighing again. He eyed Ella warily, as if she'd puked down her shirt or something.

She clenched her fists when he closed the gap between them. When he continued closer yet, near enough to touch, Ella was certain something horrible would happen. It took a moment to register the meaning when his arms snagged around her. Was he about to toss her over his shoulder? No, Jimmy stood still. *Hugging* her, for the first time in seven years.

"Don't be scared," he said somewhere above her head. He smelled like detergent and leather. Her heart swelled at the familiar scent.

Ella closed her eyes and squeezed him back, forgetting about the strange bald man. Cryptic Jimmy wasn't so bothersome, after all. She would've endured his pokes and prods forever if, at the end of the day, they parted with a hug.

"This is weird," she said.

"I know."

"And uncomfortable. Your jacket zipper is scratchy."

"Don't press your face against it, then."

"Fine," she said. But she didn't move.

He did, shifting his balance without letting go. "And you're one-hundred percent certain a wipe this big won't hurt her?" he said. Before Ella could ask what that meant, Jimmy added, "All right. Do it."

"Do what?" she said.

"Be quiet for a second, El."

"Okay."

The next voice didn't belong to him. When Ella heard it, her keys plummeted to the asphalt and lay forgotten. She absorbed Jimmy's warmth around her until nothing mattered but that voice.

"You do not remember 'Jimmy Daniels.' You do not remember this conversation. You do not remember me."

ELLA BLINKED REPEATEDLY, TRYING to clear the haze away. One moment she'd been walking to her car, and the next she felt like she'd rammed into a tree.

"You dropped your keys," she heard.

She shook her head and turned around. In the empty parking space beside her car stood a guy a few years older than her, her keys dangling from his fingers. He stood directly in the shadow of the lamppost, so she could barely make out his features. Ella was so disoriented that she found herself staring way too long, when she should have simply taken her keys.

"Oh, thanks. I must have dropped them. Obviously." She flushed and reached for the guy's offering.

"I'll see you around," he said.

"Yeah, have a nice night," she called. He was already halfway across the parking lot. A moment later, he vanished around the corner.

Ella groaned and unlocked her car. She climbed inside and buckled herself in. Then she hurried home. She had a lot of math to finish, and no one to help her with it.

CHAPTER SEVENTEEN

LIKE A SPLINTERING DAM, memories bled. They stacked one after the other in a consecutive stream, revealing the passage of time in faces. Mine, as I brushed my teeth before the mirror and thought of him. Kara's, as she protested her feelings from middle school through tenth grade. And his: first the round face of a child, then thinning, lengthening, as the years turned Jimmy into an adult. The memories did not return like a story told; they brought every ounce of feeling along. By the time the clips reached their conclusion, I'd regained the totality of my experience as Jimmy's friend. His existence breathed vibrantly, so real that the force of seven condensed years imploded in the single second of time.

I gasped. When my vision blurred and thunder beat my eardrums, I realized I was crying. Not at the loss, but the sudden gain—the influx of emotion motivated by every Jimmy-induced tear I'd ever cried. They burst like a flash, until a few more seconds passed, and the memories of Jimmy Daniels drifted to the spots they should've occupied. The turmoil stilled. My heart slowed.

He was not Banks. Not anymore. He was my best friend in disguise. He'd been my Jimmy, mine and Kara's. And, since the forgotten memories had settled in as if they'd never left, he still was.

One – I started.

"Kepler, open the ramp!"

I shot up, fingering my earpiece.

"Now!" Walker yelled.

Right. Plane, mission, ramp.

"On it!" I hopped over the table, brushing ideas of Jimmy away. The hatch button glowed red when I smacked it. Hissing, the ramp fell forward. Walker and Ethan charged onboard, Ethan swiveling to jab the button; I moved my hand in time to avoid a brutal smashing. The ramp ascended, and Walker darted toward the cockpit, calling, "Get the —"

Something silver zoomed through the narrow opening. Ethan shoved me behind him and shouted Walker's name. I regained my footing, peering around Ethan, right as the ramp finished sealing us inside with a hovering, metal sphere. It whirred, rotating in place, its shell fractured with dozens of blinking lights.

"Clearance identification, please." The request issued from the machine in a male, British accent.

"No one move," Walker murmured. He slowly reached for a strap around his throat, tight against his Adam's apple.

Ethan solidified; a bulldozer couldn't have knocked him from my path.

"Clearance identification, please," the sphere repeated.

I clutched the back of Ethan's jacket, not inclined to move either, because I saw that the machine could do more than speak. It had a gun barrel built into its casing.

"It's Eugene," came a voice from Walker's direction, though it sounded like Andrews. The strap over Walker's throat flashed.

"Eugene?" the machine said.

"Yes. Eugene. Disengage."

The machine floated closer to Walker, who kept a steady gaze, even as the barrel rotated in his direction.

"*Disengage*," Walker said.

The sphere hummed.

My tongue stuck to my teeth. *Ethan*, I said.

Take cov —

Gunfire unloaded.

Ruckus blared; bullets dinged metal. Ethan forwent his orders and charged, swinging his duffel bag like a bat. Walker collapsed, eliminating the possibility of losing his head to Ethan's strike. Ducking low, I shielded my head and hurried to Walker. The sphere circled madly, avoiding a direct blow, but Ethan kept swinging. When he finally hit home, the sphere rammed into the opposite wall. It thudded violently, then dropped to the floor in a heap of pieces, spitting wires, flashes, and a warbled, British voice.

"Hello... hello... hello... Eu—Eu—Eugene...." The pieces rolled, and an electric whirring petered out.

Ethan set right to smashing his heel into every silver chunk. Walker stirred; he appeared conscious, albeit drenched in blood. I grabbed him beneath the armpits and made to drag him to the clinic, but he shook his head.

"Cockpit," he said.

"Walker — "

"Takeoff first."

Using me as support, Walker flipped the appropriate switches, engaged the thrust, and set the jet on autopilot. Dribbles of blood left a trail on the console. With a grunt, he clutched my shoulder and muttered, "Clinic."

Ethan was still obliterating the robot, which resembled a heap of metal slivers. Probably overkill, but I left him to it and guided Walker down the hall. We stumbled into the clinic, and I set him onto a cot. He lay back, panting, and I got my first good look at him. Blood wetted his shirt and pants in multiple spots, way too much liquid for a mere surface wound.

Ethan had been in the line of fire, too. Did he look like this?

"Phone," Walker said. "Left pocket. Call Saini."

I felt along his cargo pockets. Keys, knife, screwdriver. Phone. "Asha Saini" showed as the last caller.

"Did he have it?" she answered.

"I'm in need of your medical expertise," he said.

"Allen. You should've brought more backup."

Walker waved me out. I shut the door, stepping aside as Ethan nearly bumped me.

"Does he — "

"Are you okay?" I guided him beneath a light and made a frantic search of his clothes, hunting for red splotches. After I angled his arms in countless directions, he nudged my hands away.

"It didn't hit me," he said. "I *am* smart enough to recognize that I should eliminate a machine's weapon before I attack it." He allowed a mouth twitch.

That almost-grin made my stomach dance. Before another interruption divided us, I stepped against him, hugging him by the neck. *I missed you so much, Ethan.*

His musings, preoccupied with the robot, took a halt. He held me just tight enough that I'd have to wiggle if I wanted to escape. We fit so comfortably together, his shoulder the perfect ledge for my cheek. Ethan's arms had settled, but his mind was another matter. Remorse, frustration, and uncertainty clogged every corner. He recognized that he'd made a massive miscalculation, and he figured his flaws had overwritten my impression of him. Ethan believed I considered him weak.

I shifted, keeping my wrists hooked around him and my head close so I could level his gaze. "Stop it. I will *never* think that."

"I don't deserve—"

"Well, you're going to have to accept it, because I'm not changing my mind."

A rebuttal opened his lips.

"No," I said, "I'm not just being nice. And yes, I'm sure."

He nearly protested again, but something in my expression must've kicked it to the curb. "It's hardly a fair argument if you read *and* interrupt my responses," he said, though his tone sounded far from annoyed.

"You don't get to argue on this. You're wrong, and that's that."

At last, his full grin emerged. "You're very stubborn, Kepler."

"Have you met yourself?"

"No, that's not possible."

I tilted my head and sighed.

Ethan touched the corner of my eye. "I don't know why, but I like watching you roll your eyes."

"Well, I like your smile."

"It's yours more than mine. You're the only one who makes me laugh."

"Good," I said, then recognized the overly triumphant glint and amended with, "Actually, no, you should laugh more. I'm not the only funny person."

"I never said I laugh because you're funny."

"You are so annoying."

"Only because—"

"I'd like to walk down the hall."

I withdrew my arms from Ethan and flattened myself against the wall behind me. Standing outside the clinic, Agent Walker looked as if he wouldn't have the patience for an old woman crossing the street. Sure I turned redder than Kara had ever been, I mumbled an apology and continued into the cabin.

You're supposed to be observant, I told Ethan.

So are you, he thought.

Ethan tried assisting Walker, but Walker shooed him back. He'd ripped a hospital gown horizontally in half, donning it like a shirt that revealed strips of gauze across his stomach.

"So," I said, determined to pretend away the past thirty seconds, "did you guys see anything to explain why Andrews was working with Chron?"

Midway toward sitting, Ethan stiffened. "He was working with Chron?"

"Yeah. Andrews knew where Chron lived and kept it from the MTA. I think that's why Chron has MTA weapons—he got them from Andrews."

White-lipped and tense, Ethan let out a sigh as he sat. "No. We didn't have time to search for anything other than the protean file. Did you eject the flash drive?" he asked Walker.

"Yes, it's...." Walker, patting his pant pocket, froze. He felt another, wincing in his search, and came up empty handed. He closed his eyes. "Must've dropped it." After breathing through a moment of frustration, he shrugged. "Well, Cassidy will have a hard time either way. Those robots don't fight like Grifters." He limped toward a seat. "Any progress with your telepathy?"

My automatic nod jerked to a halt. *Jimmy.* What could I say to him when we returned? He'd been content with pretending away the past, but I couldn't do that. At some point, I'd have to explain to Ethan that his frustrating ex-partner was my frustrating ex-best friend.

"Yes," I said.

"Good. Get back to your practice. When we arrive, you're talking to Chron." Walker leaned his head back and seemed ready for a nap.

"Who is Margaret Perry?"

The question arose from Ethan and had an immediate effect. Not overt, because Walker's stiffening was controlled, but it began the moment Margaret's name entered the air. A passerby would've pegged Walker for asleep, but anyone observant could see that his nerves were anything but immobile.

Slowly, his head moved. He looked Ethan dead-on and said, "A protean who deserves privacy."

Ethan returned the gaze calmly. I wondered whose stubbornness would win. "Yes, sir," he finally said.

That failed to satisfy Walker right away. His glare continued, but Ethan never batted an eye. Had Ethan been anyone else, Walker might've pushed the issue further; but, regardless of Ethan's original opposition to Whitewash—or perhaps because of it—Walker surely understood that Ethan kept to his word.

Not without unease, Walker leaned against the wall once more, though I was certain sleep was now about as far from his thoughts as Tennessee from Virginia.

ONLY ETHAN HAD THE chance to relax on the flight back; but, since Ethan was immune to relaxation, he spent the journey picking at robot pieces while I practiced telepathy and Walker pretended to sleep. Once I'd successfully communicated to everyone—avoiding Jimmy and One— the next step was faking Helix's voice. By the time we reached half an hour out, I'd refined my technique from "deplorable" to "laudable," according to Dom.

I made a show of waking Walker. "I think I'm ready," I told him.

"Let's hear it."

Chron, this is Helix, your sister.

His brows went skyward. "You're doing that by memory?"

"Yeah."

"Test it on me." Ethan tossed aside what looked like the viewing lens of the robot and stood.

Hi. I'm a Grifter. You've been messing with that thing nonstop. I don't think it's going to come to life again.

"Pretty convincing, Kepler." He scooped up the lens and started fidgeting with it once more.

"All right." Walker leaned forward, grimaced, then settled back against his seat. "After speaking with Durgan, I'm convinced we need to set this plan in motion immediately. It puts the pressure on Chron, and also distracts him from reading Andrews. You'll tell Chron to meet you at the *äng* tomorrow, oh-five-hundred."

"That gives us less than twenty-four hours," Ethan said.

"Our job is straightforward enough. I want Chron uncomfortable with this timeline. We force him to leave his territory in a rush." Walker eyed me. "Do it, Kepler. Then, I'll call the team and relay the plan. Don't like repeating myself."

After running through my script until I had it memorized, I closed my eyes. Ethan and Walker were probably staring at me; the idea set my jaw. The success of Plan A depended on this moment. If this failed, we'd have to return to Andrews' lab of British, lethal security drones. Worse, I had no way of knowing whether this had worked. Chron didn't have a Kara I could communicate with for verification.

Clutching the feel of connection Chron and I had shared before, I imagined his face and thought of Helix. *It is time, brother. If you wish to see me again, meet me at the äng tomorrow, in the fifth hour.*

Talking to Chron felt something like blindly pouring water and hoping it went straight into a cup.

Durgan had said not to worry about Chron responding back to Helix. She'd told Durgan about her efforts to keep Chron out of her head. Even if Chron wanted to reply, he'd likely never reach his mark.

"Okay," I said. "Done."

Walker tossed his phone onto the table, face-up. On speaker, it rang twice before Cassidy answered. "Get everyone to the table," Walker told her. In another minute, Cassidy declared everyone present. "Procurement," Walker began, "find the cadets tactical gear. At oh-four-hundred tomorrow, Banks and the cadets will depart for Chron's territory. This means you need to run diagnostics and fuel us up before then, Banks. The C-squad, headed by Sheedy, will search for Andrews, using the escape tunnel Kepler mentioned. If—"

"*Sheedy?*" It sounded like Vires.

"Pipe down," Cassidy said. "Continue, Walker," she added, a bit overly polite.

"If Andrews isn't where Kepler's cell was, C-squad will need to bring a conscious Grifter onboard so Kepler can read it for his location. She'll be keeping the aircraft in hover. Avary is co-pilot.

"Meanwhile, the rest of us engage Chron in Farmdale, North Carolina, oh-five-hundred. According to Durgan, Grifters rendezvous there. Kepler's already contacted Chron. He might suspect the ruse and bring backup. I hope so, because that leaves his base exposed. We keep him busy until we hear word that C-squad has Andrews. Questions?"

"Yes," Cassidy said. "Why are you sending a five-man team into Grifter territory?"

"Because five metas make less noise. Kepler and Sheedy escaped before. How many enemies did you encounter?" He looked at Ethan.

"Four," he said.

"It's early morning. Not a lot of Grifters awake, and, hopefully, half the guard gone."

"But," I said, twisting the hem of my shirt, "what if my telepathy didn't work, and Chron is still there?"

"C-squad won't engage until we give the signal. If Chron is a no-show, we'll know it didn't work."

"Let's backtrack to Sheedy as CG," came Agent Keswick's voice. "Last I checked, he was in containment and considered us an organization of traitors."

I checked Ethan's reaction and found it shadowed.

"Sheedy's been vetted," Walker said. "Now, everyone talk to Durgan about the layout. Our ETA is fifteen minutes." He ended the call.

"Why is Avary co-pilot?" I asked.

Walker leaned back in his seat and said, "Because I assigned her co-pilot, Kepler. Stop asking questions."

Ethan and I spent the flight hashing out memories of Chron's territory. Grateful though he was for Walker's faith in him, Ethan had never appeared so unsure—or unsure at all—about his role as commanding general.

Hey, I said, grazing his hand, *don't doubt yourself. You know how to lead.*

Appreciation blended with humor as he thought, *That would've been more convincing if you didn't sound like a Grifter.*

Whoops.

The jet had hardly silenced when the ramp descended. Up marched Dr. Saini, and behind her, lugging bags, Dr. Lee. Saini stood before Walker and coolly skimmed him over.

He lifted his hands. "I followed your instructions."

"Following instruction goes against your moral code, Lee." She swiveled her neck and barked the word out. "Check Ethan. Ella, change clothes first. You're covered in blood." Saini bent over Walker and helped him rise.

I took a pile of clothes from her assistant, whose job must've given him access to our nondisclosed mission. After changing in the captain's cabin, I passed Ethan on the way out. He warily inspected an anxious Lee as the young doctor tested his finger joints. Figuring they'd need privacy, I exited.

Outside the hangar, an afternoon sun hung. I headed across the sand, not at all eager. I could pretend to be casual around Jimmy, but I didn't know how to broach the subject. Did I even want to? If he felt too embarrassed to admit our former friendship, dredging up the topic might push him further away.

I rounded a wall of bramble and plowed right into the object of my thoughts. I stumbled back as if electrocuted.

"Nice skills of observation," he said. He wore his coveralls, which, now, struck me as laughable.

I gaped at him—the familiar eyes, unruly hair, typical expression of annoyance that *wasn't* because he was rude, but because we'd built our friendship on bantering. My heart stretched toward him, and out tumbled, "Were you ever going to tell me?"

"Tell you what?"

"Really. That's how you want to play this?"

Jimmy's confusion, like a sand wall weathered away, crumbled into discomfort. He turned his cheek and glowered into the sunlight.

"I'm going to wait for you to be honest for once," I said.

"I was never dishonest."

"A *police academy?* Come on!"

"What do you expect me to have said—that I work for a nonexistent branch of the government?"

"You could have told me everything and not wiped my memory, and I could've joined the MTA with a friend instead of nobody."

"A Tacemus would've read you," he muttered.

"In case you forgot, I was blocking the Tacemus, because you told me they were evil. So nice try."

He rolled his eyes.

"So everyone in Whitewash knew about this except me?" I said.

"*No,* El, and you better keep your mouth shut. All they know is I visited you a few times with One."

"Cool, so you lied to everyone else, too. That makes me feel better."

Still glaring toward the sea, he asked, "Can you give Kara her memories back?"

"Give them back?"

"Yes. With your telepathy. Why are you so dense?"

I threw up my arms. "I'm not a machine! Are you going to tell her? Never mind, of course you won't." Frustration left me, one giant huff. All this time, Jimmy had been tiptoeing around her, someone who thought he was some random meta she'd known for less than a week. I'd seen how six months of that dance had frustrated Ethan. He'd been bound by rules, but nothing prevented Jimmy from telling Kara the truth—nothing but the same cryptic ways that had always held him back.

"You have to tell her," I said.

He refused to answer, so I edged into his line of sight and waved a hand before his frowning face. When that failed to garner his attention, I touched his arm. "Come on," I murmured. "Talk to me."

He eyed the hand resting on his elbow, but at least he didn't shrug it off. Instead, he plucked my hand free. I expected him to fling it away, but he surprised me again. Jimmy held on. I let a cautious hope grow that maybe, *finally,* Jimmy would realize he could open up.

His attention jerked past me, and he dropped my hand. My ears perked. Footsteps.

"I have to check the aircraft." Jimmy darted past me.

I saw no point in calling after him. He would only ignore me.

Lee and Ethan rounded the corner, Ethan much less gruesome in clean clothes.

"So." I summoned an easygoing air. "No serious injuries?"

"Not with him." Lee jabbed his thumb toward Ethan. "Dr. Saini is still picking shrapnel out of Walker's chest."

"But he'll live?"

"Of course he'll live!" Affronted, Lee trudged ahead.

"Are you all right?" Ethan fell into stride beside me.

"Asks the guy with the injuries."

"You look sad."

I stopped walking, eyes shut.

"Ella?" Ethan's shadow pressed my eyelids.

"Sheedy!"

A shout rang frustratingly near. Footsteps pounded the sand. Seconds later, James skittered around a sand dune, Bridget close on his heels.

"How long have you been here?" James asked. "We had no idea! Why didn't you tell us, Ella?"

McFarland entered the scene next, and a tiny reunion ensued. McFarland and Ethan, two rule-following ferios, had always gotten along, and James was friendly with everyone, but Bridget seemed happiest to see Ethan. He'd been her A-level instructor, patient with her fear of heights and never shaming her for it. Her happiness bubbled over, igniting mine and making it impossible not to grin.

The five of us trekked toward base. Bridget's boisterous mood lingered, and I let it, feeling somewhat like a thief as I stole this happy moment where nothing mattered but renewed friendships. If only Jimmy and I could have reunited so easily.

CHAPTER EIGHTEEN

OH-FOUR-HUNDRED ARRIVED LIKE DUSK on a winter night. Hours seemed to stretch before us; then, they slipped, and morning arrived.

Worry had grown. The idea of facing Andrews had previously discomforted me, but my expectations hadn't traveled that far today. First, the cadets had to make it out of Chron's alive—and, before that, we had to learn whether Chron had heard my message. The rest of Whitewash was already on their way to North Carolina.

Yesterday I'd found Kara on her belly, legs high, elbows propping her upright as she read a book on the bed. Such a normal sight, transposed over an abnormal setting, made me gawk. She'd shifted and noticed me in the doorway.

"Did your telepathy session go well?" she called.

The innocent curiosity undid me. I couldn't call Jimmy a liar and then follow in his footsteps. So I sat beside Kara and tried summing up seven years in five minutes. Her gape froze once I made it clear she suffered from the same memory wipe. I'd lost Jimmy as a friend, but she'd lost him as much more.

Once I finished, she eased the book shut. Nervously, she combed her hair, which made it frizzier. "I thought he was just being nice," she whispered.

I sighed, frustrated—once again—by Jimmy's refusal to own his feelings.

"Is there a way for you to return my memories?" she asked.

"I wish. There are some I'd love to give back to Ethan, and...." An unbidden pain struck, the kind that's fuzzy at the edges, keeping the source at bay. I swallowed.

Kara, ever selfless when it came to prioritizing, found my hand and squeezed. "Jimmy told me about your parents. I'm sorry, El. You can't do anything?"

"My telepathy's not limitless."

"There has to be a way to reverse it, somehow."

I shrugged. A year ago, my every action had been motivated by the quest to restore my parents' memories. Ignoring it now seemed unfaithful to that determined Ella, but I lacked the emotional strength to invest myself in another dead-end search. When this battle ended, I'd face what Andrews had told me: no one had the power to restore stolen memories. Not even Whitewash's telepath.

As the seven of us processed toward the hangar, Ethan took the lead. Naturally, Jimmy fell to the farthest spot, giving me the opportunity to pull him back. I tugged him around a sand dune topped with tuffs of grass half my height. He'd avoided me since yesterday, both annoying and just the sort of thing he'd do.

He shrugged out of my hold. "What are you—"

Stop being weird.

Once Bridget's footsteps faded, Jimmy faced me. "Fine."

"You're still sulking."

"No I'm not."

"Yes you are."

"Why are you trying so hard?" he said.

"Because I care about—"

"*Why?*" Jimmy, a smudge of black in the shadows of morning, raised his hands. "Don't you get it? I only befriended you because you grew too old for One to visit. It was *my* idea. *I* started Whitewash. *I* recruited Walker, the one who impersonated your dad on the phone. Every moment I visited you in Briarwood, I knew you were a telepath, that we would eventually take you from your parents, and you're still pretending I'm your best friend."

One had assumed incorrectly. It wasn't embarrassment holding Jimmy back; it was shame.

Did I blame him for every Whitewash-instigated misery? Looking at his twisted expression, how could I? His was not the reaction of a heartless manipulator. Jimmy cared; he just wasn't comfortable enough to own it. Not without a little help.

"Take off your bracer," I said.

His exhale dragged. Jimmy knew where this was going, so he did nothing.

I raised my brows. He raised his right back. When I reached out, he scooted sideways, and kept twisting out of contact until I had to lunge at his arm.

"Stop," he said, yanking free.

"*You* stop! You're making me chase you!"

"I'm not making you do anything."

"Fine. We'll just stand here, then, until Ethan comes looking." I crossed my arms and waited.

"This is ridiculous," he said, refusing to look at me. He exhaled through his teeth. After glaring toward the sky, he tugged at the fingerless wrist guard. A final, hesitant pull, and the faded, red string of yarn came into view. Aged by sweat, but just as knotted as it had been when he was thirteen.

Trying not to grin *too* obnoxiously, I stepped closer with my hand extended. "Hi. I'm Ella. Let's be friends."

He expended commendable effort to keep the irritation. Something lighter — it might've been hope — wormed through. "You're so childish," he muttered. But he clasped my hand.

"What's your name?"

He sighed. "It's Banks." Then, with a shrug that seemed to slough off that final resistance, he added, "But you'll probably call me 'Jimmy' anyway, so... Jimmy works."

TAKEOFF HAD GONE SMOOTHLY, what with all the automation. The hovering part made me more anxious, though not so anxious as I was about my friends. Bridget and I got the easy job of staying put — and worrying.

I kept meeting Ethan's eyes, then forcing my gaze elsewhere. Most of the time, it went to Jimmy. It would've been easier to lose Banks in battle. Now, I cared about him too much.

Back to Ethan. Sliding into his head required zero effort now. I couldn't turn my curiosity off, but he knew I was listening and didn't mind. He was worried too, wrinkles deepening as he scrutinized each cadet. Other than Bridget and James, who shared a seat, the others had shoved as much distance between them as possible. Ethan's soldiers had lost the unity they'd once shared, and he couldn't figure out why.

It's because they realized they'd all been lying to one another, I told him. *Plus, no one likes Jimmy. I mean, Banks.*

Ethan straightened, continuing his observations, now with a different approach. If the cadets were disgruntled with one another, what must they think of *him*, their leader who'd failed to guide them? He decided their solidarity might return if he admitted his faults first.

He stood. "I need to apologize to you all." As he gathered his words, all attention — even Jimmy's — rested on him. "I misled you as your commanding officer, your commanding general, and... your friend. The MTA is corrupt, and I never saw it. If my ignorance led to poor decisions on your behalf, I take responsibility. My duty was to lead you well. I failed. For that, I am sorry."

If I hadn't cared about Ethan already, that speech would've done the trick.

"It's all right, sir," McFarland said softly.

"You don't need to apologize," James added. "You were a good CO. You never lied to us."

McFarland grew downcast. She'd been CO after Ethan.

The huff that rolled in Vires' throat could've been heard a mile away. "Stop the pious diatribe, Reynolds."

James' flush blended his complexion with his hair.

"That's enough," Ethan said. "From all of you. We are a team. If you have disagreements, either resolve them now or disregard them. I'm not letting anyone off this aircraft who's going to endanger the mission."

When Vires retorted, Ethan held up a hand. An uncomfortable stew followed. I saw how Ethan wanted to resolve the tension between them but didn't know where to begin. Perhaps I saw clearly because I'd read all their minds at one point and had pieced together the bits they ignored.

And so, the one privy to their inner turmoil, I felt I had to be the one to patch it up. "Here's the thing," I announced, standing beside Ethan. "I lied too. When I first joined the academy, I was working for Whitewash the whole time. Also, you guys lied to me when I came back. None of you pretended to know me. I'm not mad, I'm just making a point. Everyone here has lied, but we did it because we thought it was the right thing. So we should all forgive one another and move on. You're about to go on a dangerous mission, where you could die without having said all the things that should be said. And so, here goes." I faced McFarland and cleared my throat. "McFarland, when you caught me on the roof that one time, I was practicing my telepathy. Avary, I didn't meet you for practice in acro because I had to talk with Banks. Vires, I went into that clubhouse because I was meeting with Helix. Reynolds, I never actually studied for Velencia's class. Banks, I—" I caught Jimmy's raised brows, remembered Kara, and forced out, "I told her." Before his expression alone murdered me, I switched to Ethan. "I hated that peanut butter chocolate, but the gesture was sweet, so I pretended to like it. Um. That's all."

The extraction of words felt so satisfying that a jittery fervor quadrupled my pulse. My attention couldn't settle on any one cadet, all bearing a variety of expressions, from bemusement to Jimmy's outrage.

Vires crossed his arms. "So you admit to starting the fire."

"Are you serious? *That's* what you—for the last time: I'm not a pyromaniac!"

"You actually did start the fire," Jimmy said.

I swiveled. "What?"

"It was an electrical fire. A fuse blew. Your fingerprints were on the light switch."

My mouth hung. The glint overlaying Jimmy's otherwise nonchalant face clearly read, *Payback.*

"I knew it!" Vires' long finger pointed like a staff.

"I knew that too," James mumbled. "Griffin told me, but he said to keep it quiet or Vires would be even angrier." Tentatively, he checked Vires, in time to see the latter's triumphant gleam puff out. Then, James took a breath and turned to McFarland. "I get it. I forgive you."

She drew herself a bit taller, perhaps an automatic reaction to a perceived attack. Then, realizing none had come, McFarland's features clouded, and she nodded. "Thank you," she said quietly. Her attention moved to Vires next. He had to sense it; her eyes drilled much like a meta's fist might. For a brief snatch, he looked at her, then resumed his sulking. That must've meant something to McFarland, for she settled in her chair less troubled than before.

Bridget rose, wringing her hands, but never got a word out before James pulled her back down and said, "You did nothing wrong, Avary. This is on us. We're horrible role models." He dug his elbows into his thighs and plopped his forehead into his palms.

Focus aligned on Jimmy next. He let it linger; then, probably remembering the stubbornness of metas, said, "I'm not apologizing for being on the right side."

"As expected," Vires muttered.

I glanced at Ethan, but he didn't appear to have heard Jimmy. He was staring at me—curiously. And, beneath that pondering, I spotted something else that notched up my pulse.

"Kepler," he said, "I need a word with you in the cockpit."

Suddenly, I felt as nervous as Bridget.

In the cockpit, I leaned against a chair and waited for Ethan to close the door. Even after he did, he said nothing, continuing the stare that told me exactly what his thoughts would've, had I had the boldness to read them. When my heartrate neared chaotic territory, I said, "The suspense, Ethan."

He took one step forward. "You made a good point. Actually, you made several, but I'm referring to one. I've left something unsaid. I didn't think it needed saying, but you told me people like hearing things, even if they already know them."

"Are you going to say it?"

He smiled. "I just did."

"No you didn't. You—"

"I love you."

My breath hitched.

He crossed the small space to cup my face. "That's what I would have told you, had you met me on the roof. I love you, Ella. The MTA never taught us what that means." A hard line formed between his brows. His fingers tightened, but as he contemplated me, the anger faded. Ethan softened his hold and stroked his thumb along my cheek. "But I know I do. It's not a feeling but a certainty. A decision. I *will* love you until I die."

I focused on that intent certainty. That, more than anything he'd said, proved the strength of his words. Ethan pursued everything with all he had. He couldn't just say he loved me; he had to infuse his assurance into his expression, too. I understood all this about him and wished for a thousand days more to tell him so, but the MTA was a thief of time, and Whitewash was no better.

"Ethan… " I whispered, "what if you die today?"

"Then I die."

Surely he meant to follow that up with something encouraging. I stared, waiting, until it hit me that I'd wait forever.

"That was really… not comforting at all." I tried to frown. Face-to-face with him, annoyance failed, and I laughed instead. "You're terrible, Ethan!" I smacked his chest.

"What did you want me to say?"

"It's worse that you don't even know. It's going to be a real challenge, loving you forever." After saying it, I had to pause. Of course I loved him. I'd never sat down to analyze the word, but when I thought of it, I thought of Ethan.

Arms crossed, I said, "I'm assuming you already knew I love you?"

"If I didn't know that, I'd be an idiot."

"Well—"

He touched his thumb to my lips and tilted my chin up. "May I kiss you?"

I determined not to blush or gape. "You interrupted me."

"Of course. You were about to call me an idiot."

"Fair point."

Ethan stood quietly expectant, patient in this as he was in all he did.

"What if I say no?" I knew his answer. This was about letting Ethan demonstrate he intended to be a gentleman.

He dropped his hand, though not entirely—because he must've known my answer, too. "Then I won't kiss you," he said.

I smiled, enjoying that I could say no and he'd carry on unoffended. "Okay," I said. "Yes."

Ethan touched my chin again. The glint of humor gave way to a determination that deepened the blue of his eyes. He meant this moment to be decisive, a measured act rather than an impulsive one. And so, as Ethan had taught me, I waited. Patiently, even. I absorbed his deliberate care, waiting for the moment his lips would meet mine.

He didn't make me wait long.

WE HARDLY HAD A MOMENT before the nav screen flashed a warning. I sat to prepare the jet for hover. It was 0446. Fourteen minutes out. Walker would call if and when they spotted Chron.

Ethan leaned on the back of my chair and kept quiet as I configured the controls. My grip on the thrust lever had gone slick by the time the jet evened out. After locking the hover control, I palmed my face. "That was the most stressful thing I've ever done."

"You did—" Somewhere above me, Ethan's phone vibrated. "Sheedy," he answered.

I heard Walker plain as day.

"We've sighted Chron. Your move, C-squad."

"Copy." Ethan tore out of the cockpit in another beat.

A swallow stuck to my throat like tar. Chron had heard me. Each time I took a step further with my telepathy, I never got the chance to process it. We'd go a million miles an hour until this ended.

Since my work was finished, I climbed over the seat and joined Ethan for the announcement. "We're clear to engage," he said. "Are you all ready for this mission?"

The cadets stiffened with palpable, battle-ready air. McFarland stood first. "Yes, sir."

James echoed her. After a pointed look from McFarland, Vires stood, mustering visible indifference as he allowed a verbal assent. We all turned to Jimmy. Only he and I understood this could've been his mission, his operation. Now, he had to entrust Whitewash's success into the hands of someone who'd wholeheartedly resisted the operation a few days earlier.

He stood. "Your call, Sheedy," Jimmy said, with no apparent sarcasm.

Resolve clicked across Ethan's face, sliding into place. It was his battle face, this time untainted by doubt or anger. "Let's move," he said.

No one had to check a strap one last time; they'd been ready since we boarded. McFarland prompted the exit latch, and the door lifted like a jaw. The plane, despite its stationary position, roared with vibrations that mixed with the wind. Light from the cabin spilled onto the gray splotches of clouds.

One by one, the metas hopped into the vacuum of invisible space waiting beneath the plane. Bridget and I watched them all disappear. Second to last, Jimmy paused to meet my eyes.

Don't be mad, I said.

Go away. Lurching backward, Jimmy jumped.

Ethan gripped the edge of the roof. I knew what he was thinking; the same thought echoed in my head. "Talk to you soon," he said, then stepped backward and dropped.

Bridget called up the ramp, robbing me of the chance to follow the metas' inky shapes. I ignored all the negative *what-ifs* of my imagination. It seemed pointless, maybe even unnecessary. Chron was gone and didn't know we were coming. We had a shot.

"Should we wait in the cockpit?" Bridget said.

"Good idea."

We were a few steps from the door when something thudded. I checked behind. Down the hallway, a tangle of limbs and rope emerged from the captain's room.

My jaw dropped. "Durgson?"

The Grifter froze, one leg elevated. He was entwined with thick cord, some sort of net.

"What are you doing here?" I said.

He kicked the netting free with the force of someone booting a giant. "I would not expect an elak to understand." *Chron... my father's place...* he was thinking.

"You want to go after Chron," I said.

He crossed his arms.

"He's not even here, Durgson."

"I am not here for him. He — he has stolen the allegiance due to my father. I would rather die than allow one more Hela to follow *Chron*."

"He's going to jump," Bridget whispered.

I saw the idea flash, in his mind and set expression, right before he bolted.

Durgson barreled toward the exit hatch, beside which blared the inconveniently obvious button. Bridget and I leaped simultaneously. Once landed, I spun around, waving my hands widely enough that Durgson had no other option but to quit charging and face me.

"Our team is down there," I said. "If you cause a scene, they could get hurt."

"I will not bother your team. Move." Durgson might've been Durgan's son, but he lacked the authoritative tone.

"Let's talk this through, Durgson. I know — "

He let out a cry and hurtled forward.

I got this, Bridget, I told her, hoping she'd move. I stood my ground, using the two seconds before collision to spot my entrance. Before impact, I dipped low and angled my shoulder to receive the brunt of his force. Durgson's momentum radiated down my spine as his energy slammed; I swallowed my grunt and kicked back. His body had nowhere to go but over, so over me he went, toppling backside onto the floor. Sheer willpower pushed me through the ache in my shoulder. Before Durgson could regain balance, I gripped his wrists and dragged him from the exit.

"Find some cuffs!" I said, and Bridget scurried off.

When he yanked, I let myself fall onto him, elbows down. They battered his stomach, hopefully knocking the air out of him.

A burst of wind pillowed my face. Though I grabbed Durgson's limbs, the door opened. A clipboard clattered to the floor — straight from the exit button.

Stupid telekinesis!

Durgson writhed, spinning us both. We shot to our feet, sharing a tense moment of hesitance while the outdoor wind whipped feet away. A wild anxiety shivered through him before he sprinted. I leaped, wrapping my arms around his torso, but he carried my weight like a backpack. Durgson was getting off the plane, and I could either go with him or take my leave now.

Duty fought necessity during the wink of time before he jumped. I had to stay aboard — yet I owed it to Durgan to keep his impulsive son from getting himself killed.

Crap, I thought.

Durgson pelted us airborne.

CHAPTER NINETEEN

I MADE UP MY MIND as we fell. I was in the perfect position to give Durgson a swift pressure-point jab. As my fingers crept toward his neck, trees gobbled us up; branches smacked us apart. I curled, shielding my head. Twigs scored my arms and legs but at least slowed the fall. Still, I hit the ground hard enough to lose my breath. The ground dipped, sending me into a roll that seemed prepared to topple me indefinitely. I dug my fingers into the earth, finding leaves but no purchase, not until the knobby skin of a root jutted between the dirt. I snatched hold. The root tore, overcome by the momentum of my roll, but it had the strength to sever the intense pull of energy. The abrupt halt snagged my shoulder, adding a sear of pain to the general layer of discomfort pressing the rest of me. I lay face down on a forest floor, panting.

Are you okay? I sent out, picturing Durgson.

Yes.

Don't move.

His answer to that was to move. I heard the rustling and followed its source. Every step sent spikes of pain into my shoulder.

Durgson! Stop! I reached the river and saw him bounding across the boulder walkway with no sense of precaution. He had a death wish.

Feeling stuck in a nightmare, I copied Durgson's slippery steps, shouting telepathic warnings he ignored.

Do you even know where the tunnel entrance is?

I will find it.

No, you'll get yourself killed. Slow down, Durgson, and let me help you.

He hesitated on the rock closest to the waterfall's mouth and let me catch up. Water flicked static-like droplets from the spray.

I closed my eyes. First, I told Bridget we were okay. Then, I searched the tendrils of mental connection for Ethan. They relayed a series of disjointed words and scenes, everywhere from SPO-10 to the academy. Nothing in his current train of thought dealt with Grifters. He was unconscious — already? I switched to Jimmy and encountered the same cobbled-together static. Barely ten minutes into their task, and they'd been overcome. But there were five metas! *We should've had the advantage.*

I think they need help, I told Durgson. *Can I count on you to do* exactly *what I say?*

Maybe he believed the waterfall held more answers than me; he examined its relentless gush, though a Grifter's eyesight couldn't have absorbed much in this darkness.

Durgson. We don't have a lot of time.

He rolled his shoulders. *Yes.*

I breathed out. Durgson and I were going headlong into Grifter territory and without a stitch of gear. Walker hadn't wanted me joining the mission for this reason. Every cadet could die, and Whitewash could carry on—unless they lost me.

Well, I'd picked around Chron's territory once before. I wouldn't need Ethan's disguise this time.

Carry me over your shoulder, I said to Durgson. *You need to pretend like I'm your prisoner.*

I am not dressed as one of Chron's.

We'll just have to hope they don't notice.

Slung upside-down over Durgson's shoulder, I had a disjointed view of our progress. He inched forward. Buckets of torrential downpour deafened me, drenching me in an instant. Even after he passed through, it was impossible to hear anything but the roar.

I soaked in the scent of minerals and controlled my pulse. *Keep walking.*

The tunnel lacked the convenience of torches; and, upside-down, I was little help in the vision department. I strained to hear instead, anything beyond the water that grew fainter with every step.

"... more will come?" The throaty voice sounded far too close.

Stay still, I told Durgson. *I hear talking.*

"I suspect not," another answered.

"Surely Ledare does not need them alive?"

"That elak is familiar. Perhaps the others.... Bind them. Ledare will decide their fate."

"Yes, Bern."

In my anxiety, I clutched the back of Durgson's shirt. *Don't move yet,* I told him. Between the two of us, we could probably take one Grifter, but I would rather we drag out our disguise as long as possible.

When footsteps retreated, I guessed only one Grifter remained. *Go,* I said. *But carefully. Remember, I'm your prisoner. If he asks, say you're... seeking refuge.*

His pulse skipped.

Light trickled into my vision. I got a view of an avalanche of rock and a heap of bodies and a Grifter dressed in red—but my attention returned to Ethan's slack figure. Around the exit of the tunnel, every meta lay crumbled near one another, yet none of them showed any obvious sign of injury. They hadn't even had the chance to remove their night vision goggles.

"Who is there?" the Grifter called.

Durgson halted. "I am Elis. Of—of Kian. I am traveling."

"And what is that you carry, young Elis?"

"Elak." Durgson coughed. "I overcame it... outside."

"Then leave it with the others."

Durgson hesitated, but I gave him the okay to drop me. *Ask what's wrong with the metas,* I said, trying to keep my limbs loose as he flung me onto McFarland. She didn't even stir, though I felt her deep breaths.

"What is wrong with these elaks?" Durgson asked.

"An odd question, Elis." I heard the Grifter stand. "Kian has often favored the side of Durgan. You have heard of the traitor?"

"I have heard nothing of his treachery." Darkness stole into Durgson's throat.

Ignore him, Durgson.

"Yes. It would seem so." The Grifter laughed. "Fool. You believe I would forget your face, son of Durgan? I remember my conquests. Few have the privilege of destroying the spawn of filthy traitors."

Meaning rang icy clear, cold as a slap.

As Durgson's rage bellowed, I yanked McFarland's left bracer off her arm and shoved my own gloved hand into it. Fortunately, I remembered the biometric lock in time; I jabbed her thumbprint against the safety mechanism and felt the bracer engage.

I clambered to my feet, edging fully into Chron's sitting room, where he'd interrogated Durgan not that long ago. Durgson had the Grifter in a headlock and failed to see the incoming staff that charged toward his temple. Telekinesis would've come in handy. Instead, I kicked the staff clear across Chron's quarters.

The Grifter writhed and flipped Durgson onto his back. Once freed, the Grifter turned to me. I lifted my left arm and put a shot in each kneecap, which didn't hurt him, though it did cause him to stagger. He lunged at my waist; I danced around Chron's room, butting into a chair. Durgson barreled toward the Grifter from behind. The Grifter got sandwiched between the floor and a bulky two-hundred pounds of deadweight. He balked, but Durgson slammed his palm into the Grifter's head. It took only one forceful blow for the Grifter to go limp beneath him, yet Durgson struck again. The Grifter lay immobile, doing nothing but bleeding as Durgson smashed his skull into the unforgiving stone.

"Stop!" I booted Durgson over. He tipped into the wall but bolted upright with a snarl. I lifted my hands. "I'm sorry about what he did. It's unforgivable. But he's dead, Durgson."

His chest heaved. My bracer hand curled. I never could've predicted this thirteen-year-old kid had the unchecked rage to beat a Grifter to death. I doubted Durgson would have been able to predict it, either. But he'd come face-to-face with his siblings' murderer with no warning, and people were unpredictable, Grifter or not. So I kept my bracer ready.

He looked down, first at his drenched fingers, then to the body at his feet. After a gasp, Durgson dropped to his knees and recoiled behind his hands.

"I'm sorry," I said. Regret, revulsion, and remorse burrowed deep. I seemed stuck in a hollow, out-of-body nightmare.

After a sigh, I hurried to the cadets. The Grifter had been in the process of cuffing Ethan's wrists together with a metal circlet bled through with electric blue dashes. More MTA tech? Vires and Jimmy had already been bound; a stack of handcuffs waited for McFarland and James.

Ethan, wake up. I slapped his face. When that got me nowhere, I slapped the rest of them. They slept on. No injuries, but all lost in unconsciousness. How?

No time. Chron would eventually return—we needed to get Andrews.

I ran into the hallway that led to my former cell. The barriers wending across the stone door stumped me, but with enough twisting, the locks unclicked. I'd already listened for a heartbeat and found none, so I expected the empty cell before me. Chron had Andrews reserved elsewhere. Time to initiate Plan B.

Bridget, I sent out, *the team is all unconscious. I'll move them into the tunnel.* I rubbed my forehead. Could I ask her to do this? But what other choice did we have? *You need to come get them and bring them to the jet. I know it's a lot to ask, but they'll either get captured or killed if I leave them here. You can do this. Wake up Dr. Lee. He'll help you. I'll bring them down the tunnel as much as I can, and then I have to get Andrews.*

Durgson flinched when I touched his shoulder. "You need to help me bring the cadets into the tunnel."

This was how Ethan talked to his cadets—firmly, and with lots of "you need tos." Durgson had no room to protest.

Jerkily, he stood, batting my arm away. He slung Vires over one shoulder and Jimmy over the other. I scooped Ethan up and raced into the tunnel until it was too dark to see. He slept on, oblivious to my quick brush along his jaw and compliant as I stole his goggles and right bracer. By the time I doubled back with McFarland, Durgson was just returning for James.

Afterward, I surveyed the garish scene in Chron's room. We couldn't do much to hide the Grifter's blood. I carried him into the tunnel and stopped before Durgson. "You need to put on his clothes."

"I will *not* wear that scum—"

"Durgson!"

He growled and wrenched the Grifter out of my arms.

Good grief. He was worse than Vires.

While he changed, I paced the sitting room. We'd have to find another Grifter for me to read. Had I been taller, I would've donned the clothes myself and searched on my own. Relying on Durgson made me nervous.

He emerged in a tunic too long for him, stained around the shins and collar.

"Listen to me." I crossed my arms and tried to make my stance wider than his. "We are in Chron's territory, which means we're going to come across other Grif—Hela who think your dad's a traitor. You *need* to keep your emotions in check, Durgson. We can't fight off every Hela here. Okay? If they say something, just nod and keep walking. Okay?"

"I will not nod to—"

"Then say nothing. Just don't fight them. Your dad wouldn't want you to die like this."

"You do not know my father!"

"Yes I do, Durgson."

He fumed. I was lucky Durgson wasn't a protean with fire breath.

"Are we clear?" I said.

Glaring at every inch of me, Durgson managed a thin, "Yes."

"Good. Let's go."

DURGSON STALKED FASTER THAN ideal for stealth, but I didn't tell him to slow. First, he would have ignored me. Second, we needed to shave off time.

Though I expected an ambush at every turn, we stayed lucky a solid five minutes. Our first encounter was with a young female strolling and humming, tray in hand. Upon catching sight of Durgson, me hanging over a shoulder and presumably dead, she swallowed her cheerful tune.

Talk to her, I told Durgson.

He shifted me—much more roughly than needed—and grunted, "*Flicka.*"

Her chin lifted. "I am older than you." She wore a dress, not the maroon tunic of Chron's guard. A civilian, for all intents and purposes. The simplicity of her outfit triggered my telepathy like a radio gaining volume.

... idiot boy....

Shooting past present moment, I searched for Andrews. The Grifter knew him only as an idea, titles branded by her friends. Corrupt. Evil. Lawless.

My fingertips had started to dig; I waded in further. A brush of conversation from earlier today drifted up like a kite.

"*Ledare requests all youth join the adults for breakfast tomorrow.*"

"*Has he moved the monster to our refectory, Mama?*"

"*I shudder to think....*"

Following the trail of that conversation led me to a wide dining hall not so different in arrangement from the academy's. Like stepping backward, I traced a path from the refectory to a corridor, to another, to a slope, to a hallway, and at last to the bridge.

Got it, I told Durgson.

After that, the few Grifters we encountered called to him for clarification about the body draped over his shoulder. They received a brusque "Elak" as their answer. Durgson skipped their remaining questions and tracked forward. I counted seven Grifters by the last leg of the journey.

When Durgson threw himself around the final corner, all sounded eerily silent, other than his clacking footsteps. I twisted and peeked for clarification. There, not even guarded, stood a single door. The final obstacle.

Tell Walker I'm outside Andrews' room, I told Bridget.

Durgson shrugged me off. Before he decided to kick down the door, I said, "Stand guard and let me know if anyone's coming."

"Yes, elak," he muttered.

I faced the door. It operated like a black hole to my adrenaline, sucking it dry. Behind it, I'd find the man who'd lied to my face for months, whose treachery had brought Ethan close to crying. How had I wasted all this time in putting off the inevitable? Our meeting wasn't in some vague future; it was now. Here.

And I wasn't ready.

"Why do you stand there?"

I shut my eyes. Durgson had a valid point. I'd gotten onto him for letting his emotions rule; I couldn't do the same.

First, I wiped my features clean of any misgiving. He would find me confident, not scared. I set my jaw, gripped the door, and pushed. One step forward.

"Ella?"

Not that voice. That face. Even as I longed to deny it, his form took shape. The man with many names wore a dress shirt and loosely knotted tie. His shirt looked blood-spattered. The faintest shadow of stubble darkened his cheeks and further disorder undid his hair, revealing the unruly waves that gel had sought to maintain. Even in dishevelment, he perfectly captured the expression of a school principal worried that his student had gotten in over her head.

Eugene Andrews.

CHAPTER TWENTY

IN THE REFECTORY, EMPTY of all but Andrews, he was bound to a chair by metal circlets. They looped like an eight, an ankle stuck through each hole, while his arms hid behind his back. Even now, he x-rayed me. I wanted to act casual, but I couldn't pretend.

"You're not a killer, Ella," he said quietly.

He knew, then, that I wasn't coming to him as one scared cadet helping her Leader.

"I'm not going to kill you. Whitewash wants you alive."

"Then I believe I'm a prime candidate for the proverbial 'Between a rock and a hard place.' My options, it would seem, are either to remain here and be tortured by Grifters, or leave with you and be tortured by Whitewash." He spoke in a level tone, the voice of a man calmly working through an inconvenience. "Activate your pulser. The shock will disengage the cuffs."

I swallowed. I had no way to carry him like this, attached to the chair, but I felt reluctant to follow his orders.

"Hurry up, Ella," he said with a chop of impatience. "Or save yourself, and let Chron finish the job."

I thrust my right wrist forward. The bracer tingled. A tube the length of a pen slid into my palm, then uncorked. I gripped the rubber center as the pulser grew in length from each side, expanding to full height and thrumming with its charge.

He pointed his chin over his shoulder. "Hands first."

I crossed the room, an iron-clad hold on the pulser in case his telekinesis got any ideas. Instead of his arms, I aimed the bracer toward his legs. He could still run fast with his arms behind his back.

The metal bracelets whined, and the blue light sputtered. With a cough and hiss, the cuffs snapped in half and plummeted.

Andrews stood immediately. "Hands."

"No. Let's go." I turned for the exit.

"Are you certain you can trust that Grifter guarding the door?"

I couldn't walk out with a conscious Andrews. He'd fight Durgson, handcuffed or not.

I spun around. To do this, I needed close proximity. Before him, feeling insignificant under that uncannily familiar stare, I found myself saying, "What is Banks' mother's name?"

A glimmer of humor sparked in his eyes. "Did he really give you such a sentimental request?"

"Answer the question."

"Colette Barineau."

I suspected he spoke the truth. That name matched his computer password.

"Don't you want to know his father's?" Andrews said.

"It won't make a difference. Banks is nothing like you." I swung an elbow; it popped Andrews in the temple.

Got Andrews, I told Bridget, hoisting him over my shoulder. Now for our escape.

Durgson fought me in a constant battle of speed, but having a Grifter in front gave me an extra second of safety. The guards wouldn't attack right away, not until they saw me on Durgson's tail.

Our path lay empty. At each turn, Durgson tensed, but the way was clear. The lack of opposition made the hike more ominous.

The final curve came, the bend in the cavern that would lead us to the bridge—the great divide between Chron's quarters and everyone else. Durgson rounded the corridor and halted; my face plowed into his shoulder blades. I regained my footing and peered around. Before him, at the start of the bridge, waited at least three rows of Grifters.

I cycled through frantic offensive strategies before taking in the absence of movement in the army.

A Grifter in front, clad in soldier's garb, pointed toward the door the Grifters currently blocked. "Take Andrews and go," she said. I recognized Freia's voice.

Durgson froze, a string of tension tightening the back of his neck.

"If you attack us, we will resist," Freia said. "We will win. But Ledare's war has destroyed our families, and we are weary."

I stepped around Durgson, into Freia's view. She showed no reaction, but I knew she recognized me.

Thank you, Freia. Again.

She nodded. "Fall back," she said to those behind her.

The Grifters formed a line along one side of the bridge. They stretched from front to back, a railing of sentinels leaving only a breath of space for us to squeeze past. Once Freia took her place, Durgson tore off his captured tunic. He balled the bloody fabric under his arm and stepped forward. The Grifters stared after him with an anxious sort of hunger. Did they hate him? Pity him?

The bridge had no railing, other than the Grifters. If they recognized me, they didn't care, but bore me down with resignation. We straddled their territory, outnumbered and low on ammo, yet the air drooped with their defeat. Chron's vengeance had broken them.

Once beyond the line, Durgson fumbled at the stone door, white with purple lines like a palm stained with berry. It rumbled open, and I dashed into the hallway beyond. A few paces in, I realized Durgson had stayed behind. He lingered in the doorway.

"Let's go," I called.

Durgson looked back at the bridge of Grifters, then slowly faced me and shook his head. "I must stay."

"What?"

"I… I cannot abandon them. They have no hope."

Staring at his expression—a bit wide, though certain—hollow dread sank deep. If Durgson stayed, Chron could very well do what he'd bragged of and finally kill him. How could I return to Durgan without his son?

"Durgson, it's too risky. You can't."

"I must," he whispered. "My father would have helped them. So I must try. It is what a king would do." He edged backward, as if summoned by the desperation he sought to change. The door grinded when he closed it. A white and purple wall of defeat stared at me.

Panic clawed my throat. I shifted Andrews and made my way back toward the door, intent upon overcoming Durgson, somehow—knocking him out and adding him to my other shoulder.

A force yanked the pulser staff from my hand. I twisted, scrabbling for it, just as Andrews rolled off my shoulder. He righted himself quickly and never wavered as I aimed my bracer. He rubbed at his wrists, the broken cuffs at his feet.

"You can't control everyone, Ella." He grabbed my staff from the air and looked up. "Now. Shall we?" Andrews pointed in the opposite direction.

I lowered my arm and fired. Even as I shifted, Andrews slipped sideways. I took aim again as he motioned with his hand. Pain spliced my skin, sharp as a knife; I gasped and doubled over.

"This should keep you pliable." Andrews gripped the handle of whatever he'd telekinetically stabbed me with. I clamped down hard as the fiery point dug deeper into my waist, passing cleanly through my t-shirt. Andrews yanked the goggles off my neck, then maintained the pressure as he pushed me past my old cell.

I tripped forward. This couldn't happen. If I failed, we all did.

After taking a second to steel my resolve, I heeled his shin. He hissed a curse, losing his grip on the hilt. The release of pressure caused another spasm of pain. Half blinded by tears, I elbowed backwards, forcing him into retreat as I rotated. He swung the pulser. I hopped back and fired a useless shot. More ammo in the bracer cartridge hold, but I wasted no time reloading.

Andrews struck with the pulser again, and I shimmied from its reach, drawing him closer to the escape tunnel. He stopped, letting the staff rest vertically. "This is pointless, Ella. You're injured and, frankly, not the most skilled fighter. Are you going to telepathy me to death?"

Not a bad idea.

Concentrating on Helix's voice, I locked onto Andrews and released the equivalent of a Grifter shout. He started and inspected over his shoulder. I charged, ignoring the blade of pain wedged into my hip. Though yards divided us, I planned on outracing the time it took for him to turn back around. I almost succeeded. Mere inches away, his staff rose. His move flicked in half a second. The blunt edge smacked my side. I cried out and stumbled into him. Andrews yanked my arms, not courteous to my injury as he twisted me around.

"Clever trick," he said. "I'm curious to learn what else you're capable of." Something cold clasped my wrists. The cuffs throbbed with energy, a magnetic thrum that drew my arms together despite all resistance.

Finding his hold on the hilt, Andrews shoved me forward. "Let's try this again."

I dug my heels. My refusal to walk was due only in part to stubbornness—moving would quadruple the pain. But if he continued this, forcing me to walk, it would strain the injury. I was better off controlling my own way.

With a locked jaw, I walked. This wasn't over yet.

Coming out of the tunnel with Andrews in a minute, I told Bridget. *Need back-up.*

None of the cadets lay in the tunnel. That gave me hope. Bridget had heard me and moved them. Or else Grifters had.

While we walked, I couldn't forget who I'd left behind. I was less frustrated with Durgson than I was with myself for failing to stop him.

He might've considered me an annoying elak, but that didn't change my level of responsibility for him. *I'd* led him in here — and not out.

At the waterfall, agony reached its height. Still wedging the tip into my skin, Andrews maneuvered me into water no less merciful. My legs gave. He had to stabilize me.

The base of the waterfall smacked boulder and river with violent energy. The stone made for slippery purchase; I tripped, jerking the blade further.

"Try *not* to kill yourself, please." He secured my waist and jumped halfway across the river. Another couple leaps and he touched down on the bank. Andrews maneuvered me forward one step, then halted. He hooked me in a choke hold and tightened his grip on the hilt.

The grass rustled.

I searched through strands of wet hair. Relief alleviated some of the sting. Bridget had heard me.

Highlighted by the moon, four metas in helmets, each equipped with a shouldered rifle, dashed from the trees. One of them, missing his right bracer, halted before us and motioned the others forward. Two flanked Andrews on either side, while the fourth circled around him.

Andrews let me go and stepped back. Without his support, I realized I'd been relying on it. I careened forward. Ethan caught me with one arm. The other, he continued aiming.

"Pulser… disengages the… cuffs," I told him.

On his way toward shoving Andrews into the trees, Vires tossed Ethan his pulser. Once Ethan released the magnetic power and my cuffs fell away, he lifted me upright. I saw Vires and Jimmy forcing Andrews through the woods, Andrews offering no resistance. Even he knew when to accept defeat.

"We have to go back," I said. "Durgson's there."

Ethan removed his helmet and knelt by my waist, squinting. Poking from bloody shreds of t-shirt was a jagged edge of stone, not a knife after all. "They captured him?" he murmured. Gingerly, he touched the skin around the protrusion.

I sucked in a grimace. "No. Decided to stay. But he doesn't know what he's getting himself into."

"He doesn't want our help."

"They'll kill him!"

"It was his choice, Ella." Ethan rose, swiping his helmet off the ground. He moved to my other side, draped my arm around his shoulders, and started forward.

I resisted. "We can't leave him."

"We're not. He chose to stay."

"*I* can't leave him."

"You can barely walk. How do you plan to defend yourself?" He tugged his helmet on and shifted the gun to his other arm, freeing up a hand. With it, he urged me onward. "Chron is going to return soon, and we can't be here when he does."

I fought frustration with Ethan for being the bossy commander Jimmy had always disliked. Sure, Ethan had a point: I was injured, and we needed to disappear before Chron arrived. But the feeling of failure lingered.

Ethan guided me into the woods. "You've done nothing wrong. Durgson made his choice."

"I don't like his choice."

"I can sympathize. It's frustrating when someone you care about decides to infiltrate hostile territory without proper gear or back-up."

Subtlety was not Ethan's forte.

Yards down the trail, bungee ropes hung through the trees. Stepping into the attached harness had too many complications; the strap rubbed against my injury. The least painful method of ascending meant clinging to Ethan while he gripped the bungee. Up we rose, as we had twice before—both times escaping from Chron.

He'd lost five prisoners in the span of a few days. Now, we'd deceived him by manipulating his relationship with his sister. Though summer air and Ethan's warmth surrounded me, I succumbed to a shiver. Chron's rage would be terrible, and his broken, hopeless Grifters, including Durgson, would be on the receiving end. We might've finally had Andrews in our hands, but this war would never dissipate with Chron still in power.

I drew closer to Ethan, wondering when success was going to feel like success and a whole lot less like failure.

CHAPTER TWENTY-ONE

ONBOARD, I WAS THE only one without a helmet. Even Andrews wore one, a fish-bowl-like dome more suited for an astronaut. He'd been strapped to a seat, hands and ankles restricted with cuffs. With the black, impenetrable cover over his head, I could only guess how humiliated Andrews felt—though he had no way of knowing that his captors were the young metas he'd advised not that long ago.

Vires vanished into the cockpit to initiate takeoff. His retreat and Andrews were the only things I glimpsed before Dr. Lee, somehow emanating stress through his helmet, ushered me to the clinic. After telling me to lie flat, he tossed his helmet in the corner—it thudded against the wall and cracked—and bent a flushed, sweaty face to my side. A grid hovered between him and the protrusion of stone, emitting blue lines that swept over the wound.

"Regeneration's already begun," Lee said. "I—I don't have time for a local anesthetic. I have to remove it now."

"Wait, are you sure—"

The feeling of claws shredding my insides intensified so sharply that my vision went spotty. All thoughts of wishing for Saini over Lee vanished into pain. After some excruciating moments, the fire slowly ebbed away; Lee must have found the time to give me a sedative. When only a dull throb remained, I opened my eyes. Lee was waving the bloody stub around.

"... don't need to listen to someone who's never read a medical textbook in his life!" he shouted at Ethan.

"Stop arguing and do your job! She has an exposed wound."

"Well I was about to do that before you interrupted me!"

I groaned and covered my face. That prompted Lee into action. Ethan kept his opinions to himself—verbally, at least. Seeking distraction from Lee's poking and prodding, I lost myself in Ethan's thoughts. Mixed into his frustrations with Dr. Lee and even me, Ethan consciously avoided contemplation of Andrews. But a mind-reader saw all. I wasn't the only one in need of distraction.

"What knocked you guys unconscious?" I mumbled against my palms.

"When we broke through the barrier, it triggered a gas bomb. Chron was expecting intruders."

"Chron has a full arsenal of MTA weaponry," came McFarland's voice; I hadn't realized she'd entered the room.

"I have a theory Andrews gave him that in exchange for something," I said.

"He gave him protection along with weapons," said Jimmy. Was *everyone* watching Lee stitch me up?

When Lee declared himself finished and I wearily opened my eyes, I had to blink a few times at all the distraction. Bridget, James, Vires—everyone crowded the clinic, which flustered Lee to no end. He kept muttering about invasion of privacy as he washed his hands.

"Why is everyone in here?" I said.

Several uncomfortable seconds passed until James quietly said, "Better here than out there with him."

No one could argue with that.

WHEN THE HELMET WAS yanked from Andrews' face, he didn't wince at the onslaught of light. In Ethan's former room, Andrews, bloodied and tattered, stuck out. He measured each of us, revealing the slightest disappointment when he registered Ethan in the line of cadets. But his attention moved on, and the emotion dissipated.

Once his inspection ended, he said, "Ms. McFarland's presence surprises me most. I admit, I couldn't have predicted that."

McFarland stood taller, fighting poorly disguised guilt. The cadets conveyed varying emotions at the sight of their former guardian. James paled, and Bridget's apprehension tugged at my chest, thanks to the strange workings of my telepathy.

"Are you not going to defend yourself?" Ethan surveyed him with the same disappointment Andrews had shown him.

"What would be the point? You all think I'm a monster."

"What should we think you are?"

Andrews let that question reverberate and found me in the crowd. In Ethan's jacket, with half my shirt trimmed away and a hunk of gauze plastered to my skin, I doubted I resembled Whitewash's secret weapon.

"You lost, Andrews," Jimmy said.

Slowly, Andrews eyed him. His brows lifted with amusement, but beneath the sarcasm sat something eerily expectant. He stared at Jimmy long enough to make everyone fidget. Then, his attention drifted toward Bridget. "Ms. Avary joined the cause first," he said, "and the rest followed suit?"

She took a step closer to James.

"Why are you asking?" Ethan said sharply.

"I would like a word alone with Ms. Avary."

"No," James said. "You need to—to leave her alone." His voice cracked, and an eye twitch made his glare less intimidating.

Andrews spoke to Bridget as if the rest of us had disappeared. "This situation worries you. It's possible Operation Whitewash is mistaken. They'll kill me, Bridget. Do you believe that to be just?"

Beneath her freckle dusting, Bridget's tan skin lost some warmth. Words were only words, but Andrews' held power. I noticed the creep of uncertainty stealing into my gut. James' glare began to slip.

"Has Whitewash told you the truth?" Andrews continued. "No, I see that you don't know. Let's discuss this privately. I'll help you."

It unnerved me how easily doubt plagued the others: McFarland dropping her gaze, Vires growing stiffer, Ethan's troubled frown beginning to show. As I watched, he screwed his face against it. He swept the helmet off the floor, crossed the room, and dumped it over Andrews' head.

"I want a private word with him," he said.

Ethan's movement severed the uncertainty. The cadets took their cue and dispersed.

You sure? I asked Ethan.

Yes.

Okay, I said, but leftover doubt gave me pause. Andrews would play with Ethan's loyalties.

Jimmy paused near Ethan and said, "He's going to try to manipulate you."

"I know."

"What if he succeeds? I don't feel like incapacitating you again."

"He'll fail." Ethan's jaw locked. Even in profile, his features left little room for argument.

I exhaled, reminded myself that doubt was only a feeling, and booted it out. Andrews had cemented Ethan's distrust with one rock— the one he'd stabbed me with.

Jimmy shrugged and turned for the door. Together, we slipped out.

Other than One, the hallway lay empty. When cadets wanted to leave, they left fast. And when Andrews wanted to unsettle someone, he proved sickeningly good at it.

One, typically of few visible emotions, radiated worry in every forehead wrinkle. He appeared anxious for intel, though not curious enough to near Andrews' room.

"We're alive, One," Jimmy said. He set a hand briefly on One's shoulder before continuing down the hall. His random answers, combined with One's continued staring, told me that One was interrogating him. Despite that, Jimmy walked more calmly than usual. While the face-off with their old mentor had discomforted the rest of the cadets, Jimmy finally had Andrews right where he wanted him.

Was I meant to share that victory? Whitewash had overcome the final hurdle. Today, we won. I repeated that mantra and saw only the cadets' torment, Andrews' smirk, and Durgson slipping backward into Chron's territory. That sulky Grifter teen made a better leader than Andrews. He'd had a loving father as a role model, someone worth copying. None of the cadets had known a parent's love, not even in imitation. Andrews made a horrible father figure... and an even worse father.

In the refectory, he may as well have confirmed it. Jimmy's dad was Eugene Andrews. Whereas Durgan could hardly stand discussing the loss of his children, Andrews had sent his son into a daily battle he could have ended. No one could accuse him of showing favoritism.

An aching understanding slunk into my chest. Andrews had favored Ethan instead. Of course Jimmy hated Ethan. He'd never admit jealousy, but I grasped him well enough.

"Are you even listening?"

My head jerked up. Jimmy and One stood halfway across the main floor while I remained in the doorway of the galley. As if visual contact had plugged me in, Jimmy's thoughts came hurtling. They were mostly of Kara, which consoled me.

"I'm sorry, Jimmy," I whispered.

"For what?"

"That Andrews is...." The rest hung in the yards between us.

His pinched mouth whitened, and he turned his head. At his side, One offered Jimmy sympathetic scrutiny. But Jimmy ignored him, and One found my eyes instead.

Reading Andrews was my responsibility. Cleaning up his messes felt like it, too. Every heart he shattered, I wanted to re-stitch. Maybe it was an empathy thing, a stubborn thing, or just an Ella thing.

I asked him for your mom's name, I said. *Colette Barrineau. Now you can find her.*

Jimmy looked at me with a Vires-like incredulity. "Why did you do that?"

I left the doorway and drew myself up to full height before him. He still towered. "When are you ever going to accept that friends help each other?" I said.

He'd probably sooner shake hands with Koleman. Jimmy made sure to clear the emotion from his face as he replied, "'Barrineau' sounds like a word you made up."

I feigned exasperation and shook my head, blotting a tear in the process. If he saw, he kept quiet. Half my friendship with Jimmy took place in the silence of words unspoken.

Thank you, Ella, One said.

What for?

Continuing to care for him. Few are up to the task. One's small smile displayed something near amusement.

From overhead, voices drifted from the clinic—James', mingled with Kara's. Jimmy stiffened, then turned for the conference table.

"You can't avoid her forever," I called.

"Would you stay out of my head?"

"Ah, so you *are* avoiding her."

He shot me a glare first, then One, adding, "Don't encourage her."

"Come on, Jimmy," I said. "She already knows everything and still likes you. Stop making the both of you miserable."

One kept his commentary to a minimum as I clutched Jimmy by the elbow. Only as I towed Jimmy toward the stairs did One say, *He will be less embarrassed if I do not witness this. But no less annoyed.*

"When it comes to me, Jimmy's always annoyed," I said aloud, for both their benefits.

Jimmy muttered his assent.

Steering him somewhat like a kid on his way to the principal's office, I dragged him up. He didn't relax, but he didn't escape either. He wanted this reunion, even if he refused to admit it.

In the clinic, Bridget sat obediently before McFarland as the latter searched her for injuries. Vires leaned against the wall, cross-armed, spying on McFarland. The talking came from James, who was cramming Kara with an interrogation as fast as oxygen would allow.

"... an *actual* theater?"

"Um." She peeked over his shoulder and saw Jimmy, right before he wrenched open a cabinet door and ducked his head behind it. Her IV pole tipped sideways, thanks to her nervous twitch.

"Oops," James said, telekinetically straightening it.

Kara failed to notice; her eyes were fastened to the cabinet.

"Can I talk to Kara?" I called. "By the way, Kara, this is — "

"Reynolds already introduced us," Vires said. He waited for McFarland to finish dealing with Bridget, then followed the two out.

James' tact beat out his curiosity; he left Kara alone. Not alone — I was here, and so was Jimmy. Hiding his face inside a cabinet.

Kara drew in a breath, clutched her pole, and kept moving until she stood beside him. He had at least half a foot of extra height. Somehow, Kara seemed taller.

"Jimmy?" she said softly.

From my vantage, I saw what Jimmy did: piles of gauze and boxes of disposable gloves. Nothing capable of turning someone into a statue, mesmerized and unable to turn his head.

She stretched out a hand. I held my breath, counting seconds until contact. When her fingers rested on his arm, I was certain Jimmy had stopped breathing too.

His neck moved. Slowly. Jimmy let the door close and turned toward Kara. She didn't gawk. She didn't even flush. Kara smiled, the coy type reserved for a handful of people. That seemed my cue to leave. I edged backward — and rammed into someone solid.

"Ow." I clutched my throbbing wound and doubled over.

"I'm sorry," Ethan said. He steadied my shoulder.

"What happened?" Kara called.

"Let me check your bandaging. If the wound — "

I staved off Ethan's hand. *How did your talk go?*

"Would you just — " I heard him sigh, sensed his shifting, and suddenly Ethan was crouched below my waist. Carefully, he peeled away my hand. The sticky moisture and his expression told me the wound had re-opened. The injury was far from fatal, but, judging by his face, my side may as well have been split in half.

"I'm fine," I said.

Ethan shook his head. He refused to blink, so transfixed that I double checked to make sure my stomach *wasn't* carved open. The bandaging showed a few spots of blood. Nothing dire. This overreaction was unlike him.

Ethan?

In his mind, Andrews' face overlaid my injury. Ethan couldn't separate the two, not with their conversation so fresh. Even though he'd accepted who Andrews was, he'd held out for an admission of wrongdoing. Andrews had owned nothing. Worse, he'd harmed me, and Ethan had defended him days earlier—a fact Ethan had admitted, which had only given Andrews the tools to dig deeper. He'd never bothered trying to win Ethan's loyalties back; he'd called him a doormat instead.

It's not your fault. I touched his cheek.

The gesture startled him. He looked at me, so clouded by regret I lost the familiarity. *Sorry... so sorry...* he thought.

I know, Ethan. Ignore what he said. I held out my hand. *Come on.*

He stared at my palm. Drawing in air, he narrowed his expression until resolve made a stronger appearance than remorse. When he stood, he didn't need the aid of my hand, though he grasped it to guide *me* upright.

"Do you want some gauze, El?" Kara's voice pulled me out of Ethan's head.

"Sure," I said. "It's behind you, Jimmy."

"That's the second time you've called him 'Jimmy,'" Ethan said.

Right.

Jimmy shook his head, danger flashing. He should've known the warning was pointless.

"Banks was my best friend growing up because he had to monitor me for Whitewash," I said to Ethan. "My memory was wiped, of course, but I remember now. Also, I can control the Tacemus, which Andrews knows, and he's probably going to tell everyone."

Ethan's request that I repeat myself was overshadowed by Jimmy's groan.

"Why would you tell him?" Jimmy said.

"Because I'm not going to lie."

"He won't understand."

"You don't know that."

"Yes, I do."

"No, you—"

"*Ahem.*" Kara coughed into her fist. "Let's go change your clothes, Ella. You're... covered in blood."

Leaving Jimmy and Ethan alone seemed a poor idea, but Kara had donned that motherly expression. Loaded down with gauze, she steered her IV over. I hesitated, but she tucked her arm through mine.

Once inside my room, we both exhaled. "Control the Tacemus?" she said. "Isn't that what Whitewash is trying to fix?"

"What *didn't* Jimmy tell you?"

Her brows rose.

"Oh."

I rummaged for a fresh shirt while she unraveled the gauze.

"What happened?" she asked.

"Andrews."

The air grew subdued after his name filled it. One floor away, Eugene Andrews still wielded the control.

Neither of us knew how to dress a wound; we tacked more gauze on and hoped that did the trick. Kara helped me into the clean shirt, her attention distracted as she fiddled with the torn-up, discarded fabric. "I'm scared for you, Ella," she whispered.

Our eyes met. We hadn't shared a look so grave since the day I returned to the academy — the day Jurstin kidnapped her. Then, I'd been fearless. Today, I'd face Andrews and discover whether I had it in me to step inside his mind.

I should've shrugged off her comment with an optimistic response. But I was done with lying. "I'm scared too."

When we returned to the clinic, worry echoing in our ears, neither of us made any visible attempt at preparation for the no-doubt unpleasant disagreement we'd walk into. Jimmy and Ethan weren't arguing, though. The two shared similar poses, chins high, with several feet between them. But the mood felt level.

"Everything... good?" I said.

Ethan contemplated Jimmy, who shrugged.

"Sheedy hasn't attacked me yet," he said.

"He's not going to," I said.

"You're so—" Jimmy started, then surveyed Kara. His remark fell away.

After a solid five seconds of staring at one another, I made the first move. We had another quarter hour before Whitewash arrived; I had no desire to spend it in awkward silence. I leaned against the sink counter and motioned for them to join. Kara and Ethan boxed me in, while Jimmy took the end spot beside Kara.

With no distractions left, I felt mounting terror. Fears attacked as one, making it impossible to break each down and address it. I squeezed my eyes shut and tried those tricks Ethan had taught me. They did nothing against my erratic pulse.

"Andrews is going to tell everyone what I can do," I mumbled.

"No," Ethan said. "It's to his benefit if Whitewash doesn't know. Otherwise, they could use his weapon against him."

"Think so?"

He nodded.

"Sheedy's right," Jimmy said. "Andrews will only mention it if it's advantageous."

He and I exchanged a meaningful glance. Jimmy had never learned for certain whether we shared the same power, but he knew the feeling of discomfort about it. Suddenly, I was glad to bear the burden for him. Being Andrews' potential son was bad enough.

I rubbed my forehead. Even without the worry of having my ability revealed, I still had to force a connection between us. If that failed, so did everyone else. The Tacemus would be forever slaves, Durgan would die still waiting for an answer about the Grifters' origins, and every future meta would be torn from their parents—all because Ella Kepler failed at what she'd been prepped for since day one.

"What if I can't?" I stepped away from the counters and spun around to face them. "What if I don't have it in me, and this has just been a giant waste of everyone's time?"

"This is exactly how he wants you to feel," Jimmy said. "Stop giving him power. He's lost and he knows it."

Kara's face mirrored mine. I sought Ethan so his confidence could cancel our worries out. He and Jimmy could muster the boldness to carry me downstairs. But Ethan's forehead was furrowed.

"What?" I said.

"I believe you can read him." That, Ethan voiced without any doubt. But that surety bled into his next statement, and it turned my veins to ice. "I also believe he wants to be read."

"Don't listen to Sheedy," Jimmy said. "He always assumes the worst."

"I could lie and tell her there's nothing to worry about, but she needs to understand her enemy." Ethan's glance, somewhat like bedside concern to a dying patient, failed to convey any encouragement. Though he did try. "You're strong enough to read him," he said. "Just be on your guard. Andrews isn't nervous, and that concerns me."

Jimmy had no chance to convince him otherwise. The intercom blared with Whitewash's arrival.

After eighteen years, it was time to crack open Eugene Andrews.

CHAPTER TWENTY-TWO

EVERY WHITEWASH MEMBER, INCLUDING the three I'd never met, crowded outside Andrews' room. They still wore their tactical gear, as if they'd jumped straight from their bikes to the hallway.

The windows of Andrews' bedroom were clear, exposing the MTA commander in his chair. He stared flatly at the hulking tower of Walker.

"... like a spectacle," Andrews was saying.

Walker chuckled. "Feeling self-conscious? I can cover the windows."

I found Durgan in the crowd and felt another jolt. He'd have to be told about Durgson. Even after Andrews, so much remained to be fixed.

One, out of sight from Andrews, noticed Jimmy, Ethan, and me coming down the hall. *Are you prepared?* he asked.

I have to be.

He does not need to be read now, Ella.

I shook my head. Now or never.

Walker peered at the glass, spotted me, and motioned me over. All eyes turned. I moved through the cluster — no, they moved for me, even Agent Cassidy. The agents cleared a path, until nothing blocked the gap between Eugene Andrews and me. I stood before him. His gaze was only one, but it burned more than the dozen pressed at my back.

Ethan was right. He didn't look nervous at all.

"Are you positive you can read me?" he asked.

"Yes," I said, wishing it felt like the truth.

"I nearly want you to be right. But I have my doubts. Have you tested your ability on everyone in Whitewash?"

"Yes."

"Again, I'm skeptical," he said, but he did not look it. Shrewd introspection glinted in the hazel eyes the same shade as Jimmy's. Andrews took a steady breath, then inspected me with the air of someone weary of waiting. "I'm afraid Operation Whitewash is going to be disappointed. I don't know how to emancipate the Tacemus."

"He's lying," Cassidy said.

"What point is there in lying to a mind-reader? Go ahead, Ms. Kepler. Read me, and tell them they've wasted men and resources on a dead-end pursuit."

He did it so effortlessly. We were the pawns and he our master. I could've been convinced he meant what he said.

Soft footsteps padded around me. When One stopped before Andrews, the latter betrayed not the shock I would've expected, but a hint of amusement.

"A Tacemus? You should know better, Ella. They can't read me."

One gave him the inaudible answer. I watched Andrews' confidence fracture, the humor flee, the uncertainty creep faster than a shadow fell from light. "You...." He turned upon me. "How many have you freed?" he murmured. Softly, as if he believed the metas polite enough not to eavesdrop.

"Cut the act, Andrews," Walker called. "Kepler's reading you."

Between Andrews and me stretched a tightrope, and on it I teetered. Then, Andrews shifted, and the rope snapped. He took in One, then Durgan beyond the window. "Is this the Grifter who wants peace?" Andrews laughed. "You're searching for a Grifter's purpose, a meaning to your existence. I will give you your answer freely, Durgan. Save Ms. Kepler the trouble." He rolled his neck and spoke. "Grifters are the collective mistake of Doctors Johansson, Fitzpatrick, and Bergström. My father always said Johansson and Fitzpatrick knew what they were doing, and it was Bergström's fanatical persuasions that ruined the project. My father was also a cynic, so his judgments leave much to be desired." His expression soured.

He mentioned a father, which no meta had the luxury of, but I disregarded it for now. "Collective mistake?" I said.

"Yes. Bioengineering. Poorly done, in this case. Grifters were intended to be the first physically strong metahumans in centuries; the abilities associated with the gene had gone dormant. Come late seventeenth century, three doctors found themselves on the cusp of scientific discovery. Our three good doctors exploited the genetic discoveries of another and decided to apply them to latent metahumans. Test group nine proved viable, though so deformed that the project was terminated, and the subjects to be discarded. Dr. Bergström took them away for disposal. As to what happened next—well, we may look to your ally. Centuries later, Grifters are thriving, and Bergström is very much dead."

Andrews' explanation found itself rebounding in a choked silence. He took this with a hint of satisfaction. He'd stunned us, and he knew it. Eventually, reactions hissed like escaped steam.

Months ago, I'd read a library book at the academy written by Eugene Andrews—a name that had meant nothing at the time. That Eugene, assuredly a previous MTA commander, wrote a history about the origin of Grifters. He'd claimed they were deformed metas born of ill mothers. These accidental creatures were hardly human, devoid of all compassion and reason.

That Eugene, same as the one in front of me, must've known the truth. And he'd blatantly *lied*.

"I've read Bergström's work," came Dr. Saini's voice.

I turned, too sick to continue staring into Andrews' face.

Saini stood outside the window and seemed, alongside half of Whitewash, ready to barrel her way inside. "He wouldn't have discarded living subjects, particularly life *he* created. The only evidence for your theory can be found in textbooks produced by the MTA."

"You're forgetting Bergström supported the project," Andrews said.

"Initially, but he was devoutly moral. He wouldn't have understood the consequences."

I forced myself to hunt for Durgan amid the army. His openly pained expression fell on Andrews. *I'm sorry,* I told him. Then, stirred by a slosh of anger, I swiveled back to Andrews. "So the MTA created Grifters, then tried to destroy them. Hundreds of years later, we're still trying to kill them—and why, because they're 'deformed'?"

"Because Grifters should never have existed. Some may be civilized, but most are barbaric. It isn't a lie to tell metas they're monsters, Ella. Consider what Chron did to Kara, to you."

"That makes sense. One Grifter is evil, so we should kill all of them."

"It is better for the wellbeing of society that Grifters disappear. But that was the MTA's aim when Grifters were a minor threat. We can't launch a full-scale attack on every Grifter territory. They've encroached too much upon civilian life. Therefore, we keep them at bay. If Grifters are allowed to survive, they will do so in anonymity."

"Is that what you tell Chron whenever you meet? 'Stay quiet and we won't kill you'?"

The assured smoothness that had conducted his behavior lost strength. "Now," Andrews said quietly, "how do you know about that?"

"We know you've been giving Chron MTA tech," Walker said. "What's he given you in exchange?"

Andrews said nothing.

"You're working with Chron," I said, "who's obviously intelligent, and you still think he's an animal?"

An odd hesitance tested his words before he set them free. "Even a dog can learn how to sit."

The shell encasing him cracked, giving way to Eugene Andrews' core. I wished he'd glue the mask back on. A man who could compare Grifters to dogs had little humanity himself.

"Speaking of Chron...." Andrews touched the back of his shirt collar. "You'll want to scan me, Dr. Saini. He injected something into my skin. A tracker, I assume."

My pulse dropped.

"What?" cried Cassidy.

The door swung open. Saini's caramel eyes shone of anger. They zeroed in on something and froze. She rushed forward and gripped the back of Andrews' head, exposing the skin beneath his collar. Her laser pen flew from her pocket; she passed its invisible light onto Andrews' neck and said, "He's right."

A pocket knife spun from the doorway to Saini's outstretched hand. "Cut it out," Walker said.

She flipped open the blade, angling Andrews' chin toward his chest.

"I wonder, Dr. Saini," he said, "do your associates realize you're a pro—"

Saini dug the blade, and Andrews went rigid. His head shot up, jerking against the knife. The veins in his eyes spread. Then he stilled. His head lolled sideways, and his shoulders went stagnant.

Saini held a bloody knife. Above her other hand floated a microchip, whose spindly wires touched Andrews' neck like claws. Both knife and chip plummeted to the floor as she gripped Andrews' shoulders and gaped over his slacken face. "Lee!" she shouted.

I stared at the scene, refuting the evidence—the *absence* of evidence. The absence of a heartbeat.

Her young assistant crashed into the room and skidded, on his knees, to the chair. I stepped back, feeling eerily detached as Lee and Saini unbound Andrews and lay him flat. Saini beat his chest, surely not enough times before she stopped, her head drooped.

"He's dead."

PART II

SAECULORUM

CHAPTER TWENTY-THREE

THIS PROCLAMATION MET MORE silence and one that seemed unwilling to end. Disbelief fogged my mind like condensation clinging to a mirror. I replayed the final scene. Had Saini severed an artery, or had the chip somehow killed him?

"How?" Walker said, and his voice neared dull.

"Chron must have installed a kill switch in the chip," Saini said.

I searched for Jimmy. No matter how much he hated Andrews, the man was likely his father.

Had been his father.

At first glance, Jimmy was nowhere in sight. When I stood, I saw him against the wall of the hallway, doubled over and gripping his head as if it'd combust if he let go. His face lay hidden, but anguish radiated off his posture. Despite everything, he mourned, bent over in evident pain. No one noticed him but me and One, who steadied Jimmy by his shoulder. The rest had moved forward, gaping through the window, leaving Jimmy a strangled, isolated figure in the background — and One, the silent Tacemus offering comfort only Jimmy could hear.

WE GATHERED AROUND THE conference table, more bodies than chairs, but most probably felt like standing, anyway. Durgan had returned to his family, not before I'd pulled him aside to tell him about Durgson. His demeanor had been bleak since Andrews' speech; I hated tacking on more pain.

"I tried to stop him, Durgan."

A long moment passed before he lifted his head. "My son cannot be persuaded. Stubborn, like his mother." Durgan then excused himself.

Jimmy had disappeared outside. He'd be battling enormous conflict, and I wanted to help — but I'd learned that sometimes people needed space, especially from a mind-reader.

We kept mostly quiet. What could be said? Andrews had died to some fluke of technology. Yes, Chron would be unable to track us, but what was "us" now, without a goal? Eighteen years of planning snuffed out in an instant, swift and merciless.

The cadets stayed mute. Ethan kept looking to Andrews' room out of sight. One seemed detached. He'd watched the senior Eugene Andrews die, and now another.

Dr. Saini, sitting mutely at Walker's left, failed to keep the flinches of guilt at bay. Dozens of reassurances had followed her from Andrews' room to here, and she'd nodded and told us she didn't blame herself, but still she randomly grit her teeth against an invisible torment. Walker accepted full responsibility. He'd tossed Saini the knife and told her to cut the tracker out; he'd permit no accusations to fly her direction.

"Explain again," Cassidy asked Saini, "how you saw the tracker?"

"That's irrelevant," Walker said. "We're lucky she removed it before Chron found us."

"It's not irrelevant. The tracker was beneath his skin. Invisible. For all we know, Andrews has a bomb implanted and needs a full-body scan."

Seats shifted, but Dr. Saini quietly said, "He doesn't have an internal bomb."

"How do you know?" Cassidy asked.

"Because I would have seen it."

"How?"

"Because I'm a protean."

My eyes, absently observing the conversation, widened.

"You too?" Cassidy shot from her chair. "How many proteans are in Whitewash?"

"I humbly admit that I am not a protean," Dom Bist said with his hand high.

"You're probably lying. Kepler, read everyone here and tell us —"

"Sit down, Cassidy." Walker rose. Unlike half the table, he appeared unfazed by this information. I had an inkling he'd already known — he and Dr. Lee, who was busy hiding behind a book.

"I am not a protean," Walker said, "and I don't care if anyone else is. So long as you don't use your ability to sabotage our plans, you're welcome in Whitewash."

Cassidy remained standing. "You're *not* a protean?"

"Wait," said a woman, one of the unfamiliar Whitewash members, "you thought Walker was a protean?"

"Wouldn't put it past him," said the man next to her.

"What exactly is your ability?" Agent Porter asked Saini.

She sighed at Walker, whose brows went up. After some internal probing, she said, "Civilians register a small frequency on the electromagnetic spectrum. Metas, a bit more. I detect x-ray, ultraviolet, and infrared wavelengths. This means I can see things others can't, in proper lighting."

"You have x-ray vision?" I said.

"No, I have x-ray *detection*."

Porter nodded. "Neat."

"This is *not* neat," Cassidy said. "It's an invasion of privacy!"

"Kepler can read minds," Porter said, so bluntly that it stumped Cassidy into silence, and she sat.

Saini couldn't have chosen a better time to reveal her secret; no one cared too much about it in the grand scheme of things. Gradually, the conversation shifted back to Andrews. At least the MTA now had the potential to elect a better ruler, though Amy Lane quickly reminded us that Andrews always chose his successor. Whoever would take the reins next had already been decided.

When Jimmy finally came in, we'd run through enough theories to border on conspiratorial. In truth, none of us had any idea what would happen next. Jimmy joined a group more subdued than the one he'd left. He leaned against the wall behind me, which kept him invisible, unless I felt like craning my head. I'd caught his expression during his walk over, though it betrayed nothing. He'd lost the clenching anguish in exchange for something unreadable, as blank as a Tacemus.

Are you okay? I'd asked.

He'd nodded right before stepping out of sight.

The *ping* of an electronic notification sounded. Amy Lane, whose sandy hair formed a frayed ponytail, pulled a grid from her jacket's inner pocket. Her eyes widened as she read the screen. A nub of hair found its way into her mouth, and she chewed without seeming aware we all watched her. "Rodriguez says she received an email from Andrews twenty minutes ago. Apparently, all academy leaders did."

"You accidentally said 'Andrews,'" Dom said, frowning.

"It wasn't... an accident. She forwarded the email." Amy cleared her throat. "'To all: If you are receiving this email, it means my Internal Vitals Biometric has deactivated. This can only happen as the result of my death.'" Amy lifted her head. "Wait—"

"He had another chip embedded in his wrist bone," Saini said. Earnest intrigue overtook her former guilt. "It must have been an IVB."

Cassidy *tsk*'d and rolled her eyes.

Amy continued. "'Upon the commander's death, the successor must be immediately instated. He will carry on the legacy of Eugene Andrews and preserve the Metahuman Training Academy's perpetual ideals. My choice of successor may seem unexpected, but it is to be enforced without question. I trust you all will abide by my wish for the well-being of the MTA.

"'For my successor, I choose....'" Here Amy paused, mouth stuck open. In unison, we leaned forward, as if our collective anxiety could summon the answer faster. Amy gawked at her grid a moment longer, then looked up. "William Banks?"

One by one, heads redirected to the wall behind me. I was the slowest to react, uncertain who William Banks was before memory hit.

"Read that again, Amy," Dom said. "I must've misheard."

"It says William Banks. Then it lists his ID number. Eight-seven-three-three-two-nine. Is that yours, Banks?"

I turned around. Jimmy appeared neither shocked nor thrilled by this news but hid beneath the empty expression he'd carried in from outside. "Yes," he murmured. His attention rested on a speck in space.

Andrews' choice made sense—and yet it didn't. He'd certainly been arrogant enough to assign a successor from his bloodline, but Andrews had been far more practical. If he'd wanted to pick a young, male successor, Ethan made a better fit than Jimmy, who had given up even the responsibility of leading Whitewash.

"Well." Cassidy sighed and crossed her arms. "There's no point pretending to be blind anymore. We never said anything to your face, Banks, but all of us have thought for years you look like Andrews. This email confirms it. Congratulations, you're the son of a snake."

An awkward film covered the air. None of Whitewash's veteran members clamored to deny Cassidy's statement. McFarland gaped. Ethan had donned a frown as soon as he'd taken a seat. Jimmy, however, continued to look disinterested.

Dom seemed unaffected by the discomfort. "You could have said that more politely, Miranda."

"I don't have the energy for civility right now," she muttered.

"His son?" McFarland said.

"Don't tell me you never noticed the similarities," Cassidy said. "Banks is a spitting image. He's either his son or his brother."

"Could be a cousin twice removed," Dom said.

"No, definitely thrice removed," Hina Akamu said.

"You're probably right, Hina."

Walker rubbed his mustache. "You're quiet, Banks. What are your thoughts?"

After staring down the invisible speck that had enraptured him, Jimmy's focus drifted to Walker. "Yes. He was my father."

A pang went through my chest. He'd never admitted to it before; but, once outed, maybe he figured denial would come across as petty.

Jimmy dipped his head, solemn and polite. "Finish the email, Amy."

My brows drew together. He rarely used *my* first name.

Amy twisted a clump of hair. "'Banks is currently AWOL, though I have full confidence he will adapt to his new position without difficulty. Wait for him to contact you. This should take place within twenty-four hours of my death. Once he has made contact, preparations for his installment should begin immediately. Whatever questions you may have, he will answer.

"'As always, I thank you for your service to the MTA. In perpetuum, Eugene Andrews.'" She set the grid down. It made a firm clack on the table.

"Something's not right here," Cassidy said.

Dom lifted a finger. "It could be—though perhaps I walk out on a tree limb—you're confused that Andrews appointed a factionless, undisciplined young graduate as his successor."

"Obviously, you dolt!" Cassidy flung a pen at his head. "The MTA doesn't practice nepotism."

"I thought Andrews hated Banks," Hina said, stroking her chin. "It *is* odd."

"You're all ignoring the lovely note of positivity in this strange turn of events," Dom said, absently sticking the pen into his thick poof of curls. "Banks—if we accept the email as fact—is now in charge of the MTA. Which means, my dear chaps, *Whitewash* is in charge of the MTA."

It seemed a gesture of comic relief, but Dom looked earnest. By putting Jimmy in charge, Andrews had literally handed Whitewash the keys to the MTA, so ridiculously convenient a move it had to be a trap.

Beside me, Ethan seemed well on his way toward premature wrinkling. ... *Leader assigned Banks CO to test his leadership... Banks failed... Leader would never place him in charge of the MTA.* Ethan straightened, letting his hands fall to the armrests. "Andrews knew Banks was in Whitewash. This wasn't a sentimental move. He wanted us to get overconfident. Lower our guard."

"I agree," Walker said. "We can't trust it."

"But the other leaders will," Amy said, "even if we don't. This is the tradition of the MTA. The commander always appoints his successor."

"Can the leaders vote him out?" I asked.

"No. It's not a democracy. Andrews was once Michael Bailey, a twenty-nine-year-old mechanic with little leadership experience. When the former commander chose him, he immediately quit his work and moved to Georgia. The leaders will expect Banks to do the same."

I glanced at One, who'd been there to receive the new Andrews. One was busy studying Jimmy.

"Michael Bailey wasn't rogue," Dr. Saini said. "It goes against the MTA's best interest to appoint Banks."

"Not to their knowledge." Jimmy, as if by the nature of his new title, commanded the room's attention. His detachment had begun solidifying into the barest hint of confidence. "The MTA leaders— excluding the ones Amy has approached—are ignorant of Whitewash. Outside of Agent Chang and a few others, Andrews never discussed it. Doing so would've admitted he had a problem he couldn't deal with."

"How do you know that?" Dr. Saini asked.

"Because I understand how he operates." Jimmy left his wall perch and strode to the head of the table. Walker raised his brows but let him speak. "When Andrews appointed me CO, he told me I'd one day be MTA commander. I ignored him. And here we are. It *was* a sentimental move, but not toward me. Andrews loved himself more than anyone, and he thought his DNA was potent enough to override whatever defects he found in me. He thought, when the time came, I'd accept this role because... because I'm an Andrews." A flutter of discomfort slipped around his budding assurance, but Jimmy shut his eyes and exhaled. When he surveyed us again, the discomfort had vanished. "He doesn't want me leading—he wants him*self* leading, through me. Andrews expects me to follow in his footsteps, but obviously he's wrong. I won't be anything like him."

An odd picture overlaid my thoughts. Jimmy stood before an audience of metas, not irritated or tossed about by emotion, but unwavering. And they *listened*. Maybe this was the Jimmy he'd always denied—a leader, sure of himself and willing to prove it. Andrews had been the weed strangling Jimmy's growth. Now, his roots could spread.

One, the Whitewash member deserving of the most input, gave none. He continued examining Jimmy, though it mattered little. He couldn't read Jimmy any more than the Tacemus could read Andrews.

"What of the Tacemus?" one of the unfamiliar Whitewash members said. "Could it be that Banks now controls them?"

"Possibly," Saini answered. "Banks was a poor choice, but perhaps Andrews' *only* choice. The ability could be hereditary."

I peeked at Jimmy. *Should I tell them about me?* I said.

His head shook a fraction.

"I don't know," Amy said. She'd studied the email enough times to have it memorized, but again she pulled the grid to her face and searched. "Andrews doesn't mention the Tacemus."

"Maybe the connection is broken," Saini said to Walker, "and Andrews was unable to transfer his ability, or however it might work."

"Or," Cassidy said, "Banks is the only one controlling the Tacemus now. Either way, we win."

Words rose in my throat, fast and sour as bile. Jimmy wanted me to keep my ability from Whitewash. So did One. But I couldn't hide this forever. *I have to tell them,* I said to One.

Do what you feel is right, One answered. He was so absorbed by Jimmy, I wondered if he followed my meaning.

Ethan? I said. *Should I tell Whitewash I can control the Tacemus?*

I think... tell Walker. Not now. Privately.

I relaxed. It may have been best to conceal it before, but the time for a revelation had come, especially if I was the Tacemus' only master.

"None of us know what will happen," Jimmy said. "We'll play it by ear."

Even Walker nodded. Jimmy was in charge now.

I'd have to get used to that.

CHAPTER TWENTY-FOUR

THE AIR AT WHITEWASH'S Virginia base hung ripe with trepidation, but most potent was a sense of vanishing time. Assuming leadership of the MTA, effortlessly as that change of command had arrived, took planning, and metas weren't known to skip conferences. Most of the meetings were exclusive. All of them involved Jimmy, Amy, and Walker, who found additional opinions—namely Cassidy's—a nuisance, and ordered everyone elsewhere while the three of them took up Andrews' former room.

That night, Ethan and I waited for their meeting to finish. Dr. Saini waited with us; I wanted her present for this conversation. Her phone beeped with a notification a little after midnight. "They've finished," she said, standing with her mug of tea. One, Jimmy, and Amy exited the galley a moment later.

Before I could catch Jimmy's eye, he moved closer to Amy. "Can I see the speech again?" he asked. They walked away in conversation.

I recognized his avoidance tactics and couldn't help feeling annoyed, a reaction my empathy tried overriding. Of course Jimmy felt confused, and clearly wanted alone time, but when would he learn the purpose of friends? At least he tolerated One's presence.

A few hours after the death, Jimmy had asked to bury the body. Walker felt uncomfortable with the idea, but Saini convinced him. Jimmy and One took Andrews to the beach. No one else had cared to accompany them. I'd asked, but Jimmy requested privacy, even from Kara.

How is he doing? I asked One now.

Not well, Ella.

Should I corner him or something?

I do not understand the question.

You know, get him alone for a private —

"Shall we, Ella?" Saini said.

Meeting in Andrews' room, where hours before his dead body had lain, put me ill at ease. But we had nowhere else for privacy.

Chairs and a square table cluttered with papers had been moved into the room. Walker, massaging his neck, gestured the chairs and said, "What is it, Kepler?"

I remained standing. It wasn't intimidation holding me back but the imagined disgust from Walker. I reminded myself that he could handle proteans and telepathy. This was simply an extreme version of what he'd already allowed into Whitewash. Right?

I focused on Saini. "When Andrews and I were in novum last year, he brought a Tacemus to read me. I told the Tacemus to stop. And he listened. Andrews realized that... I can control the Tacemus too. He knew the whole time. So do One and Jim—Banks."

Like a jaw steadily dropping, her mug had lowered, until it clunked on the table. Dr. Saini wore a shrewd interest that lightened the amber flecks of her eyes.

"Integer knows?" Walker said. He shared none of Saini's scientific giddiness, but he wasn't ripping out his mustache, either.

"Yeah," I said.

"Why keep it from us?" Saini asked.

"Because...." I felt naked beneath her gaze. Did I have to unveil myself even further? Saini's attention told me yes, I did. "I didn't want to admit that I can do the same thing we hated Andrews for."

"We didn't hate him because of his potential, Ella. We didn't hate *him* at all. We hated what he did." Her mug scooted aside, clearing a path for her elbows. Eagerness played at her mouth. "You are the most fascinating protean I've encountered."

"It's probably why the old Andrews was there when I was born," I said.

"We drew the same conclusion, regarding your telepathy, though it doesn't quite make sense. The gene is discernable, but not the ability. He had no way of knowing what you could do. And yet, as far as we know, you're the only metahuman whose birth warranted a visit from the MTA commander."

"He doesn't visit other proteans?"

"Not that we've observed," she said, and I felt an Ethan-like frown emerging. Walker's concerned energy distracted me; he folded his arms and began pacing.

"If Banks has the power to control the Tacemus, he'll be reluctant to admit it. I guarantee he'll lie. Likely for the same reason he never told us about you. He's afraid we'll want to control them. But he wants them free, so he'll do what it takes. We might wake up one morning to search-and-rescue orders for a thousand roaming Tacemus. So we wait, see what Banks does. If it's apparent he doesn't have the control, it'll be your turn. Might be you can force them into freedom."

"It won't be that simple," Saini said.

I shook my head. "I can't just order them free. One would hate that."

"Oh, would he?" Walker muttered. "He conceals valuable intel, yet he thinks he has the right—"

"Agent Walker," Saini said calmly.

He huffed, letting his focus drift to Ethan. "Sheedy twist you into telling us?"

"No," Ethan said.

"Now that Banks is commander, we figured it was a good time," I added.

"Smart move," Walker said. "Don't trust anyone else with this information. There are plenty who'd do unspeakable things to access your power."

"I'm sure that's exactly what occurred to One," Saini said, not meeting Walker's eye while an amused smile played around her mouth.

That stumped him for a moment. Saini's smile grew. Somehow, she was the only one in Whitewash who could get away with teasing Walker.

Once he got over his annoyance, Walker shook his head. "A mind-reader with an army of obedient wipers at her command. You're a fearsome thing to behold, Kepler. We're blasted lucky you're on our side."

I never thought I'd see the day when Walker called me fearsome.

ONE, WALKER, JIMMY, AND AMY left in the afternoon. Things were hectic up until their departure, giving us zero time to chat. I managed to snag Jimmy on the way to the hangar. Walker fretted about time constraints, but Jimmy waved him and Amy forward, though One lingered. Jimmy seemed only half present during our walk along the sand dunes.

"I know I've been distant," he said. "It's because I don't want you reading me, analyzing my thoughts about Andrews."

"I figured. But I wouldn't do that, Jimmy."

"I'm sure it was tempting."

"Not really."

"Then... I'm sorry."

"Wow. That's the fastest you've ever apologized." Playfully, I bumped him.

His smile looked tighter than a cord.

"Did you say bye to Kara?" I asked.

"No. She...." His control faltered. I could see him fighting it, trying to force a neutral expression and failing miserably. "I need to leave," he said quickly. "Bye, Ella. Come on, One."

One inclined his head to me.

Make sure he's okay, I said.

Yes, Ella. One followed after Jimmy with no more farewell than that. He was acting distant, too.

I frowned after their retreating figures. This felt wrong. Whitewash was meant to have won, yet this stank of the beginning of a battle.

"Jimmy?" I called. "You don't have to accept this position."

He grew taut, from his neck to curled fingers. "Yes, I do."

"But it's a lot to handle."

"I'll survive." Jimmy grew a sardonic simper painfully reminiscent of Andrews. Then, after a nod, he turned.

Even after the jungle brush swallowed them up and the roar of engines faded to the distant crash of ocean waves, I stood there, wishing Eugene Andrews were still alive.

SINCE WHITEWASH NO LONGER worried about Andrews targeting them, its members resumed former duties. Saini and Lee to their medical research, the agents to their safe houses, Dom Bist and Arthur Finch back to England — where, I discovered, the MTA's original headquarters operated. When I asked why he didn't have an accent, he gave a simple answer: "Because we're not civilians, though it is *quite* fun to pretend."

One by one, Whitewash left, until six cadets, three Grifters, and one civilian remained. Base felt small without the bustle.

Kara and Ethan had an actual, formal introduction, accompanied by James and Bridget. James, because he took every chance to converse with Kara, and Bridget because she went wherever James did, comfortable as a shadow.

"I'd pictured you as a redhead," Kara said once she and Ethan finished shaking hands.

"Why?" Ethan said.

"Because you remind me of Ella."

"First," I said, "my hair isn't red. Second, Ethan reminds me of *you*, so that can't work."

"*Me?*"

"What color do you call it?" James asked, touching his head.

"Red-brown," Ethan answered.

"Otherwise known as 'red,'" Kara added.

I automatically turned to Jimmy. This seemed the sort of thing he'd side with Kara on. But of course he'd left.

The day of his inauguration, it took us a frustrating thirty minutes to configure the projector. McFarland and Vires handled most of the set-up, an offer that filled Kara and me with trepidation.

"The manual instructs that this cable—"

"I don't need the manual," Vires interrupted. "This process is straight-forward."

"If that were the case," McFarland said, "the cable would be in the correct spot and not still in your hands."

"Only because your nagging—"

"*Por favor!*" James dug his fingertips into his hair. The cable soared out of Vires' hands and writhed, like a worm, on the floor. "Will you two ever stop bickering? It's driving me mad. McFarland, he loves you but he's too vain to admit it. Vires, she... she would love you if you weren't so... so pigheaded." James went red as his hair. Beneath his discomfort, he looked reluctant. He kept himself angled away from McFarland, and when the awkward shroud grew too thick, he strode the long way around the table to wrench open the galley door. There Ethan stood, tucking his phone into his belt.

"*Disculpe,*" James mumbled, squeezing past Ethan until he disappeared.

"Agent Walker said everything is on schedule," Ethan spoke after him. When James failed to reappear, Ethan frowned at us. "Is something wrong?"

Vires was melting the projection screen with his fieriest glower and refused to acknowledge anything, especially McFarland, who gaped at him and, for once, ignored her former CO.

"We're good," I blurted.

Glad James said something, Kara was thinking. *Wasn't sure how much more I could take.*

Yeah, but poor James.

Why poor James?

I kept that explanation to myself. Sometimes I forgot my telepathy gave me answers that others seldom thought to ask.

The video footage streamed on a private MTA channel, the only one programmed at base. Cadets never watched television; the channel was for graduates who cared about staying on top of MTA events. The election of a twenty-two-year-old commander would draw even the most uninvolved viewer.

We moved to the table. James slunk back inside and took a seat far from McFarland and Vires, neither of whom made any sign they'd seen him.

A metal thunk along the stairs told me Durgan approached. With Walker gone and a handful of young adults for company, Durgan had mostly stayed in his room with Ly and Tam. The latter two had taken the news of Durgson harder than their father. Ly's open-channel, telepathic protests had reached my ears and continued long past Durgan's reassurance that all would be well. Whenever the Grifters did emerge, Ly unhappily dragged her little brother along. Tam had perked up whenever he saw Agent Porter, but now even he had come and gone.

"Papa...." Ly rushed after Durgan, who shook his head. He gave her a silent answer, to which Ly's shoulders drooped. Slowly, she returned to her room. Durgan lingered on the stairs, watching her depart. After, he sat at the foot of the table. Though the cadets never made outright comments, Durgan was smart enough to recognize that these metas hadn't adapted to the Grifters' presence as easily as older Whitewash members had. Other than myself, Kara was the only one to speak directly to him. James had made a few half-hearted attempts, and Ethan had made eye contact with him once, but Vires refused to be bothered, McFarland failed to hide her discomfort, and Bridget looked ready to pass out every time Durgan neared.

The live video stream began with an image of the MTA's logo. Its outer shape had sixteen points — a "hexadecagon," according to James. Within it was a pale brown trim, a series of strokes framing the central logo, which I first mistook for some ancient hieroglyphic before I recognized the M, T, and A that formed the shape. The letters, stacked over one another, would probably be indecipherable to anyone not looking for them.

After the logo faded, a stage came into view. The camera was positioned at the back of the room, pointed down over several rows. The seats, set at angles as if in a theater, faced the stage. A flag with the

MTA's logo hung from a podium, the stage's only prop. Men and women in suits gradually filled the auditorium over a fifteen minutes punctuated by soft chatter and the creak of furniture.

Once nearly every seat had a body and a formal silence permeated through the projector screen, figures stepped from the invisible backstage. First came Agents Walker and Chang, followed by two agents I recognized and one completely new to me. Amy Lane came next, dressed in a collared shirt tucked into her gray skirt. She looked nervous enough to faint; but, as her sandy hair was woven into a bun, she couldn't chew the ends. They formed a line at the front of the stage, attention cast behind them. When Jimmy strode into view, a whip seemed to snap every audience member into high alert. Bridget gasped.

"Unbelievable," James murmured. "He looks just like him."

Jimmy wore a black suit I was fairly certain Andrews had once donned. His shirt was white and the tie the same beige color from the MTA logo. As he stepped to the podium and straightened the flagpole, the intentionality behind the matching colors grew clear.

"There's no way we can pretend they're not related," I said.

Ethan scrutinized the screen as if expecting someone to launch a bomb at Jimmy. He opened his mouth. Then, clapping began.

The audience carried a brief welcome, each clap exactly in sync. They stopped after five seconds.

"Thank you." Jimmy made as if to touch his tie knot, then dropped his hand inside his blazer. He withdrew a grid and spent some seconds propping it against the stand.

Hanging in the background, easy to miss, stood One. I knew it was him, because One was meant to stay by Jimmy's side.

We'd all memorized Jimmy's speech word for word. Before leaving, Whitewash crafted the role Jimmy would play. The academy leaders— not to mention the entire MTA—would be suspicious of Andrews' choice. Jimmy's age, lack of experience, and undisciplined behavior made him a terrible candidate for commander of the MTA. To admit that Andrews was motivated solely by his relationship to Jimmy would raise another red flag; therefore, we'd keep that secret under wraps.

Amy wrote his acceptance speech. She and Walker created his entire persona: a young commander, true, but one who couldn't be manipulated. We figured plenty of metas would be itching to worm their way into Jimmy's head. By presenting him as firm and one-hundred percent dedicated to the MTA's cause, he'd seem much less moldable.

Of Operation Whitewash, he'd make no mention. A few agents, including Chang, knew we existed, and that Walker was its head and Jimmy its member. Those agents needed some convincing and were the reason Jimmy needed to appear unwavering.

"He can't upturn the entire infrastructure on his first day," Walker had said. "There'd be a coup. We'll work subtly. Convince the likes of Chang that Banks won't make any changes, but he will. Slowly."

We'd prepare ourselves for the eventual showdown, once Whitewash made its presence known. In the meantime, the MTA would be run by Whitewash's original leaders: an independent Tacemus united with a rebellious meta willing to break the mold.

After a motionless stare at his speech, Jimmy eyed the camera. "I can imagine those of you watching this—either here or abroad—are confused. Why did Eugene Andrews elect such a young, inexperienced successor? To that question, I phrase another: Why do we have such little faith in our youth? Andrews understood that cadets make up twenty percent of our population and provide incalculable aid in the war against Grifters."

I checked Durgan. Not once had he spoken of what Andrews had revealed about Grifters. The MTA had not only engineered them; it had tried destroying them, then spent the next couple hundred years covering its tracks. Grifters had just as much claim to the MTA as metas did. They *were* metas. That couldn't have been the answer Durgan had wanted. The weight of it shadowed his expression.

"Without our young metas," Jimmy continued, "the MTA could never flourish. We are not a body of decay, but of vitality. The youth give the MTA its stamina, and I will do the same.

"As to my seeming lack of experience, my record says otherwise. I was commanding officer my final year at the academy. Prior to that, I was a student instructor and commanding general on a dozen missions. Eugene Andrews recognized this, and that is why, when he appointed me CO, he told me I would one day stand before you."

Heads turned, and Jimmy spoke louder. "Yes, I knew I would be here, ready and willing to continue the MTA's legacy. I proved myself in school, and I will prove myself to my staff. And so, why did Eugene Andrews elect such a young, inexperienced successor? The answer is simple: he knew what he was doing. If you doubt that, perhaps you should reconsider your loyalty to the MTA." He held the camera's gaze, every bit the unyielding commander he needed to portray.

"To the matter of appointments," Jimmy said. "My first officers remain the same: Agents Chang, Walker, Langley, Graham, and Rand. All academy leaders also retain their titles, for the time being. To cover my predecessor's former post at academy four, I appoint Amy Lane. I will now swear her in."

Amy edged forward. Sweat, dancing across her forehead, shone in the spotlight. Jimmy began an introduction of her strengths.

"If I hadn't known that was Banks, I'd guess it was Sheedy," James said.

"*What?*" I said.

"Because he's a good leader," James quickly added. "Does anyone else agree?" He scanned Kara and Bridget with the desperation of a fighter searching for his second. Ethan returned his glance with bemusement.

"He's behaving exactly as he always has," Vires said. "Banks is an actor. He played the role of indifferent cadet, and now he's playing the opposite."

I glanced at Kara. Regardless of her lack of memory, mine had been sufficient to convince her she'd cared about Jimmy, and he'd cared in return. She'd taken to my memories as if she remembered every detail.

Presently, her attention zeroed in on the projection. *Actor…* she was thinking.

I turned away and gave her musings the freedom to unfold.

AFTER JIMMY'S SWEARING IN, I dragged Kara and Ethan outside before he sought out McFarland for a sparring match. Since Andrews' death, Ethan had doubled down on the exercising. We said little about it, and we didn't have to. Ethan knew I could read him, inside and out.

Dusk came late, but as summer drew closer to autumn, daylight hours had begun shedding. Above the expanse of the ocean, the glow seemed to stay forever. We trudged down the beach, Kara and Ethan steering the conversation while I retreated to my latest ponderings.

Understandably, Whitewash's concerns centered around Jimmy. A lot of fires needed putting out, and we only had so many allies. We couldn't free the Tacemus amid instability; we had to time this right. That meant no one currently thought much about the Tacemus — except me. I couldn't be the only one. But Whitewash's Integer was out of range, evidently. Whenever I tried communicating with him, I hit a wall of static.

"Ella?" Kara called. She and Ethan stood in the sand, several yards uphill, which meant....

I looked down. Water sloshed around my shins, soaking my boots. I'd walked right into the ocean and hadn't noticed.

"Thanks for telling me," I said, wading out.

"We wanted to see how deep you'd get," Kara said.

"You need to learn how to multitask," Ethan added.

"We tried. At SPO-10." I waved a hand. "Never mind, you don't remember. I'm trying to reach One. I've *been* trying, and all I get is static. Maybe he's too far away?"

"Why do you need to talk to him?" Ethan asked.

"Because everyone's so focused on smoothing over Jimmy's inauguration, and no one's doing anything about the Tacemus. We still don't know if he can control them."

"Agent Walker would have told us if that were the case."

Perhaps not. Walker might not have a clue. In his last update, he'd told Ethan that Jimmy had begun pulling Tacemus from academies, freeing them from MTA duties one step at a time. "Which blatantly disregards the concept of laying low," Walker had grumbled, "though I don't know why I'm surprised." According to Walker, there was no clarity on whether anyone else had control over the Tacemus. I had an inkling Jimmy was too afraid to test it out. I felt tempted to ask, but he'd never been a fan of my voice in his head.

"Look," I said, "I didn't read Andrews—"

"You didn't fail," Ethan said.

"Okay, but I still didn't read him, and... if I *am* the only one left who can control them, I need to figure out how to fix this."

"What if you can't? What if there's nothing you can do?" Ethan asked the tough questions because a soldier had to consider every outcome.

I, on the other hand, refused to see any solution except the one where I kept my promise. That was the behavior of a soldier too, right? "Then I'll just have to magically develop another protean ability," I said.

"Maybe Ethan's a protean," Kara said with a smile.

"I'm not," he said. "Agent Walker searched for my name in the lab."

"Did you see any other familiar names?"

He betrayed himself by letting his mouth open a sliver before he closed it. Ethan had, but he'd never divulge another's secret.

"He won't tell us," I said.

"You could always read him," Kara teased.

"No thank you. He'd lecture me for —"

"Sheedy!"

Dashing across the sand, McFarland waved for our attention, her alarm clear in the fading sunlight. Panic brightened her eyes, and she called, "There's been an air raid on Dewey National Forest. Chron's territory… it's completely gone."

CHAPTER TWENTY-FIVE

WE DIDN'T BOTHER SITTING. The seven of us huddled around the projection screen, where James' grid broadcast a local news channel. A reporter spoke over helicopter footage of angry clouds of orange striking through the evening glow.

"... national parks around the US are closing as fear of terrorism spreads. While no casualties have been reported, a strike at the heart of the beloved Dewey National Forest will cause catastrophic ecological damage, destroying the homes of formerly peaceful wildlife. Fire Marshal Kevin Monroe is here to weigh in on the growing wildfire crisis. Fire Marshal, how far do you think these fires will spread?"

None of us spoke until the news went to a commercial break. Even then, we took a moment.

"Turn this off." Ethan glanced toward the second floor. I knew why. The truth pulled at me like stitches ripping apart.

Durgson had stayed behind.

I bit my knuckle—fully healed now and free of gloves—as James unplugged his grid from the projector. Who had led Durgson into Chron's? The same person who'd have to tell Durgan that someone had just dropped missiles on his son.

"What are the chances Durgson escaped?" Bridget whispered.

"Slim to none," Vires said.

My vision went foggy. Kara touched my shoulder.

"An attack that deliberate... it must have been the MTA," McFarland said.

"Why?" I said croakily, then cleared my throat. "No one knew Chron was there."

"Except Whitewash," James said.

Seven grave stares shared unity.

"I'll call Agent Walker." Ethan headed for the stairs, his phone already glowing.

"Stay, Sheedy," Vires said. "You're not CO. Walker's not Leader."

Ethan stilled with a foot on its way toward the stair. At the academy, he'd handled emergency conversations privately with Andrews. Walking away had been a knee-jerk reaction. Ethan nodded and stayed put. Six rings went by with no answer from Walker.

Vires turned the projector on again, though he was considerate enough to mute the volume. The news channels streamed a variation of the same crisis: national forest destroyed, terrorists suspected. Ethan dialed Walker again.

"Walker's not going to tell us anything we haven't learned," Vires said after Ethan left a voicemail.

"He—"

A buzzing phone interrupted. "Sir," Ethan said, setting Walker on speakerphone; Vires couldn't complain about that.

"What airstrike?" Walker blared.

"Civilian news reported it. Chron's territory has been attacked."

"When?"

"An hour ago. It wasn't the MTA?"

"It was not."

Kara and I shared a look. The news report made a ghostly filter over her cheeks.

"If Chron's still alive," Walker said, "he'll retaliate, and he'll have nothing left to lose. We need boots on the ground."

"Where should we go?" Ethan asked, but Walker had hung up.

"If it wasn't the MTA...." I trailed off.

"Could the civilian government have found Chron?" Kara asked.

"Unlikely," Vires said.

"It may have been another Grifter," Ethan said. "If Andrews gave Chron the tech—" His phone chirped. "Sir?" he answered.

"One of our fighter aircrafts is missing," Walker said. "This was an inside job. Unsanctioned. Someone in the MTA knew Chron's location."

A heavy beat of silence passed as we absorbed that intel.

"Give the phone to Durgan," Walker said.

Ethan hesitated, finding my gaze. "Yes, sir."

"I'll do it." Features blank as I could manage them, I took the phone. Only in the safety of the landing did I wipe my eyes.

Durgan had already lost his wife, three children, and home. Why couldn't that have been enough?

The door opened a moment after my knock. Privately, I said, *Agent Walker wants to speak with you.*

Durgan stepped into the hallway and let the door close. The phone flew to his hand. "Agent Walker?"

I'd taken the phone off speaker, but hearing would've been simple, an action of little strain. The temptation to eavesdrop never occurred. A mind-reader already heard enough.

Durgan's response lacked the emphasis of a question; he was subdued as he said, "Do you know the culprit?"

I kept my head ducked. Should I have left? The idea came too late. My legs refused to work.

"Thank you, Agent Walker."

Durgan's outstretched arm entered my peripheral. He handed the phone off. *Call ended* spelled out on the screen.

Durgan remained in the hallway, now the one with the bowed head. Dressed in MTA clothes, he could've been an agent with scarring.

"I'm sorry." I hated how useless the words were.

He moved. I thought he meant to return to his children, but his figure neared. Before I could remind him what I'd done, Durgan gathered me into what must have been the first embrace between meta and Grifter. In this momentous occasion, I stood immobile against his chest.

"You continue to blame yourself for the crimes of others," rumbled his voice.

"I took him there."

"And he chose to stay. Do you have a father, Ella Kepler?"

My eyes shut. *Yes.*

"And does he love you?"

He had, but now he was Joe Smith, and Joe Smith had no daughter to love. I couldn't tell Durgan that. Instead, I lied.

"Then," Durgan said, stepping back, "you know he could not be angry with someone who saved his daughter and fought for her unto the end." He tilted my chin higher. I could hardly feel the roughness of his finger. Durgan waited — for a reaction, I realized. So I nodded, and he nodded, and then he left me in the hallway, aching for parents who were no longer mine.

I DIDN'T MISS THE former bustle created by Operation Whitewash. After the airstrike, those of us who remained managed to make just as much commotion.

The projection screen aired civilian channels around the clock. Initially, we'd wiped the screen when Durgan's lopsided stride could be heard, but he was adamant about staying informed. Despite everything, Durgan retained that authoritative tone that no one argued with.

The news cycled the story endlessly. "… investigating these sources, but none have been confirmed. Until then, all national parks have been closed. The National Park Service has issued a statement speaking out against terrorism and its impact on innocent wildlife."

"These reporters have wasted more time discussing wildlife," Vires said. "What of their fellow civilians? Where are the reports on *human* casualties?" His questions, unfiltered in his agitation, revealed the Vires that McFarland must've glimpsed once or twice. Vires cared enough to worry about someone other than himself.

"The MTA is controlling their focus." Ethan kept his phone nearby, in case Walker called. He'd had the opportunity to update us just once, and he'd given us grim facts.

Grifters had escaped. No one knew how many, or which ones, but their moves seemed as unpredictable as the fire raging across South Carolina. Not one peep of staff-wielding monsters had breached civilian news, and the MTA was keeping it that way, contacting reporter plants to ensure the focus steered clear of the Grifter revolution that had broken into the civilian sphere. There *had* been deaths, civilian deaths — emptied pockets and stolen cars around the radius of Dewey National Forest. Whoever had fired against Chron had not only failed in eliminating a Grifter threat, but had even expanded it.

Jimmy's career as MTA commander received a forceful jumpstart. The issues we'd prepared to deal with disappeared, set on hold until the MTA contained the situation. Jimmy's potential control over the Tacemus was neither explored nor questioned as all efforts shifted gears. In some ways, it made Jimmy's promotion less of an issue. The protesting voices went mute, convenient for us. *Too* convenient. After all, the only people who'd known of Chron's location were either dead or in Operation Whitewash, which gave life to a theory that made everyone uncomfortable in their chairs: Someone in Whitewash had attacked Chron to distract from Jimmy's strange promotion.

Vires accepted it first, no surprise there. I was shocked when Ethan took to it next. A month ago, he never would've assumed someone could betray the MTA like this, but Ethan had paid the price of naiveté. The more we discussed the idea, the more it took root. James came next, which meant Bridget jumped onboard. McFarland tried defending Whitewash, but even she had to admit she'd known its members as little as her fellow cadets had.

"Ella knows them best," Kara said. "I mean, Kepler," she quickly added.

Kara did what she could to erase all assumptions that she was a random seventh-wheel trying to wheedle her way into MTA business. No one really thought that except Vires.

"And who cares if he complains?" I'd told her.

"Me. I don't want to be helpless. If I can't go back to Briarwood… " she'd gathered her breath and aimed for straighter posture, "I might as well try to fit in here."

As it was, she spoke more than Bridget, and at least she wasn't a Grifter. Vires responded better to her presence when Durgan was around.

Since I'd interacted with Whitewash most, it was up to me to defend their innocence. Some, I'd only briefly met, but the rest I'd developed a decent feel for. Every time I wanted to eliminate suspects, Agent Miranda Cassidy's face cropped up. She'd researched the protean lab without Walker's permission. As an agent, she'd have access to an aircraft and weaponry. But was she heartless enough to obliterate an entire Grifter settlement, knowing Durgson was there—Durgson, whom she'd helped reunite with his father?

"It's possible the information about Chron leaked when Andrews was still alive," I told the table. "Chang could've found out, though I don't know why she'd do it."

"What if it was an act of revenge?" James said.

"Enacted by Andrews," Ethan said.

McFarland tilted her head. "It's possible he arranged for a contingency plan, should Chron ever violate their arrangement."

"No," Ethan said, "faking his death was the contingency plan."

The air stilled. Everyone looked at Ethan, who kept his eyes low after slipping that theory so quietly into the room.

"What?" I said.

"Banks requested the body. None of us verified that he buried it."

A chill touched a finger along my spine, but Kara's incredulous tone brushed it away. "You think Banks would go along with that?"

Vires scoffed. "I disagree with Sheedy, but you don't understand Banks like we do, Watson."

Vires was lucky Kara lacked a meta's strength. Even so, her stare had the force to knock down a building.

"Hold up," I said. "I know Banks isn't your favorite person, but remember, he started Whitewash with One."

"What does that have to do with anything?" Vires said.

"He's been on the right side longer than any of us. He wanted to bury Andrews alone because he was his dad, okay?"

"I wasn't suggesting Banks has any malicious motives," Ethan said. "I'm suggesting Andrews does."

I took a steadied breath. "Andrews is dead."

"Or had the appearance of death." Ethan failed to pick up on my *You sound crazy* expression and continued without abashment. "The MTA fakes our deaths when we're born. Andrews would be familiar with the process, and," he spoke through the swelling shadows of anger, "he knows enough about Banks to extort him."

I started to protest. And then I remembered Colette Barineau. What *wouldn't* Jimmy do to find the mother he'd much rather have a relationship with than Andrews?

"You think Andrews is blackmailing him into keeping him alive and... doing his bidding?" Doubt and worry vied in Kara's tone. She got it now, too.

"Yes," Ethan said. "Andrews knew Chron implanted the kill chip. He wanted to appear dead so Banks would be promoted and Whitewash would believe it won."

Vires crossed his arms and gave Ethan his finest incredulity. "This is the most asinine thing I've ever heard."

"But Sheedy has a point." McFarland's low voice melted some of Vires' outrage. "Andrews would have known how to appear dead."

"Dr. Saini is a protean," said Bridget, twisting her fingers around and too nervous to look up from them.

"Good point," James said. "Saini would've seen his heart go out. Andrews couldn't have faked it around her."

I exhaled, relieved. "Exactly. And a few hours passed before Ji—Banks buried him. Pretty sure a heart can't stay stopped for that long."

"*Pretty sure?*" Vires said. "Your medical expertise is astounding."

"Why are you arguing? I thought this was the most asinine idea in the universe."

"He just wants to argue with someone," McFarland said. It was the first time she'd spoken about Vires since James' outburst—and the first time something close to mischevious humor dared glint in Vires' expression. But it didn't last long. We turned back to the news, resuming other theories. Ethan, a silent bystander to our discussions, thought of Andrews.

You're giving him power he doesn't have, I said.

I don't want to repeat the same mistake.
You won't.

If Ethan had believed me, he would have nodded. He was too honest to pretend. So he turned back to the screen and thought of Andrews once more.

A FEW DAYS AFTER the airstrike, we received the summons. Every member of Whitewash was to head to D.C. for questioning.

Immediately.

None of us had visited the Department of Homeland Security, a place Kara and I considered intimidating, whereas the idea of strolling into government buildings left the cadets unfazed. Though they'd never actually worked under the government, they'd believed it all their lives.

Durgan, enemy of Chron, was still a suspect; so, Grifters, metas, and a civilian piled into the transport van and began the three-and-a-half hour drive from Virginia to Washington. Vires drove and Ethan took passenger side. The rest of us sat on the floor of the cab, where lack of windows kept the Grifters out of sight.

The Department of Homeland Security did not greet us as one formidable structure but a series of buildings tacked onto a tan, brick center that could've passed for an eight-story school. Beyond the windshield, sunlight beat upon a fairly empty street. Trees decking the lawn shielded much of the compound; we only got a clean glimpse when Vires jerked left into the entrance. My eyes followed the trail of adjacent buildings, then bumped down to the security bar that obstructed the drive. A uniformed guard leaned from his box and flagged Vires down — a *familiar* guard.

"Budge over," squash-nosed Agent Keswick said as he climbed into the back with us and squeezed his massive bulk between James and Bridget. "Follow the back entrance route," he called up to Vires.

According to Walker, a Whitewash member — Keswick — would escort us into a private room. There, One and I would conduct the questioning. From Jimmy to Walker, everyone would receive equal treatment — except One and me, who couldn't read ourselves. I'd read him, he'd read me, and Whitewash would have to trust the mind-readers weren't playing tricks.

One had told me he never wished to read another mind. Today's emergency must've sidelined that promise; or, he'd let me do all the reading while he observed.

The one-way strip of road ended at a row of dumpsters. Keswick motioned us out. Propping open a door beneath an awning, Agent Cassidy ordered us to hurry up. Nothing in her mannerism *seemed* shifty. By the end of today, I'd know for certain whether Cassidy had hijacked an MTA aircraft.

We filed into a hallway of linoleum floor, cream walls, and overhead lights that flickered. Cassidy sent us to the first room on the left, reminiscent of a classroom, with a series of desks where the Whitewash team congregated. I barely got the chance to search for Jimmy before Walker gripped my shoulder and steered me into a room off the first, which turned out to be a soundproof supply closet. Pressed against wire racks of lightbulbs, tools, and walkie-talkies, One and I made room for our first subject, Dr. Saini. We didn't even have space to sit.

Where's Jimmy? I asked One.

I do not know.

Isn't he —

"Let's keep this under an hour, shall we?" Saini said, scanning her watch.

Do you want me to do the reading? I said to One.

He blinked. *I will read her.*

You sure? I don't want you to have to break a promise.

I will read her, he said again.

I hesitated. His behavior seemed off. The prospect of following Walker's orders must've bothered him more than he'd admit.

We moved through Whitewash's members to the tune of six questions, honing in on motive, means, and alibi. One, able to read present thoughts as they came without strain, performed his job much swifter than I did, particularly when it came to the three members I'd briefly met. However, Zachary Holt, Dr. Marie Webb, and Luke Bender had nothing to hide.

My suspicions of Agent Cassidy reluctantly grew as she continued diverting questions about her alibi; but, when I finally broke the barrier, I understood why. Agent Keswick didn't share her embarrassment and readily spilled more than requested.

"It took a lot of convincing, but we've been going to the studio for three months now. She's cracked a couple smiles. It's progress. Call Louise at Detox Dancing for an alibi check. Any further questions?"

I coughed into my elbow to disguise a laugh. "No. Thank you."

After Keswick strode out, I had to grin. I found it a relief to cross her off the list.

Since Ly and Tam accompanied Durgan, I questioned him telepathically. Durgan had the strongest motive; even he admitted that. What saved him was the undeniable truth that, even if he'd come by MTA-grade weapons, he would have aimed them nowhere near his son.

Walker entered last. "On August eighth, I was in a meeting. Lane can confirm. I first heard of the attack when Sheedy called." He continued his explanation, and One pronounced him truthful. A minute later, I'd sifted enough to reaffirm.

"Unless you and Integer have been fooled," Walker said, "we have to start considering that Andrews told someone other than the ranger. It'll be hard to seek an audience with Chang, but I'll see what I can do." He reached for the door.

"Did Banks arrive?" I said.

"No. He'll be in meetings the rest of the year."

"So we aren't going to read him?"

"Having second thoughts?" Walker asked.

"It's only fair. We said we'd question everyone."

"They know you've already read him."

"What? I haven't read him."

Walker sighed and said, "I don't understand this conversation. I'm referring to this morning."

"What about it?"

"Your briefing with Banks, in which you vetted him and declared him innocent. Why am I having to explain this, Kepler?"

"Walker... I was in Virginia this morning. I haven't seen Banks since he left base."

His mustache was starting to bristle. "You trying to be coy? I have no time for this." He yanked the door open, but I stepped into the doorway and pulled it shut. My pulse had taken an unpleasant hike.

"Wait," I said quietly. "Did Banks tell you that I vetted him?"

"He didn't have to. I was there. What—"

It dawned on us at the same time. His coal eyes grew minuscule. After frowning at each other, Walker and I turned in unison to One. The Tacemus blinked, mild as ever.

"One," I said, "did you give Walker a fake memory?"

You asked me to be sure that Jimmy is okay.

"That didn't mean lie and fabricate!" I said, and Walker groaned and scrubbed his face. "Why did you do it?"

You asked me to be sure that Jimmy is okay.

"What's he saying? Integer, explain yourself." Walker demanded questions of the Tacemus. Whether or not he answered, I didn't concern myself with it. In the tiny closet without room to hide, the Tacemus matched my gaze and forgot to fake emotion.

Cold, sickly dread worked into my veins. I should have detected it as soon as I'd spotted him. Yet he'd checked off the appropriate boxes: on our side, speaking the way One should, and aware of the conversation we'd had the day One and Jimmy left Virginia. But hadn't I thought he'd seemed off, even then?

"Are you One?" I asked. "Integer?"

I am One.

"Were you in Virginia?"

He gave no answer, proving he wasn't One with every empty blink. But how? He must've played the role for days; he'd referenced my conversation with One, when I'd asked him to make sure Jimmy was okay.

No, I'd *told* him to.

My mouth dried up, though my palms grew sweaty. "Clap your hands," I told the Tacemus.

He did nothing.

Walker set his hands on his belt, where his knife was holstered. "What are you thinking, Kepler?"

I was still deciding. "He's not One," I said, "but he's talking in the first person, and you saw that he won't... obey me."

Walker motioned the exit. "Wait outside," he told the Tacemus.

The bald head turned to me. He remained motionless.

"You try, Kepler," Walker said.

I wished Walker didn't have to witness this. "Can you... " I swallowed, "can you please wait outside?"

Yes, Ella. Promptly, the Tacemus exited.

"So he prefers that you're polite. Noted." Walker released a sigh that sounded heavy enough to fill up the cracks in the shelves. "Well, I was right. Banks has inherited control, and he's covering it up." His scowl darkened, and he muttered, "Wish I understood that kid. He makes everyone his enemy."

"That Tacemus was in Virginia. I thought One was acting strange...." I chewed on my next statement. Ethan's outlandish theory seemed less farfetched when confronted with a Tacemus impersonating One. Forcing myself to match Walker's stare, I said, "We never saw Banks bury Andrews. He could've faked his death. I think he's still alive, controlling the Tacemus and blackmailing Banks."

"Dr. Saini confirmed — "

"Did Andrews know about her protean ability?"

Walker smeared a finger over his mustache. His silence, an answer in itself, was deafening.

Theorizing with the cadets had felt eerie but safe. To see Walker consider this idea gave it merit, and with that came the horrifying possibility that maybe we were right.

"Where's Banks?" I said.

"My memory tells me he's in Maryland, which leads me to believe he's here, in his office. Room seven-oh-two."

"I'm going to talk to him and get to the bottom of this."

"You don't have clearance to roam this facility."

"Do the Tacemus?"

Slowly, Walker nodded. "But they seem inclined to disobey."

"I'll ask politely." I reached for the door. Walker palmed the doorframe, blocking my way.

"Take Sheedy with you," he said. "Don't breathe a word of this to anyone else. We wait until we have the facts."

I agreed. These no-nonsense metas wouldn't be held back by ideals of loyalty and friendship. If Jimmy *was* hiding the truth about Andrews, Whitewash wouldn't give him a break just because he pulled the "missing mom" card.

"If this goes south," Walker added quietly, "you'll be safe at seven-three-one Meyers Street. Somerton, West Virginia. Key is in the rooster's mouth. Gear in the basement. Stay the same course we've plotted from day one: free the Tacemus, save the MTA. Understood?"

I only considered a back-up plan once Walker gave me one. His lifeline worsened my anxiety rather than alleviating it. "Yes," I said.

His hand moved to my shoulder. Fingers, solid as steel, dug into my clavicle. "You will enter the house first and hide two photos. The first is on the computer in the basement. The second is on the nightstand in the master. But I never told you this, Kepler. The house belongs to an anonymous MTA operative. Tell anyone it's mine, and I will personally tend to your demise. Doesn't matter if you're our only hope. I'll find myself another telepath. Got it?"

"Yes, sir," I said quickly.

He released his clutch. I withheld my grimace.

The makeshift classroom was abuzz as if Whitewash had never stopped its planning. Keswick, currently under Cassidy's fire, called her attention to our entrance. She spun around, pink in the cheeks, but straightened up and said, "I thought you said innocent until proven guilty, Walker."

While others offered commentary, I found the Tacemus. He'd drifted to the edge of the room, content with his isolation. *Take me to Jimmy's office,* I tried.

He blinked at me.

Can you take me to Jimmy's office?

Yes, Ella. He moved toward the exit.

Without getting caught, I hurriedly added, *or alerting him that we're coming?*

Yes, Ella.

All right. For some reason, direct orders failed. Sometime recently, Andrews must've forbidden the Tacemus from obeying me, but I'd stumbled on a loophole. His command had forgotten requests.

Next, I searched for Ethan. *I think you might be right about Andrews,* I said. *We're going to talk to Jimmy.* I switched to Kara. She wanted to be involved, but that wasn't the reason I sought her help. *Will you come with me to talk to Jimmy about... well, Andrews being potentially alive?* I asked.

She scanned those standing nearby and came back to me with furrowed brows. *Are you sure that's a good idea? I'm not even a....*

He always listened to you better than anyone else.

Kara chewed her lip. Then nodded.

After catching my eye over Cassidy's shoulder, Walker made a point of calling everyone's attention toward him. Ethan, halfway across the room, paused.

This way, I said, tugging his arm. I corralled Kara, nodded at the Tacemus, and, like four thieves foolishly believing the searchlights can't see them, we slipped from the room of observant, ever-alert metas.

CHAPTER TWENTY-SIX

THE DOOR AT THE OPPOSITE end of the hallway opened to a floor where escalators climbed and strips of conveyer belts chugged. I could imagine we'd stumbled into airport security. Civilians chased escalators and waved their phones around in obvious panic. High on the walls, TV projections recycled news footage with an additional, red banner blaring the words "NATIONAL THREAT LEVEL: SEVERE."

The MTA had never felt more surreal. We shared Homeland Security with real, never-heard-of-the-MTA government officials. How had the MTA lasted centuries without alerting the world?

The Tacemus, that's how.

He made for the nearest metal detector as if he owned the place. Upon seeing his approach, the uniformed guard perked and fiddled with her computer. A beep sounded; the metal detector powered down. The Tacemus walked through the archway while we lingered on the safe side.

Follow, the Tacemus said.

I passed through first. When the guard noticed I'd caught her gaping, she averted her gaze and mumbled an apology.

... shouldn't stare... she was thinking. As far as she knew, anyone accompanying the "short, bald guy" earned high-security clearance, no questions asked.

We joined the escalators behind a woman on her phone. Up we climbed, travelers in this sea of movement. I searched the upcoming floor for a marker that would indicate whether we'd just come from ground or level one. My attention spun to a butter-white ponytail. Cement glued my heart to the floor.

Lydia Burnette stood on the opposite escalator. She dropped; we lifted — and we were about to pass within an arm's length.

I stared, pulse so violently kicking that anyone with meta hearing would sniff me out — yet Lydia seemed unconcerned with me. Her eyes fixed on Ethan. For his part, Ethan was preoccupied with the approaching floor and didn't notice her.

The moment zoomed near when we'd be exactly beside each other. I turned my head, forcing a neutral expression. I could feel the scorch of her gaze during that agonizing blip of unity.

Once she was below us, I touched Ethan's arm. *Lydia just went down the opposite escalator.*

Lydia? Here?

Yes. She saw us.

He started to turn, then stopped himself. His profile grew sharper.

She can't do anything, can she? I said.

I don't —

"Ethan."

The low voice behind us may as well have been an exposed wire; Ethan went rigid, and the muscles in his neck tightened. His lips made an impenetrable line. Because he wouldn't budge, I gathered an inhale and turned.

Lydia had bypassed half a dozen patrons to sidle beside us. Forgetting her usual disdain, she wore a mask of urgency. At such proximity, I stumbled around wisps of awkward tension, but she didn't spare me a bitter glare.

"I thought you were dead," she whispered.

Ethan acted as if he hadn't heard; his mind busily hatched a plan. He was also saving the escalator patrons from witnessing the most awkward interaction of their lives — because Ethan had nothing to say to Lydia. Rather, he had only one thing to say, and he meant to say it when he was certain she'd listen.

He shifted, pushing me up a step. "Go."

I read his plan. "Come on," I said to Kara, then asked the Tacemus to hurry. We pressed upward, squeezing around the lady on her phone and the group above her. I didn't monitor behind but moved until level seven arrived. We stepped off the escalator and picked up a stride.

"Who was that?" Kara asked.

"Lydia."

"*What?* As in —"

"Yes. Ethan's making sure she doesn't interfere with us."

We hurried around a corner to a hallway lined with doors. The search for room 702 proved simple: second on the left. I didn't want to burst in unannounced, but lingering in the hall, where government officials could surge upon us at any second, seemed a bad idea.

Thank you for helping, I told the Tacemus.

Yes, Ella.

After a quick auditory search that revealed we wouldn't interrupt a meeting, I knocked once, then twisted the knob. Locked. A familiar voice called, "Come in" just as the lock gave way. The door swung forward.

And there, looking more than ever like the man who'd once sat at a similar desk and told me everything would be all right, was Jimmy Daniels. Formerly William Banks, and now Eugene Andrews.

Kara and I darted in.

This shade of office was neither the sterile white of the MTA nor the classical-era of Andrews' but a room as standard as the building. In one corner stood the American flag and in another a Tacemus. A single glance and I knew he wasn't One; he kept his eyes downcast, unresponsive to our entrance. Filing cabinets piled with binders took the place of elegant bookshelves. Jimmy's desk was lopsided, covered by an ancient computer and more paper products than electronics.

Jimmy, immersed in his grid, let us stew in trepidation before he set the grid aside and looked up. Shock punched his eyes wide open.

"Hi," Kara said.

For a moment, Jimmy looked at her with a soft familiarity. He lifted a hand, as if to smooth his hair. Unnecessary; gel now held every previously chaotic wave in place. The composure, along with the suit, aged him a few years.

"Where's One?" I asked.

"I thought he was with you."

Jimmy didn't know, which meant Andrews was pulling the strings more than I'd suspected. That filled me with both relief and unease.

"You busy?" I said, dragging a chair closer to his desk.

"I'm always busy," he said. "Especially now. Why are you here?"

"To talk." I plopped down. Kara took the other seat. Jimmy dragged his gaze off her and scratched a pen cap on paper, making circles. "Is this room private?" I asked.

"Why wouldn't it be private?"

"Andrews could've installed cameras or something."

The pen cap paused on its journey toward full circle. "He didn't," Jimmy said, slowly resuming his invisible doodles.

"Are you okay?" Kara asked.

"I'm stressed. We can't find Chron."

"Any headway on who attacked him?" I said.

"No. I was hoping the briefings would reveal some insight. Since you're here, I assume you learned something significant."

I swallowed. Now before him, my idea seemed callous and forced. How could we segue into a conversation about his supposedly dead dad?

Kara, not oblivious to my muteness, bumped my foot. *Let me*, she was thinking. "Jimmy, we have — um, a theory. About Andrews."

The pen cap disappeared inside his fist. Jimmy churned an inaudible answer in his mouth before letting it free. "What theory?"

She inhaled, clenching folds of her pants. "He's still alive. Isn't he?"

Jimmy stared at her. The emotion that darkened his eyes from green to hazel seemed to bubble. Waiting. As the gaze continued, it seeped away, chaotic passion hardening into something indecipherable. He turned his head, and as he did, a tiny buzz — so brief it could've been summoned by my imagination — tickled my ear.

Movement stirred in my peripheral. The Tacemus had come to life. He inspected me, then Kara — who, still waiting for Jimmy to deny her claim, never noticed.

Jimmy wasn't going to deny Kara because he couldn't. Somehow, Eugene Andrews had faked his own death and pulled Jimmy into his spiral of darkness.

"Is he threatening you?" I said. "You can tell us. We want to help you."

"Help me," he said quietly, face shifting with confusion — the same he'd worn when he'd realized I wasn't going to reveal my suspicions about his relationship with Andrews. Even now, Jimmy couldn't fathom the benefits of friendship. "Who all have you told of your theory?"

"Walker and the cadets," I said. "We know it sounds crazy."

"Yes. It does." He rubbed his temples, eyes closed. "What do you want me to say?"

"The truth," Kara said.

"And if I tell you the truth, what will you do next?"

"Whatever we can to help," I said.

"I see." He nodded.

Kara and I had concluded our part of the conversation. The rest lay with Jimmy. He had the power to lie to our faces, but that opportunity had passed. Truth, that bane of Jimmy's existence, waited hand-in-hand with silence.

Another vibration buzzed. Kara failed to notice, but I glanced to the Tacemus again. Our eyes locked. His mouth opened. Without words, they spoke. But with them, they stole.

"Stop," I blurted. "Please, can you stop?"

The man's mouth sealed. Obedient as a lamb, he bowed his head.

I shot upright, bumping back the chair. "Jimmy, he was about to...." Prickles dotted the back of my neck. This room *wasn't* private. Andrews was watching.

Where's Andrews? I asked Jimmy.

His eyes tightened.

Come on, Jimmy, I said. *Let us help you. We can free the Tacemus and—*

"Why is it always about him?" Jimmy slammed a fist on his desk. The pressure made it grind along the floor like a rusty anchor. "I want my own freedom!"

Kara gaped, which unsettled him more. Jimmy gripped his head, breathing turbulently, as if crushed beneath a mountain.

Unhinged – the word slid into my mind, a warning sign.

Kara moved around his desk. He continued heaving into his fingers as she leaned beside him. "It's okay," she whispered.

Beneath her touch, his shaking desisted. His breathing slowed to the rhythm of Kara's strokes. She and I shared a look.

Freedom, she was thinking.

Jimmy felt as enslaved as the Tacemus. But where was *his* master?

"Is Andrews still alive?" I said.

His fingers dug deeper. With jagged movement, Jimmy nodded. "I can't help you," he said, thick and emotive. "You shouldn't have come."

"Of course we—" Kara's voice stalled as the door kicked open.

Warning flashed up my spine. Dark-haired Agent Chang, weapons evidently immune to the metal detector, stepped into Jimmy's office. With the heel of her palm, she sealed us inside.

"Ella first." Jimmy wouldn't look up.

Even before Chang turned her attention upon me, I felt frozen.

"What are you doing, Jimmy?" Kara said.

I curled my fists, relieved I still could, yet Chang had me in the line of her dark eyes. Beneath her telekinetic control, I'd do whatever she wanted. But I still had my telepathy. Gathering steam, I shouted into her head, imagining my voice like a bullet. She winced, and the connection fractured. I leaped over Jimmy's desk and pulled Kara behind its cover. Even Chang needed visual contact. Without it, her power waned.

Something squeaked from the direction of the filing cabinets. I braced myself for Chang's next maneuver. When the sound of a heavy weight thwacked the carpet, I imagined her forming a battering ram of cabinets ready to obliterate the desk. I peered up at Jimmy, who paid no attention. She'd have to avoid hurting him in the process, right?

Out of nowhere, a binder soared over his downcast head. It jerked around like a disembodied hand itching to slap someone. Finding no purchase, it sunk, skimming his hair. The binder reared back, then clipped him repeatedly until Jimmy crashed forward on his desk.

Had Chang sent the binder after him?

I craned my head over the desk. Chang was sprawled on the floor. Blood dribbled down her forehead. She hadn't controlled the binder, and neither had Jimmy. Kara and I obviously lacked telekinesis, which left the Tacemus, but he was oblivious.

"Did Chang leave?" Kara raised her head and got the same view as me.

"I have no idea what—"

Again, the door swept inward. Lydia darted in, surveyed the slack forms of Chang and Jimmy, then kicked shut the door. Noting our shock, she hesitated, fidgeting as if beneath the stare of someone far more intimidating.

"Where is Ethan?" I said.

"In a closet. Listen, you—"

"A *closet*?"

"Yes. It was the safest place to stow him. He wouldn't let me speak with you, so I knocked him out. Don't argue, Kepler. I'm doing you a favor. Do you want to live or die?"

"I want to make sure my teammates aren't stuffed in random closets where someone could discover them."

"Fine. I'll bring him here." Lydia spun out the door.

Taking an assessment of the unconscious bodies, I groaned. *Why* hadn't Jimmy asked for help, just once? Andrews was twisting this situation out of control.

Agent Chang's belt and pockets held a number of gadgets whose uses I had no time to guess. If she awoke, we were good as captured. I searched for the electric cuffs that Chron had used to bind Andrews.

Kara knelt beside me. With trembling fingers, she tugged the collapsed, silver circlet out of Chang's thigh pocket. Blue flashed on the bands, and a magnetic pull yanked her arms together. However, her hands were not her primary weapon. Chang's pockets were missing a convenient blindfold. I opted for her belt.

Lydia dashed back inside, carrying Ethan. His arm drooped toward the floor, but Lydia secured his head in the crook of her elbow. "Listen, Kepler," she said. "You need to go. Right now. It's a ruse. Banks is letting Whitewash lower its guard, but you're all targets. The MTA has orders to capture if any of you are spotted. I can escort you downstairs. No one will suspect if I'm with you." Her features, pinched with intensity, appeared genuine as far as I could tell, but this was the girl who loathed me for a variety of reasons, had once told me Kara was better off dead, and had obstinately refused to join Whitewash not that long ago.

"I thought you didn't believe in Whitewash," I said. "Why help us?"

A furrow of defiance streaked across her face. "I've never liked Banks."

Of course she hadn't. He'd been Ethan's unappreciative partner.

What do you think? I asked Kara.

Don't see why she'd be lying. If she wanted us captured, that agent was about to do the job.

Kara had a point. Ultimately, this situation boiled down to lack of time and a heap of pressure, which meant I had to make a decision about Lydia and stick to it.

"Hold on," I said. I dug my palms into my eyelids. Whatever was going on with Jimmy, we could get him out of it. He tended toward seeing his options as limited, but we could take him from Andrews and fix this mess. However, I doubted he'd come happily, which meant he needed to remain unconscious during transport. How, exactly, did one carry around an unconscious government official in the Department of Homeland Security?

Do you trust Lydia enough to go with her? I asked Kara.

I don't think she'll kill me. If that's what you mean.

That was very reassuring. I switched my focus to the Tacemus. *Can you go with Kara and Lydia? And if Lydia makes any obvious attempt to hurt Kara or a member of Whitewash, can you...?* What weapon could a Tacemus wield, other than his words?

Yes, Ella, he said, because he'd followed the train of my thought.

Not of anything important, I quickly added. *Just wipe her of... the past minute. And only if it's necessary.*

Yes, Ella.

He didn't bat an eye. But I *hadn't* commanded him. The Tacemus agreed on his own.

Next, I squared Lydia, in case she got it into her head that she was calling the shots. "Here's what's going to happen. You escort Kara outside, where our car will be waiting. This Tacemus will go with you. I'll wake Ethan up, and we'll take Banks through the window."

"This is a secure building," Lydia said. "Even civilians will fire if you kidnap a government employee. Besides, the window's armed."

"Meaning an alarm will go off?"

"Yes."

I sighed, inspecting the window. If that set off an alert, it gave us little time to hightail it out of here. "I'll have to be fast, then," I said. "Hurry, before Banks wakes."

By some miracle, Lydia nodded without a single argument. She carried Ethan around Chang and lay him carefully on the floor. In another few seconds, Kara, the Tacemus, and Lydia were gone. I was left in the lull of three sleeping bodies.

I raised the blinds shielding Jimmy's window. The parking lot looked like a checkerboard from this height. *Bridget,* I said, *it's Ella. Can you tell Vires to pull around to the east side of the building? I'll be jumping from the seventh floor and need a quick getaway. The window is across from a yellow car.*

Naturally, the window refused to open. To break it, I needed a force that would do the job with one blow; I couldn't risk an alarm blaring to life after a sliver in the glass. Jimmy's computer looked up to the task.

When I turned, Ethan was clambering upright. He cast a wild inspection around the room and said, "Where's Lydia?"

"Long story. We need to get out of here ASAP, with Jimmy. I'm going to bust this window open, which is going to sound the alarm, and then—what, do you have a better idea?"

"Kidnap him?"

"Yes. No. It's not kidnapping if it's out of love."

He dragged a hand down his face.

"Let's debate this later," I said. "Do you want to break the window, or should I?"

"You mean, do I want to mutilate government property in addition to abducting the MTA commander?"

"Okay, I'll do it."

Ethan edged around the desk and pressed a palm against the window. After skimming the surface of the glass, he said, "Are you sure?"

"If we leave him here, we leave him to the mercy of Andrews."

"He's alive, then?"

"Yeah." Saying it aloud gave me a chill.

His expression shifted. Wide at first, then narrowing just as firmly. Ethan placed his hands on either side of the windowpane and sighed. "You can't fix everything, Ella."

"But I can try." I hooked Jimmy under the arms and dragged him off the chair. "What would you do if it were me?"

He lifted an eyebrow, but the gaze beneath softened. "I wouldn't have clipped your forehead." Ethan touched my hairline.

"That wasn't me. A floating binder took out Jimmy and Chang."

"Floating binder?"

"Yeah. I think it was Lydia. She must've been peering underneath the door or something."

His hand dropped; Ethan turned to the window with features muddled somewhere between bitterness and regret. "There's an explanation for that." He appraised the window again. "All right. Stay behind—"

A wail whooped from an overhead intercom, then grew to a shriek. Recessed lights near the doorway flashed blue and red. Yet Ethan hadn't broken the window. In unison, we peered outside.

Below, our white van zigzagged around the parking lot, dangerously teetering in its efforts to avoid cars and the spray of gunfire from the guards sprinting over the asphalt.

"What are they doing!"

"It's too risky down there," Ethan murmured.

"We can't stay here. If we get caught, with him unconscious—"

"We stick to the wall of the building. I'll jump first and catch Banks. Get ready." He reared his arm back and, as if throwing a bolt, thrust the hard edge of his palm into the window. The glass exploded, spraying the sill with pointy flecks. Ethan leaped out.

I lugged Jimmy to the window, kicking slivers of glass that twitched like icicles. He groaned when I heaved his body toward the opening, and plummeted like a ton of flour. Once my hands were free, I pulled myself over. The fall felt like a breeze on my sweaty skin; the landing jarred my legs.

Ethan, pressed against the brick, had Jimmy thrown over a shoulder. On the east side, we were on the corner, invisible to the employees fleeing from the front entrance. The sirens blared from outside speakers, mixing with gunfire and shouts to create the definition of cacophony. From our vantage, we couldn't see the van, but I heard tires squealing.

We're outside, I told Bridget.

Someone called my name. Darting into view, Lydia and Kara hurried in our direction. The Tacemus followed as quickly as he could.

"Where's your transportation?" Lydia hissed.

I pointed — and ended up poking Jimmy's head; Ethan had stepped between us. "This doesn't concern you, Burnette," he said.

"I don't need to justify myself to you. Now, *Kepler*, if you're planning to carry Banks into the fray, I can cover you."

"How?" I said.

Lydia waved her fingers. "Animos aren't useless without weapons. Unlike some cadets."

All things considered, I was glad she was still her normal self.

"I counted ten," Ethan said.

"I just have to see them once." She set her shoulders, glaring at Ethan, me, and whatever else landed in her path.

"There's the van," Kara said, craning her neck.

"Get behind me." Lydia moved over the grass and onto the sidewalk with her arms splayed.

I had no idea how she intended to cover four of us from ten guards, but Ethan seemed confident in her ability, so that had to count for something. *Stay here,* I told the Tacemus, then remembered to make it a request.

Yes, Ella, he said.

We crept after Lydia. Emerging around the corner, we became visible to anyone looking. Fortunately, most were preoccupied by the parking lot commotion.

The van came pealing down the road that enclosed the parking lot, aiming straight for us. I caught Vires' wild face behind a cracked windshield. McFarland leaned a head out the passenger side, contorting her arm about. She might've been the reason none of the bullets had hit the tires yet, though plenty dented the side.

"Now!" Lydia dashed onto the street.

I covered Kara in a side-hug and ran with her. We made slower progress than Ethan, but the van was nearing fast. Vires swerved parallel to us, tires barreling onto the sidewalk, leaving streaks in the grass. The door rolled open.

"Come on!" James cried.

Instead of diving into safety, Lydia jumped on top of the van. In the blaze of sunlight, she stood in clear view of every pointed gun.

"Burnette?" Vires yelled. "What is *she* doing here?"

Ethan tossed Jimmy into the cab, then stepped aside to wave Kara and me in. I heard gunshots, though no *plinks* against the van. As everyone frantically made room and McFarland told Vires to go, I took stock of our missing numbers.

"Where's Durgan?" I asked Bridget.

"He was with the others. It happened so fast...."

"What happened?"

"Is Burnette coming?" Kara called.

We received our answer by glimpsing out the windshield. A cluster of guards in gray uniforms writhed about in the air, all of them stuck to the sky by their guns. Instead of letting go, the guards fought for control over the weapons that dragged them higher and higher. Below, the crowd gaped. Some shouting, others trying to ground the airborne guards by tugging on their boots.

Vires slowed, peering upward. "What the...?"

"How is she doing that?" McFarland said.

"Move!" Ethan shook Vires' shoulder, and the latter threw the gear into drive and floored the gas.

"She'll fall off!" Kara said.

"She won't." Unlike the rest of us, Ethan wasn't gawking out the window.

Near the parking lot exit, more guards sprinted for the security box. The bar stayed a staunchly lowered arm. I noted a stirring in the asphalt and knew what came next.

"Spike thingies!" I said.

"Use real words, Kepler!" Vires shouted.

"They're gonna slash the—"

A bullet made a *ping* against the windshield, and Vires jerked the wheel left, just as rapidly autocorrecting. We headed for the only exit, where we could probably withstand the security bar, but not the spikes growing out of the ground.

I blinked. The scenery changed, as if we'd tilted backward—or lifted upward. Vires raised his hands; the wheel spun on its own. The security box was one moment ahead of us, and the next below. We weren't zooming over the asphalt any longer. We were *flying*.

The few guards manning the box simply stared, drop-jawed. I couldn't blame them. They must've been civilians, unacquainted with telekinesis. I'd seen my fair share, but a flying van put those to shame.

"Get ready, Vires!" came Lydia's call from above.

He returned his hands to the wheel, a bit hesitantly, as if worried the wheel had teeth.

Once we surpassed the security box, the van descended at a choppy rate. Everyone braced themselves for impact by holding onto chairs or one another. The tires touched down without much drama. For a moment, the van moved too fast and veered into the opposite lane, but Vires regained control.

The side door slammed shut. Lydia settled on the floor behind Vires without a scratch to prove she'd just saved our skin.

"Well, that was… conspicuous," James said.

"Cleverly said, Reynolds," Vires muttered. He drove us away from the Department of Homeland Security and toward the calm beyond.

CHAPTER TWENTY-SEVEN

"**YOU NEED TO TRIGGER** the vehicle's evasive features." Lydia leaned over the center console, but Ethan yanked her back.

"Don't touch anything," he said.

McFarland and Vires shared the same scowl, their first hint of unity in days. Even James had crossed his arms. Bridget alone showed no desire to hurl Lydia out of the car.

"I don't need your input, Burnette." Vires stabbed the blue icon hovering in the navigation screen. A shimmer rippled up the hood, which seemed to bubble like plastic melting. The white faded to a forest green dented by rust and scrapes, as if we'd traded the van for one in a junkyard.

"Refresh the license plate display, too," Lydia said. "This one will be tracked. Banks gave us the records of every vehicle Whitewash acquired."

"Why would he do that?" James said.

"Ask him yourself."

We all turned to Jimmy. What with the sirens, jostling, and gunfire, it was a miracle he'd stayed unconscious as long as he had. He'd scooted to the corner, where he observed the group with indecipherable scrutiny — everyone but Kara, whose pointed gaze he ignored.

"We need to go back," he said, clambering upright. "This whole 'interview' was a trap set up by Chang and the Society. Everyone in Whitewash is going to be arrested or killed if we don't get them out."

"He's lying," Lydia said. "Have you searched him? He probably has his phone, if not a tracker." Jimmy's watch band tore free and soared to Lydia, who smashed it to pieces. "What's in your pockets, Banks?" She moved closer to him.

Ethan blocked her. "Pull over, Vires."

"We don't have time for this!" Jimmy's unhinged mania rebounded.

Kara and I met eyes, then quickly looked away.

Vires turned down a residential street, where the van fit in as easily as a smudge on porcelain. He stopped in a cul-de-sac.

Ethan leaned around Lydia and thrust the side door open. "Get out."

She paled, though her features puckered with forced anger. "I'm trying to help your squad."

"Does anyone else take issue with Burnette leaving?" Ethan turned to the others like she hadn't spoken.

"No," McFarland said, loud for once.

Vires, on the other hand, lacked a snippy response. He glared out the window. James shook his head. Bridget murmured, "No, sir."

"Wait." I shielded the open door, in case someone got the idea to hurl Lydia to the pavement.

"She helped us escape," Kara said.

"Burnette's unreliable." McFarland crossed her arms, and then I understood.

While these cadets had learned to choose practicality over emotion, their distrust of Lydia stemmed from resentment. She'd been alone with Griffin, Vires' partner and best friend, when a Grifter killed him. Since his death paved the way for Lydia's position as J-level instructor, Vires and McFarland—probably James and Bridget, too—held the belief that Lydia had let him die. Ethan had defended her against their accusations, but he had other reasons for distrusting Lydia.

"What are you waiting for?" Jimmy said. "She's in the Society! We can't trust her."

"I'm not the one who summoned Chang," Lydia said.

"I didn't. Andrews did. He's manipulating this situation."

"You're confirming Andrews is alive?" McFarland looked ill.

"Yes. He staged his death. *He* assaulted Chron, hoping to pin it on Whitewash." Jimmy swiveled to Bridget, who cowered under his reignited passion. "Please," he said to her—an odd choice, given their lack of relationship, but maybe Jimmy sensed she was the only cadet unaffected by a grudge. "We have to turn around, before it's too late. Andrews will kill Walker and everyone else unless we stop him. You don't want that to happen. We need to go back. Everyone in Whitewash is depending on us."

Darker shadows of doubt clogged Bridget's eyes. I wasn't immune to Jimmy's reasoning. Our whole team was back there.

"He's right," I said to Ethan. "We can't leave them to Andrews."

Ethan said nothing. He focused, strangely narrowed, on Bridget and Jimmy.

"There's no guarantee they're still there," McFarland said.

"What do you mean?" I said.

"Agent Walker got into an argument with some agents after you left," James said. "They wouldn't let us leave. Walker didn't like that. That's when the fight broke out." He rubbed his nose, where a smear of dirt and sweat darkened his freckles. "More agents came, and civilian guards. We didn't know how to act around them, so we all started running. Then Avary heard your voice and told us to bring the van around."

"What happened to the Grifters?"

"Agent Porter ran like a bull with the little one on his back. They hopped a fence."

"But," I breathed through the worry, "they escaped?"

James nodded.

"We can't attempt an extraction," Vires interrupted. "We have no gear, and this vehicle's garbage."

"Let's return to base and plan from there," McFarland said.

"The MTA knows you're in Virginia Beach," Lydia said. "None of your Whitewash hideouts are safe."

The chirp of a crosswalk outside could be heard. If we couldn't rely on Whitewash or the MTA....

I paused, remembering Walker's final piece of advice. If this didn't qualify as "south," I could apologize to him later. The only question was how to convince the others that my anonymous "friend" had a safe house.

Mentally, I nudged Ethan. *I know somewhere we can go and get gear. Someone in the MTA told me about it, but I can't say who. Trust me?*

... trust her... I do. Are you sure it's safe?

Yes.

The others will need something more definitive, Ethan thought.

They'll go along with it if you do.

I'm —

A clap from the driver's seat made me start. "Stop having private conversations," Vires said. "You do this frequently. It's irritating. What's our move?"

Ethan ignored him. His hesitation spelled out plainly. Though his attention strayed from Lydia, his thoughts didn't.

Let her come, I said. *She just wants to help. It'll be good to have her perspective.*

... don't trust her....

I know. But give her a chance. We'll keep an eye on her.

His protests butted with the knowledge that Lydia could provide us with intel no one else could. Ethan inhaled before saying, "We're relocating to a safe house."

"Whose safe house?" Jimmy said quickly.

"That's need to know. Before we leave," he stared Lydia down, "you lose anything traceable. All of us should, even if we acquisitioned it from Whitewash."

"You're letting *her* come?" Vires said.

"Yes."

Complaints issued from the front of the van, but Ethan held fast. Lydia unclasped her bracers, stomped on them, then flung them onto the road. The rest of us followed suit, losing our watches, and Ethan his phone.

With the amount of distrust fomenting in the van, it was incredible anyone could breathe. Lydia owned one corner of the floor, Jimmy the other, and he wasted no time hashing out his plans for taking back Whitewash. His fervor hadn't abated; the wildness seeped through the rest of him, loosening his hair from its gel. He talked over Ethan, sidelining all his input. A week as MTA commander had evidently sunken in.

"This plan is idealistic," Ethan finally cut in. "There's no guarantee the safe house will have that artillery."

"If Kepler would tell us what she knows...." Jimmy glared at me.

"Surely you guys understand confidentiality." *Calm down,* I privately added to Jimmy. Not the wisest thing to tell someone close to combustion. I was surprised when he retorted with an apathetic turn of the head, then resumed spewing plans.

These cadets, so used to viewing Jimmy as the MTA outlaw, had a hard time responding to the guy who'd concealed Andrews' agenda. They knew nothing of his mom, of course. Then again, neither did I. We had only theories.

The conversation eventually turned cyclical; I could zone out and return to find them spouting the same pros and cons. My attention went to One, wherever he was. Jimmy had no idea, which had me worrying about what Andrews might've done with him. However, my telepathy hit the same fuzzy blockade.

I tried intermittently throughout the drive. No answer. I'd have to drag One's location out of Andrews when we returned to D.C.

Once daylight had cycled forward to early evening, we reached a rural neighborhood of farmhouses on stretches of rolling land. Each brick home sat on several acres alongside horses and dense trees. Meyers Street only had two houses. The road dead-ended at a Colonial style home with pillars and a wrap-around porch.

"Seven-three-one," McFarland said, pointing toward the numbers on the mailbox.

This farmhouse belonged to Walker? The neighbor had cows.

Jimmy beat me to the door, but Ethan shook his head. "Kepler goes first."

That news contorted more brows than Jimmy's. His fingers hesitated on the handle before he moved aside.

Alone, I strode up the path decorated by globe lights strewn along potted trees. The front porch, whose rocking chairs and throw blankets screamed anything but "MTA safe house," would've fit all nine of us without anyone having to huddle close. Carved into the pearly door was a rooster knocker. I twisted the beak. A key fell into my palm.

Sweet cinnamon and vanilla spilled through the threshold. A lamp illuminated the decorative rug that stretched across the foyer, a high-ceilinged entrance bedecked with cozy paintings and a plant on the table. Despite the key in my palm, evidence of Walker's words, I worried I'd stumbled into the wrong house.

I skirted the living room and stairs and began testing doors. After finding a bathroom, linen closet, and office, I opened one that revealed a flight of descending, concrete steps. Basement first, then the master.

Walker was proving to be the most unpredictable part of the day. His decision to trust me with his oddly homey safe house still confused me less than his orders to hide two photographs. What could be so secretive, so incriminating, that none but me could witness it?

When I rounded the corner into the basement, I knew I'd entered the right house. Walker had raided a gun shop and relocated it here. The pegboard wall of guns made up only a fraction of his stash. Glass cabinets displayed stacks of bursts—MTA grenades shaped like metal triangles. Beyond weapons, the shelves supplied watches, cell phones still packaged up, binoculars, walkie-talkies, and helmets. Along another wall spanned a narrow table, upon which sat two computer monitors. Stacks of paper covered the rest.

The photo in question sat tucked into the corner of a monitor. Its single subject stopped me in my tracks. She was a copper-skinned young girl, probably seven or eight, with a firm set of her mouth. The MTA's logo made a watermark over the image, and her ID spelled out below her name: Margaret Perry.

She was the protean Walker had clammed up about, after lancing Ethan with a death glare for broaching the subject. I hadn't imagined the name belonged to someone so young, someone with a familiar sternness not so different from what Walker wore half the time....

A lump got lodged in my throat. Margaret Perry was his daughter. As to Margaret's mom? I could make an educated guess.

Margaret explained why he'd put Whitewash off the search for the protean lab. And now he'd given away his biggest secret to keep us ignited.

Feeling as if I reached for treasure and not a tiny square of paper, I delicately unstuck the picture. I tucked it into a pocket and double-checked the zipper, then made for the stairs. He must've had another photo of her in the master. Nightstand, he'd said. Hers was the last face he saw before falling asleep.

The master bedroom released a floral breeze when I cracked the door. More elegant touches to the décor, but I bypassed the admiration and aimed for the bedside table. The ivory frame bordered two people this time. My heart and eyes competed for which could swell larger.

A youthful Agent Walker and Dr. Saini huddled close beneath an ivy arch strewn with flowers. Her white dress was simple, his suit nondescript. Their expressions made the scene. Their eyes were locked, faces a couple inches apart. Walker nudged Saini's chin with his thumb, not quite smiling, but he didn't need a beaming grin to indicate the happiness evident in every bit of him.

I must've swallowed a dozen times. Somehow, they'd done it: defied the expectations of metahumans and fashioned something close to normal for themselves. The proof rested in my hands, and it turned my thoughts to Ethan.

I slid the photo from its frame. Not the time.

With two weights in my pocket, I returned outside. Had a carful of impatient people not awaited my reappearance, I would've set the two photos side by side, noting the similarities. Did Margaret know, or was she another ignorant MTA victim?

I expected Vires to hold the most suspicion—indeed, the accusations shot as soon as I opened the van door—but Jimmy surpassed him. Whose house? Why had I entered alone? Were we sure we could trust this mysterious contact? I offered only vague answers. Walker might've threatened me into secrecy, but his trust in me acted as a stronger motivator.

Nobody cared much about the interior decorating except James. At the basement door, I gestured them in. Ethan waited at the rear. Instead of entering, he took my hand, shut the door, and pulled me away.

"What's up?"

He shook his head, searching. The ascending stairwell satisfied him. Ethan continued into the hallway off the bedrooms and chose the one that rested farthest from the stairs — and just so happened to belong to Walker and Saini. Touching my pocket, I strode into that room with the now empty frame. Ethan crossed halfway and spun around near the dresser.

"You need to read Banks before we agree to his plan."

I'd resisted peeking at his thoughts, but I felt stupid for not guessing them. I knotted my arms and said, "At some point, you're going to have to accept that he's not your wayward MTA partner. Jimmy is on our side."

Ethan stared at me a lengthy moment, displaying his usual solemnity. The pause meant his next words were still being pieced together. I steeled myself. When he spoke, the rush of information made up for his hesitance.

"Bridget is a protean. She doesn't realize it, but Walker and I saw her name at the lab. She has the ability of mood control. Andrews documented several successful encounters of manipulating her in order to control a crowd. He tried doing that in Virginia, and Banks tried in the van. Notice he spoke to her directly. I saw Bridget falter, and I started thinking we needed to turn back, which is what Banks wanted."

My mouth had dried by the time he finished. Bridget, a protean? I'd assumed my telepathy had been the force behind how often I'd keenly felt her emotions. Apparently not. I could learn what others thought, but Bridget could actually manipulate emotions. This tiny meta carried a dangerous tool, one that could manipulate a crowd...

... into joining an operation?

Andrews had asked whether Bridget joined Whitewash first. James and McFarland had followed immediately after — and, once at base, McFarland had seemed unsure of that decision. Bridget and Vires might've been the only cadets to join Whitewash without any emotional inspiration. Andrews had known. According to Ethan, so did Jimmy.

"You're making some huge assumptions here," I said.

"You can verify whether I'm right."

"Or, I can have a normal conversation with him and not treat him like the enemy."

"You tried that already." Ethan paused again and obviously weighed his next words. "Why did you kidnap him?"

"To get him away from Andrews."

"Why didn't you *ask* him to come with you, then?"

I turned my head, not intending the direction of the nightstand, but that was where it went.

"Because you didn't think he would come willingly," he said. "That isn't the way to treat someone you trust wholeheartedly, Ella."

"You're putting words in my mouth."

"I'm—"

"I'll talk to him." My interruption came abruptly, as did the mood shift. Irritation pricked my skin, annoying as an unexpected drizzle. Ethan's suspicions of Jimmy nettled. Not as much as what he had left unsaid: that I seemed just as suspicious. I turned to leave.

Ethan touched my shoulder. "If Andrews is manipulating him, we can only trust his plan once we're certain it's coming from him and not Andrews."

"Jimmy wouldn't betray us like that. Especially not Kara."

"I hope you're right."

He spoke of hope, but the meaning rang of anything but. I clenched my hands and continued out.

We'd just stepped off the bottom stair when someone barreled into view. I glimpsed the gas mask, registered the person wearing it—and, most alarming of Jimmy's accessories, the assault rifle held at elbow level.

For metas, reactions could begin and end within half a second. We stepped off the stair, Jimmy came around the corner, and Ethan pushed me behind him, all within a blink.

Keeping the rifle aimed with one arm, Jimmy swiped the mask off and tossed it to the floor. "Letting me leave so easily?" His voice and expression had lost the fervor. He was calm, unnervingly bland. "I know you, Ethan."

My mind's racing never reached a conclusion. Ethan pulled me low as a shot fired. I flattened myself on the wall. Then, Ethan darted after Jimmy, who'd vanished into the foyer. Another gunshot cracked.

Panicked questions — no time for those. I bolted toward the archway that led into the foyer, then leaped aside as the rifle skittered along the wood floor. I kicked it out of sight of the battling metas. The carpet runner slipped under their feet, and a lamp wobbled on the foyer table.

A quick assessment told me what I'd predicted. Jimmy, as he'd done throughout their partnership, had the upper-hand. Ethan's moves were deflective. Maybe he relied on Jimmy tiring himself out, but Jimmy's former wildfire didn't translate into this fight. Every swipe came measured.

To Jimmy, I mentally shouted nonsense. He faltered, and Ethan seized his opening. The lamp flew. Ethan caught it, angled it, and swung hard. Porcelain shattered upon impact. Jimmy swayed, and Ethan smacked him the rest of the way toward unconsciousness. Six feet of mass collapsed on the rug.

"Check on the team," Ethan said, "and find something to bind him. Wear the mask."

I removed myself from the scene as if he'd chased me.

When I put on the mask, it felt sticky and smelled of musk. I wiped my unsteady hand on my pants. Photo paper crinkled.

A horrible, cold swell was rising faster than loyalty could allow. To contemplate the past two minutes hurt. So I thought only of the basement door. And when that arrived, I staggered to the next point. A spherical, metal object hissed on the top step. Nothing visible issued from it, but it must have done something. There were no sounds from below.

I leaped to the floor and swiveled left. Kara and the cadets lay in various forms of discomfort, from twisted limbs to James' facedown slump. I darted to the closest — Bridget — and felt her pulse. Bridget the protean. Maybe he'd tried convincing her and failed.

No speculating.

Everyone breathed raggedly, but they breathed. Removing the gas bomb would hopefully help. First, I searched for handcuffs. Agent Walker had some on the bottom shelf of the glass case. I wildly snatched and came out with four sets.

Gas bomb, I told Ethan. *Hold your breath.*

Another jump put me at the stop of the stairs, where I grabbed the bomb and wrapped it in my shirt hem. The basement door collided into Jimmy's sprawled figure.

"Hold it under his nose for a minute," called Ethan from somewhere. "Then get rid of it."

I had to close my eyes the entire sixty seconds. The face my knuckles brushed—it wasn't Jimmy's. The gradually thickening inhales—not his, either.

Once sixty ticked by in my mental count, I ran to the front door, over the off-center rug, grinding porcelain into the thread fibers. Outside, I skimmed the yard. Walker's house was isolated near a plain that disappeared into trees. I aimed for those trees when I threw.

Back inside, I considered my next objective. I'd dropped the handcuffs by Jimmy; Ethan had probably bound and relocated him. That cleared the way toward the basement.

In twos, I carried the others toward the living room, not pausing to talk to Ethan except to tell him not to enter the basement yet, in case the gas lingered. He'd set Jimmy, wrists and ankles cuffed, on a loveseat. I made sure to avoid it.

When my last load passed from me to the couch, Ethan asked for water to revive the team. He'd stay in the living room. Someone had to monitor Jimmy, he said.

Enemies needed monitoring.

I returned from the kitchen with an armful of water bottles from the fridge. Ethan strode over and reached around my head. The mask lifted. I'd forgotten it was there.

Starting on opposite ends, we worked through the unconscious group. It took the bottle's entire contents, but the cold water did the trick. McFarland groaned. On my end, Vires swatted my wrist away. They stayed foggy while Ethan and I finished the process, delaying the inevitable, the moment someone would notice we weren't reviving Jimmy. It didn't appear that the cadets knew who'd attacked them.

Kara was my last patient. One bottle gone and she hadn't awoken. I ripped another out of Ethan's hand and mercilessly dumped. With a twitch and a splutter, she opened her eyes and immediately coughed.

"You okay?" I helped her rise.

She stared around the room, rubbing her throat. "What happened?"

"Gas bomb," Ethan said.

A bottle soared to McFarland. She started for Jimmy.

"No," Ethan said sharply. "Banks stays unconscious."

"Why?" James asked.

I let my eyes go unfocused. If Ethan did the same, maybe no one would realize—and if no one acknowledged it, then we could pretend it had never happened.

"He said he was going to the bathroom," Kara murmured. I could sense her head turning my way. "He did this?"

Lydia remarked first. The rest of the conversation faded out. I let it dissipate, break apart like a withered tree. The effort was meant to ward off the truth. In the silence of my mind, even the barest hint of it screamed.

Something was wrong with Jimmy. Something had been wrong with Jimmy since Andrews' death. Supposed death. I'd noticed it as soon as he'd strode to the head of Whitewash's conference table and began taking charge. Every action since that day had been calm and thorough. Honestly, attacking his peers and attempting an escape seemed the most normal thing he'd done lately, only because it had been reckless. I could've dismissed it all as the desperate plan of an emotional Jimmy except for one fact.

My Jimmy would never hurt Kara.

After voicing that, even mentally, the cold inside returned. I didn't want to admit it. I'd gotten annoyed with Ethan for considering it, but continued denial was unfair to the people he'd just hurt. My duty was to sift out, not cover up, and I could either stand here speculating, or I could do my job. Even if it hurt.

I inhaled, feeling the ice spread. All at once, I felt tempted to retreat toward the hot plain of ignorance. The pull came so strong that the only way to combat it meant taking an immediate step. I tugged the water bottle from McFarland and stood before Jimmy. Ethan protested, but I broke the cap's seal and flung the water at Jimmy's face.

He started, head jerking as he shook off droplets. When he came to awareness, his cursory scan of the room did nothing to his expression, not until his attention locked on me. He turned stony. Resigned.

"Don't." Jimmy said it quietly.

"Why not?"

"The truth won't change the facts."

I wanted to smack sense into him. *Why are you doing this, Jimmy? How long are you going to keep this up?*

His head turned. "Saecula saeculorum," he whispered.

"That's Latin," James said. "It essentially means 'forever.'"

With understanding came a chill on my neck. Eugene Andrews' motto was inked into his coat of arms as much as his name, which passed on and on —*forever*. But it was only a name. Jimmy didn't have to own it.

Not forever, I told him. *Remember what we talked about, Jimmy? It doesn't matter if he's your dad. You get to choose how you act.*

"You don't understand."

Then help me understand.

"You're going to read me. Explaining it would be redundant."

We'd reached the impasse. He refused to offer anything, and I wouldn't uselessly badger him.

I would've preferred to do this without everyone watching, but this was their business too. So I closed my eyes and pretended Jimmy and I were alone. Shutting out that detached, foreign Jimmy helped; he was difficult to understand, unlike the Jimmy who'd watched me grow. That boy, I could empathize with.

Entering his mind proved easier than sorting it. I'd read him before, specifically searching, and had encountered that warehouse-like compartmentalizing that divided his memories. Walls had kept them distinct. Now, his mind resembled a limitless library of information with nothing to keep it from mingling. Somehow, he seemed to have accumulated a gazillion more memories. I'd drown if I didn't narrow my focus. What I wanted revolved around the day of Andrews' "death." Releasing an exhale like it had the power to stretch, I found the scene.

Jimmy watched through the window as Dr. Saini cut into Andrews' neck.

"I wonder, Dr. Saini: do your associates realize you're a pro —"

The MTA commander stiffened, flinching under Saini's knife. Andrews' back arched. Then, his chin drooped.

At once, agony struck Jimmy's skull, causing him to cry out. Doubled-over, he heard One's concerned inquiry. It was the last thing he registered before the memories exploded.

CHAPTER TWENTY-EIGHT

"WILL IT HURT?"

He endeavored to voice the question as Father might, an inquiry of scientific curiosity and nothing more. A tremble of fear ruined his efforts, and he resented it.

"No, Master Eugene. You shall only feel the needle's prick." Nurse Lockwood smiled upon him, sweeping back his hair.

He felt some trouble fade, then cursed himself. It would not do to allow himself to draw comfort from the nurse as if he were namby-pamby. What would Father think of him?

"Eugene," a man called sharply. Nathaniel Andrews stood in the infirmary's doorway. His pale hair was tied with a ribbon to match his cravat. His livery shone a blue shade that strengthened the vibrancy of his eyes, though he currently glanced elsewhere. He rarely bestowed a thorough observation upon his son.

Eugene thrust back the nurse's coddling hand and gave the man his most confident nod. "Father," he said, pleased to hear a measure of composure returned to him.

"Has Nurse Lockwood detailed the procedure to your satisfaction?"

"Yes, sir."

"Excellent." Father inspected the timepiece that hung from his coat. He'd developed an attachment to it; Eugene had observed that during their few interactions.

"Shall I leave you to your privacy, sir?" the nurse said.

"Carry on, Miss Lockwood." Father waved a hand. "Eugene knows I possess no illusions of sentimentality."

Eugene's throat curled. Father could not spare him a word even this morn. Eugene understood that he, with his inept body, displeased Nathaniel. Though likewise lacking a metahuman's strength, Father could at least operate telekinesis. Not so for Eugene. He carried the hope that the proceeding experiment would redeem him. The doctors intended to rectify nature's mistake so that Eugene no longer differed from the metahuman students at the Andrews Academy. They couldn't belittle him if he joined their ranks. True, the pupils never dared openly criticize an Andrews, but he could see their scorn, even with his weak eyes.

"Another experiment? That sounds foolishly dangerous," Emmett had argued when last they saw each other. "Can Father's approval be worth your life?"

To which Eugene had persisted that Father would *never* allow the doctors to conduct an experiment that endangered the life of his son. But he hardly expected his brother to understand. Though Emmett also lacked the metahuman strength, he made up for the loss a hundredfold with his telepathic capabilities.

Nurse Lockwood wetted a muslin square and wiped the cloth against the inner skin of Eugene's elbow. "My first measure will be to sterilize—"

"Do refrain from coddling the boy, Miss Lockwood," Nathaniel interrupted. "And do hurry. I have more important obligations."

A flash of ire darkened Nurse Lockwood's fair countenance, though she hurried with a curtsey. "Yes, sir." She maintained a gentle touch, despite Father's disapproval. Some within the Academy did not allow Father's position to intimidate them. Emmett was one such intrepid lion. Such bravery, however, was not to be found in Eugene.

"Egad!" he swore when she withdrew a pointy needle from her frock.

"Only a pinch," she murmured, although she stayed her hand, and distress wrinkled her fine features. Her fingers shook violently. Why was she so afraid? *Eugene* would be receiving the injection, not she.

"Shall I assign another to your duties?" Father asked with undisguised exasperation.

Not wishing Father to associate him with such a fretful woman, Eugene grasped the nurse's hand. "Get on with it," he said harshly. Afterward, he peeked over. Nathaniel, still intent upon his timepiece, had not noticed Eugene's false display of indifference.

Tears bloomed from the nurse's eyes. "Godspeed, dear boy," she whispered. "I pray you live." She drove the needlepoint into his flesh.

"Why shan't I...."

Eugene collapsed before he could finish the question.

"EUGENE? CAN YOU hear us, love?"

He recognized Nurse Lockwood's voice and moved toward it. "Yes," he murmured as he strained to open his eyes; they felt so very heavy. "I hear you."

The sound of his voice startled him. It sounded quite soprano, as if he were younger than thirteen.

When he found himself able to focus, he peered at the figures before him. Some were the laboratory doctors; he could tell because their white overcoats. Nurse Lockwood sat at the edge of his bed, and towering above the foot stood Father.

"Do you recognize those you see, Eugene?" Nathaniel peered down, stern lines around his mouth, as if Eugene had done something wrong.

He strained to flex his fingers, hot with dread that the experiment had failed. As he did so, clarity spilled into his eyes and focus into his ears. Those in the room grew sharper in detail, and Eugene could have sworn he heard Father's heartbeat, measured and broad, contrasting Eugene's thin staccato.

"Of course, Father," he replied, still in that high tone.

Nurse Lockwood gasped and covered her mouth. Was his voice so shocking? He cleared his throat and spoke again. "Was the procedure successful? Am I strong now?" Inwardly, he cursed himself, annoyed to find his pitch had not lowered.

"I certainly hope so." Nathaniel glared at Dr. Dietrich.

"We shall test him, ya?" the bearded doctor wheedled with wringing hands. "Can the Master Eugene summon the object?" He indicated a cup on a shelf across the room.

Eugene's heart thumped. Father, Emmett, and all the students at the Academy could wield telekinesis. Thus far, Eugene had proved horribly useless at the power, something that vexed Nathaniel to no end. If he should fail now, after the experiment... he shuddered to imagine the extent of Father's disgust.

His arm stretched forth, though it reached not as far as he willed. Somehow, his limb appeared shorter. Ignoring this strangeness, Eugene focused on the cup and ordered it to fly his direction. *You best obey,* he thought.

It did. Pliable as Emmett.

The doctors clapped and cheered, all but Nurse Lockwood, who maintained her horrified gape. Eugene ignored her. He glowed with relief. Father, however, was not yet satisfied. "Break it," he commanded.

Eugene barely squeezed the porcelain, yet it shattered in his palm. The doctors cheered louder still. Even though his skin ached, Eugene flushed at the thrill of new strength. He was a metahuman now. The Academy students could not disdain him any longer.

Nathaniel looked at the doctors. "Bring him."

Two of the men left, returning in a moment with a newcomer. Emmett Andrews, steered into the room by the fierce grip of Dr. Dietrich, took a gander at Eugene upon the bed. The muzzle obscuring Emmett's mouth could not disclose his expression, but his eyes—a muddled blue, like Father's—grew wide.

You've shrunk, Emmett said to him.

And you've grown, haven't you? Eugene thought; for, indeed, Emmett appeared taller, his breeches seeming to stretch endlessly before they met his hosiery. Though Eugene preceded his twin in age by four minutes, Emmett had acquired Father's height swifter. Even so, Emmett had never seemed so tall, his unruly, blonde curls creating an additional inch or so that, previously, had never seemed a vast difference to Eugene.

I've not changed, Emmett said. *Eugene, you idiot. Father's turned you back into a child! Now he'll want to know whether this new body can manage me.*

A... child? Recalling his altered voice, Eugene felt a rise of alarm. He searched Nurse Lockwood's expression. Her continued horror made him inexplicably angry. He wished he could see Emmett's mind to learn what his brother currently beheld, but he did not possess any insight into Emmett's mind. The connection they shared was entirely his twin's doing. Eugene, on the other hand, held the ability to command Emmett into obedience—a gift Father loved, Emmett despised, and Eugene exercised sparingly. He did not like forcing his brother into submission, but it pleased Nathaniel, so Eugene obliged when loyalty to his twin failed him.

Yes, Emmett said. *You don't look a day over eight!*

But... but I am thirteen!

Not any longer. Oh, Eugene, why did you let Fa—

"Sharp to!"

At Nathaniel's rough call, Eugene flinched, and Emmett gave their father a withering stare. He'd never cared for Father's approval and surely did not mind at all that the twins had ignored their superiors in exchange for private discourse.

Eugene brought a hand before his face. It did seem smaller, did it not? Paler, too, closer to Father and Emmett in their fair coloring — for, while they resembled each other, Eugene's brown hair, hazel eyes, and warmer skin tone must have come from the deceased mother he'd never known.

"Now, Emmett," Nathaniel was saying, "do not embarrass yourself with silly hysterics, or Eugene shall have to quiet you."

Emmett must have silently communicated to Father. Eugene did not concern himself with it; he turned his attention upon Nathaniel and said, "Why does Emmett say I am a child?"

Sighing, Nathaniel motioned to Dietrich.

"An effect of the surgery," the doctor said smoothly. "Your body has... ah, what is the word for *verkleinern*?"

"Reduced," offered another doctor.

"Ya, reduced." Dietrich nodded. "You are young again, Master Eugene."

Eugene swallowed. "How young?"

"Currently, you —"

"Does it matter, Eugene?" Father interrupted. "You are no longer weak. You wanted vitality, did you not?"

Eugene, in his shock, could not answer. Emmett spoke for him, raising his hands in visible consternation and mentally badgering Father.

"Yes," Nathaniel answered, "and he will age properly — not into the inept creature that he was, but an able-bodied man who can carry the Andrews legacy without disgracing me."

Inept, Father had called him. But, in the same breath, he spoke of something grander. Now, Father considered him worthy of his name. That praise dulled some of Eugene's perplexity.

"Oh yes, Emmett," Father said to his brother, a strange glint in his gaze. "*In perpetuum,* indeed." He turned to Eugene. "Go on, then. Tell him to jump."

Of course — the doctors would want to know whether Eugene could still control Emmett. His brother had predicted as much.

Eugene glanced at his twin. Both boys understood how this game operated. Eugene had tried to end their connection years ago, but a command to be free proved the only order Emmett could ignore.

Please, Eugene thought, hoping his brother read him. *It's only a jump.*

It's always only a jump, Emmett replied. *Only a jump, only a memory. Here, I'll obey before you ask. Father shan't have his way in perpetuum.* Emmett thumped the floor, causing a shower of dust from the rafters.

No, stop!

Emmett continued jumping. Eugene could think whatever he liked; it bore no impact. He wielded no power until he spoke.

"Stop jumping, Emmett," he commanded. His young voice sounded somewhat like Father.

Emmett ceased at once. He glared at Eugene, who felt regret burn so sorely, he feared he might embarrass himself by weeping.

The doctors clapped again—all except Nurse Lockwood. "Very good, Eugene," Father murmured. The note of pride in his voice drew Eugene right away from his sorrow. Unless he were mistaken, Father looked quite close to jubilant.

Father's impressed, Emmett said. *I'm sure you're not sorry any longer.*

Eugene had to admit that Emmett had spoken truly: he was not sorry at all.

It was the first time Father had smiled at him.

EUGENE WAS KEPT FROM public view after the procedure; it would not do to alarm the students with his eight-year-old body. Whilst the budding attendance of gifted metahumans studied a life of adventure and intrigue, Eugene was relocated to Emmett's quarters beneath the Academy's ground floor. While he enjoyed this new freedom to see his brother daily, he bitterly missed the pleasure of living around others who, though they may have believed him to be Nathaniel Andrews' inept son, had nonetheless treated him with the respect of his title. Eugene longed to prove that he was stronger now; but, alas, he could not show himself until those who recognized him had moved on from the Academy. This infuriated him, and he consoled himself by breaking things.

Emmett did not find Eugene's youthful body a fascinating topic of discussion. He only spoke of it to bemoan that the procedure had occurred at all. He grew convinced that the doctors had done far worse than they'd divulged, evident in that Eugene no longer bore a scar he'd received around the age of four. Eugene failed to see what an absent scar proved, but Emmett would not let the matter be.

"Can you truly admit nothing odd about it?" Emmett said aloud; the doctors did not fit him with his muzzle in Eugene's presence, for they knew he would never use his power against his brother. He sat behind a desk he'd outgrown; his long legs—Eugene did envy his brother for his taller, older body—sprawled like fallen branches. "You ought to have that scar, even if Dietrich did *verschluken* you."

"*Verkleinern*," Eugene amended. "Your German is quite poor. How ever did you occupy your time down here?"

"*Latine loqui*." His brother grinned. "*Et français, monsieur*."

"Your pronunciation of both is horrid. Will I have to instruct you?"

"I can't have a tutor half my age. That's hardly appropriate."

"I'm your elder by four minutes," Eugene said, annoyed.

"Not so anymore, little brother."

For all Emmett's height and age, he behaved like a child. Glaring, Eugene resumed the mental levitations of his writing quill. Often, he telekinetically toyed with it. He liked to see that he still could.

"Oh, Eugene." Emmett made to thwack his twin's arm, but Eugene easily avoided the blow, finally outmatching the brother who had outshone him with all his mental prowess for thirteen long years. "I know you're not really angry with me," Emmett said. "This isolation vexes you. Don't fret, brother. Father wishes you to lead the Academy after he's dead. You'll have your freedom then."

"Does he? Truly?" Eugene could not hide his pleasure at that. Mind-reading certainly had its uses. The quill he twirled danced higher. "Well," he added, "I suppose we must first see the outcome of the war abroad. Father says those revolutionaries are as much a plague as the Grifters."

"I'd sorely love to be a Grifter or a revolutionary. Anything to remove me from this confinement."

"I wish you wouldn't speak like that, Emmett. It's so morose."

"Command me into silence, then."

The words riled him. Despite Nathaniel's repeated insistence, Eugene had denied his father this single request. Emmett had begged, saying he would rather don the muzzle than lose all faculty of speech. So much of Emmett's happiness lay in Eugene's hands. His brother's powers could cease by Eugene's word—and, by default, so would Eugene's own power over memories and thoughts. For, as Nathaniel often said, a master is only as powerful as his tool.

"You know I shan't," Eugene said quietly.

The two shared a long gaze; and, while Eugene lay exposed, Emmett shared none of his thoughts.

Eventually, Emmett sighed and freed himself from his desk. He crouched and gently clasped his brother's wrist. "I would do anything you wish," he murmured. "You needn't ask. You know this?"

Eugene turned his head. He'd always had difficulty deciding whether his brother's unfailing devotion left him feeling honored or uncomfortable. "Yes," he said.

"Anything, Eugene. Except what you have me do. I cannot bear it. Their minds—"

"Not this harangue again. They are only civilians, Emmett."

"And were you not like one of them before this monstrous experiment morphed you?"

"No," Eugene said sharply, withdrawing his hand. "I was not. I still possessed the proper gene."

"It is hardly their fault for lacking it." Emmett's volume dropped lower still. "We are not better than they, Eugene. These gifts do not make us gods."

"But we do have gifts, Emmett, and they must be protected. In these quarters, you have been blind to the dangers wrought by frightened civilians."

"You forget I see far more than you, dear brother. I have observed the thoughts of those you have me manipulate. They are frightened because the Academy lies to them. Some believe we have stolen their children."

"That is absurd. Father would never allow such a thing." Eugene, uncomfortable, shifted in his seat. "What we do is for the wellbeing of society."

"No, it is for the wellbeing of the Academy."

"And why does that trouble you?"

"Because the Academy is unjust. And I fear it will consume you."

Eugene could not answer; an interruption made them draw apart. The warning bell along the wall had rung, indicating someone's approach. Emmett would need to resume his muzzle, for no one trusted him to restrain himself except Eugene.

Once certain his brother's muzzle strap lay securely fastened, Eugene opened the schoolroom door.

"Come, *junge Meister*," Dr. Dietrich said.

The boys knew the doctor's purpose. Emmett's ability was required—meaning Eugene's was in turn.

It struck Eugene as ironic that Emmett's perceived enslavement gave them their only moments of freedom.

Though Eugene made to follow the doctor, Emmett clung to his desk.

"Oh, pish," Eugene called. "You know this makes it worse."

Emmett refused to budge, and Eugene was forced to persuade him in the manner neither of them enjoyed. "You brought this upon yourself," Eugene said, and Emmett sulked.

As soon as Father had realized the extent of Emmett's abilities, the young son of Nathaniel Andrews had been fitted with a muzzle and relocated to the Academy's laboratory for observation. There, he had spent most of his childhood, allowed leave only when Nathaniel determined his other son's special power. Upon realizing Emmett had no choice but to obey whatever Eugene said, Nathaniel understood that one who could destroy and recreate memories at whim provided the Andrews Academy with unlimited defense against inquisitive eyes and ears. For nearly a decade, those who learned more than Nathaniel preferred about his elite Academy promptly forgot, due to Emmett and Eugene. One son performed the function while the other induced it. A symbiotic relationship, Dr. Dietrich said.

Both sons—one thirteen, and the other now eight in body—followed after Dietrich. The man led them upstairs, toward the barred door that would take them directly outside without fear of chancing upon students. Eugene had crippled this door once, per Emmett's encouragement, but their breath of freedom had not been worth Father's rage. Emmett still chortled about it, but Eugene usually gave the newly fitted door a liberal berth.

"Tell him to silence, and remove that mask," Dietrich said, pointing to Emmett. "We are going into the outside. He cannot be seen in that fashion."

Emmett's eyes pleaded. *Don't do it, brother.*

"Only for a moment," Eugene said. "I'll revoke it once it's safe to don the muzzle."

Nay, you'll revoke it when you command me to destroy another poor soul's memory.

Eugene sighed. It was this sort of sentimental rhetoric that had disposed Emmett to a life of confinement. "He has his mother's spirit," Nathaniel frequently remarked. Emmett, shut in for years, had not endured the same tension as Eugene and the rest of the metahumans: the suspicious whispers at the market, the incriminating newspaper headlines, the bricks thrown through windows. Civilians did not like Father's Academy because they feared what they did not possess.

You needn't command me, Emmett said, his mental voice adopting a solicitous tone. *I'll stay silent.*

But what of Dietrich? Eugene wondered.

We shall trick him. Slyly, Emmett winked.

The doctor admonished the boys for delaying. Raising his chin high, Eugene firmly said, "Do not speak aloud until I say otherwise."

Uncertainty flashed in Emmett's eyes. He obediently bowed his head as Eugene unclasped the latch, and Dietrich turned to the door. Stowing the muzzle under his arm, Eugene raised himself on tiptoe and whispered, "Speak however much you like."

Emmett's grin came quick with relief. "Yes, Master," he whispered back.

Outside, Eugene heard the ruckus before Dietrich and Emmett; neither showed any reaction as the three crossed through the courtyard, boots clacking on the cobblestones cracked with weeds and age. As Dietrich tended to the iron gate that proudly proclaimed the Andrews crest, Eugene closed his eyes and listened.

"... rotten devils, the lot of ya!" a man shouted.

"Murderers!"

"Miscreants!"

The crowd threw insults as surely as they threw stones; Eugene heard the shatter of glass and Mr. Bennett's calming timbre. But Father's secretary could not repel the civilian's vicious fears. Only Emmett could.

By stealing their memories, his brother mentally spoke. *They are right to call us miscreants.*

They can't remember well enough to accuse us. Now come along, Emmett.

His twin's steps fell obediently after.

They stole along the road bordering the Andrews manor, shielding themselves from a faint drizzle. The gray sky reminded Eugene of a Grifter's coloring. He had never seen one himself, but he'd chanced upon a diagram in Father's study. "A pity Bergström allowed so many to survive," Nathaniel had said.

If only the foolish civilians recognized that the metahumans protected them. But the civilians could not know the danger that lurked, a threat far stronger than the revolutionaries instigating war with their motherland. The Andrews Academy had to monitor the repercussions of its scientists' failed experiments.

Before the manor, angry civilians thronged at the expansive iron gate. The crowd jeered so loudly, Eugene wondered how their fragile ears withstood the cacophony.

The sight of them stumped Emmett. He rarely saw others, and certainly not a crowd of this volume.

"Do you mean him to address them all at once?" Eugene called to the doctor. "There are too many."

"To the gate, the gate," Dietrich ushered. "He shall attend to them from there."

The three companions could not easily skirt the crowd; they were forced to make their progress by edging along the gate. Eugene knew he could overcome them all, but it would not do to rile them further.

"You!" a man shouted, and Eugene turned to glare. The peasant, filthy in the face with his cap crinkled in his hands, pointed to Emmett. "Spawn of Andrews! Fancy yerself better than us, aye?"

Emmett's face shone white with horror, and he uttered no defense. *The poor people*, he said to Eugene. *I cannot think how to help them.*

They do not deserve your pity, Eugene thought.

If not I, from whom else can they receive it?

Dietrich cursed the skies, and Eugene pushed Emmett through the increasingly agitated peoples. They did not take note of Eugene, nor how he commanded his brother to keep walking. Whilst both boys wore noble attire, everyone knew Nathaniel had twins. Certainly an eight year old could not be kin to the boy who bore such remarkable likeness to the man cursed by the civilians.

"Slimy spawn!" The same man pounced through the crowd.

Eugene turned, deciding he ought to silence the fool for having the audacity to address an Andrews in such a manner.

"Please." Emmett gripped his brother's elbow; the doctor likely could not hear him speak in this chaos. "Do not hurt him. He knows not what he says."

"He knows plenty well, Emmett. Now, stop—"

"Please." Emmett touched Eugene's mouth. "Obey *me*, brother. Just this once."

Eugene hesitated. He heard Emmett's pulse and the man's fiery cries.

His brother smiled and lowered his arm. A show of faith. Uncertain, Eugene searched for the peasant. His eyes fell upon the black pistol in the man's outstretched hand.

Eugene did not have time to wonder whether he had the speed of a bullet. He threw himself before Emmett as a violent noise rang. A woman screamed, and Eugene readied his command that Emmett find safety.

Would you command me to be a coward, too? Emmett said, and Eugene felt his brother shift around him. *Am I not even free to love your life more than my own?*

"Emmett—"

The gun's discharge pierced again. Emmett's lanky form collapsed. In his shock, Eugene failed to catch his brother, who dropped prostrate. His eyes lay open, and blood wetted the ground.

Eugene stiffened. He barely noted the pain that lanced his skull just before his vision turned rapidly to darkness.

HE DREW IN A shuddering gasp. The effect burned his throat as oxygen arrived. Something obstructed his face. Eugene raised an arm to claw at the suffocating mask and found his limb reluctant to obey. The more he persisted, the more feeling returned to him. He seemed to be underwater. His limbs drifted, his eyes stung at each attempt to see, yet he did not drown, even as minutes faded.

Emmett? he thought. *Are you here?*

His brother did not answer. Eugene could not bear to consider the meaning of that silence.

When Eugene regained proper mastery over his limbs, he set to exploration. Someone had placed him inside an enclosure hard as glass that gave when he beat upon it. A great gurgling began about his ears. He heard the water now. It drained, and Eugene felt himself sink. Cool, hard objects brushed his bare torso.

Once his eyes could endure the sudden light, he saw that he lay covered in broken glass. He wore no clothes, and strange wires dug into his damp skin. Eugene had somehow come to be inside a tank, flat on his back, affixed to foreign mechanisms. Perhaps Dietrich had confined him in some sort of healing machine. That would explain why Eugene could not feel his recent injury.

He wrenched the obstruction off his face and gagged as a tube emerged from his mouth. With tremendous effort, he pulled himself upright, blinking furiously. His efforts lagged, and full sight did not return. Over several more moments, Eugene detached the wires from his skin, and then stood. He staggered and fell at once over the side of the tank. Throbbing painfully, he panted on the cold floor and sought to gain his bearings.

"Is... anyone...?" His voice rasped, an ugly croak. He could not manage the rest of his inquiry. It would benefit him to exercise his detection capabilities, but Eugene found his senses woefully frail.

He knew not how long he lay shivering. At last, voices worked around the blockage in his ears. Someone heaved him to his feet, and he stumbled.

"Fetch him a blanket. He is a sniveling rat," came Nathaniel's voice.

"F-Father." Eugene detected Nathaniel's form, though it remained hazy in outline. He needed so desperately to inquire after Emmett, but he could not voice his question quickly enough. "Where... Emmett?"

A heavy fabric draped over his shoulders, and his balance faltered again. Why was he so pitifully *weak*?

Gathering the blanket about him like a cloak, Eugene strained and squinted until the film left his eyes. He saw Nathaniel bickering with Dietrich and an odd, bald lad between them. Searching the room for Emmett, he beheld the large objects decorating the floor. Lined beside the broken tank he'd emerged from sat another half-dozen vessels. They hummed, emitting soft light, illuminating the sleeping figures within them.

Eugene's mouth dried. Four of the figures looked identical to him — to his eight-year-old body. The other two creatures resembled the bald lad. A certain familiarity struck Eugene at the sight of them. Had his gaze lingered, he might have reached recognition.

"Come, Master Eugene." Dietrich cuffed his shoulder. "'Tis not the place for you. Dreadfully cold and wet."

Tripping after Dietrich, Eugene observed the bald boy — the conscious one. He stood quite short. The lad had Emmett's forehead and coloring but none of his wild, blond hair. He, too, wore a muzzle.

"Emmett?" Eugene whispered.

The boy gave no indication that he'd heard.

Eugene pulled away from the doctor and nearly collided with his father. "Who are those... where is my brother?"

Dietrich flushed and strummed his white beard.

"Are you blind, rat?" Nathaniel's nostrils flared as he gestured in a direction Eugene had not yet explored. "Emmett is dead. That civilian wretch murdered you both. Two Andrews, defeated by a worm."

Eugene followed his father's motion and saw two figures on the floor. He recognized both lads, but he focused only on the taller one. In his mind, he envisioned Emmett's lifeless body outside the gate and realized he'd already known. Some inept civilian had murdered his twin, and Eugene had not prevented it.

A hand, colder and less forgiving than the inside of that tank, flattened Eugene. He could neither breathe nor moan. His father's mention of *two* murders did not coax him from the wasteland. Only when Eugene remembered the bald boy, so similar to his brother, did desperate curiosity rejuvenate him enough to speak.

"Who is that creature?" He pointed.

"Your brother's copy," Nathaniel said. "Dietrich failed to retain his exact physique as he did yours, but Emmett's abilities are intact."

"I do not understand."

"Yes, I expect not. Emmett was the astute one."

Was – the word struck Eugene like a blade.

"We have duplicated him, Master Eugene," Dietrich said. "So, you see, it is not so bad, ya? Emmett lives! This copy has been awake for five years now."

Eugene stared at the pale boy, who apparently possessed not an ounce of Emmett's astute perception. The lad's vacant expression and downcast gaze lacked all familiarity. He seemed a mindless sheep.

"No," Eugene said, "that creature is not awake."

"Ya, the subject is not meant to be much animated." The doctor gazed greedily at the boy. "Master Andrews did not want your brother's unruly disposition to interfere with his purpose."

"What purpose is that?"

"To serve Andrews unto the end of ages." Dietrich clapped.

"So long as they are alive," Nathaniel said, indicating the bald lads in the tanks, "you are eternal."

"Those creatures ensure your survival, Master Eugene," added the doctor. "Their collective consciousness allows for your anamnesis to, ah, *verschmelzen*... to pass into your next body. They are why you awoke in the tank with your memories intact."

Eugene's focus returned to the dead lads on the floor, and he allowed himself to accept what he had recognized before. The shorter body belonged to him, identical to the forms in the tank. He searched his elbow for the scar Emmett had fussed about and did not find it. This body likewise did not feel the pain of his recent injury — for he no longer wore that form.

"Then that experiment did not reduce me," Eugene said. "It murdered me, and I awoke in one of my duplicates."

Nathaniel smirked. "Perhaps you have some wit after all."

Eugene could find no pride in that compliment. Emotion throbbed his temples and boiled his veins. A flame of rage lit his insides, a painful oppression that thickened the more he beheld that sickly duplicate of Emmett. If he could burst, unleashing his anger upon this room until Nathaniel, Dietrich, himself, and every last duplicate of him and his brother were reduced to ash, he would gladly succumb.

To every disparaging remark Emmett had spoken of their father, Eugene had offered a defense. Though he knew Nathaniel disliked them, Eugene had, like a child, clung to the expectation that their father must feel some attachment to his only sons. Foolhardy, Emmett had warned. Eugene did not need that admonishment now, nor did he wish for Nathaniel's heart to change. He suddenly hated the man who had confined his brother, duplicated his sons without their knowledge, and called for an experiment that directly murdered his own flesh.

Trembling, he forced himself to address Nathaniel. "And if we woke another now?" he said, indicating a vessel that contained his figure. "Who would he be?"

"A very confused little boy," Dietrich said. "Until your current form is deceased, your duplicates are autonomous. It is why they must remain sleeping so they do not develop an identity. Otherwise," here Dietrich loosened a chuckle, "you would be battling another personality for dominance!"

Eugene understood the doctor's rationale, but he determined in that moment never to awaken in a vessel again, pitiful and shivering.

He spied the mindless, bald lad. "What of Emmett's anamnesis? Can it be regained?"

"No," Nathaniel said. "Emmett is lost. If I had wanted him to be immortal, I would have made it so."

"But why must I be immortal?"

"The Academy will always need a telepath, and he will always need you."

In that indifferent manner of Nathaniel Andrews, Eugene's future had been crafted. His father would remain pragmatic above all else. For the Academy to thrive, society must be manipulated. Only Emmett could do so, and only Eugene could force his brother to perform what he detested. And, if Grifter, civilian, or Death himself should come for either twin? The brothers would endure. They were immortal now.

No, only one brother survived. The doctors had not preserved Emmett's true self.

Eugene's fingers curled. "Where is the man who killed him?"

"I do hope you are not intending to avenge him," Nathaniel said, giving his timepiece a lazy inspection. "You have already allowed a civilian to kill you once today, Eugene. I cannot endure the embarrassment twice."

Hatred stormed within Eugene. Like a tempest, it scattered his thoughts until he could only rest on a sole objective. He grasped the blanket and strode directly to Emmett's strange duplicate. Certain that enough strength had returned, he forwent the latch and sized the creature's muzzle. "Be silent," he said, "unless I order otherwise."

Its eyes flickered upward, as if suddenly awoken. *Yes, Master Eugene,* it spoke. A dead voice, nothing like Emmett's.

Eugene ripped the mask free, clutched the creature by its neck, and spun it before him like a shield. Dietrich staggered backward, but Nathaniel stood his ground.

"Do not be a fool, Eugene," he said.

"No man may kill an Andrews without consequence." Eugene searched his father for fear, for he'd meant it as a threat.

But Nathaniel smiled for the second time. "You have my spirit after all," he murmured.

Eugene loathed that smile.

"Read them," he ordered the boy, "and tell me the name of the civilian who murdered Emmett."

Henry Cook, the creature answered after a moment.

"Good." Eugene's fingertips tightened. "Make them forget I learned Cook's name."

He walked away as the creature began to speak.

Foolish Nathaniel had reversed the truth. Eugene did not wield power because of Emmett. He wielded it by his own design. For a tool was only as powerful as his master.

AFTER ENSURING THAT ONLY Dietrich and Nathaniel remembered the scientists' strange experiment, Eugene made himself the duplicates' sole caretaker. Nathaniel had been averse to that proposal; Eugene handled his dissensions by having them erased. A lad with Eugene's power could achieve anything he wanted.

Eugene freed all six bodies from their tanks and sent his own duplicates across England. The four boys bore an identical story of an orphan left with neither family nor memories—though each was fortunate enough to have a wealthy, anonymous benefactor who could procure an education for them. If Eugene had to eventually share a personality with another, he would at least have the duplicate educated.

As to creating more, Eugene decided to repeat the process every decade. The genetic material for both Andrews had been meticulously preserved; Eugene need only conduct a bit of science with the tanks when he wished to grow another. Once his new copy reached two years of age, he would be anonymously given to the Academy and raised as a metahuman, as was his right.

Emmett's duplicates were not given the same freedom. Their future copies would not be freed from their growth vessels until they reached twelve. Eugene had no desire to surround himself with mindless children—although, for all appearances, he was a child himself.

Time faded by. Eugene awaited his death, nearly precipitating it on several occasions. He was curious to discover what should happen once this body ceased and his anamnesis drifted to the next duplicate, someone who'd lived without knowing his true origins.

When his body reached sixteen—though Eugene's consciousness had lived two-and-twenty years—something akin to a spell overwhelmed the three bald duplicates of his brother. Though Eugene had not commanded it, every copy arose from his bed and marched. Eugene placed himself before them and said, "All but one, desist."

The creatures halted. All but one. This one, Eugene followed.

"Where are you going?" He had to ask aloud after ordering the creatures never to penetrate his mind. They did not deserve that privilege.

To her.

"Her? Tell me who she is."

We do not know.

"Then why do you go to her?"

She calls.

Eugene found this curiously strange. To further questions, the creature revealed that he was not aware of his destination, only that he must heed the woman's call: *Ah, Emmett, viens à moi.* The creatures understood enough French to obey.

After the copy, Eugene followed.

The journey delivered them to port, where Eugene was forced to pay the captain a generous sum in exchange for a destination of whim. His companion did not stir until they reached the port of Saint-Malo the following morn. After half a day's walk through Brittany, they approached an incline, the top of which displayed a handsome château whose elegance boasted strict fortifications. The duplicate disregarded etiquette and set his hands upon the gate.

Eugene stopped him. "Is this where the woman lives?"

Yes.

"Cease, then. We cannot enter in this fashion."

He waited for the mail carriage and was given the name of Monsieur Tabouillot. As to any ladies of the household, such were Madame Éva and her two daughters. Now supplied with the appropriate information, Eugene *then* surpassed the gate with the duplicate upon his shoulders.

After some mental persuasion, the footman escorted the two Andrews into the salon. Neither one admired the rich furnishing nor partook of the offering of wine but awaited the entrance of the three ladies, one of whom had summoned the duplicates from across the channel. Such a woman, with an ability to match Eugene's, must be studied.

The arrival of feminine voices drew Eugene's attention toward the glass windows that overlooked an orchard. Beyond it, two lasses peeped curiously while their mother questioned the footman.

"Je n'attends pas un invite…." Madame Éva's head motioned the direction of Eugene and his companion. Likely she could not clearly discern them. Eugene, with his superior eyesight, saw perfectly.

The Madame was younger than Father but roughly twice Eugene's age, of an olive complexion far darker than Father's fair skin. Netting bound her hair: a thick, chestnut luster. Her hazel eyes, that brief glimpse of them, struck Eugene strongest.

They were his own.

He stood abruptly. With the duplicate upon his back again, Eugene fled through the side door.

WHEN NATHANIEL ANDREWS ENTERED his office two late evenings afterward, he expressed only slight surprise — and certain annoyance — at finding Eugene and his companion reclining near the fire.

"What inspired this intrusion, Eugene?" Nathaniel sat at his desk and took to its contents.

"I have returned from France."

"Have you?"

"I saw Éva."

"Do find your point, Eugene, or a more forbearing listener."

"Can you not bring yourself to feign affront even once?"

"To what end?" A sheaf of parchment hid Nathaniel's face. "What is your purpose here?"

"I am not surprised you lied concerning my mother's death, as—"

"Your mother?" Nathaniel lowered the parchment. "You did not mention your mother."

"Is Éva not she?"

"I have never heard the name." Shrewd comprehension stirred in the man's light eyes, and he softly said, "But it is the sort of sentimental notion she would oblige, choosing 'Éva' to represent her new life. Was she mad enough to return to France?"

Eugene arose rapidly, lashing a hand. The paper disappeared from his father's fingers. Over Nathaniel's curses, Eugene said, "My mother lives, then."

"Yes, boy, now where in France?"

Energy trembled in Eugene's veins. The crossed swords adorning his father's mantle, resplendent in the Andrews' crest, flew to his hands. Nathaniel sought to free them with his own power, but the man's telekinetic skill proved a foolhardy practice against Eugene. He crossed his father's study and dug both steel tips into the soft flesh below the man's shoulders. Blood bloomed generous stains upon the blue silk robe.

"Do not forget that I am stronger." Eugene longed to move but an inch; such movement would have Nathaniel writhing in agony. "You are fortunate Emmett's duplicate is here. I would not have him witness his father's murder. Now. My mother's name."

"Why not set your obedient hound upon me?"

"And deprive myself the pleasure of this conversation?"

Nathaniel sweated and snarled, cheeks paler still. "Barineau," he spat.

"Christian name?"

"Colette."

"And how does she live, *Father*," Eugene twitched, and the swords pierced deeper, "when flames corrupted her body when Emmett and I were but three?"

"That was a lie, you fool. Colette was confined to perpetual sleep until Emmett's death. That induced a madness which prompted her escape."

"You kept my mother prisoner when she had committed no crime," he said. *And*, he thought to himself, *years after Emmett's death, she still calls for him.*

"She could control Emmett," his father said. "Controlling a memory fabricator makes one a cruel weapon, Eugene."

This logic Eugene could not argue with.

"Did she see you?" Nathaniel inquired. "Emmett inherited his thought perception from her. If she entered your mind—"

"She saw nothing." He stepped back, casting the blades to the tile. Eugene realized then he could never meet his mother again. She should not learn that the creatures lived. If one expression of longing had called the duplicates from England to France, what could the woman do to enact revenge upon the Academy which had imprisoned her?

Nathaniel, now safe from the sword, maintained his remaining shred of dignity by not immediately tending to his wounds. Maroon disfigured his fine gown, but he seethed upon his son.

"You will never find her." Eugene found the duplicate's gaze. "Relieve the man of this conversation."

Yes, Master Eugene.

AT FIVE-AND-TWENTY YEARS OLD, Eugene's body died in the war against Grifters. They proved stronger than the Academy's metahumans, who were forced to retreat until better weaponry could be constructed. The Andrews Academy had succeeded in eradicating the local threat, but the remaining beasts had taken control of the new country across the sea. Eugene would have to leave his homeland in pursuit of the enemy, on enemy soil to boot. Naturally, he would take his experiment with him.

When Eugene awoke after the Grifter's blow, his consciousness met an immediate obstacle in the identity of the unsuspecting Patrick Davis. Eugene's duplicate did not take lightly to the sudden invasion upon his mind. Eugene found the mental shift between himself and Patrick cumbersome. At times, he had his wits. In weaker moments, he longed for a pretty lass by the name of Mary Beth. Over time, Eugene learned to quiet Patrick.

If you do not silence, he thought within himself, *I will kill your beloved Mary.*

She is only a civilian! Patrick argued.

I feel no repugnance toward shedding civilian blood.

Patrick silenced. For he could see Eugene's memories, too.

Before departing from England, Eugene visited his father one last time. Nathaniel Andrews, ravaged by disease that no metahuman would ever encounter, had been made as comfortable as possible. He lay on his chaise covered by furs, while chambermaids stoked the fire that caused Eugene to sweat. He kept a respectable distance from Nathaniel and waited until the last servant had shut the chamber door.

"Are you well, Nathaniel?"

"You mock me." The wrinkled man coughed into his silks, soiling their elegance with phlegm.

Distaste curled Eugene's lips. He could hear the weak rattle of his father's chest. How time had wrecked the once strong figure of Nathaniel Andrews.

Patrick Davis, of a gentler disposition, pitied the man.

"Mortality is a curse you will never know, Eugene," Nathaniel said. "I have spared you this pain."

"I suppose you expect some exclamation of gratitude. Very well, Nathaniel. Thank you. There, has your pain dulled?"

The man still managed to sulk, though the glower hardly affected Eugene as it once had. "Why have you come, Eugene?"

"I wanted to increase your suffering. I thought it fitting to destroy your heart using your own weapon." He threw a furl of documents at Nathaniel and relished at the man's floundering inability to catch them. "Colette Barineau is dead. Yes, I know she did not die by fire. If the knowledge of her death fails to wound you, to that I add that she loved a man who is not you. She bore him two daughters who will never know the name Andrews."

Spasms of hatred pitted Nathaniel's face; his features morphed in an unsightly resemblance to a Grifter. He flung the documents toward the fire, though his strength failed him. They sailed to the carpet a foot from the chaise. "Depart at once, and do not return. I have no desire to see you again."

Eugene bowed. "As you wish." With a smile, he turned.

"I should not warn you, ungrateful wretch, but I am swayed by weakness. Not for you, but for posterity's sake."

Eugene waited, amused by the man's attempt at a final threat.

"Your mother's ability will surely endow her legacy. There shall come another with a power to rival yours. The mutes may yet choose another master."

"You should have spared yourself the pain of speaking, old man. I have already researched this. Neither of her children bear even the metahuman quintex."

"And what of her children's children? The gene is protean. None can predict upon whom it seeks to bestow."

Perhaps Nathaniel's warning bore merit. If another inherited Colette's power... well, Eugene could wait for such a day. He had time in excess.

"Your concern is noted," he said. "Goodbye, Andrews. Do not think of me at your last breath. I will certainly not think of you at mine... whenever that may be." He turned to the small man neither of them had bothered addressing, though they spoke of him. The second son of Nathaniel Andrews did not receive nor utter a parting word.

"Come, Tacemus," Eugene said.

And his Tacemus obeyed.

CHAPTER TWENTY-NINE

I FOUND MYSELF WRENCHED backward; the movement severed me from the memory. A hiss raked my ears. Someone quivered, rapid bursts of inhales and exhales. When my mouth closed, the hissing stopped.

"Ella?" Ethan loomed over me and patted my cheek incessantly.

I lay on the floor. Quivering. Sweating. Even my lips felt drenched.

Vaguely, I registered Ethan calling for a rag. A moment later, he began blotting my nose and mouth with a paper towel. It grew red. Was I bleeding? It seemed irrelevant. I searched past Ethan and found Jimmy, still bound on the couch. He didn't look ashamed so much as unflinching.

"Now you see," he said.

That voice, he'd borrowed it from someone born centuries ago. Leader, Sanders—he had truly died, but Eugene Andrews had not. *Saecula saeculorum.* Forever and ever, without end.

One clone after the next.

Suddenly terrified of bearing this truth on my own, I caught Ethan's hand. *Clones,* I said. *He's not his son. He's Eugene.*

Ethan stared at me. Finally, a horror appropriate to the one that iced my insides.

I squeezed my eyes shut and gave in to the trembling.

Eugene had been asserting the control since Leader died. Jimmy was trapped. He never would have turned us over to Agent Chang, gassed us, or commanded any of the Tacemus.

Emmett. One was the closest to resembling Eugene's brother. Did that explain why Jimmy had been drawn to him, separated by centuries and memories but unconsciously craving that brotherly bond? It struck me as heart-wrenching and disturbing all at once—and just the reminder I needed. Jimmy would fight back, for One's sake if no one else's. He'd been trying to save One since twelve years old. Andrews hadn't barred his path then, and he wouldn't now. Sure,

Eugene held centuries of power. So what? Jimmy had a choice to be like Andrews or not. Someone needed to remind him of that.

Renewed purpose gave me a sense of calm. I knew how to talk to Jimmy. He could fight this. Eugene might've conquered in the past, but nobody got forever.

I opened my eyes. Ethan stared at Jimmy now, perhaps waiting for him to admit it.

Help me stand, I said, because Ethan currently blocked my ability to rise; but, once he slid a hand beneath my elbow and lifted, I realized I needed the aid. My legs wobbled, and my knees refused to lock. It felt as if I'd run a marathon on an empty stomach and no sleep. Only then did I remember the blood. A peek into Ethan's thoughts showed that the dive into Jimmy's head had lasted longer than a second. I'd begun convulsing, my nose bleeding, and might've collapsed had Ethan not wrenched me out of the memory.

Once stable, I met Jimmy's gaze. He tilted his head. *Go for it,* he seemed to say. Mocking.

This was not Jimmy but the shell encasing him. We'd dent it soon enough.

"He's a clone," I said, "a clone of the original Eugene Andrews who lived in the seventeen-hundreds. He could control his twin, so their father had them cloned to make sure the MTA would always have an Andrews in charge, with Tacemus under him like slaves."

Kara gasped. Lydia and McFarland stepped back. Bridget covered her mouth. This time, I paid attention to the pinch of horror in my belly. *Bridget's* horror, which she unknowingly shared with the room.

James, lips parted in wary doubt, said, "Only in body, right?"

"His consciousness goes into the new body. He remembers everything, all the way back to his original self."

"Then he would know everything Leader knew," Lydia said.

"Correct, Ms. Burnette," Jimmy said. The title, dictated as Leader had always done, caused a stiffening throughout the room. The cadets were accustomed to fighting, but who was their opponent?

"I want to talk to him. Alone," I added, avoiding Kara.

Vires, McFarland, Lydia, James, and Bridget seemed eager to leave. Naturally, Ethan hesitated, and Kara stared at Jimmy as if afraid he'd morph before her eyes. *It'll be fine,* I told them both. After more reluctance, Ethan and Kara exited.

Touching the couch triggered an instant flight response, but I quelled it, scooting close. We shared a cushion as we'd once sardined ourselves on the old school slide.

"Remember that green baseball cap I used to wear? You said it made my head look like a carrot."

"Those memories won't linger, Ms. Kepler."

"Stop pretending you're him, Jimmy." I ignored the trepidation as I dropped a hand on his wrist. I had to fold his jacket sleeve back and tilt his arm around to catch the right angle, unobscured by the magnetic cuff. But I found no strip of red, even when I searched higher up.

"It was a silly string of yarn," he said. "A token of a weak mind. Jimmy will fade, Ms. Kepler. They always do."

He'd removed his bracelet. Stupidly, that tiny betrayal stung more than the pointed rifle. I had to turn away for a moment, stare at the curtain tassels until I could manage, "Do I descend from Colette?"

"Yes."

The idea of my however-great grandmother created a blend of wariness and respect. I was her descendent—and she was Jimmy's mom, which meant we were, in a confusing, eerie way, related. Eugene Andrews and I shared some of the same genes.

I moved quickly from that realization.

According to the memory, Eugene started spacing the clones apart by ten years. Jimmy was twenty-two, by the MTA's method of tracking age. If Leader had been forty-two, what about the man in between?

"Isn't there someone between you and Leader?" I asked.

"He is dead. I wanted William Banks as my successor, not Blake Moor."

Meaning Blake Moor had been killed. I shuddered and wished Ethan had stayed in the room. "So there's a twelve-year-old and a two-year-old in the MTA. And the rest are... at the lab?"

Jimmy's expression darkened.

"With Emmett's clones?"

"The Tacemus are not him," he said.

I started to disagree, noticed Jimmy's curling fingers, and changed tactics. "How do we free them?" I said.

"You saw my memories, Ella."

I caught what he indirectly referenced. When they'd been younger, Eugene had tried ordering Emmett to be free. It had done nothing.

"Yet there's obviously a way. And you—you were there." I had difficulty voicing that truth. "You were there when One was freed, which means...."

Had he not waited with such a cunning glint, I might have taken longer to piece it together. Comprehension shivered through me. He couldn't remember the events that led to One's freedom because One had stolen the memory from the day I was born. That memory still existed, though, in One's mind.

Which was now static.

Andrews hadn't realized his memory was wiped, but Jimmy knew.

"What have you done with One?" I said.

He grew a smile so self-satisfied that he ceased to look anything like Jimmy. "Poor, foolish One. Consider, Ella, how Operation Whitewash could have gained its answer years ago, if only One had understood."

"Where is he, Jimmy?"

"I'm not foolish enough to possess that answer. My agents have taken him far beyond my reach, and thereby yours."

If he was lying, he did it so well. Thirty minutes earlier, I'd gotten annoyed with Ethan for assuming Jimmy was a liar. Now, I had to consider that unpleasant alternative. "He was with us in Virginia," I said, "and you somehow replaced him. Now all I hear is static when I try talking to him. What did you do?"

"If you want answers, Ms. Kepler, you know what method to employ."

Although I'd had enough motivation to free the Tacemus, I felt doubly determined now. Dr. Dietrich said Eugene's consciousness was dependent upon the hive-minded workings of the Tacemus. That meant, free the Tacemus, save the MTA—and Jimmy.

I shut my eyes and searched for the bridge which would guide me into his forested memories. His mind would open, and I could dig One's location out of him. If not that, maybe Jimmy *did* know the cure, somewhere deep in the vault.

The wire pulsed, hunting for connection. And there it waited, attached to nothing. It seemed I poked iron at an empty fireplace. Rather, the wrong fireplace. I couldn't read Jimmy right now; I had to read Eugene Andrews, the very objective Whitewash had tasked me with. I might've succeeded, back in Virginia, but now? Now, I understood too much about him, and saw little worth empathizing with.

I shifted on the cushion and pushed again. His mind had the —
Pain smacked my temple. The forest fell to darkness.

THE MOMENT CONSCIOUSNESS STIRRED, I sat up. Room, ceiling, bed, Ethan. He moved from his perch by the door.

"He knocked you out and attempted to hold you hostage."

My head twinged. I felt for the edge of the bed, which proved to be a twin cot. "I need to talk to him again." I swung my legs onto tile, pale like the walls.

"Not right now," Ethan said. "It won't be fruitful."

"I just haven't said the right thing yet."

"Stop, Ella."

"No! I can't stop until he's free." I sidestepped Ethan. The movement sent a spike of pain up my neck, and the pause in which I grasped my head gave Ethan the chance to box me in with classic Macto elegance.

"Listen to me." He palmed my shoulders. "We'll go to the protean lab. If any place holds answers on freeing both the Tacemus and Banks, the lab will."

"I can fix him."

"Andrews consumed every personality since the eighteenth century, Ella. A conversation isn't going to convince him."

"You don't know that." Parrying with equally proper Macto form, I disengaged Ethan. He sighed as I swept out the door.

In the living room, McFarland, Vires, and Lydia were stationed around the loveseat. Three guards seemed overkill, but I refrained from pointing it out.

Jimmy sported a busted lip that no one had bothered to treat. He maintained decent posture against the seatback. Had it not been for the cuffs, he, in his suit, would've fit in this decorated room.

"You're not allowed in here," Vires said, drawing himself to giant height.

"Good, you're back," Jimmy said. "How is your head, Ms. Kepler?"

Involuntarily, my attention roved elsewhere. It found Lydia, who returned my wayward search with something very shy of her usual disdain.

I settled before Jimmy and resumed my mental search for One. There lay the forest, but thorns barricaded it. The access of earlier was nowhere to be found. Two tense minutes passed with his mind refusing to sway an inch in impenetrability. Perhaps the lack of visual contact deterred the empathic connection.

I looked at him and tried again. Thirty seconds ticked by.

He began smirking. "You can't do it now, can you?" he said softly. "You would have failed, then, in Virginia. You were right to doubt yourself."

Jimmy voiced the conclusion that threatened to crush me. He was better than a telepath. He could expose me without straining one nerve.

"Give up, Ms. Kepler," he said. "Jimmy Daniels will be shortly gone, no matter what you do."

"And what does he have to say to that?" said Kara; I only then realized she'd been in the room, crowding the arched entrance with James.

"He says nothing," Jimmy said.

"He'll fight you."

"Be rational, Kara. Aren't you the rational one? Two centuries later, and I'm still here. Let that be your indication of my strength."

"None of the other victims you invaded had us."

He sighed. "Charming. If only you'd possessed this spirit in your childhood instead of letting Kyle crush you."

The words slapped shock across Kara's face.

A *whoosh* like cloth falling came from the window, where the rope tassel unwound from the curtain. It flew to Lydia's hand. She strode around me and yanked Jimmy's head back. The tassel got stuffed into his mouth, then she tied the attached cord around his face, securing the gag.

"You're pathetic, whoever you are," she said.

Jimmy, cheeks indented by the cord, spat against the tassel but failed to dislodge it; the rope cutting across his mouth kept it in place. Realizing defeat, he leaned back in the cushions and resumed the air of nonchalance.

My hands tremored. How dare he speak to Kara like that, stealing Jimmy's face and voice?

"Everyone gear up except Kepler and Avary," called Ethan. He stood to the side of the room, a troubled-looking Bridget cowering near his elbow.

While the cadets trooped past Ethan, I read him. Bridget's trepidation became clear. Ethan had seen my failure to summon empathy, and now he wanted to test whether it could be faked—by a mood manipulator.

Are you sure about this? I asked Bridget. Ethan had evidently told her about her ability. She'd taken to the news with giant eyes and mouth clamped tight, like she bottled a shriek. But she nodded when I asked.

I rested a hand on her shoulder. *Don't try too hard, okay? I think it happens without you realizing it.*

"All right," she whispered.

I couldn't decide whether the apprehension in my gut was mine or Bridget's. It overwhelmed any hope that this might work.

We stood before Jimmy, whose smug eyes said everything currently prevented by the gag. He had more hope than we did—hope that we'd fail.

I closed my eyes and told Bridget to do the same. *Imagine someone you can relate to,* I said. *Someone you understand.*

She pictured James first, then scooted him aside to make room for me. That image didn't fit, either. To her, I was the brave Fallow, the J who'd breezed through the MTA's obstacle courses. The Ella in her head didn't need empathy.

I searched for any emotion overriding tumultuous fear and found none. Bridget was projecting, yes, but not empathy. This task was more daunting than level B. She'd failed that multiple times; why would today work any differently?

You're not a failure, Bridget, I said.

A remorseful, aching sort of feeling overtook the terror. I tensed, trying to barricade the overhaul, but I struggled to sort between her mood and mine. Emotions, surging faster than I could analyze, made me want to run to Ethan and cry. Had I not understood the mood swing's origin, I probably would have.

This isn't working, I told him.

"All right, Avary," he said. "We'll try again later."

I opened my eyes, relieved, but the feelings lingered, and Jimmy's victorious glint stared right back at me. With effort, I followed Bridget and Ethan out of the room. She stopped after a few steps.

"If my emotions can affect the team...." Bridget swallowed but set her head higher, staring out of glassy brown eyes. "I should stay behind," she whispered. "I'm d-dangerous."

"You're on this team, Bridget." Ethan gripped her shoulder. The way he peered at her, firm yet kind, reminded me what sat in his core, so often drowned by a mind that never stopped planning. "We're not leaving you behind. You'll learn how to control it. I'm sure Ella has ideas."

"Really?"

"Absolutely," I said.

Bridget covered her face and burst into tears.

Ethan and I shared a glance. At least he felt it too; he went fidgety with the effort staving off her overflowing anguish. Bridget was somehow happy and weepy at the same time.

"Go gear up," he said. "I'll watch Banks."

On the way downstairs, I rubbed Bridget's back and tried to cheer her. At least she couldn't feel *my* emotions; my encouraging mood felt faker than anything she could've created.

In the basement, McFarland had taken to Kara's preparation like any responsible cadet would've. She showed Kara how to don bracers and explained the contents of Walker's cabinets. Meanwhile, Vires and Lydia argued over the next step in our itinerary: the lab.

"No one promoted Sheedy," Vires said.

"No one else offered to take his position."

His eyes flashed. "And no one wants you here, Burnette."

Lydia stalked toward the wall of guns. Then, spinning around, she burst, "The mission was yellow. There weren't supposed to be hostiles. By the time I fired, it had already killed him." She searched McFarland. "I didn't let Griffin die."

A quiver pulsed beneath McFarland's dark skin, yet her jaw locked.

"What were his last words?" James asked.

Lydia inhaled. "He was laughing."

McFarland twisted, hiding her face. A somber quiet touched the room, saturating it, a suffocating reverie no one could break. Bridget probably contributed to it. The fracture came when Vires snatched a duffel bag off the counter. Contents dumped on the floor, and he kicked past them, stomping all the way upstairs and exiting with a slammed door.

CHAPTER THIRTY

AFTER TAKING ADVANTAGE OF Walker's well-stocked artillery, we departed for another road trip, this time to a tiny town half a dozen hours away to battle some British security drones—courtesy of the Andrews Academy, no doubt.

Kara offered to drive. I understood her desire to feel useful. It had to be frustrating: the sole civilian among a group of metas who could toss this van skyward if they got the urge. She overpowered them in other ways; half of them couldn't explain the difference between the dollar bills we'd taken from Walker's stash, and *none* of them knew how to fuel up at a gas station.

Jimmy kept to himself in the corner. As far as he'd been informed, we were headed to D.C. to rescue Whitewash. That had been our initial plan, until Lydia told us of the last Society meeting she'd participated in. Jimmy and Agent Chang had planned to take all Whitewash members into custody and had rallied them to D.C. under the guise of questioning. We alone stood between Eugene Andrews and his never-ending reign.

I considered sending the team a telepathic message, but we couldn't be sure who'd been captured. We didn't want to risk the MTA learning anything about us. If anyone had escaped, they'd be off-grid by now. The rest would be heavily guarded by the MTA. In other words, untouchable, unless we convinced Jimmy to work with us.

Cue Plan B: kick Eugene Andrews out of Jimmy's brain.

Stealthily, in case another Tacemus monitored him, I returned to my search for One. His mind remained a static mess, warbled sounds occasionally cracking through. Out of range, asleep—or, prohibited from communicating with me.

When I looked over, I found Jimmy watching me. Light from the windshield, unevenly washing half his face every time we passed a lamppost, morphed his features. He could've been leering or expressing nothing at all.

What did you do with One? I asked.

"You're not a very useful telepath, are you, El?" He delivered the jab with that same impassivity, knowing it hit home and letting me see that he didn't care one smidge.

I leaned against the wall and stared at the roof. *Fix this, fix this....*

When we needed my ability most, it decided to check out, all because I *couldn't* do what Whitewash had expected of me.

A gloved hand domed my fist. Ethan wedged his fingers between mine. His urgent squeezing confirmed he wanted me to read him.

... Tacemus, he was thinking.

I don't know if I can do that either.

Try. Mission accomplished, Ethan withdrew his hand.

Long-distance reading worked with those closest to me. I barely shared a relationship with the Tacemus. Or did I? Hadn't Colette communicated from France to England, and hadn't I inherited her ability?

Bolstered by a new determination, I thought of every Tacemus, spokes of a shared wheel. They shared a hive-mind, which meant I could access just one to reach them all. How hard could it be if Colette could do it without trying?

I envisioned the Tacemus, reminded myself that Colette was my ancestor, and tried until Kara hit a bump, jolting me back to reality. Minutes had disappeared. The Tacemus loomed just as unreachable.

I dug my fingertips against my eyelids. *I can't,* I told Ethan.

He doesn't know that.

My head perked as Ethan said, "What are you going to do with the Tacemus?"

Satisfaction lingered in Jimmy's features long enough for the passing light to catch it. "Even obedience can't draw them through a locked door, Ms. Kepler," he said.

His tone set me ill at ease—not that I hadn't been since Walker's.

"You've imprisoned them?" Ethan said.

"I've prevented Ms. Kepler from accomplishing what she's currently attempting."

Walker had told us Jimmy started pulling Tacemus from academies. We'd thought he meant to free them from their chores. Jimmy must've suspected I'd attempt some communication with them, so he put them somewhere out of reach. Even then, he'd been one step ahead of us.

"It's a pity you've lost your usefulness," he said to me. "Operation Whitewash was depending on you. How did you put it, Ms. Burnette? If Mr. Sheedy had proven a half-competent mentor, Ella might not be such an idiot."

I looked down to avoid witnessing her reaction, or Ethan's. She'd said that to Leader, last year. Jimmy had been absent for that conversation, but Eugene had been there all along.

Hours into the trip, interstate traffic began to slow. Opposite the median, it vanished completely, painting a drastic contrast between our clogged lanes and their empty ones. We reached an eventual standstill.

McFarland craned her head out the passenger seat window. "None of the cars are moving."

The time read nearly midnight, not the standard rush-hour window. "Maybe an accident," Kara said.

Antsy quiet lapsed, though distant commotion reached to fill the void. When I focused, the noise broke apart. Thuds crashed ahead, blending with... were those screams?

McFarland's torso was halfway outside. "Civilians are running. There... someone's using telekinesis!"

Cadets butted heads on their way out the side door and onto the roof.

Beyond the line of locked cars, the scene bled horror. Vehicles spun like coins in the sky, tossed aside to the empty lanes across the divider. Pockets of civilians ran in every direction, abandoning their cars, dispersing to the woods bordering the highway — but even those shifted with danger as trees uprooted, unleashing the spittle of debris on the fleeing drivers. As we gaped, a tree writhed above the chaos and swung right for a cluster of civilians.

Ethan's arms lifted, but Lydia never had to move hers. The tree smacked an invisible wall. It trembled for a moment, tugged in two directions, seeking the strongest magnetism. Lydia grunted, and the tree exploded. Chunks of bark and twig sprayed the highway, and as I followed a trail of wood, I saw the owner of the telekinesis Lydia's had just disrupted.

Grifter.

"Gear up!" Ethan shouted.

We clambered back inside to load bracers, cram our pockets with spare ammo.

"How many?" Jimmy asked.

"Four," Vires barked.

"Five," Lydia said, debating between two rifles.

"Not encouraging numbers," Jimmy said. "Expect more out of sight."

"So we follow protocol," Ethan said. "Ranged first."

"Ms. Burnette *is* quite the deadeye. What next?"

"We use our environment."

"You do have the element of surprise."

"Not now. They know we're here."

"Then you approach this boldly. Grifters expect calculation from metas. Don't let them dictate the field."

Perhaps they'd forgotten we weren't at the academy, strategizing in Leader's office.

Starting with McFarland, the cadets declared their readiness. Bridget quivered at James' elbow. Her fear was palpable, affecting even Ethan. Strain beat against his jaw and puckered the veins in his neck. If we quaked in our boots, we'd lose.

Bridget's affecting everyone, I told Ethan. *She should stay behind. Someone needs to guard Jimmy.*

Ethan hesitated. He thought about the tricks Jimmy could pull if left alone with a mood controller. Bridget's ability could prompt Kara into releasing him. She might actually be more dangerous if left behind.

"I'll watch Banks," I said. "You guys are more experienced than me."

"The girls as well." Lydia crossed her arms.

"No, I meant—never mind. Yes, everyone's more experienced."

Ethan's forceful stare told me he wanted his thoughts read. ... *alone with him?* he wondered.

I'll keep him tied up.

A few tense beats vanished before Ethan summoned a duffel bag and tore the strap off. He tied the band around Jimmy's eyes, then stepped back.

"Lead your team well, Ethan," Jimmy said.

The first name drop sent a spike of bitterness across Ethan's face. He shook it free and raised a fist, prepping the departure signal. "Ready?"

"Sir!" McFarland, James, and Bridget chimed in unison.

Vires rolled his eyes.

"Ready," Lydia said.

Ethan nodded. "Move out."

The six of them hopped into the night.

For a moment, I listened to their footfalls, slipping around parked cars with all the delicacy of shadows. Music floated. A snippet of the news, then a commercial, then jazz—the wafts of radio from cars still idling. With clashes and screams, the contrast of peppy music was disconcerting.

"So," Jimmy said, and I pulled my focus back to my job, "will you let me free and give your team one more able body, or will they be left to the mercy of Grifters?"

"If you want to help, Jimmy, just say the word."

His lips thinned.

The front seat squeaked. Kara climbed over the center console and crouched at his side. "We never got to have our date," she said. "Where would you have taken me?"

I had no idea what she was referring to, unless she'd magically regained her memories. Or was she acting as if she had to coax Jimmy out? Either way, it unsettled him. He pressed himself against the wall but found nowhere to hide. His exhales grew sharp.

"Jimmy." Kara stretched a hand toward his face. He couldn't see, but he must have sensed her approach; fervor worked through his veins and clenched fists. He squirmed like a kid avoiding a shot.

Her fingers touched his cheek. With a vehement gasp, he froze. The whole van did, all three of us balancing on the taut rope of expectation. I kept my eyes open. Even a blink might rupture the moment. Jimmy hadn't recoiled like he had with me. He seemed incapable of doing anything.

"Kara," he whispered. Jimmy's voice.

Hope surged in my heart. I could read—

Thunderous energy slammed outside. Then, I was spinning.

The van somersaulted. It threw me against the ceiling, then wall, tossing me around the mix of equipment like a shoe in the dryer. I caught a glimpse of the night sky but never had a chance to wonder how I could see it. The violent clanging stopped. The air felt freer, my ears less congested, but I was still airborne. No longer spinning, though, which allowed me to establish my bearings before landing. All of it took seconds. Explosion, spinning, sailing.

I curled as my body smacked the dirt. Rolling lasted another couple seconds. When momentum died, it left me on my back.

I groaned. The ground tickled my skin. Soft. I tested a hand, ensuring it still worked, and felt grass. In the chaos, a door must've opened, flinging me outside. Between the van and my tumble, I felt smashed to a pulp's pulp—and I was a meta.

"Kara!" I dragged myself off the ground.

The van had tossed me onto the shoulder that divided the woods from the asphalt. As to the van itself, it had landed atop a few cars several yards from where we'd parked.

I covered my mouth and raced, not the only one running. Civilians dashed into the woods or to the clog of traffic, all screams and terror. They moved so slowly; I sidestepped them, sometimes leaping when fear kept them from budging.

The cars beneath the van were caved in, but it appeared their owners had already vacated them. That knowledge unwound some of my tension.

"Ella!"

I swiveled. The lone stationary figure in the mass of fleeing, Kara braced herself on a truck. Distant firelight silhouetted her.

"Jimmy's gone," she called. "He got out of his handcuffs."

I clutched my forehead. "Which way?"

"There." She pointed toward the opposite lane across the median.

"You're okay?" I said.

"Yeah."

"I'll be back." I scrambled over the nearest car. Its hood was still warm.

A semi-truck lay strewn around the median, crushing the metal railing, decorating both sides of the highway. Up the road, trees and car parts spun like tornados, figures in black leaping in and out of the chaos. I wrenched my focus from the battle.

I figured calling Jimmy's name would warn him to run faster, so I kept my footfalls light. The fighting drowned everything out anyway. Minutes passed in a back-and-forth frenzy up the shoulder and down again. In searching for his current thoughts, I butted against that same blockade. Jimmy and his thoughts were nowhere. I lost myself in the edge of the woods before I admitted the ugly truth.

Jimmy was gone. This forest stretched miles, and metas knew speed.

I rested my hands on my knees. The team would kill me, accident or not. At least I could join the fight. Kara would be safe where she was.

Going to help the team, I told her.

By the time I reached the last car before the center of destruction, the banging had silenced. Beyond a pick-up truck stretched a crater in the asphalt and piles of metal, bark, and miscellaneous debris. I saw no one, Grifter or cadet.

I helped an elderly woman down from her truck; she frantically motioned to the borderline unconscious driver. His wrinkled face shone pasty white, dotted with sweat, and he mumbled incoherent phrases. I untangled the three young kids from the backseat before returning to the driver.

"You all right, sir?"

As if jabbed with a shocker, he gripped my wrist. "Monsters," he wheezed.

There was no hiding the truth, not after this.

A shadow swooped overhead, and I shoved the civilians low. One glimpse of the pockmarked form, and I thrust my bracer arm forward and fired. The Grifter already lay immobile, bleeding; someone else had shot him mid-flight.

At a creak of metal behind, I twisted around and shot again. Lydia absently flicked the bullet away. My chest heaved with a combination of relief and panic.

She stood in the bed of the old man's truck and surveyed the Grifter.

"Is it over?" I said.

"That was the last one. Where's Banks?"

"The van flipped. He got away."

Lydia ground her teeth and spun around.

"Grampy? His skin's all burned." The youngest civilian was prodding the Grifter with his toes; his grandparents were too faint to notice.

I bade them farewell, then turned toward the crater.

Lydia crouched by another Grifter's slack form, feeling along his pockets. Holding each other by the arm, James and McFarland limped from another overturned semi. They looked bloodied and weary, but nothing dire.

"Where are the others?" McFarland called.

"This way." Lydia pointed. We headed for the highway shoulder. "This is Banks' doing," she muttered. "He instigated this war by antagonizing Chron."

After centuries of silence, Grifters had rejoined the civilian scene. Jimmy had said Eugene Andrews bombed Chron's territory, which meant Jimmy had done it. Andrews, master of secrecy, was smart enough to predict that Chron would retaliate if the MTA launched an attack. That sort of rash behavior—blowing up an enemy's land—I'd expect that from someone far less calculated than Andrews. Perhaps our previous theory was correct. Someone *had* wanted to distract from Jimmy's new position; just not the someone we expected.

I couldn't sit by that idea, though. Jimmy knew Durgson had stayed behind, and he wasn't a Grifter-hater like other metas.

Yeah, but he's not exactly in the best frame of mind right now.

I sighed and followed Lydia.

Three figures emerged from the woods. Bridget and Ethan supported a writhing Vires. They moved into the light of a lamppost, and my stomach turned over. A spoke of metal jutted from Vires' thigh. The wound glistened red, and the spoke didn't look willing to budge.

McFarland soared across the divide and landed next to Bridget.

"He s-saved me." Bridget, trembling, stepped aside so McFarland could take her place as Vires' support.

Ethan saw me and called, "Banks?"

"Gone," Lydia said.

"*Gone?*" Vires said. "What do you mean, gone? He was your responsibility, Kepler, and—" His toes scuffed the asphalt. He let out a series of unintelligible words right before he passed out.

"He needs a medic." The streetlamp's glow shone off McFarland's sweaty face.

"The lab has aid. Burnette, take Vires." Ethan waited for Lydia to take his place, then he hurried uphill, wincing every other step. "Where'd you lose him?" It resounded with typical Ethan bluntness, but it felt accusatory all the same.

"An explosion flipped the van. I got flung outside. When I got up, he was gone."

"But where?"

I swallowed. "Over there. I've already—"

Ethan took off.

We scoured the radius for ten minutes before Ethan would accept that Jimmy had escaped. He made me repeat the incident a million times, until I wondered if Bridget was nearby, pelting the highway with suspicion, jitters, and frustration.

"Look, go ask Kara, okay?" I said. "She saw him."

Along the way, we picked up any equipment that had fallen from the van. Near the shoulder, McFarland kept Vires upright while

Lydia used her telekinesis to reposition our vehicle. Another day, I might've gawked.

Kara hadn't stuck around where I'd left her. I peered across the median, at the trickle of civilians working their way along the vacant highway. A series of blonde heads bobbed, but none of them Kara's. She'd probably assumed the worst and taken cover.

Where are you? I sent along the invisible channel between our minds. The disconnected warble of her words sounded like flashes of a dream. Somewhere, Kara was unconscious.

Breathing through a rise of unease, I closed off my surroundings. Kara's present thoughts continued their drifting as I skipped inside her past.

KARA WAS STILL DISORIENTED when Jimmy pulled her from the van. During the tumble, she'd felt his fingers on her arm. Securing her.

One of the glowing staffs floated on its own and pierced the connection between Jimmy's wrists. *Not good.* Next he tended to his ankles.

She blinked through all her twinges and staggered closer to him, unsure of her intentions. She didn't possess the strength to overcome him.

He sidestepped out of her reach. "Stay away from me," he spat. Gripping the staff, he turned and ran.

She watched him escape, fingertips plucking at the red yarn around her wrist.

When Ella found her and asked in which direction he'd gone, Kara lied. Ella would kill her, but Kara was certain she could handle that. *Not to say I don't find you threatening,* she thought.

She limped across the interstate lanes, wishing she had a meta's strength and speed. *Would you have wanted this life for me,* she wondered to her parents, *had I been a meta and the MTA actually gave you the option?*

Her parents couldn't answer.

Through the prickle of thorns and ferns, she strode, picking her way toward a black straggle of shapes, sure to feel for that red yarn with every step. Vines lacked any compassion, licking her cheeks and arms. To have the sight of a meta! She may as well have walked with her eyes closed.

"Jimmy!" she called.

"Why are you following me?"

Her heart leaped toward the stars; Kara clutched her throat. Light made a paltry attempt to squeeze between the trees. She saw him in partial shadows. "I wanted to say goodbye," she said, slipping a finger beneath her bracelet.

"Forget Jimmy, Ms. Watson. He's dead." Footsteps resumed. Though her hearing was frustratingly average, she could tell he walked left.

She chased him, inwardly amused by how ridiculous this felt. Her hair must've resembled a nest, and the feeble nature she tried in vain to ignore made its presence known with every rasping inhale.

When a vine caught her by the ankle, she readied herself for a humiliating face plant. She staggered—and tilted into arms that didn't let her fall. Her heart grew light as air. All was not yet lost.

"I wanted to give you—" she began.

He wrenched her close, harshly enough to ache her already bruised skin. "Actually," he said, "you may be useful leverage."

Kara felt a grip near her neck. *Well,* she thought, *not exactly what I had in mind... but it works. You can find us, El.*

As spots blackened her vision, she took comfort from the yarn tightly looped around her wrist. She'd meant to give it to Jimmy. Now, it looked as if she'd be going with him, which meant Ella's team could still follow his movements. Her plan hadn't amounted to total disaster, after all.

There *was* a benefit to being a civilian: No one expected you to have any interest in trackers, and no one watched when you hid one in your bracelet.

Fatigue turned her triumph patchy, then chased her into sleep.

MY NECK BURNED, THE ghost of her pain. Kara was a genius. She was also, yet again, gone, in the hands of someone currently sharing a conscience with the man who had no problem shedding civilian blood.

A shadow fell over my feet. "Where's Kara?" Ethan said.

"He took her." I clutched my head and sought for composure, not caring that the cadets watched. I wanted to surge after Kara, falling into that familiar pattern once more.

"Do you know where they are?" he said.

"She put a tracker in her bracelet."

"What's the serial number?" asked Lydia. Before I could answer, she slid open the van door and hopped inside.

McFarland and Bridget guided the unconscious Vires into the van while James, per Lydia's commands, went hunting in the street for the tracker's packaging. Ethan and I broke apart to join the search. James found the package beneath a car, and we reconnected by the van, Lydia with one of Walker's grids lit up in her hands. Pinning down the signal ate up time. Even with MTA tech, locating the tracker required more than the click of a button. I didn't keep count of the minutes bleeding by; Ethan's mental calculations did the job.

Finally, Lydia jabbed a finger at the screen. "There. South, and moving quickly. They're airborne."

"Airborne?" Ethan tilted the grid away from her. A blue circle blinked over a map, inching its way down.

"How'd he get an aircraft this fast?" James asked.

"He's MTA commander," Lydia said. "Every vehicle in this country is at his disposal."

Every vehicle — and now Kara. Yet my legs stayed idle. When Leader first told me Grifters had kidnapped Kara, I'd run out of the academy and only stopped once I'd found her. Today, I stood still, glued by trust. Jimmy wouldn't let Andrews hurt her.

McFarland leaned around the passenger door and asked why we hadn't left yet. Lydia spoke over James' explanation.

"They're too far away," she said to Ethan. "Vires could lose his leg if we take a detour."

I bit down on my tongue. Pragmatic, efficient — those words belonged to the MTA, and a meta never deviated. It *was* impractical to go after Kara when we'd come this close to the lab, with an injured cadet to heighten our need for speed. Lydia saw that, and so did Ethan, who worked his way through other solutions. He considered splitting up but knew we needed every available fighter against the security drones.

His eyes met mine, and I nodded. We'd go after Kara and Jimmy later. For now, I had to carry the trust for the cadets, because Lydia thought Jimmy was a psychopath, and Ethan had never learned to trust his old MTA partner.

Don't let him hurt her, Jimmy, I sent out, not sure it left the confines of my head. *Please.*

Even if he gave an answer, I couldn't read it.

CHAPTER THIRTY-ONE

GLOOM FOLLOWED US FROM the highway to Tennessee, onto the dirt road heralded by the *No Trespassing* sign. Fog clung to the base of trees, scattered by the headlights. Andrews' private road looked narrower, as if the trees had crept from their perches to block our passage.

"Less than a mile." Lydia straightened the wheel.

I turned from the passenger window and eyed the dashboard. It produced the only light inside. The only activity, other than Vires. His incoherent groans, snippets of words breaking from his groggy state, were a reminder of what we stood to lose if we failed.

In that diminishing mile, I searched for Kara again. Still unconscious. And, according to James, moving southeast.

No one could deny the ingenuity of Kara's plan. She'd predicted his escape long before we had. I just wished she hadn't gotten dragged along in the process.

Ethan leaned over the center console. "Keep going. It's—" He stopped.

The break in the forest was correct but not the shape that lay in curls of fog, obscured and entirely unrecognizable. When Lydia swung right and the headlights pierced the shroud, my mouth parted. We'd brought weapons to fend off any security robots, but we wouldn't need them.

Naked beams supported themselves and nothing else; the rest of the lab made a mound of metal, wood, and ash. I couldn't tell whether smoke lifted from the debris or if the tendrils that trailed through the air were fog. Even within the car, the stench of burning rubble stung.

Horror pinched my throat closed. Had there been living Tacemus in that lab? Clones of Emmett, swallowed by flames?

"Are we there?" McFarland called from the back. "Reynolds, help me—"

"No." Ethan gripped my chair so tight I heard it rip. "The lab is destroyed. Banks must have... but he didn't know our destination."

"Banks didn't do this. Chron did." I reached over Lydia and dimmed the brights. With the harsh glow lessened, the softer shine of the headlights painted the charred letters in the grass.

Your mind was weak.

His message scorched me, too, and would linger long after new grass swallowed his parting words. Chron had set our plans aflame. Answers the lab could've held had shriveled and vanished to the wind.

"Revenge," Lydia said.

"I don't know." James peered over her headrest. "I think that's fog, not steam, which means the debris isn't hot anymore."

"Your point?"

"This fire was started before the airstrike."

"Chron attacked first," Ethan said. "Banks retaliated."

"How'd Chron know about this place?" James asked.

"He must've read Andrews while he was captured," I said. "Sheedy's right. If this was retaliation for the airstrike, Chron wouldn't have needed to leave a message. Banks would've known...." My musing drifted.

Bombing an entire territory of Grifters—some villains, others innocent like Durgson and Freia—seemed the action of one motivated by emotion. Jimmy surely came here right after Eugene Andrews awoke in him. He would've seen Chron's message and known that the Grifter just murdered all the copies of the Andrews twins. Supposing Andrews *had* kept their clones there. Surely he had, in this secret lab none but he knew of. After seeing the destroyed building, rage would've stamped compassion away, prompting Jimmy to retaliate without considering the cost.

All the duplicates, other than those already living—gone.

I surveyed the ashes, the only evidence Chron had allowed to remain. Whether or not Chron had known of the cloning, he'd understood its importance. Destroying it was the sharpest taste of revenge after we snatched Andrews from him. Jimmy had felt it first. Now, we got burned.

McFarland didn't care much about the war; she wanted to know how we'd help Vires. Even in her desperation, she hesitated when Lydia offered aid.

"I'm just as telekinetic as you are," McFarland snapped. Covered in Vires' blood and perspiration, her composure slipped.

To that assertion, Lydia's focus went askance, and she clammed up.

Ethan stood, absorbing Vires' fading pallor, then trading that sight for Lydia's locked lips. His brows dipped; his thoughts looped, weaving a circle between *animo, protean, Lydia,* and *necessary.* I connected the dots right before he spoke.

"Burnette can help. She's a protean."

Lydia swiveled to Ethan, glaring. "So you can admit it now?"

"Good grief!" James cried. "Is everyone we know a protean?"

McFarland's fist thudded against the wall. "Focus on the task at hand! Can your ability help Vires?"

"She can safely remove any shrapnel." Ethan looked at Lydia. "You saw it?"

"Yes." Lydia, graceful as a deer, hoisted herself over the console.

At her approach, McFarland firmed her grip around Vires; his head sagged in her lap. "What does your ability do?" she asked.

"If I see something once, I can wield it even out of range."

Telekinesis without the visual requirement. That explained the floating binder in Jimmy's office.

Ethan motioned for us to exit, though James asked to stay.

Outside, acrid air lingered even when I breathed through my mouth. Ethan, Bridget, and I walked over beams and half-burnt walls. All this destruction spawned from Andrews, one way or another.

After asking Bridget to look for salvageable medical supplies, Ethan nudged me in the opposite direction. He spent the walk preparing his thoughts, and I spent the walk reading them. By the time he paused near a smoldered wall, I had my rebuttal prepped.

"When the van flipped, he protected her," I said. "And right before, we could see him fighting it."

"That's my point, Ella. If he's had moments of clarity, that means it's possible to resist. He's letting Andrews lead."

"No, he...." Pain tightened the knot around my heart. That knot had been waiting, loose and patient, since Walker's house.

Ethan touched my cheek. "I know you care about him, but don't make excuses for his behavior. You need to prepare yourself – "

I stepped back. "Don't say it."

"We're in a war. I have to say it."

I turned toward the rubble. Heap upon heap of Eugene Andrews' legacy, smoldered away. This *was* war. Not everything survived — except him. We battled a villain who should've died centuries earlier; yet, because of who currently gave Andrews life, we should've had the upper hand. Easily. Jimmy had fought Andrews' control his entire life.

Why not now?

Ethan's words had unearthed the roots I'd buried, drawing them toward the surface. Andrews was powerful, cunning, well-practiced, and cruel — but Jimmy was Jimmy, the guy who'd created an operation to spite the MTA. Could fighting really be so hard? If he'd resisted in some occasions, why not all?

Maybe he didn't want to. He'd never liked taking charge.

I dropped to a crouch. Without the lab or One's location, we had no idea how to fix Jimmy. Andrews only needed a moment behind the reins. One moment and he could decide Kara was unnecessary baggage. If he killed her, I lost two friends at once. Jimmy would never recover.

Bridget was nowhere nearby, but despair pulverized me full-force. My fingers sunk into the dirt, squeezing. "I don't understand," I whispered. "Why isn't he trying harder? Doesn't he realize he's hurting everyone? *We'd* fight it, Ethan, wouldn't we?"

"Yes, Ella." Ethan knelt, dirtying his pants so he could lift my chin. "We'd fight. But Banks isn't us. He's not used to accepting responsibility for his actions."

"These are Andrews' actions, though. Right?"

"If Banks is allowing it... I can't answer for him."

I wished someone could.

Kneeling in the dirt, too beaten down to stand, I felt more useless than ever. To think, Walker had called me a fearsome thing to behold.

Arms shaking, I stared at the earth and willed not to cry. A glint overlaid my vision anyway, a sparkle in just one eye.

I squinted. No, not a tear. Half-buried in the ground, something reflected the distant starlight. I reached for it. Ashes and dirt and rubble clogged my grip, and something hard nudged my palm. I spread the handful wide. Amid the grit lay a silver flash drive, smudged but intact, far enough from the brunt of the heat that it hadn't suffered the same fate as the molten computers.

Flash drive....

Walker had dropped his.

Ethan pulled out his grid as soon as he registered the object. He inserted the device. An icon bearing the title "PROTEANS_UPDATED" appeared on the screen. Only that. We split a jittery moment before Ethan tapped the file.

A document popped to life, blank for a moment before words settled. Names trailed into sight, each one struck through with a red line.

Ackbert, Richard: pyrokinetic discharge
Akande, Busayo: TBD
Avary, Bridget: mood projection & manipulation

Ethan flicked through the pages. Name after name, all crossed out. Margaret Perry was nowhere, nor Dr. Saini, but I bet they'd been there before Walker got his hands on this list.

Toward the bottom of the document, the names changed.

Chron (Chron): telepath, inconsistent
Peo (Chron): life sense
Saga (Kian): ethereal
Fjalar (Durgan): TBD
Marko (Durgan): TBD

"Grifter names," I murmured.

"The parentheses... " Ethan said.

"That might be who their ruler is. I recognize Kian's name."

The shorter list of Grifters were also struck through. The document concluded with an incomplete entry, the only one without the red strike.

Mind-linking: female Grifter

The final entry was the inverse of the rest. Andrews could identify the protean gene through DNA tests, according to Saini, but the dozens of "TBDs" told us he couldn't figure out the ability. In the last case, he knew of an ability but not its owner.

Intriguing though this document was, unless one of the proteans had *Can disengage evil psychopath's mental clutches* or *Frees Tacemus from said psychopath* as their ability, we were no better off.

Ethan handed me the grid while he and Bridget searched the rubble for surviving computers. I cycled back to the top of the list. Andrews had determined roughly seventy-five percent of the abilities. The remaining TBDs stuck out like nails. If one of them possessed an ability we needed, we'd never know.

When I neared the end, Ethan returned to check my progress. I held out on giving an answer. Grifter after Grifter scrolled by, all TBDs or wielders of random powers.

After staring at the last line, I answered Ethan's unmentioned inquiry. "Other than Chron and me, the only other ability that has to do with telepathy is this female Grifter, so unless we can... wait." A memory snagged. Expectation thrummed in my pulse as I skimmed the Grifters' names once more. Peo was the only identified Grifter of Chron's community.

"Helix's name is missing." My fevered breath fogged the screen. "But she told me she has an ability. Something about helping Chron with his telepathy. 'Mind-link' might mean she can help me read Jimmy. What if *she's* the female Grifter?"

"Helix is MIA."

"Yeah, but I can try contacting her. I reached Chron—why not her?"

Ethan shifted, as unmotivated by this as I was rejuvenated. "Banks might not have been lying when he said he doesn't know how to free the Tacemus."

"So we figure out where he put One."

"Another thing Banks claims not to know. And even if we find One, there's no guarantee he has the intel we need."

"What else are we supposed to do, Ethan?"

"I don't know!" He spread his hands out; then, eyes shutting, dug his fingertips into his forehead, posture caving. "I'm sorry," he murmured.

Amid worrying about Kara and Jimmy, I'd forgotten that Ethan's plate was full, too. Even so, he rarely lost his composure. But that was the old Ethan. Andrews had whittled him down, and he'd yet to build himself back up.

I stepped closer and settled my arms around him. It took him a moment to return the hug, but he did.

"You don't have to know everything," I said.

"I've always known what to do, and why I did it. Since joining Whitewash...." His hold tightened, but he drew as little comfort as possible, peering over my head instead of resting his own against it. "I can't accept that every system is flawed," he said.

I thought of Durgan. He was the least corrupt leader I'd met. Even he hadn't been good enough for his Grifters.

"I wish I had the answers," I mumbled. "I don't know how to do this either."

Ethan shifted, nudging my face higher so we could see each other. A thousand worries clogged his features, painting him fifty years old instead of twenty. I longed for the day when we could share a gaze free of hardship. "We have to rely on ourselves for now, Ella," he said. "So long as we stay focused and resolved, we'll succeed."

"But I *am* resolved. So was Bridget. Jimmy is too, or was. Why do we keep failing?"

"Because you need to trust in yourself more."

Normally, I could've nodded at this, but a jolt of uncertainty had me wondering whether it was as simple as Ethan believed.

"Sheedy!" Across the grass, James waved an arm out the van. "Vires is awake and wants to—"

"*Want* is not the word, Reynolds," came Vires' waspish voice.

"He's much more manageable when he's unconscious," Ethan muttered.

"Do I detect impatience, CG?"

"You're right. Thank you for the reprimand." Smiling slightly, he thumbed my jaw, then added, "Contact Helix."

"Got it."

He turned for the van.

Be more resolved, I reminded myself. I was beginning to appreciate Ethan's old reliance upon an authority with all the answers.

It'd be nice to trust in someone other than my confused self.

CHAPTER THIRTY-TWO

SITTING ON A CHARRED beam, far away from Vires' nonstop complaints, I searched for Helix. Like ushering water along a stream, I took my words and merged them with the small shoot representing our relationship. I tried a series of greetings and hoped I was talking to more than a ghost. *I need your help. Can you meet me —*

A voice interrupted, like sunbeams sneaking into morning. *I swore to stay in shadows, but that was a fool's promise. What do you need, Ella Kepler?*

I bolted off the wooden beam; it rolled into a glob of a chair and toppled it.

You hear me? came Helix's voice.

Yes, I said. I found my beam, sat, and got to know Helix, twin sister of the most dangerous Grifter alive.

Essence bonding — that was what Helix called her ability. It acted as a drill, tunneling through mental blockades so one mind could connect to another in a two-way bond. I'd experienced it firsthand, when Chron and I met in the library. I'd chalked it up to a telepath thing, and it had been, though of an unexpected source, as unexpected to Helix as it had been to Chron and me. She only understood the extent of her telepathy at that moment.

We discussed Jimmy, but another idea wriggled out of the box I kept locked tight. Helix could give people complete glimpses into one another's minds. Thoughts, secrets — memories.

Someone could see something they'd forgotten.

I forced myself to put that idea on hold. There seemed no point to considering a life beyond the MTA when Eugene Andrews still roamed free.

Helix felt certain of her power to connect me to Jimmy. Because she wasn't about to hole up with a bunch of metas, no matter who I was, she'd meet on her terms. Helix and her allies were currently secluded two hours west. The metas would have to endure another road trip, and to a safe house stuffed with Grifters. Even James couldn't look thrilled about that.

"You're letting a *Grifter* manipulate your mind?" Even with a fresh hole in his leg, Vires salvaged his haughtiness.

"What if she sees MTA intel?" McFarland asked Ethan.

"Don't you guys get it?" I said. "Helix has zero interest in overthrowing the MTA. Besides, the MTA's already falling apart."

Shadows cloaked every cadet's features, and none could summon a response. They fought the MTA's corruption, but loyalty ran thick in a meta's veins.

Lydia drove, Vires grumbled as if severe injury had rejuvenated him, and I reached for Kara. She was awake now, alone and unmonitored. Jimmy had stuck her in a room and left her there.

Are you mad? she wanted to know.

I drummed a knuckle on the window. *No, Kar. Of course not.*

Silly though? Don't even remember him... doing this for you.

For me?

You spent months trying to save me. I can spend a few days here.

My eyes stung. *We've gotta get out of the MTA. This place is crazy.*

Don't you have to save the world first?

Not sure I'm good at this whole "hero" thing. Pain smarted my skin. I withdrew my hand from the window, noting the glob of blood on my knuckle and the spider web of broken glass where I'd just tapped.

"If you need to exert your frustrations," Lydia said, "Vires has been talking too long."

"Say that louder, Burnette," he called from the back.

"I thought metas had good hearing," I said.

Lydia's mouth twitched. That marked the first time in over a year that I'd elicited a positive reaction from her.

"I *did* hear, you inept," Vires said.

A random swoop of loyalty descended in my chest. Not sure who I'd be defending nor why I had to speak, I peered around the seat. Ethan beat me to it.

"Kepler is not an inept," he said, more sharply than usual, "and you've been monopolizing all conversation for thirty-four minutes. Either go to sleep or stop talking. Though you are free to apologize to Kepler."

"I have every right—" Vires began.

"*Si dice una idiotez mas, lo voy a estrangular!*" James stood, hands tugging his hair, face as ruddy as sunburn.

McFarland reached for his elbow. "Reynolds."

"*Ahora no te pongas de su lado!*" He pierced her with his twitchiest glare.

"You're slipping," she said.

"*Que?* Oh." He exhaled a good five seconds, then said to Vires, "You are the most obnoxious, arrogant, self-centered person I've ever met. Good *grief,* how have any of us endured you for this long?! You can barely walk and you're still convinced you're our superior. Get over yourself, before one of us murders you."

The urge to laugh was flattened by the anger simmering between them. In fact, *everyone* looked angry, even Bridget, as if we'd jumped headlong into a vat of rage.

"CG?" Vires snapped his fingers at Ethan. "Are you going to allow him to speak to me like this?"

Ethan stared between the two, then said, "Yes."

Vires' mouth dropped. Still, I felt frustration over hilarity, that nagging itch to defend someone. It spurred me along, affecting my mood, and....

I checked Bridget. She squinted. Other furious pinches took residence between her freckled cheeks. Vires' insult toward me had riled her — and everyone else.

Bridget, I said. *You're impacting us.*

She clapped a hand over her mouth. Like I'd wrenched the plug from the vat, anger swirled straight out of me, letting reason float upward.

After swaying, James sat, scratching his nose. "Sorry," he mumbled. "I don't know what came over me. I only... I'm saying this because I care about you, Vires. I just wish you cared about us."

A different mood overtook the van, this one somber and seemingly free of Bridget's influence. Vires' glare took on a marble quality, as if someone had etched the expression — and, later, returned to chip it away. Before any of us got the chance to see what came next, he dropped his chin into his palm and angled his face toward the shadows.

Jimmy would've loved to witness the day someone put Vires in his place. But he'd turned fleeting as emotions, and not even Bridget could draw him back.

LYDIA DROVE THE VAN up the hill that obscured the dilapidated barn from the highway. Its weathered face, crooked with disrepair, glowed in the cracks from an internal light source. It looked cozy as a rat's nest, oozing none of the MTA's sterility.

One of the entry doors slid aside. The haze of firelight dusted the dirt. A young Grifter motioned for Lydia to park behind the barn. Once the engine cut, the Grifter hurried to the passenger door.

"Durgson!" A heave of relief pushed through my permanently cold chest. I curbed the desire to hug him, knowing he'd likely throw me into the highway. "You're okay!"

"I'm fine, elak," he muttered, waving a dismissive hand. "Where is my family? I do not see—" Durgson faltered. His gaze rested near the hood where Lydia stood frozen, blanching beneath his stare.

My smile went rigid. A memory, this one Durgan's, plugged my enthusiasm. I hadn't realized he'd be here. Otherwise, I would've warned her.

Durgson couldn't speak; and, as no one but Lydia and I understood why, the cadets awkwardly shifted.

"Is there, um, a doctor?" I said. "Our friend's injured."

I was hoping Vires' adamant refusal of Grifter aid would disrupt the uncomfortable air, but he chose this moment to practice silence.

Durgson wrenched his focus from Lydia and walked in the direction of the barn, skirting her so obviously that surely everyone noticed.

"What'd you do to *him*, Burnette?" James laughed.

"Let's get Vires inside," I said loudly. I tugged Vires' arm around my shoulder. *Now* he'd cause a scene, drawing the attention away from Lydia's shell-shocked face—but Vires complied with irritating ease.

A wave of heat smothered my skin when we stepped inside. The barn stunk of sweat more than animals; the absence of hay and manure indicated the length of its disuse. From a metal basin in the center of the space, fire spat. Grifters waited around the flames while others slept in the rafters. Shadows clung to the empty horse stalls in the back. Durgson had disappeared, though he'd evidently warned the Grifters of our arrival. Those present carried taut postures, monitoring our entrance and no doubt searching for weapons. The cadets entered behind me but lingered by the door.

A tall Grifter strode from the firelight. Freia, niece of Durgan, disregarded the tension. She came right over and cuffed my arm. *I am relieved you survived, little älskling.*

The stink of the barn wasn't as choking when I sucked in a relieved inhale. "It's good to see you, Freia. How many escaped Chron's?"

Many did. Many did not. Her demeanor darkened. She passed an inspection over the rest of the team and said, "Your friend is injured. We have a healer."

Vires edged back, dragging McFarland and me along, finally asserting that he felt perfectly fine.

"We're here for Helix." Ethan stepped forward. Every Grifter eyed him.

"I am she." Another Grifter left the firelight's glow. She wore gym pants and a hoodie, but civilian clothes couldn't disguise the familiar, scarred features, feminine though she lacked hair and rippled with strength.

At her voice, the uncomfortable atmosphere recharged into something harder. Freia stepped away. The other Grifters barely acknowledged her. Helix noticed, and her shoulders sagged as she motioned me toward the exit. "Come, Ella Kepler," she said.

I extricated myself from Vires. A collective exhale passed around the barn as Helix and I exited.

She directed me to the hill. Helix didn't slouch but gave the highway her best posture. We were alone now, free to speak, but she continued staring into early morning as darkness pulled away. Finally, I wondered whether she wanted me to start the conversation. The realization sent anticipation reeling. I could ask her about mind-linking and memories. A few shared words between us and I'd know. But what if she gave an unpleasant answer? My emotional strength was spent on Jimmy and Kara. I couldn't carry another setback.

"Did you know Chron was working with the MTA commander?" I shot the question out, afraid I'd go another direction if given any more freedom to think.

She turned her cheek and murmured, "Andrews found us when we were young. And foolish. He would have killed us, but his mind-seer glimpsed my brother's ability. Andrews promised us Chron would be the most powerful Hela. He required only that my brother find one who could save the mind-seers. They are dying."

Understanding hammered, striking as the line of sunlight brimming in the east. Andrews hadn't wanted proteans to build an army; he'd been searching for a cure for the Tacemus. Every time One had wiped him, a Tacemus had died; and, since Andrews hadn't known of One's rebellion, he'd been unable to explain the Tacemus' sporadic deaths.

"Andrews is also unwell," Helix continued. "He falls into amnesias he cannot explain. So he seeks a cure, for himself and the mind-seers. Chron helped him toward this goal. He divulged the secrets of Hela and received weapons for the price of innocent blood. I helped him accomplish this."

My thoughts, spinning with these developments, halted at her tone.

Helix's head dipped. "I bear that guilt," she whispered. "My duty now is to atone for it."

Responses popped in and out of my head. In this situation, words felt woefully inadequate. Helix *had* done wrong. I couldn't pretend otherwise, and she wouldn't want me to. Even if I had, the testy Grifters in the barn would make sure Helix remembered her crimes.

I rested a hand on her back. Violently, she shook her head.

"You would not dare touch me if you understood what I have done. Hela died by my hands." Helix's tone had enough venom to intimidate. I was tempted to move my hand—better yet, return to the barn. I forced the wariness away.

"You asked me to show mercy to Chron," I said. "Why can't that apply to you too?"

"Because...." She covered her face. Tendons worked as she squeezed. Her thoughts sprouted; I ignored them.

We remained in our stiff poses until footsteps made noise in the grass. I searched the bottom of the hill. A lurch of happiness massaged the ice out of my chest. Looking every bit the fun uncle toting his nephew around, Agent Porter walked with a sleeping Tam on his shoulders; the little Grifter slumped over Porter's head and snored. Beside them, Ly helped Durgan climb.

I patted Helix, warning her that we'd lost our privacy. She smoothed her fingers over her bald head and stood. However, when she saw the incoming party, she fell to the ground and pressed her face in the grass.

"My harsk. I am not worthy."

Durgan slowed at the crest of the hill. He slid his arm from Ly's and knelt beside Helix. Even before he lay a hand on her head, she trembled. He kept his fingers stationary, for all appearances saying nothing. Slowly, Helix raised her face.

"Come, Helix." Durgan cradled her chin.

"You are here now. That is what matters. I will leave."

"You are needed."

"If you wish, I will stay."

"I wish it."

"Then...." She gathered her strength and pushed off the grass. Durgan touched her elbow as she rose. Helix was too strong for that little aid to make much of a difference, yet it seemed he carried her.

"You have food and water?" he asked.

"Yes, my harsk. And your son. Durgson lives."

Ly gasped and hopped. "Papa!"

Durgan's joy overwhelmed the somber mood. He grasped Ly and made down the hill, but I stopped him.

"Wait, Durgan," I said. "Could I speak with you?"

He motioned for the others to continue. Porter nodded at me and trooped down the hill. Ly snagged his hand, and he held fast.

I faced Durgan, clenching back a shiver of nervousness. *Lydia Burnette is here. The meta you told me about.*

His attention, distracted by his children, took a slow path back my way. *Does she remember?* he asked.

Yes.

Durgan drew one extended breath, then said, *I have longed to see her again. Though not in this way.* His head dipped. *Thank you.*

We started down the hill. I offered my shoulder; he didn't appear used to the prosthetic yet. Outside the barn, showered in the glitter of rising sunlight, a crowd gathered. Grifters formed a line on the grass, all of them drawn toward our descent. One by one, they crouched on one knee.

"*Leve vår kung!*" Freia cried.

"*Leve vår kung!*" echoed the Grifters.

Durgan turned stiff as a cardboard cutout. A storm of his thoughts swirled with flashing images, and my telepathy took hold. Above feeling touched, he wished his wife was here.

It seemed impolite to keep standing, but the strength of his grip prevented me from kneeling. Behind the crowd, the cadets remained standing, as well. Lydia's lips were pinched. When Durgan saw her, his thoughts converged on that pale, bitter face.

One Grifter broke from the line. Durgson climbed toward his father. Morning light framed the fabric he carried, a bundle of colors belonging to a cloak, and that cloak belonging to one Grifter. Durgan didn't break the reverie by words or movement; he let his son cast the garment around his shoulders, covering the MTA apparel with the robe left behind at Chron's. Durgson tied the strings across his father's chest and forgot to glare at me.

The sun made the only movement, stretching its reach. In his cloak, he shone like a lighthouse. Sweat beaded my neck before he could speak.

"There is a story I have long desired to tell," he called. "Cowardice and shame concealed it, but they have run their course. You must hear. You must understand." His hold lessened, giving me the freedom to step from the center of attention.

I did so quickly. I knew this story.

"I hated the metahumans as any other. They were born my enemies, and bearing that title they died. Until one aided my son. He had followed, unseen. When the metahumans discovered him, their violence was unjust, as always. I had cast away hope that they were capable of compassion. This despair remained with me when I witnessed one metahuman's gentle touch. This metahuman... she comforted Durgson, as I should have done. In return—for I was weak, and cowardly—I allowed my soldiers to torture her for long minutes before I intervened. It was a miracle I was not too late. Her life came close to passing, by my orders. My hands." He glanced down at them. Beside him, Durgson stared at the ground.

The crowd below waited, rapt. Surely not Lydia, but I didn't want to draw attention to her by scoping out her response. Plus, I wondered whether I should witness it.

"I do not know that I will be given the chance to thank this metahuman," Durgan continued. "Perhaps I do not deserve this privilege. Instead, I honor her by sharing this memory. By her touch, I know compassion. By her name, I fight for peace. As do we all." His gaze lifted, as did his fervor, sharp with command. "Do not forget!"

Cries, a variety of affirmations, moved through the Grifters. I searched beyond them and caught a swish of blonde ponytail before Lydia disappeared around the barn. Ethan watched her go. Anger cut his expression sharper than I'd ever seen. The reaction seemed random. But, as his mind unveiled, I understood. This anger came on her behalf, directed toward Durgan. Ethan knew what memory haunted Lydia. Now, he knew which Grifter had caused it—the Grifter we'd allied ourselves with.

He regrets it, Ethan, I told him. *Go talk to her. She needs a friend.*

Confusion pulled his frown back. He searched for me around the clamoring Grifters. Once our eyes met, I didn't have to push him further. His tension evaporated, and he hurried after her.

Morning had come, and stomachs were rumbling. We relocated inside, where the Grifters set to passing around jerky, nuts, and tea. Agent Porter joined the bustle as if he'd done so all his life. The cadets stuck to the background. In the far corner of the barn, where scrap metal and a rusty wheel barrel resided, we breakfasted amid cotton pallets, waiting for Ethan to return with the grid so we could track Jimmy and plan our next move. Eating seemed far from everyone's agenda, likely thanks to Vires' leg. We kept staring at his stained skin.

Not a single bite had been consumed when Vires suddenly said, "Reynolds."

James' telekinesis, spinning an almond in circles, cut out. He peeked at Vires. "What?"

"Help me stand."

"Why?"

"Because I can't walk to their doctor on my own, you idiot."

James brightened. "Oh!" He scrambled upright, bounded over, and stuck out a hand.

Glowering at the extended limb, Vires took hold. He failed to hide the wince when James pulled, but the rest of us were smart enough to withhold additional support. James balanced Vires and, as eager as Vires was annoyed, carted him toward the Grifters. McFarland watched them go, smiling. Bridget and I smiled too. After everything that had fractured this group over the past few days, it felt nice to see some mending.

A single thought of Jimmy, and my smile vanished.

After breakfast, Agent Porter crouched in our corner to touch base. He guessed every other Whitewash member had been apprehended. "No one contacted me on the SOS line," he explained. When I told him about Jimmy, his expression morphed with disgust. Sensing a disparaging remark, I spoke before he could voice it.

"So, Helix can use her ability to...." I paused, distracted by the entrance of Ethan and Lydia.

"... but Kauffman never cared what you thought," Lydia was saying.

"No one did," Ethan said, and they chortled. Both stepped lightly, unburdened by bitterness. They hadn't chatted this easily in over a year.

"Figured she'd come around eventually." Porter observed Lydia's approach. Her mouth shot open; then, she turned her cheek and let it go. "She saved your life," Porter said to me, "when that cadet fired at you."

Though she wouldn't have wanted me to, I couldn't help staring. She refused to meet my gaze. "How did—" I started.

"Which cadet?" Ethan spun on McFarland and Bridget, who shrunk back.

"Koleman," McFarland said.

Next, Ethan swiveled to me. "Koleman aimed a gun at you?"

"And fired," Porter said, "but she—"

"When?"

"Relax, Sheedy." Lydia crossed her arms. "She's obviously alive."

"Redirected the bullet," Porter continued, unfazed by the interruptions, "which should've been impossible."

"I thought all animos could do that," I said.

"For a close-range shot, the kinetic energy's too powerful to manipulate, even for a meta. That's why we're ranged. If not for her protean ability, it wouldn't have worked."

Lydia stiffened.

"You saw her file?" I said.

Porter stretched his arms behind his neck. "What file?"

He'd figured it out on his own. Somehow, I wasn't surprised. Porter made an interesting agent, though not as curious as Lydia. She could've let Koleman kill me, but the girl who'd appeared to hate me had kept me alive.

Our eyes met. She let the contact linger.

Thanks, I said.

Her glance flicked away, but that moment had been enough.

"I suppose...." McFarland worked her jaw, then stood, stretching a hand toward Lydia as if hoping for a low-five. "I'm happy you're on this team, Burnette. That's more than one life you've saved."

No one had taught metas how to accept a peace offering. Lydia inspected McFarland's hand like it concealed a knife.

"No, McFarland. Like this." Butting his way into the group, James readjusted her hand, then took Lydia's and brought the two together. "Handshake," he said, steering them up and down.

Sheer willpower must've kept Lydia from wrenching her fingers free. The two continued their awkward handshake until James let go.

Lydia quickly clasped her hands behind her back, but McFarland had realigned her attention on Vires.

"It's a pointless civilian gesture regardless," he said, keeping to the edge. Brown, frayed fabric wrapped his thigh; the pant leg below had been cut off entirely, revealing how long and tan he was.

"How is your leg, Vires?" Ethan asked.

"It—"

"She said whoever extracted the foreign object did an excellent job," James interrupted. "Regeneration's going well. He just needs to avoid putting weight on it. Which reminds me." James tucked an arm around Vires, who muttered and griped but let himself be lowered to the ground. I couldn't decide who looked more satisfied: James or McFarland.

Ethan hardly let a moment of peace reign before he took out his grid. "Kepler," he said, "check on Kara."

A SHARP RAP PRECEDED the door's opening. Kara stood, reticent to be seen doing nothing—which she did most hours. She'd bolstered her strength for Jimmy's arrival; but, when he moved into the room, her vigor faded.

Neither spoke. His pallor was wan, contrasting the smudge beneath his eyes. He'd attired himself like an executive but lacked the energy of one.

"Jimmy?" she said.

"No. Goodbye, Ms. Watson. I don't expect I'll see you again." He made to turn.

"You're leaving?" Kara hurried across the room, untucking a plan as she did so. Ella already knew Kara's location, but that helped little if Jimmy went elsewhere. If she wanted to send him off with a tracker, she couldn't appear too eager to part with it. Perhaps a distraction first. It could work. He had, after all, come to say farewell when he needn't have bothered.

"Something to remember me by," she whispered, craning on tiptoe.

He turned his cheek away. Her lips met air. Kara felt relief over disappointment. She had no real desire to kiss him in this state, and the rejection gave further credence to her next move.

"Never mind that," she said, loosening the final knot in her bracelet. "Something to remember *you* by." She took his hand and pressed the yarn there, then curled his fingers over it. Whether he accepted it or discarded it to the floor, Kara didn't witness. Her interest couldn't be too eager. She returned to her bed and kept her eyes on the floor until she heard the door close. Jimmy was gone.

So was her bracelet.

I REMINDED KARA AGAIN and again of her brilliance while the cadets and Agent Porter pooled their knowledge of MTA bases. Jimmy had left Kara in Florida, and now he headed northwest in a nearly perfect slant. We had a van and he used a plane, so we couldn't hope to catch up, but any amount of head start helped.

"I still don't see why he would've kept the yarn," James said again.

I picked at my own bracelet and offered no answer. Maybe Jimmy was holding on. Or maybe Eugene had shoved the string into a pocket and forgotten about it.

The conversation reached a lull. McFarland traced a finger from Florida and followed it straight to Montana. Her head shot up at the same time as Lydia's.

"Orbis," they said in unison.

Lydia nodded. "We know where he's going."

CHAPTER THIRTY-THREE

BY CAR, TRAVEL TO Orbis would consume a hefty thirty hours. We had zero shot of beating Jimmy there, but that didn't kill our plan. According to Lydia, the isolated research lab offered the perfect place to hide information. If Jimmy was headed there, days after the protean lab burnt to the ground, we had a good chance he'd stay put.

No one had any idea what to expect of Orbis—whether it stood heavily guarded or could mean a simple in-and-out. We would plan our entrance once we had an idea of the layout. Helix would join us, but it became clear the other Grifters had no desire to, despite Durgan's confidence in us. There'd been protests, Grifters reluctant to risk their necks for the metas whose organization created then discarded them.

None of us could pinpoint the last time we'd slept, but Ethan said we'd take shifts during the drive north. His eagerness to leave had to do with our current company. The cadets shared his readiness; I'd never seen them agree to a plan so quickly.

Ethan oversaw the Grifters who packed us food for the journey, probably ensuring none of them snuck a bomb into the bundles, while Agent Porter said his goodbyes to Ly and Tam. The other cadets had scampered to the van as soon as Ethan gave the signal. Durgan appeared nowhere around; Helix and I searched outside the barn, hoping to say farewell. We found him near a copse of trees, engaged in conversation—with Lydia. They murmured to each other and didn't notice their observers.

Helix and I turned toward the van in sync and said not a word.

Ethan joined us shortly and tossed a stuffed knapsack into the back. He searched the van's occupants, tallying.

Talking to Durgan, I answered.

He tensed, making to turn around, then stopped himself with visible effort.

Lydia slid the side door open after a couple minutes. She kept her head low and settled immediately in the far corner, but I caught the red veins in her eyes. Yet they didn't seem the angry type.

"Ready?" Ethan said. Though he addressed all of us, Lydia stole his attention.

"Yes, sir," Vires answered.

Every cadet stared at Vires, who continued his folded-armed nonchalance a moment before realizing we gaped at him. "What?" he said.

"You just said—"

"I know what I said, Reynolds," Vires snapped. "Am I not permitted to speak now?"

"I'll get back to you," James said, grinning.

Porter revved the engine, and Ethan settled in the passenger seat. Helix's presence, while not entirely discomforting, gave Bridget enough trepidation to stir my stomach. It would be a long drive.

"Wait." James scrambled toward the driver seat. "Sorry, Porter. We have to turn around."

"What are you doing, Reynolds?" Ethan said.

"There's something I have to tell Durgan first." He eyed me over his shoulder. "Will you come with me?"

Ethan gave us two minutes, but James said he needed less than that.

We walked into the Grifter's circle around the fire pit. Their conversation slowed at our approach. A few looked annoyed by the interruption, but Durgan flourished his arm and they silenced.

"I wanted to say, before we left...." Beneath their observation, James fidgeted, though he continued forward. "I think Andrews lied. The phrases and words you use—'elak,' 'svag'—where did you learn those?"

"We have always known them," Durgan said.

"Right, well, they're Swedish. So was Dr. Bergström. But it sounds as if the experiments took place in England, meaning Grifters would speak English. Unless someone taught them otherwise. I—I don't think Bergström took you away to discard you. I think he was protecting you from the MTA." Observant James must've noticed how the Grifters eyed one another, and then him, renewed curiosity perking up their posture. "How long have you been calling yourselves 'Hela'?" he asked.

"As long as we have existed," Durgan said.

"I've read it before. That's what Bergström called you. It means 'whole.'"

"Whole," Durgan repeated softly. He dipped his head and trembled.

This had been the answer Durgan wanted. Grifters had an unnatural beginning, but someone had loved them enough to save them.

The Grifters began a back-and-forth. James couldn't hear the telepathic broadcast and stood at a loss during the inaudible debate. In the end, Durgan had the final say. *Without healing,* he said, *there can be no peace.*

It was decided: the Grifters were coming with us.

"Congrats, James," I murmured. "You just negotiated your first treaty."

WE SHARED A BUS HELIX had acquired from one of Chron's hidden caches; he had several scattered around the southeast. She'd raided it for clothes, food, and weapons. Combined with our gear from Walker's, we seemed decently prepped for a fight, though hopefully we could avoid one.

Night fell somewhere around Nebraska. The cadets had sequestered themselves to the back of the bus, though Porter snored somewhere in the middle, Ly and Tam slumped on either side of him.

I sat with Ethan in the front. He'd told the team to rest but wouldn't partake himself; instead he urged me to talk to Helix. He couldn't grasp why I resisted.

"What if she can't?" I whispered.

"You know she can."

"What if she *won't*?"

"Then I'll talk to her."

"What are you going to do, make her run sprints unless she helps me?"

"You're creating unnecessary stress for yourself, Ella. Ask her, or I'll make *you* run." Though his tone was light, sincerity bled through. He'd once pushed me off a pine tree; he'd drag me to Helix if he thought it would help.

Approaching footsteps caused us to shift slightly apart. Durgan settled in the empty bench parallel to ours. Ethan went rigid as a spring. He harbored no hatred for Grifters; he simply didn't know how to process "Grifter" and "ally" in the same sentence—particularly when that ally had bad blood with Lydia.

"You are their leader?" Durgan spoke, a quiet voice breaching the lull of snores and heavy breathing.

Ethan answered when it became clear Durgan would keep staring. "Yes."

"I see."

Silence resumed. Ethan looked as relaxed as a guy on a bed of nails.

"And whom do you follow," Durgan said suddenly, "if you believe your Academy to be corrupt and the leader of Operation Whitewash misguided?"

Ethan shifted. "Myself."

"You trust yourself entirely?"

"I trust my resolve."

"A strong will cannot subsist forever. We are all weak, and our will fails us when we need it most."

Ethan's mouth, already open in preparation, let nothing escape. Not even air. His frown reached maximum strength. Then, unexpectedly, it withered. He finally looked at Durgan. "Then what do we rely on?" he asked.

Durgan smiled. "Come, Ethan Sheedy."

Meta instinct kept him rooted even as Durgan stood and walked away. I nearly prodded Ethan's foot, but something told me this decision needed to stem from him. He unfurled his knuckles, breathed out, then followed Durgan down the aisle.

Words continued tumbling long after Durgan walked away. He had a way of oversimplifying. In a way, he resembled Ethan. Things were or weren't, no in-between. Either determination alone could see us through, or... Bridget couldn't project empathy, I couldn't read Eugene, and Jimmy couldn't fight back, no matter how hard we tried.

I liked Ethan's logic better.

I AWOKE TO A backdrop of mountains, cutting angles behind swaths of fluffy, pointy trees. Everywhere I looked, greenery dominated. Crystal lakes sparkled; a cloudless sky blanketed the mountaintops. My idea of Montana included snow, but summer had yet to fade, even this far north.

Beside me, Ethan's head sagged. Though exhaustion clung to his pallor, he didn't appear stressed. Evidently, he *could* relax, even if in dreams alone. Carefully, I tiptoed over his legs and let him sleep.

In the rear, past the drowsy Grifters, McFarland paced the whole two feet of the aisle's width. "Where's CG?" she called.

"Asleep."

"Good," James said. "I don't think he's slept since Virginia." Yawning, he skimmed over Vires, squashed against the window beside him. "Did you want to say something?"

Vires pursed his lips.

"I could remove Reynolds' hair if he's annoying you," Lydia said. Seated beside Bridget, she spoke as if to anyone listening.

Despite that, Vires replied directly to her, losing his glare in the process. "I wouldn't mind."

Satisfaction tugged at her mouth. She eyed James, who entwined his arms around his hair and ducked. "I didn't mean from your head," Lydia said.

He froze. The five of us watched him, waiting. Would Lydia do it? To smooth things over with Vires, I guessed she might.

Suddenly, James gave a little twitch and clasped his knee. "Ow! Point taken, Burnette."

Vires snickered, shoving James into the aisle. "Annoy me again, Reynolds," he said, "and Burnette will ensure you resemble a Tacemus."

McFarland helped James stand, then took his seat so she could reprimand Vires. He seemed just fine with the close proximity to her. James shook his head at me, Bridget giggled, and Lydia was smiling.

The last leg of the drive brought us into dense foliage that eventually consumed the dirt road. We had to park and hike the remaining mile. Amid the noise of Grifters waking and checking supplies, Ethan awoke. He found us in the back and demanded to know why none of us had roused him.

"We'd rather you not fall asleep in Orbis," Vires said. "Are we exiting this bus or not?"

Ethan motioned us out, catching my arm as I passed. He waited to speak until after the bus emptied. Exhaustion lined his eyes, but he held the steady focus I'd always associated with Ethan. "Helix will help you read Banks," he said. "But if she can't, and you can't read him, and he can't defeat Andrews—it's all right."

I'd expected a back-up plan. His lack thereof made me tense. "No, it's not," I said.

"Yes, it is. Andrews is weak too. Maybe we won't defeat him today, but he'll lose eventually."

Eventually? Since when had Ethan considered anything but the here and now, an objective he could touch, grab, and conquer? "What did Durgan do to you?" I asked.

"Informed me that my ninety-eight percent accuracy is... inaccurate." He smiled, the gesture as unexpected as his absent gloomy warning.

Suddenly *I* was the frowning one, feeling the need to defend the gravity of our situation. "Are you going to tell me to lighten up next?" I said.

"No," he said, drawing me close, "just that I love you."

For once, I wanted to wriggle free and remind him of what we stood against. I forced myself to feign relaxation, ignoring the frayed nerves that screamed at me for standing still.

"When you see Banks, don't do anything rash," he murmured.

"Likewise."

"Am I ever rash?"

"Well," I said, stealing my chance to lean back. His smile lingered. I tried reciprocating and felt my mouth protest. "You know what they say. Love makes us blind."

OUTSIDE, THE AIR SMELLED CLEAN, and the leafy branches shielded us from a sun that beat our necks with none of Florida's intensity. Montana had the ideal summer climate: warm enough to swim without being too blistering. Trusting Helix's compass, we trekked the scenic distance to Orbis.

A few paces divided us from Helix before I realized Ethan had been steering me in her direction. She held up the rear, separated from the Grifters who considered her a traitor and the cadets who were still learning how to walk alongside their enemy without attacking. Ethan gave me a significant nudge, then hastened forward in the procession.

I chewed my cheek, allowing the group to put us further in the rearview. Maybe Helix was grateful for the company; she slowed to my pace.

Ethan was right. Delaying this only added to the stress.

"A Tacemus took my parents' memories," I blurted. "After all this, could you mind-link them with him?"

The question sounded clumsy and forced. Surely Helix hadn't understood. I wished I could scrape the words away from the air.

Her answer interrupted my mental search for a better-phrased question. "I am sorry, Ella Kepler," she said softly. "My ability will not give you what you desire."

I stopped short.

Helix couldn't match my gaze as she added, "They would see what they have forgotten, but it would be a life seen. Not a life lived. And, with time, those scenes would leave them. Do you recall all you saw in Chron?"

Mercilessly, my brain replayed that day with Chron, when Helix had accidentally linked us. The only certain facts I recalled were his name, Helix's, and his relationship with her—all things I'd learned afterward, anyway. I must've seen more, but the details had grown hazy. My parents could retain their memories just as fuzzily, and only as a movie they'd watched and let slip away. Their memories wouldn't be *theirs.*

Andrews had been right in telling me they'd never truly remember. Would he win every battle? Put our efforts to shame and remind us of our failures?

"Are you willing to link them anyway?" Ethan had eavesdropped; he'd drifted from the group and stood near us.

"Yes." Helix bowed toward me. "I offer my help as often as you need it."

They awaited my response. I drew the anguish back inside and gave Helix a nod. She'd promised to help, and that meant everything. Even if my parents never absorbed their memories, anything was better than a blank slate.

We caught up to the group, and though uncertainty pinched my chest, it slightly loosened when I told it to go away.

The woods gave way to a plain that sloped down, at its base a rounded building shaped like a sphere cut in half vertically. Silver paneling and endless glass sparkled with a lake's reflection. Orbis had its own lake, forest, and mountainous wall. Smackdab in the middle of nature, without a highway pass-thru, the facility avoided scrutiny in typical MTA style.

We peered at the two-hundred-yard dash between our wooded cover and objective. The windows peppering Orbis' walls, climbing along even its roof, twinkled like mocking eyes.

"Stealth will be impossible," Ethan said.

I searched again. The distance between us and Orbis didn't become any less exposed.

"There may be another entrance," Freia said. "We will scout. Come!" She and four companions proceeded deeper into the trees to scope out Orbis' back.

Helix motioned me away from the discussions. "Only you and I are necessary," she said. "You could bring me to the building as a metahuman would deliver any Hela prisoner."

"I don't have clearance here. If they find out who I am, they're not gonna let me go." I rubbed my head. We'd based our plan to find Jimmy assuming that we'd have sneaking as a possibility. As soon as any of us left our cover, the metas inside Orbis would spot us.

A sharp inhale rasped from Helix. She gripped her forehead, as if pained.

"Helix? What's wrong?"

Seconds passed. When she lowered her arm, it fell like a weight. "Chron. He is here."

My heart pumped harder. "Where?"

"Less than two kilometers."

I swallowed my unease. "Does he know we're here?"

"No. He does not realize I can sense him."

"At least we know. We'll stick to the plan and hopefully avoid any confrontation with him."

"You do not understand, Ella Kepler," she whispered. "He is here for vengeance. He has brought an army."

"An... army? How — how many?"

Helix moved a trembling hand to her heart. "Five dozen."

Five dozen. We had roughly thirty. Some of those were children.

Metas never panicked. They kept cool heads in the face of danger, even the lethal kind — the kind that made survival an uncertainty. Panic blared louder than Helix's words nonetheless. Since she stood equally frozen, I spun toward the clearing of congregated allies and shouted, "Chron is leading an army of five-dozen Grifters here. They're less than two kilometers away."

All chatter ceased. Everyone stared at me. The spell of panic did not sever easily. The forest collected us in it, locking us in dread.

A Grifter aimed a finger at Helix and cried, "You betrayed us!"

Helix froze, seeming to shrink as other Grifters began muttering their approval of that idea.

"Silence," Durgan said, and their voices faded. "These suspicions cause only division." He looked at Ethan. "How do you suggest we proceed?"

Ethan spent ten seconds in furrowed concentration before saying, "Chron is likely here to kill Banks. We need to stop him. If we can make it to Orbis, we'll have an advantage on the roof."

"The metas inside will sound the alarm as soon as they see us," Lydia said.

"We could make a white flag out of someone's shirt," I said.

Everyone shared equal confusion except James, who shook his head. "The MTA won't recognize surrender," he said.

Ethan surveyed the distance to Orbis again. Finally, he said, "It's a risk. We have to take it. If —"

From somewhere in the woods, a shot rang out. It sounded far closer than two kilometers.

"Run to Orbis!" Agent Porter hooked Ly's elbow and scooped Tam right off the ground. "Everyone, run!"

Anxious energy flurried as the Grifters closest to Durgan argued over who should protect him. Ethan darted to my side. I urged Helix forward, but she retreated.

"I must find him," she said. "If he could be persuaded...." She carried little conviction, even before her sentence trailed off.

I knew I merely reflected her thoughts when I said, "He came all this way, Helix, with an army. I'm sorry, I... I don't think he'll be willing to listen."

Her cheek turned like I'd lashed her, but she nodded. "Then we run."

We burst out of the woods and onto the plain, the last trio aiming headlong for Orbis. I ignored the burn of exposure from the front and back. Ahead, Durgson and another Grifter half-carried Durgan in an awkward sprint. McFarland had a hold on Vires, picking up the slack of his wounded leg. Bridget and James were nearly at Orbis, passing Agent Porter as he carried Ly and Tam, one under each arm.

Somewhere behind, another gunshot cracked. Durgan teetered as the Grifter on his left dropped facedown. Barely a second passed before a third shot fired. Pain nicked my arm; I cried out and stumbled. Ethan caught me, asking where I'd been hit. Lightning gunfire echoed over my answer.

"Go!" Ten feet ahead, Lydia flipped around and stuck a palm in the air. A bullet halted an inch from her hand, then tumbled to the grass. "I'll cover you!"

Ethan shoved me and Helix forward. I winced and cupped the sticky wound as he pushed me along.

"Protect the harsk's family!" a Grifter shouted. He'd taken the place of the fallen guard, hauling Durgan alongside Durgson.

Another shot rang. I glanced at Agent Porter in time to see him collapse. Running one moment, sinking the next. Durgan's children rammed into the ground with him. Though they moved, he didn't. But metas always got back up.

Regret squeezed oxygen out until my lungs hurt.

Ethan and I reached Porter and the young Grifters. Ly had wrapped herself around Tam, who kept shaking Agent Porter's shoulder. I blinked past tears, letting the gunshot wound distract me from the icier pain inside. The stinging multiplied when I toted Tam away, kicking and screaming. Ethan carried Ly.

Beneath the full Montana sun, between water and mountains, we raced. Scenery bled by, and Orbis, that domed building, stood grounded in my vision. We could still do this. Get Jimmy, and then— and then what? We couldn't leave with an army on the doorstep.

I leaped for the roof and set down Tam, whom Durgson was quick to wrestle out of my arms. Ly wriggled away from Ethan and flung herself at her father. As McFarland ushered the Grifters away from the manhole hatch that capped the dome, Vires darted to it. Though he never touched it, the cover swung up, and a middle-aged man draped in a lab coat stuck his incredulous face through the opening.

"What on *earth* are you doing here?" the man said.

"Use your eyes, you idiot!" Vires seemed ready to punch the man back down the hole. "This building is under attack!"

Ethan swept past Vires and spoke over the old man's spluttering. "There are five dozen Grifters approaching. What are your defenses? Do you have weapons?"

"Grifters are already on the roof, boy!"

"These are our allies. Do not attack them. Weapons?"

"Th-this is a research laboratory! We don't require defenses!" The man tugged his earlobes and muttered, "Grifter allies?"

"We have our objective," McFarland called. "Kepler and Helix will find Banks. We defend Orbis."

Ethan nodded absently as he surveyed the grounds. His expression relaxed when Lydia jumped onto the roof, sweaty but breathing.

Below, a few bodies lay in the grass. Figures crept from the forest's outskirts. Leading the army that blemished the scenic view....

A Grifter with only one arm.

Something plinked on the roof; a pane of glass shattered. Ethan cried for everyone to assume defensive positions, animos in the front. Freia had yet to return from scouting, but, after Durgan made a gesture, the Grifters listened to Ethan. He took my arm, motioned Helix over, and pushed the old man aside. We dropped down into a hallway.

"Where is Andrews?" Ethan asked the researcher.

"Well... in his office, I presume."

"Take her and this Grifter there immediately."

Registering Helix, the scientist stumbled back. He would've turned-tail and fled if not for Ethan grabbing him by the shoulder. The man fidgeted and swung a chop toward Ethan's arm. "See, here," he said, wagging a finger, "you're very ironhanded for one so young!"

Ethan ignored him. He cupped my neck and pulled me close. "When you find Banks, you leave. We'll keep the fight isolated to the front. If there's an opening out a back entrance, take it."

"And leave everyone here, fighting?"

"Yes. You, Banks, and Helix need to survive."

I... I can't leave you, Ethan.

"Don't think about me. Stay focused." His eyes, bright and wide, caught a flicker of light from the sun. Ethan nodded once, then hopped backward and up. The grate slid shut, and the sounds of battle diminished.

I stared after him, searching for the phrase that would call him back. None of this should have happened. No casualties, no bullets chasing our heels, no vengeful Chron.

Images of Agent Porter fastened to my eyelids. I had to shake them free, take a breath, and get this job done. Jimmy, though he didn't realize it, needed me to focus. All of Whitewash did.

So I opened my eyes and pretended the images had disappeared.

The old scientist was inching along the hallway. I darted past him and blocked his escape. "Listen." I held up my hands, and my arm twinged with an unpleasant reminder. "I don't like reading people's minds without permission, but this is an emergency."

His wrinkles stretched as he gaped. "You're the telepath." He quivered his nose. "They're all on the second floor, in containment! Room nine. Take it, and go." He flung a badge at me, flailed his arms, and ran out of the hallway.

They? Was Kara here too?

The hallway veered left. Helix and I reached a landing, which overlooked the building's four floors. Through the rounded windows facing the lake, Chron's army surged closer. Helix emitted a pained moan.

Below, metas in white coats sprinted every direction, yelling questions. Yes, metas would always be metas, but these researchers had likely not seen a day of training since their time in the academy. They might've been able to fend off a civilian intruder but not sixty Grifters.

Helix and I swung over the railing; who knew where the stairs were? We flipped onto the second floor. Room nine lay toward the back of the hallway. I swiped the scientist's badge. The door hissed and slid sideways.

Cold air gave me goosebumps, and the contents of the room kept them prickling. Containment chambers, each stocked with a body, lined the far wall. The bodies, hooked up to tubes and suspended in goo, varied in size. I checked the first tank, and my stomach churned.

Agent Walker. They were all here, every missing member of Whitewash. In the last tank, One floated.

Jimmy had come here for more than research. He'd stashed Whitewash here, too. Maybe we wouldn't need Helix. I could read One now and see if *he* had the answer.

Each chamber had a "disengage" lever. I tested Walker's first. The machine gurgled. Liquid drained. When the water level dropped below his bare torso, a claw-like mechanism affixed under his armpits, keeping him elevated.

It took a minute for the last drop to swish down the drain. I wrenched the handle in the glass. It opened like a freezer.

Walker's eyelids fluttered. Drenched, gray hairs stuck to his temples. Hesitantly, I fiddled with the mask over his nose and mouth. It popped off with a squelch. He started coughing.

"Walker?" I said.

He slipped and staggered. Helix and I helped him out of the tank. Streams of water followed his footsteps.

"Find me... " he coughed again, crushing our shoulders, "clothes." He wore a loincloth and nothing else. The women fared the same, with an additional chest cover.

"Chron's attacking," I said.

"Come again?"

I gave him a choppy explanation as I disengaged One's tank, then moved down the row. Helix worked in from the other side. Cassidy, Dom, Saini, Lee... everyone but Porter. If we could get them clothed and equipped, we'd gain over a dozen additional fighters against Chron.

Walker, wrenching open every drawer he found, stopped only to help Saini. He guided her from the others and draped a towel around her.

"Why does *she* get a towel while the rest of us freeze?" Agent Cassidy rubbed her arms.

"I'll warm you up." Agent Keswick scooped Cassidy off her puddle and carried her to the drawers. All of them had been emptied. No agent gear, but Walker tossed around towels and black medical scrubs.

He repeated the updates I'd given him. Helix filled in the gaps. I focused on One, handing him a towel. A waxy glisten clung to his cheeks, which had thinned along his bones.

What do you remember? I asked.

One's eyelids twitched. He was roughly three times Emmett's age when he'd died, bald and short, but I could see his former self. See Colette, too, in the curve of his chin. The stormy blue eyes, however, were taken from Nathaniel.

Banks, he said. *He is... Agent Chang was on the beach.* Like ants crawled beneath his skin, spasms flecked his face. *Banks did this to me. I do not understand....*

It's okay. I'll fix him. I'm going to read the memory you stole the day of my birth. We'll free the Tacemus today.

One's gaze lost its sleepy grip.

"Where's Porter?" Cassidy called.

Even drenched, my mouth went dry. I couldn't form the answer. My eyes shot to One, imploring. He looked past me and gave Cassidy the silent truth.

"Dead?" Her pitch rose. "How?"

"Chron," I mumbled.

"Porter will have justice," Walker said. "Let's see to it. Kepler, Helix, and One: hunker down until this is over. Then, you run fast and do what you need to do to free the Tacemus."

"Walker, we...."

When Cassidy's voice broke, I turned around. All her glowering demeanor had fallen away to something childlike. "Look at us," she said. "We're in medical scrubs. Wet. Hungry. Barefoot. No weapons. How do you expect us to survive?"

All eyes focused on him, except Saini's. She turned her head. Walker noticed; his jaw locked, but he breathed through it. "I don't," he said. "But I expect us to get the job done. Chron's likely here for Banks, but if he sees Kepler and Helix, he'll realign his focus. We keep Chron from getting his hands on them, and we've succeeded." The bleak message, delivered in his no-nonsense manner, buoyed the team nonetheless. Cassidy set her shoulders and fiercely nodded. Hina Akamu ruffled Dom's hair. Dr. Lee seemed on the verge of collapse, but his knees never buckled.

"If the Tacemus aren't freed, the corruption never ends," Walker said to me. "You see that it does, Kepler. Understood?"

I matched his gaze, the man who'd impersonated my father while secretly playing that role to someone else. He'd held this group together for years, until the very end.

"Yes, sir," I said.

Walker tipped a salute to his temple. "Operation Whitewash, move out."

A team of metas clad in MTA black trooped from room nine. Helix, One, and I watched them go. Walker held Saini back.

"You stay. We'll need a doctor, and Lee's a moron." He stroked her chin, easing it upward.

"He's not a moron. He only—" Saini's voice gave. Her hands trembled.

Walker pressed her fingers against his lips. Then, he leaned toward her ear and whispered something. She nodded. Walker lingered near her cheek a moment longer, then left.

CHAPTER THIRTY-FOUR

EVEN WITHOUT STRAINING, I heard the battle outside. Jeers, gunfire, thumps. Wars make noise.

"Go, Ella." Dr. Saini had paled. She tucked her damp hair behind her ears and looked nothing like her business-like self.

"I have to read One first," I said.

He nodded. One had craved this moment since the day he awoke a free man.

Lightly, I touched his temple. I understood how this worked. It would only take a second.

EUGENE HAD SEEN COUNTLESS newborns, all of them kin. Eleanor Jane Kepler looked nothing like his mother.

Only the crude cogs of science had delivered this reunion. It offered only a copy, a shadow, the closest Eugene had striven toward his long-deceased mother. It had taken more than two centuries for her gene to manifest, but here it was, borne of two civilians who could not appreciate their daughter's gift.

The baby in Eugene's arms whined. Emmett would have comforted her, but he, too, was a shadow. Living and yet dead. Present and yet absent. The young man at his side was not Emmett.

He is, you sick psychopath, spoke a voice.

Eugene's eyes narrowed. He had not heard this duplicate's voice in some time.

And this is what you've done to him, David Shepherd continued. *He worshipped you, and you've enslaved him for an eternity.*

Eugene almost squeezed the girl too hard.

Oh, I know just how to get under your skin, Eugene. You don't like it when we remember Emmett. Know what he'd see in you now? Nathaniel's lapdog. Still a sorry little kid trying to please Daddy.

Thomas Kepler, busy humming to the baby, did not notice how Eugene's fingers had stiffened—how his aged, wrinkled face contorted as he sought to drown out the voice. How had David found an entrance? Eugene thought he had silenced the man. No matter. Eugene would ignore him.

"So small," he said, returning his focus to the child. "One, come meet Ella Kepler."

I'm going to free him, David whispered.

This provoked a reaction, if only to remind the duplicate of his folly. *Speak all you like,* Eugene said. *You know it is impossible.*

Yes, I saw your halfhearted attempt to free Emmett. You didn't mean it. Even as a little boy, you liked power too much. He knew, too. He knew you'd never let him go. Yet he still loved you.

Rage filled Eugene, though not with its familiar fire. His insides grew cold instead, as if he'd been doused in ice. He felt weak. Like a sniveling rat. He hated David for witnessing it.

Nothing you do will matter, he hissed. *The Tacemus will never hear you.*

You're probably right, David said. *But you know what? Worth a shot.*

As the Tacemus' hand brushed Eugene's, and the baby's wail finally softened into coos, David spoke.

I release you, Emmett.

A shudder harassed Eugene's mind. The effect ended in an instant, and as it faded, it seemed to pull him along. A memory from his youth—Nathaniel's sharp tongue—followed this wind. And then it vanished, and Eugene could not recall what memory he'd revisited. Another tugged at his consciousness, this one belonging to Patrick Davis. It disappeared as quickly as the other, and Eugene watched a third memory come and go, and so the memories swam and dissipated, one per each consciousness contained within his mind. This continued until his latest identity. David Shepherd remembered his first speech as commander, and then forgot it.

He looked to One, the maker and keeper of memories. The face tilted toward his own had ceased to resemble its bland copies. This Tacemus, he *gazed*. He *saw*.

Eugene opened his mouth to wonder, and One did the same. He spoke to Eugene for the first time in more than two hundred years.

"You do not remember entering this room. You do not remember ever discovering Eleanor Jane Kepler."

Even as Eugene fought, clarity mutated. "You cannot. You are under my control. You cannot...."

His limbs weakened. He would drop the child.

Child... what child....
His consciousness slipped.

THE MEMORY SEARED ME with continual heat, even after the replay ended. Understanding took slow root.

Eugene *did* have the power to free them. If he'd given an honest effort in the past, Emmett might've been freed. Now, Eugene hated the Tacemus—but Jimmy didn't. He could free them, just as David had freed One.

I clutched the towel around One's frame. "Jimmy can do it. He can free them."

Then he needs to remember, One said.

"Can you link One and Jimmy?" I asked Helix.

She nodded. She couldn't restore memories, but she could make sure Jimmy saw what Eugene had forgotten.

It felt wrong, leaving Dr. Saini alone as Helix, One, and I headed out. The scientists had dispersed; all that remained below beeped or swiveled, computers and chairs that occasionally rumbled from the commotion outside. I felt a simultaneous appreciation and dislike for the giant windows that illuminated the clashing bodies on the lawn. We turned our backs to it.

I pointed to the doors that peppered the hallway. "He might be—"

A thunderclap cut me off, and the air ruptured. Hot energy threw me airborne. The world was a mess of debris and ash, flung against my skin as I sailed. I smacked into a rigid surface, then tumbled another direction. It must've been down; pain and the nonstop ringing disoriented my bearings. The momentum died when I crashed onto another surface and lay still.

My chin ached, and the pain in my arm quadrupled. I'd landed on my stomach, face first. As I recalled different parts of my body and tested their strength, chunks spat at me, nicking and bruising as the ceiling rained. By the time it finished, I lay covered in plaster.

Beyond the ringing, I detected yells. The floor rumbled, as if an army of hundreds marched. Everything was chaos; my nerves had caught fire. I had to move.

The first attempt made my muscles seize. I pushed off the floor again, shaking. A puff of dust followed the movement. I coughed, flitting my eyes until the haze cleared. Debris fell from my clothes when I stood. My jaw felt wet.

Orbis had erupted, and I'd landed on the bottom floor. Bits of the ceiling and walls still groaned and settled, peeling off where it shouldn't have, causing more shoots of dust each time another scrap fell apart. People were running, metas and Grifters—I couldn't tell whether friend or foe. They kicked through rubble. Computers, tables, fractured doors went flying, causing more mayhem. The explosion had thrown me far enough into the wreckage that nobody paid me any mind.

I crouched low. *One!* I called. *Helix!* We'd been standing near each other. Shouldn't they have landed close by? Any one of these heaps of construction could've concealed them. I began picking through beams and glass, calling their names. Neither answered.

An object whizzed overhead. I dropped flat and shimmied toward an overturned desk. Splinters of wood and glass sliced my arms. *Weaponless* arms. No bracer guns or collapsible staffs. Those had been given to the cadets, since the highway attack had diminished our munitions, and we'd figured they'd need the weapons more than the telepath who was supposed to avoid any battles.

The desk skidded sideways, clipping my head. I got thrown onto my back, stunned. It seemed I blinked a million times, hunting for clarity.

Something yanked me off the ground; my collar cut a line in my skin as a Grifter hoisted me into the air. Not an ally. I recognized this face. Jurstin's gaze conveyed a disgust that could burn.

"The elak puppet," he said.

Durgan's former first officer, who'd handed his king over to Chron after breaking my fingers like twigs. He'd show me no mercy.

I swung my feet and launched off his chest. Fabric tore as, once again, I soared. This time, I braced myself for impact. Jurstin hurried after, but metas were quicker. I landed, rolled out of his reach, and flung the nearest, largest object at him: a computer monitor. Jurstin swiped an arm, disrupting the screen's trajectory.

A figure, blonde ponytail swishing, barred his path. Lydia was airborne, graceful as a dancer. Her feet met their mark on Jurstin, who tipped sideways. She glided off and prevented him from an easy recovery. Wood and plaster took nosedives at Jurstin's face, a shooting range for the animo who never missed.

Partnered for months, Lydia and I had fought together only in class. That had been weeks ago, but both of us appeared to remember how to step around each other, sliding in Macto stances as if proving our teamwork to Leader. She kept up her target practice while I fell into the routines of a ferio, regretting the lag from my injured arm. I kicked his legs in, and he went down amid a hailstorm of debris.

A Grifter's strength doubled a meta's, and Jurstin knew it. He was back on his feet in a blur, shaking off Lydia's tornado that swirled around his head. She stayed back, letting me engage in hand-to-hand. I might've been faster than Jurstin, but I hadn't practiced in weeks, and he could see my injury. He grabbed my upper arm and shoved a thumb into the wound. Pain spiked, fog hazed my vision, and I wobbled. Lydia must've done something to distract him; he let go, and I smacked against the wall, disoriented by agony.

"Get up, Kepler!" Lydia yelled.

With gritted teeth, I gave myself over to meta instinct, not bothering to cycle through counter attacks but letting muscle memory do its job. I tossed a broken beam at Jurstin while barreling toward him. Another figure met me halfway. Her posture in perfect Macto form, McFarland launched herself at Jurstin, landing snug on his back and hooking him in a headlock. Beyond them, Vires flung his pulser like a javelin, and Lydia telekinetically guided the throw.

"Come on!"

Fortunately Ethan had shouted first; otherwise, instinct would've prompted me to slug him when he pulled me away. In the midst of his frantic energy, I wanted to tell him how happy I was to see him alive, but we had no time.

"Get out of here! Helix is—" His voice halted, like a brick had jammed his throat. Something foreign—unnerving—clicked in his eyes. They focused past me, over my shoulder. He staggered back.

I turned. Saw the blonde halo around a fallen body, the tottering staff pinning that body to the ground, and understood.

Jurstin, unhindered by McFarland, unsheathed Vires' pulser from Lydia's chest. Its sticky point dripped her blood. When it swung, red washed the air like rain.

Ethan shouted and charged past, so swiftly I teetered. McFarland had the foresight to leap for safety, right before Ethan planted a boot between Jurstin's shoulder blades. The Grifter got launched into the wall, which exploded as he sailed through. He kept going, maybe blasting apart another wall, but I didn't check. I pinned Ethan's arms to his side and yelled for him to stay put. He detangled himself as if my grip were string and surged forward, but Vires blocked him. He had never looked so pale, nor small.

"We'll—we'll manage the scum." His eyes had grown giant, unyielding in their determination to avoid the bloody pulser on the floor. His weapon, covered in Lydia's blood.

McFarland joined him. The two nodded at each other, checked their bracers, then raced through the hole in the wall.

"Ethan," I said, shaking his shoulder. "*Lydia.*"

At her name, he jerked his glare away from Jurstin's retreat. The expression stiffened when he saw her. Ethan knelt. His hands hovered a moment before he pressed them against her, trying to stopper the gurgle of blood staining Lydia's torso. She writhed, coughing a red dribble.

"Stay still." Ethan's voice had a sharp energy to it.

"Don't be... a dictator." Lydia took in a moist, rattled breath. The movement caused a fresh swell of blood from her chest. Ethan scrabbled to compress it, but she groped for his wrist. "Where... Kepler?"

My legs could barely carry me over. They gave after two steps; I crawled the rest of the way. Why did the battle rage, pounding the floor, when it should have ceased?

Lydia retched; the strain stole her oxygen, and her fingers dug into the chopped up tile. "Kepler?" She searched, frantic, though she relaxed when she saw me. "I'm sorry... too."

I nodded. *It's okay. It's okay, Lydia.* Soon I couldn't see beyond the tears.

"Tell... Durgan...." His name hung on her tongue. She began to convulse, sucking in harsh gasps. The last wheeze drew in, and then out, slow but not steady; loud but not purposeful. Oxygen simply fell out of her. Her eyes were still open, brown muted by tears, by pain... then nothing.

I kept waiting for her request, and when it never came, I searched her thoughts for it. Nothing pulsed on the other end of the line. Not even a buzz, or a warble. My telepathy went nowhere.

"Lydia," Ethan whispered. He didn't move. Nothing happened for some seconds. When the pain finally conquered, it broke him all at once. His jaw trembled. Every mastered facet of Ethan's emotions unraveled, bringing water to his eyes and failing to prevent it from dripping free.

I touched his cheek. He gripped my fingers. Mentally, he apologized a dozen times. I didn't know what for. His thoughts whipped by, disorganized and relentless, a valve that refused to close.

"If you can't fight, you need to move somewhere safe. Okay?" I spoke firmly, faking it for both our sakes. "Ethan. *Please.* Move."

"I won't leave her."

"Then take her with you. But I have to go." I pulled my hand free, though I rested my head on his shoulder. Just for a moment. *Please be safe*, I said.

Walking away hurt just as bad as crawling toward her. At least he'd been at her side when she died.

Died. I'd already accepted it.

Lydia Burnette was dead.

Regret ruptured. Why her, of everyone here? If she, powerful though she was, could die from a well-aimed blow — then who was safe? Not our Grifter allies, not Agent Porter... I dreaded the end of this day, when the tally would be counted.

I tensed at approaching footsteps and ducked around. Ethan's eyes shone; he looked lost.

"What are you doing?" He darted in front of me. "It's dangerous. I'm covering you."

"Ethan —"

"Stay behind me."

This was not an Ethan capable of listening.

Sequestered in Orbis' left wing, we had several yards to go before we breached the thicket of the action. With the center of the building blown away, the fighting outside had nothing dividing it from spilling over. Figures clashed on the lawn and over debris. Black scrubs mingled with civilian clothes, lab coats, and two MTA outfits that meant James and Bridget hadn't met Lydia's fate.

We played a game of constant ducking to avoid flying bullets and whatever else, Ethan always shielding me, his movements more chaotic than usual as he pushed me to the floor. Overbearing — I could dodge on my own. But his thoughts ran on one track: *She can't die too.*

Keeping to the shadows and waiting when necessary, we made slow progress to Orbis' rear entrance, where Ethan had spotted Helix earlier. Even with the building split open, the fighting still stuck to the front. Helix and I should make a run for it, Ethan said. He would find One and Jimmy.

Ten yards from the glass door, somehow still intact and gleaming in the sunlight, a Grifter pounced from a hole in the ceiling. He waved a gun, slim-nosed and pulsing with blue electricity. One gun for Chron's solitary arm.

Ethan knocked me back as Chron's first shot barreled past. The second skimmed his hair. The third came right for his face, a cause for alarm if the target had been someone other than Ethan Sheedy: fast, ever alert, and capable of dismissing the bullet as any telekinetic meta could.

He didn't.

The bullet pricked.

Ethan jerked sideways and fell.

I forgot Chron. My concentration existed for my arms, making sure they moved properly. I caught Ethan, all his uncontrolled weight. Gingerly, I laid him on the floor, guiding his head. Blood drenched my palm. His blood. It poured from his eye, the one bordered by the freckle I'd always wanted to touch. I reached for it, felt the barest hint of contact.

Chron kicked my jaw. My head snapped, and the force slammed me backward. After crashing against my shoulders, I hurried to rise, to return to Ethan. Chron slammed a foot on my chest and pinned me to the floor. *I promised you, Ella Kepler,* he said. Smiling, if a monster could. *You will watch him bleed.*

I stared into the barrel of his gun. He'd stared into mine a year earlier, but I'd redirected. Chron wouldn't.

Instead, he flew backward as if tossed.

I scrambled upright, a fraction of me caring that Chron had seemingly vanished—a fraction overwhelmed by every other nerve shouting for Ethan. Before I could near him, a force hooked my navel. Sucked by an invisible vacuum, my body shot airborne, through the cleave in Orbis that led directly out the roof. The roar of engine and whirring blades chopped overhead. Metal bellies streaked in the clouds.

"Ethan!" I twisted against the power that conducted me. Useless. Someone was controlling my body. Agent Chang had arrived.

Bodies tumbled from one of two aircrafts overhead. The blurs shot past me; a blunt edge smacked my arm. MTA agents, dressed in full gear, unleashed gunfire as they dropped.

"Stop!" I shouted, because they couldn't have known which Grifters were allies. But the wind stole my plea, and the agents wouldn't have listened, anyway. They showed no favoritism. Grifters, scientists, Whitewash: I watched them all fall.

My head clipped a hard surface, then a grip beneath each armpit dragged me out of the Montana sun. I glimpsed black boots, brown dress shoes. Swatting the hands away, I clambered to my feet. Agent

Chang stood in the helicopter. So did Jimmy, dressed like an executive out for a business trip.

"Turn around!" I yelled. "Ethan—"

"He'll either die now or by evening. No more Operation Whitewash." An indifferent divot formed between his brows. Our few days of separation had continued the scuffing away of Jimmy; he looked closer to Andrews than he did my friend.

He motioned to Chang. "Restrain her." He returned to the cockpit, obscured by the headrests of three seats.

By evening. He meant to eliminate Whitewash once and for all.

"Jimmy, please!" I said.

"That isn't my name, Ms. Kepler."

I tried to follow, but Chang kept me rooted in the center of the tiny space, where the wind outside the open door kept lashing my skin. At least my mouth worked, but the endless shouts did nothing to draw Jimmy from the cockpit.

"They're your friends!"

"Jimmy's friends," he said. "I should have killed them earlier."

Chang forced me into one of the chairs. A harness pinned me to the seat like a roller coaster strap. Once Chang looked away, I could fidget, but my arms wouldn't reply. Though my legs could flail, my torso was stuck. A hum emanated from the harness.

Sitting like a fool, I wept, not given the freedom to hide my tears. Eugene Andrews had rooted his claws deep. Unless Jimmy fought back, we had no hope for him, for Ethan, Bridget, James, Kara—everyone I loved, wiped away, and not even a telepath could bring them back.

For some reason, Jimmy had summoned me out of the fight below, setting me feet from my objective. But nothing could happen without Helix or One. My only companions were bad memories. Over and over, I watched Ethan jolting, falling, immobile on the floor with blood covering half his face. This was Chron's punishment for escaping him. Ethan paid the price. Who knew to what extent? I had one sure way to check, but I couldn't bring myself to telepathically reach. What would I do if his mind gave the same silent answer Lydia's had?

Please be alive, Ethan. Please hold on....

"Ten o'clock, Suyin," Jimmy called.

She moved to the open side door. I strained, but she stayed beyond kicking reach. Her arm stretched, controlling something out of sight. I thought of Lydia, then wished I hadn't.

A writhing form rose into view, tossed about by the copter's wind. Helix clung to One, who slumped, unconscious, in her hold.

Desperate hope struggled for momentum. Helix, One, and Jimmy, all where they needed to be.

"The stowaway is fighting me," Chang said.

"Bring the Grifter," Jimmy said.

Agent Chang tossed the duo on board. They crashed into a chair. Helix shimmied out from under One.

Careful, I told her. *She can control people's bodies.*

Helix froze. Then, she hoisted One's body as she hopped upright. Using him as a shield, she charged.

Chang looked down, and Helix's feet skidded. Falling backward, Helix shoved One at Chang. This forced Chang to readjust her attention, unless she wanted One to go flying off the copter. Helix had her opening. Sensing her intentions, I groped for One's legs with my feet, securing him the moment before Helix punched Chang off the helicopter. Getting socked by a building would probably hurt only slightly more. Chang launched into the wind and dropped.

"Man overboard!" the pilot cried.

Helix found an object stuck into One's neck—a blue disc the size of a coin—and pulled it free as Jimmy clambered out of the cockpit. When he saw Helix, One stirring to awareness across her lap, disgust darkened his face. "Don't touch him," he said.

Though his hatred simmered, Helix spoke as if unburned. "You have been searching for me, Eugene Andrews. I am Helix, sister of Chron, and it is *my* ability you want."

Slowly, comprehension worked through the hardness of his expression. While it took its time, I focused on One. *Helix is going to mind-link you,* I said. *Are you ready?*

One's bleary gaze contracted. *I do not wish to see who lives in his head. But I will do what I must.*

Helix's news, once absorbed, served to turn Jimmy more condescending. I hated to see that look on him. "You can hardly blame me for failing to recognize you," he said. "You creatures all appear the same."

"We are creatures, yes, equal to you. But you are not Hela. We are whole in—"

"I am not interested in the philosophical drivel of a pest." He turned toward the cockpit and called, "Give me your stunner, Ward."

By the time he had his desired weapon, Helix had risen to full height, bearing One with her. "The man who shows no humanity is a far more pitiful creature than a pest," she said.

"And a pest who—" Jimmy's response halted. Helix had thrust One closer to him. The two locked gazes and froze.

My single instance of mind-linking with Chron hadn't operated like telepathic retrieval. It had taken longer than a second. As the two stayed bound and Helix concentrated, I could only watch and hope. This was our final effort. If Jimmy couldn't be convinced by what Eugene's memory revealed, we had no other option, short of abducting him again and keeping him isolated until Helix, One, or I figured out the next step. Maybe that was my future. On the run with two clones and a Grifter.

The pilot flew on, evidently unaware of the telepathic exchange behind him. Wind and commotion chopped at each other beyond the open door. I didn't listen too hard. For now, I had to set my fears on hold and hope.

Helix's sudden gasp died to the wind. She staggered back as One clutched his head. Jimmy stared down at him, a layer of Eugene chiseled away. I latched onto the sliver showing through the fractured mask.

"Jimmy?" I said.

The muscles in his cheek twinged. That emotional spasm had to belong to him.

Come on, I said. *Fight this. You can. Remember?* I strained for conviction, feeling the weight of everyone relying on this moment. My efforts came up short. Dread pulsed in my chest, and my plea sounded dull. I had to fake determination and hope it grew genuine at some point.

Jimmy twitched like recoiling from an unexpected shiver. I saw, with painfully sharp meta vision, his doubt retreat. Cunning stole the stage again. He leaned closer to One, who shrunk toward Helix. "Free them?" he said. "Do you truly believe them capable of a virtuous life? A freed Tacemus wreaks just as much havoc. How many *poor souls* have you robbed, One? How many Tacemus have you killed during your crusade?"

One shuddered. Pain broke across his face. As he lowered his chin, a tear raced down one cheek and dripped off.

"Precisely," Jimmy said quietly. "I owe you my gratitude. Because of you, my conviction is strengthened. So long as I am alive, they will *never* be free."

Eugene's long-ago command that the Tacemus stop speaking prevented us from hearing just how successfully Jimmy had broken One, who covered his face and trembled.

I couldn't recognize Jimmy anymore, nor Eugene, the young boy who'd once loved Emmett. I'd thought that boy might've survived all these years, but Eugene *had* died, by his own hand. He'd strangled his goodness and allowed his father's favorite strengths to thrive. If Eugene loved Emmett now, he loved him as anyone loves the object that keeps them alive.

We'd done all we could. Jimmy had seen the truth, and it had only turned him harder.

He aimed his gun at Helix. I opened my mouth to plead, knowing it was useless. She flung herself outside as his shot fired. Then, a tug from below jerked the aircraft.

"Sir," the pilot called, "we're experiencing some drag."

Jimmy peered outside. "The Grifter must have found purchase on the skids," he said to the wind. "Stay sharp, Agent Ward." He pocketed the gun and returned to One. Jimmy forbade him even a moment to grieve; he thrust One into a seat and buckled him with rough motions, unconcerned with the fact that he might've wanted to keep his face hidden.

The helicopter suddenly lurched.

"Bogey!" the pilot cried.

Glass shattered, and the world tilted.

CHAPTER THIRTY-FIVE

WEDGED INTO MY SEAT, I didn't go spinning like Jimmy. It was an odd, uncomfortable feeling, watching the chaos while immune to it. One and I stayed plastered to our chairs, but the tailspin flung Jimmy outside. I shouted his name.

The scenery flashed and collided, the sky and ground blending, a reflective surface joining the picture as the helicopter's swinging grew faster. I closed my eyes and fought the nausea.

When the wind's shriek plummeted, I braced myself for impact. It hit from one side, then the other. The copter bounced; a spray of water doused me in an off-and-on rhythm, like we tumbled around a puddle. The motions decreased to a jostle, and finally a slight rocking.

Even before opening my eyes, I knew we'd landed sideways. Gravity thrust my legs in an awkward direction, and my pulse roared louder in my left ear. I cracked open an eye. Beside me—more like below me—One shook his head.

"One?" I coughed. "Are you okay?"

He glanced up. A trickle of blood zigzagged over his forehead. *You are bleeding.*

"So are you. Can you... " I groaned and uselessly shifted, "can you see a way to get this harness off?"

Jimmy had strapped him in an ordinary seat. He undid the buckle and limped toward the cockpit. After fiddling around with the controls, he found the switch that deactivated the magnetic harness. I would've toppled sideways, but I caught myself on the edge of my seat and scooted off. The scene flipped. Water reached my shins.

The windshield had shattered; the pilot had disappeared. I swallowed and helped One through the jagged mouth of glass. Once out, I dropped off the copter's nose, then guided him into the water. We'd landed in the shallow bed of a lake. The scenery could've gone on a postcard. Water that sparkled pale blue, lush trees framing it, and, like a miniature mountain, a rocky outcrop. The gray stone formed an uneven wall beyond which, if I had to guess, lay Orbis.

"We have to—" Pain flared behind my eyes. I bent over, resting my hands on my thighs. "We have to... find Jimmy and... and...." Air quivered out my nose. Adrenaline faded fast, and panic was emerging. I tapped a slow beat and blamed the thinning air on the Montana altitude.

The immobility gave my thoughts a dangerous freedom; they started roaming over that outcrop, toward Ethan, but I quelled them by jerking upright. One, wearing oversized scrubs drenched in blood and water, looked even smaller beside the lopsided helicopter. Contrasting the machine's black paint and his dark clothes, he seemed translucent.

If I'd had the strength to muster emotion, I couldn't have guessed what I'd feel. Determination, that ingrained meta grit, disintegrated. I didn't know where we were, whether anyone in Whitewash was still alive, what to do now—and if there were even a point to resisting.

That last confession came unexpectedly, and it hit hard. I stumbled a few steps until my knees gave. Even the icy water, drenching my folded legs, failed to snap me out of it.

Free the Tacemus, save the MTA. Walker's command swirled. Free the Tacemus, save Jimmy. But Jimmy had never allowed me to save him. And now, he seemed beyond redemption.

I detected One's quiet voice but couldn't focus on it. Blood dripped onto the lake's surface. I watched it cloud the water. Colette's protean ability had skipped generations and eventually settled on me. Its power expected me to liberate the chained, even if my world got sacrificed along the way. Whitewash had never given me an option. I *had* to buck up, face Jimmy, and convince him to fix this.

But I can't. I'm so tired. Tired....

I lacked the energy to flinch when a hand brushed my cheek. One's touch came gentle, wispy as hair. Maybe he spoke and my brain pushed the words out. Maybe we shared the crippling silence, as we must've done dozens of times, all those childhood memories he'd stolen from me. Something like this moment could have already happened outside my memory: me, too tired to stand, and One, offering his tiny hands in encouragement. *He* had formed Whitewash. Jimmy might've organized it later, giving it a name and new members, but One had taken strides long before Jimmy entered the scene. From the beginning, Whitewash had been a Fallow and a Tacemus. That was how it would end.

I met his stormy eyes. *I'm tired, One.*

I know. You must try a little longer. Then, you can rest.

Metas fought until the end. Lydia had. Ethan would, if he hadn't already. *Until I die,* he'd promised, and he never broke his word.

My heart twisted. *I can't,* I said, but I forced myself to sit upright. Fatigue and water fought against me. Every movement ached. Duty alone pushed me to my feet, the recognition of what I had to fix—if not for any remaining member of Whitewash, then for One. A thud echoed in my chest. A robot's heart, beating because it was programmed to.

When I stood, dribbling water back into the lake, I heard distant sloshing. Not Jimmy; he was gone. Eugene Andrews marched across the lake with his bracer raised. A gash split his lip open; his other arm might've been broken.

"We're leaving, One," he called.

One gripped my hand and stayed put.

Eugene glared. I just stood there as he approached, until his fist came to rest against my forehead. The black padding of a bracer clothed his wrist. It let out a low hum.

"Don't interfere, One, or her death will be slower." His knuckles were flexing. Sweating. They pressed harder into my forehead. "I don't need you alive anymore, Ms. Kepler. You were a curiosity, and I've been sated."

It should've hurt to look into my friend's eyes and find hatred; to feel his weapon buzzing at my skin; to know one twitch of his finger would mean he'd decided my life was useless. Jimmy's disgust would be the last thing I saw if he made it so, but I couldn't stir up any emotion.

The bracer dug. His entire arm was trembling. If he managed not to kill me, he'd bruise my forehead at the least. Eugene's eyes reached a narrowness that seemed ready to precede an explosion. "Get out of my head, One," he spoke through clenched teeth. A pause, then, "I can't be burdened by regret." He laughed dryly. "Love? Eugene Andrews doesn't love anyone."

Small fingers wrapped around Eugene's wrist. A Tacemus was no match for a meta, and Eugene made that apparent by not letting his arm waver a centimeter. But One continued pulling, and then... Eugene's arm lowered, lowered, until it came to rest by his side. His face shone with sweat, and his eyes—they conveyed every ounce of emotion currently drained from me, the most drastic of them despair.

He collapsed in the lake, hunkered over, knees and palms buried in the mud. Sweat dripped off his hair, undone now, a disheveled state that matched the rips in his suit. At first glance, it seemed his telekinesis was frothing the surface. His arms did the trick just fine. They trembled so violently, I wondered how he could prop himself up.

"I'm sorry, sorry, so sorry...." The words were slick, like he'd swallowed a mouthful of the lake.

One crouched beside him, a dangerous position, but Eugene didn't attack when One embraced him. Eugene leaned into the hug, clutching One's frame like he'd sink without it. The two of them couldn't have been comfortable—Eugene with his broken arm, and One crushed by the weight.

I stared at the scene and felt nothing. Either Eugene was acting, or we were getting a tiny glimpse of Jimmy. He'd emerged before. He'd had moments of clarity, yet he'd handed the control back to Eugene every time.

Anger roused me from the haze. I encouraged it, fanning the exhaustion away, embracing anything that could prompt me to stomp across the water and tug One free. "Don't touch him," I said, hiding One behind me. "How dare you."

Eugene glanced up. Behind his bloodshot gaze, an anger equal to mine swirled. He curled his lip, then yelled, "Stop controlling me!" Up he shot, flinging water in every direction. "You're probably bothered that you aren't the cure. That you aren't the one who has to fix them."

"At least I'm *trying*."

"What do you think I'm doing?"

"Nothing!"

"I don't know how, Ella!" He raised his arms, shouting for anyone to hear, if they'd been alive to listen. Wild and panting, he glared at me, though Eugene had centuries of practice in controlling his mood swings. Perhaps the explosion had caught him by surprise; he seemed unsure what to do with it. His arms fell, shoulders drooped, and emotion drained away. "I don't know how," he whispered.

I heard his words, cycling on repeat—and then, louder, Durgan's words, directed to Ethan but meant for me all along. *Saecula saeculorum*, the Andrews motto boasted, but nothing truly lasted forever. Not even our own willpower.

Jimmy's release of frustration carried mine with it. We'd gotten caught up, as we always had. Maybe the familiarity of our arguing had given him his inch of independence—and, more notably, the freedom to admit what he never had. Jimmy *had* been trying. And failing. Because Ethan had finally pinned it right, after an MTA career of getting it wrong. It had taken a Grifter to convince him, but I'd needed Jimmy's admission to force the truth into my stubborn head.

Sometimes, situations were outside our control. We were weak. Resolve wasn't enough. Sometimes, despite every intention to succeed, we utterly failed. None of us wielded the strength alone, not even the meta who'd plotted his own course from day one.

The truth came clearer than the crystalline, untainted lake around my shins. Jimmy couldn't defeat Eugene by himself. He simply lacked the strength.

And that was okay.

I stepped closer, arching my feet, trying to find some equality with his height. "It's okay, Jimmy," I whispered. "I get it now. You *can't* fight him. Not on your own."

It seemed an eternity before he could look toward me. "Then," he said, meeting my eyes like an ashamed cadet facing punishment, "will you... help me?" A spark of fear removed years from his face, painting him childlike, as if he'd never known the MTA.

I took hold of his shoulders and leveled him with my surest expression. "Yes, Jimmy. You're going to free the Tacemus. Right now."

His frame shook; I couldn't have held him steady if I tried. "I c-can't," he said. "He won't let me."

"Think about Emmett. Like David did. Push Eugene away."

"Emmett...." Jimmy searched past me.

One sloshed to Jimmy's side. Rather than encouraging him, the sudden nearness made Jimmy's head violently shake. "Eugene's stronger," he said.

"Maybe he is," I said. "But even he has to fail at some point."

A desperate hunger splayed open his expression. Gone was the mask of Banks, Eugene, and even Jimmy. Hiding under the layers of his tacked-on identities, he was terrified, unsure of himself, as afraid of failing as I'd been. "He... never... fails." Jimmy released the words through clenched teeth. Something darker flicked across his face. Strength—and not the hopeful kind—began closing around him like a cage.

One lashed out, the movement so jarring and unexpected that I couldn't follow his intention until I heard the slap resound. He'd struck Jimmy square across the cheek, the motion completed without a hint of anger or impatience. Jimmy flinched, gawking at One, who stared calmly back. It couldn't have hurt; One's arms carried little strength, but it had succeeded in swiping Eugene away before he finished emerging.

Jimmy and One shared a long gaze that ended when Jimmy nodded, elevating his shoulders and letting out a shuddering exhale. His air felt controlled, though not by Eugene. "We have to do it now," he said to me.

"'We'?"

"Don't you realize? David Shepherd only succeeded because you were there. You're connected to them. Like my... like Colette was."

The compass had spun full circle. Eugene's memory had given me the idea that David had done all the work.

"O...kay," I said slowly. "So where are the Tacemus? Let's go."

"We don't have time. You can reach them from here."

"From here?"

"Stop being dense, Ella."

Now that everything relied on me once more, I cowered. "Jimmy," I said, "I've tried communicating to them long-distance. I can't do it."

"Are you going to make me quote you again?" He tried to tweak his brows, as if I'd asked for homework help and he found me tiresome.

Somehow, seeing him try made me more determined to put forth my own effort. "Okay," I said, mentally fanning away my uncertainty.

His gaze drifted, though he appeared to absorb none of the scenery. "Give this to Kara," he said, drawing the yarn bracelet out of his pant pocket. "He knew you were tracking him, but don't tell her that." Jimmy traced a thumb over the twined threads, telling me to take it but not letting it go. "He wanted you to find him," he murmured. "He called Chron. Invited him here. The goal was to eliminate every setback at once."

The news of Eugene's further manipulations skimmed by me. It no longer mattered. "You can give her this yourself," I said.

"You don't get it. I shouldn't tell you. You'll try convincing me otherwise." Wind gusted his hair, shuffling the strands that already lay in knots. His head was slow in turning back to me. It took even longer for his focus to settle. "The Tacemus are what keep my memories intact," he said.

"Eugene's memories."

"Mine too, now."

"What does that mean?"

"You know what it means, Ella." Jimmy continued that raw eye contact. The exposure was dangerous, unveiling too much. His words didn't hit a wall; they sunk right in.

The Tacemus held Eugene intact, but Eugene was part of Jimmy now. If he disappeared, he'd pull Jimmy along.

That conclusion reached, I switched to the solution. We had answers to memory issues. "One can wipe you," I said calmly. "Then, later, Helix can link you, and you'll remember everything."

Jimmy shook his head as One said, *I cannot take Jimmy away. Only Eugene will be left. He will not free them.* His anguished expression carried too much. One had understood also. I'd been the last to know.

"How... how much are you going to forget?" I whispered.

"I don't know," Jimmy said. "It doesn't matter."

It *did* matter. More than anything.

An argument rolled out. I didn't hear it, had no idea what I'd said. Jimmy's unwavering stare told me it failed to convince him.

"Don't, Ella. Don't make this harder." He gripped my shoulders. "We have to do this now."

"No."

"Yes."

"But I'm a telepath!" I shoved his arms away like they were prison bars. "One can create memories! Helix can link minds! You're telling me none of that matters?"

"Yes!" Jimmy yelled. The tumult spilled into his voice, his posture, flinging his arms skyward once more. "We don't get to end this without a sacrifice. We're metas. Nothing is easy."

I wanted to yell at him, and I opened my mouth to do so. A sob came out instead, and a shriveled, unwanted truth slunk in. The Tacemus deserved freedom, this was the way to do it, and I couldn't stop it. Why? Because the Tacemus needed us. Because it was the right thing to do. Because I was a meta, and metas saw the bigger picture.

Do not fight him today, Ella. One's voice, soft and somewhat chiding, somehow made noise over my blaring reluctance. *Let him save them. This is what he has always wanted.*

My heart revolted, and I nearly screamed my objections. Retracting them from my mental voice proved harder, but I had to quell this for Jimmy's sake, because One had it right. *This* was right. Eugene didn't love the Tacemus, but Jimmy did, and he'd lead them by letting them go.

I spoke the only way I could. *Okay*, I said to Jimmy. My heart pricked over the simple word — a civilian word, really. Metas never said it. None but Jimmy, but he'd never been a proper meta. *I'll help you, Jimmy. And, after this, I'll ask Helix to link us.*

He released a noise that could've been a laugh if not so anguished. "I don't know if you realize, Ella. Her ability is invasive. I'd see everything in your head."

Who cares?

Jimmy hesitated, then quietly said, "I would."

Good thing I'm not you, then.

"Yeah. You're not." He attempted another laugh that gave up somewhere inside his throat. He swallowed. "Kara's in Florida. The Tacemus are in California. Check the jet's travel logs. And tell Walker he's in charge of the MTA. Remove the blue disc in his skin. He'll wake up."

It felt out of place, the wiggle of hope in my chest, but it tried. "You mean... " I whispered.

"The agent used stunners," Jimmy said, "on everyone."

Meaning Eugene hadn't obliterated all of Whitewash in one fell swoop. After this, some amount of normalcy could resume. Except for those already taken before the agents arrived. Agent Porter, Lydia, and....

My hands went icy, and my expression must've conveyed the rest, because Jimmy said, "Sheedy's too annoying to die."

My lips ached with the effort of forcing a smile.

"For what it's worth, he...." Jimmy let the sentence hang before he shook his head and added, "No, my last words can't be that."

"S-stop acting like you're about to d-die."

You both need to hurry, One interrupted.

Evidently, he gave Jimmy the same warning; Jimmy's eyes grew wide enough to betray his fear. He looked down at One, and his resolve visibly crumbled. "I'm doing this for you," he whispered.

Whatever One replied, it was for Jimmy alone.

My fingers flexed, a show of strength that mocked what trembled inside. "Close your eyes," I said, "and think of One."

Obedient as he'd never been, Jimmy squeezed his eyes shut.

I imagined their familiarity. Could I read him, or would I fail again when he needed me most?

Once I entertained the doubt, a dozen more uncertainties revealed themselves, as if I'd blindly followed an ant to its hive. What if this was all a ruse, another of Andrews' manipulations? He hadn't batted an eye, had prompted his own death, because he'd wanted Jimmy to resume his mantle. Everything in Andrews' plans could have been targeting this moment.

Ella. One's voice disrupted the panic. *Are you going to worry forever?*

I thought you weren't reading me anymore, I said.

There are other ways of reading you. Have trust.

In what? Desperation took a stronger hold over my doubt. If not my telepathy, what could I trust to fix this? I'd never heard Durgan's answer.

Trust that help will come. A cool, tiny hand wrapped mine.

I absorbed that small comfort, though One hadn't reached out solely to show kindness. This was an offering. It was aid. But a remedy did nothing unless accepted. So I accepted One's hand, careful not to squeeze too hard, and let him help.

At once, the entryway to Jimmy's mind breezed open, like it had been cracked all along. Leaving my doubts in the doorway, I stepped through.

Eugene's essence was squared and quartered away, patrolling the outskirts, searching for his opening. Jimmy's mind coalesced, a steel trap warding off invasion. Memories of One kept the trap alert.

I am here, One said to Jimmy, and I sensed him stabilizing Jimmy with his spare hand. Somehow, though tiny, he kept us standing.

I'm here too, I added.

Jimmy went on the defensive, a kneejerk mechanism. It wasn't past faults Jimmy wanted to conceal; it was his current reluctance to do what he knew was just. The inner struggle made mine look pitiful in comparison. Jimmy didn't want to go. Now that instances, even the painful ones, were temporary, he craved them all the more, particularly because he foresaw no happy ending. Jimmy believed nothing sat at the end of his final moment but a dead brain.

Braindead—I couldn't think the word. I had to be the traitor, the one egging him on toward the edge of the plank. *Remember why you're doing this,* I said.

I know. He strained for focus, so intently my mind ached. Scenes of Kara drifted by, memories of the way color flushed her cheeks when he complimented her. She was the rope mooring Jimmy to Whitewash, a few happy memories of the academy, and, right where he'd always been, One. There, Jimmy found his center.

El.... he thought. *Not just them.* A snippet of red yarn breathed over his memories.

In a jab of movement, I dropped One's hand and slung mine around Jimmy. He squeezed back. He was tall enough to tower clean over me, but he stooped so our heads butted. This felt nothing like an embrace between two friends. Jimmy was a little boy and I his matted teddy bear.

I care about you too, Jimmy. I should've said it more.

I should've showed it more.

I held him tighter. It didn't escape me that he'd instigated our solitary other hug for the same reason I hugged him now. He'd supported me while One stole my memories. Now, I could return the favor.

We shifted in unison. *Ready when you are,* I said.

He wasn't ready. Never had he so fiercely longed to rebel. Battling himself more than anything, he jumped into action. Though he pictured the Tacemus, One inspired his efforts. *I want you to be free,* he said, not to me. *Take your voice back. I don't want it anymore.*

Unless I acted, his words would go nowhere. Eugene had gotten that part right. One never would've heard David's voice if not for me.

I envisioned every Tacemus, spokes of a shared wheel. I felt pressure shift to my elbow and knew One was doing his part to prop us up. On our own, we would surely fail. Resolve was only half the battle, so we fought what we could and let the rest come from wherever it did.

The term "hive-mind" took form the longer I let my imagination do its job. In the center floated a magnet, and branching off were hundreds of metal pieces. Where the magnet moved, the pieces followed. I registered the connection between us as tangibly as my own consciousness. We were distinct from each other, but they couldn't claim the same. And yet, it felt as if more than a single entity waited on the other end of this link. They *were* multiple; I could see each part and how it connected to the whole. Separate and united. Individual and conjoined. A clover with hundreds of leaves. Instead of dissecting the pieces, I honed in on the magnet and let Jimmy speak.

I release you, he said. *Saecula saeculorum.*

It came not as a domino effect, one crashing into the next. Maybe, had they kept some autonomy, their freedom might've unfolded consecutively. Instead, a shockwave disintegrated them all at once. As they scattered, so did his memories. Mountains of scenes hung in Jimmy's consciousness and then vanished, quick as a snap. Like a collective entity, the memories disappeared—except One. Images of him centered Jimmy, tethering him to reality.

The event lasted mere seconds. I felt each Tacemus, each memory, then nothing but One and Jimmy.

His weight plummeted. I went down with him. We toppled into the lake, me bearing the two of us, keeping him from sinking. Tentatively, I positioned him across my lap. The water carried most of the weight— and a red cut of yarn, floating on the surface. He'd clutched it until the end.

The Tacemus, One said. He moved a shaking hand toward Jimmy's brow. *They are free?*

Mentally, I tugged at the presence that had overwhelmed mine moments earlier. It was gone, and when I searched, never appeared. "Yes," I said, feeling strange that such a small, commonplace word concluded this battle.

And Eugene Andrews? One asked.

He and I stared down in sync. Jimmy's lips were parted, eyes vaguely opened, features as relaxed as someone sleeping. He remained conscious, but barely.

Before attempting a mental scan, I knew I no longer needed One's aid, just as I knew what I would find. In Jimmy's head, a single idea was rooted, unwavering as a tree that had grown comfortable after years of cultivating. Jimmy knew One. Everything else had vanished alongside Eugene, but One hadn't budged.

Eugene's gone, I told One.

He dug into my arm. I couldn't tell whether he meant to prop me up or keep himself steady. The movement stirred Jimmy; he rapidly blinked.

"Jimmy?" I whispered, lightly shaking him. "Are you okay?"

His gaze trekked sideways, an agonizing crawl that took forever to land on me. The empty recognition hurt worse than Eugene's hatred, but the pain lasted briefly; his attention drifted onto One. There, it settled. His eyes widened. "One?" he said. He appeared to register his surroundings—that he lay in the lap of an unfamiliar girl. Jimmy twisted away and must've received another shock at finding himself in a lake; but, with all the agility of a meta, he scrambled upright and looked down at us in his sodden suit, his hair a drippling tangle.

"Who is this?" he said, gesturing to me.

I turned my cheek and assumed One gave an answer.

"No," Jimmy said. "All I remember is... you."

During the silence that followed, I gathered the strength to examine Jimmy again. He was staring at One with a frenzy that seemed unfitting. "I remember promising to help you," he said, stumbling closer. "And I'm going to. But I don't... I...." Shame painted over his intensity.

One stretched out a hand, but the comfort made Jimmy wilt further. To whatever One must've been saying, Jimmy shook his head. He didn't realize that we'd succeeded — that *he'd* succeeded — because he couldn't remember what battle he'd promised to fight. Though scenes of One dominated everything else in his mind, those were fragments of a larger spread he couldn't piece together. Not without the other memories that had defined him. And, even now, Jimmy was still unwilling to ask for assistance.

I stood, wondering when water had become so heavy. "I know you're confused," I began, though Jimmy seemed deaf in his frustration. "It's because your memory is... a little complicated. But don't worry. You kept your promise."

His head rose, and he sought me out. A light bulb never flashed; he didn't spontaneously remember me. But he met my eyes with something close to hope, and that kept me standing. "I did?" he said.

I smiled. "Yes. Yes, you did."

CHAPTER THIRTY-SIX

SUNLIGHT WARMED MY NECK. A pleasant pulse, like a hand. Ethan's hand. I could pretend he stood behind me, scolding me about lagging when a job needed doing. There were still MTA agents in Orbis, after all. We'd won the first step, but what about the second?

Though... what else awaited us at Orbis? *Death and destruction,* I thought, then tried to disregard it. I could just as easily ignore the sun's heat on my skin.

I needed distraction. Something solid and familiar. *Kara,* I thought.

Her mind spluttered with confusion. *Ella? Are you okay? What happened?*

We did it. The Tacemus are free. Eugene Andrews is gone.

And... Jimmy?

He's alive, I said.

Her relief worked on me like wind: calming when it blew but leaving me discontented again once it passed by. Her next questions were about Ethan and everyone else. I had no answers. I told her we'd come for her soon and left it at that.

Come, Ella. One, striding to me as if carried by the water, had lost all sense of worry. The Tacemus were free and Andrews gone; One might've felt that anything else we fixed would only be a cherry on top. *If we hurry,* he said, *we may intercept Andrews' agents before they do worse.*

"How?" I said. "There's too many."

They will submit to him. He motioned Jimmy, who crossed his arms.

"Who will?" he asked.

While One set to explaining, I waded toward the fallen helicopter to search for weapons. On my way, I plucked Kara's red yarn off the lake's surface. It seemed a mercy she'd never regained her memories of him. Losing *that* Jimmy would've been a thousand times harder.

The helicopter provided nothing but a waterlogged gun that, when tested, made a squelching sound. We'd have to rely on Jimmy. He took to One's plan with plenty of suspicion and hesitance. If One hadn't been doling out the idea, I doubted Jimmy would've listened at all. In the sparse minutes I'd spent with this new Jimmy, I recognized Banks more than my friend. At the same time, Banks had understood the MTA. This Jimmy didn't. He knew only One. Everything else working through his mind was snippets of faded concepts.

One took the lead toward the outcrop, the wall that hid the view of what lay beyond. Once I saw that rocky ledge, my heart seemed to wither.

Death and destruction.

I longed for One's buoyed pace. Every step felt leaden. One noticed and slowed. His expression of concern made every pain sharper.

Be happy, he said. *We have won. He can make new memories.*

I nodded. The motion was a lie. Not that I disagreed with One's point. Jimmy was alive, and I was grateful for that. But what of everyone else?

The memory of Chron shooting Ethan haunted me, replaying with unpleasant clarity, giving me no room to refute the evidence. Not even a meta could survive a head shot.

"Chron was aiming at me. Ethan...." I brought my fist to my forehead. Nothing stabilized the shaking, not with that memory so potent. One could make it disappear. I felt halfway tempted to ask.

He touched my arm; Jimmy silently watched the exchange. *Ethan would not regret it,* One said.

"I know."

Ethan would've done it again. And again. As many times as that memory replayed, he would've taken a bullet for me.

Pretending my legs had muscles and not silly string, I forced momentum, carried by an odd, disconnected purpose. The beautiful scenery, so full of life, taunted.

Sparkling through a wall of fir trees, Orbis' reflective shape came into view. One steered us around a barricade of shrubbery. For a moment, we stared at the heaps of bodies strewn around in a fifty-yard radius, from the building to the lake beyond it. Everyone, from those in the tunics of Chron's guards to the elderly metas in white coats, lay passed out. Maybe Andrews had figured instant sleep was more effective than taking the time to kill everyone. Or maybe he'd wanted to leave everyone alive so he could later sort out who deserved death and who might prove useful.

A chunk had been taken out of Orbis, like a peach whose pit had ripped clean through. Its domed form was still intact, though dozens of windows had shattered, and a hole blasted open a section of the back. Unless he'd been moved, Ethan would be on the first floor, near that hole.

We continued, picking slowly over the grass. I wouldn't reach out to Ethan. This unending, bumpy walk in the unknown was agonizing, but not as painful as that potential truth. I'd keep that at bay as long as I could.

We approached Orbis' backside and froze when a figure dropped from the roof, but the agent was busy checking her bracer and turned for the front without pausing.

Her, One said.

I searched her mind and drew out a name. *Agent Ross,* I told Jimmy.

He called across the grounds.

She turned, shielded her eyes, and replied, "Sir?"

Jimmy swallowed. Just once, the only hint that he needed a moment to steel himself. "Tell the others to return to their posts immediately. I will manage this on my own." He spoke smoothly, not a wobbling word to be found.

Of course. He'd always made an excellent actor. Some things never changed.

It spoke to the commander's power that Agent Ross promptly replied, "Sir" and set off.

We stood in the grass, listening to Agent Ross calling out Jimmy's orders, watching the agents congregate around the solitary aircraft. An engine kicked on shortly after. I hoped it could be as simple as that. They'd leave, and we'd sort them out later.

But, as Jimmy had said, nothing came easily for metas.

Bruises shining, Agent Chang stalked into view. We saw each other at the same time. She drew a rifle over her shoulder.

"Are you injured?" she called; the question was for Jimmy.

Call her "Suyin," I said to him.

"I've taken care of it, Suyin," he said. "Join the others. That's an order."

"From whom, Banks or Andrews? I can tell when he's asserting control." She swung the rifle over. "For instance, Andrews wouldn't blink if I killed Kepler. But Banks would."

Chang had it wrong. He wouldn't blink either way. Not over some random girl he'd just met. In a way, I felt relief. Ethan had already taken one bullet for me today.

Before Chang could test her theory, a shot interrupted the quiet. She suddenly staggered, one leg caving beneath her. I darted forward to take advantage of her distractedness, but Jimmy beat me to it. He looped her in a headlock and knocked her unconscious with deft precision.

"If she's a threat," he said, carelessly dropping her, "why didn't you wipe her, One?"

The aircraft took off. Maybe the agents figured Chang had snuck onboard, or else they didn't care that they left her. These weren't Whitewash members or ungraduated cadets, united by loyalty and friendship. If someone dared to stay behind, whether intentionally or not, these agents had no obligation to wait around.

Past Chang's unconscious body, ignoring the aircraft's takeoff and Jimmy's sharp discussion with One, I searched the grounds for our rescuer. Dragging a rifle as stiffly as his legs, Walker hobbled across the plain.

"Walker!" I hurried to him, but he held up his palm. The rifle floated horizontally, its target Jimmy.

I spread my arms wide. "Wait," I said. "Andrews is gone. He's just... Banks, now."

Walker squinted at me. His mustache twitched.

"Also," I added, "you're in charge of the MTA."

"Oh, really?" He flung the gun aside. "Quit standing idly, Kepler. Stun Chang, then wake up our allies."

"How did you avoid the stunners?"

He raised his eyebrows in a way that suggested, *Because I'm Agent Walker.* Then, he limped off toward Orbis.

Chang lay still when I tugged the gun out of her holster. Its orange barrel tapered oddly, and it weighed less than a bracer. When I fired, a blue coin attached itself to her hip.

One and Jimmy headed toward Orbis' front while I moved to the next closest body on the grass. Agent Cassidy sported the disc on her neck. Light flickered to the tempo of her pulse. Like a sticker, Cassidy's chip pulled at her skin when I tried removing it. With a firm yank, I peeled the disc free. A blood globule clung to the stinger in the middle.

She gasped and sprung to her feet, scooping up her staff mid-leap. When she registered me, her face fell. "We're the only survivors?" she said.

"No, the rest are —"

"Why didn't you start with that, then?" Using her staff, she budged me out of her way and marched toward the building.

Fortunately, Chron's army wore a uniform; I avoided black tunics as I scurried to wake our Grifter allies. Once conscious, they darted off to search for friends. Neither Durgan's family, Freia, nor Helix were in sight.

Upon registering the first outfit of black MTA gear, I froze. McFarland's cheek pressed the grass in either sleep or... worse. A disc stuck her in the hand, but Andrews' agents had shot everyone, alive or dead. When I reached, my fingertips brushed warm skin. I coughed out my fear and ripped the disc off.

She rolled onto her back, panting.

"You okay?" I extended a hand.

She ignored the aid and hopped to her feet. Inspecting the grounds, she said, "Where's Reynolds? And... " her speech slowed, "Vires?"

"I haven't seen them yet."

The soldier in McFarland gave way. She'd never appeared so much like a teenage girl. "Avary?" she whispered. "Sheedy?"

My throat sealed.

Her wide eyes spoke volumes, though she was the quiet one. She clipped the worry, for which I was grateful. "Come on, Kepler," she said, squaring her stance. "Let's find our team."

James and Bridget had collapsed by each other, a sight that drew McFarland and me up short. We both knew the other could hear heartbeats, but it seemed she couldn't bring herself to listen, either. She dropped beside James while I tended to Bridget. Her chest evenly rose and fell, the warmest sight in the world. She blinked as the stunner's shock seeped away. Her relief at seeing me alive did massage my chest, but dully. I felt the emotion as if feeling a stranger's.

Coughing drew our focus. Blearily, James sat up, not managing a full rise before McFarland looped her arms around him. "You're all right, Jamesie," she murmured.

He rubbed her back absently, scanning Bridget. "Okay, Avary?" he croaked.

"Okay," she whispered.

We found Vires near Orbis' corner. Even after McFarland wrenched the disc from his shoulder, he remained unconscious.

"Simon!" She slapped his cheek, a fierce thwack that smarted just hearing it.

His eyelids flickered, wide for a flash before they focused on her.

She released a strangled word. "Get up." Her voice cracked. "We need you."

"I know *that*," he said. "Now help me stand."

She pulled his arm, but he paused once their faces neared, maintaining a half-elevated stance. Though McFarland tugged, he resisted, until she finally said, "What are you waiting for?"

"You," he said, a bit uncertain, almost like a question.

McFarland stilled. They stared at each other a long moment. Then, she tipped her head, a brief nod. And Vires, regaining his cocky smirk, let her help him to his feet.

"Where are Burnette and Sheedy?" Bridget asked me.

My chest cinched painfully narrower.

"Burnette fell," McFarland said.

Bridget covered her mouth. A drawn-out moment punched the silence before James spoke.

"Sheedy?" He looked to me, so hopeful, as if certain I'd laugh and say Ethan waited right around the corner.

Even after five swallows, my throat still felt nonexistent. "Chron... " I tried. I wished Bridget could project something happier.

"Chron what?" Vires said sharply.

"Head shot."

That made Vires angrier. "CG can't die," he said. "Where is he?"

"Toward the back."

"Let's go, then."

My footsteps were ungainly; it took several moments before I smelled the smoke and metallic tang emanating from the charred hole in the building. Hope and dread played a vicious match for dominance. I let them fight, not allowing favoritism. My heart would be locked in neutral territory until I combed every inch of Orbis.

Yards away from the back entrance, my legs decided to regain speed. I hurried around James and Bridget, bypassed McFarland, and nearly shoved Vires aside. For the remaining distance, I closed my eyes. If I looked too carefully into the building, scoping out that back hallway, I might see Ethan's body. And then I'd know.

I'd surpassed speed-walking by this point and probably looked ridiculous, closing in on Orbis with eyes squeezed tight, but I didn't care, not even when I plowed straight into someone who'd decided to exit the building the same time I entered it. I mumbled an apology and made to walk around the person, but he held on, not allowing my escape.

My brain knew instantly, pinpointing the familiarity. My heart, still too scared to hope, took longer. I heard Vires call me an idiot amid the other cadets' jubilant voices, then tuned everyone out and gave my telepathy a cautious prod upward.

... *Ella,* he thought. That was all.

Finally, squashed by the strength of his arms, I clenched the front of Ethan's shirt and cried.

Indecipherable commotion stirred around us. Murmurs, random bumps against my back. All at once Ethan and I were swallowed by various limbs. The space between us grew smaller as the cadets wormed their way into the hug. Ethan resisted, securing me tighter. Maybe near-death had something to do with his lack of caution, because Ethan was a squeeze away from cracking me in two.

James' insistence of a group hug continued, Vires loudly arguing, until Ethan called, "Everyone, move."

They obeyed. The air around me breathed again.

Ethan eased back. I stayed put. He had to speak around my head, ordering everyone to report to Walker inside. Once they left, Ethan nudged me off his chest, maneuvering us until we faced each other.

I winced. A square of gauze, stained red, covered his right eye. Ducking into his thoughts, I found that he couldn't see out of it. The wound burned like fire, licking far into the socket.

"Are you injured?" he murmured, scanning me as well as he could. "Dr. Saini should examine you."

"I'm fine. Ethan, Chron was—"

He caught my face, somehow managing one of his intense stares. "What else would I have done?"

"Not let Chron shoot you?"

"I did slow it. If I were an animo, I...." His face contorted, fighting off pain from both fronts, gazing out of the only eye that worked now. It held enough heaviness to count for two.

"I'm sorry," I whispered.

It pained me how intently his jaw worked, monitoring the trembles. I wished he'd let himself mourn. That would've come easier than fighting off the anguish. But Ethan always chose whatever required the most perseverance.

"Come on." He took my hand and turned around, for he wouldn't be Ethan if he ignored matters of business.

I resisted his momentum. "You can lean on me," I said. Then, before he disagreed, I looped my arm through his and guided him down the hall.

He cut off my pace. "No, Ella. I'm going to carry you now." And, though he suffered the worse injury, Ethan lifted me.

I rested on his shoulder and gave up.

Inside Orbis, everyone who could was moving. Grifters and metas worked together in dragging every tunic-wearing Grifter into one area. Along one wall, Saini and the Orbis researchers resembled a swirl of white coats as they bustled to and fro, dumping gauze and medical kits on a salvaged desk. Spread throughout the rubble, our numbers appeared insignificant. I found it difficult to focus on anyone long enough to determine who they were. I didn't want to know who else had fallen.

On the opposite end of the building, Walker looked more bear-like than ever as he loomed over One. Jimmy stood nearby, absently attuned to the conversation, the rest of his focus on the commotion around the floor. He glanced briefly at me but didn't linger.

Ethan paused. He'd seen Jimmy too. "Banks is Banks?" he said.

"Not exactly." Swallowing my sigh, I shimmied out of Ethan's hold. "I have to go to California. That's where the Tacemus are."

Once we emerged from the hallway and had a better visual of the room, we halted again. The wall had hidden what now lay painfully visible: the fallen, set off in one corner. Arthur Finch, still wearing his headphones. Dr. Lee, who could've been napping again. And, attended by the cadets, Lydia.

Ethan lurched. We reached the side wall in seconds. The cadets made room, inching from Lydia somewhat warily. When Ethan and I knelt, though, they closed back in.

"We killed the scum, Sheedy," Vires said quietly.

Then Jurstin was dead. That brought no hint of peace. Ethan's jaw only grew tauter.

More people crowded the area, some bringing additional bodies. I caught sight of Freia, somehow emanating strength even in death. I had to bite my knuckle and look elsewhere, but that only revealed more pain.

"... still with those dratted headphones," Dom Bist was saying, blowing his nose at Arthur's side while Hina Akamu rubbed his back.

Agents Cassidy and Keswick kept silent vigil over Porter. Dr. Saini arrived, saw Lee, and covered her face, not moving until Amy Lane gently took her elbow and guided her forward.

Soon, it seemed all of Whitewash had arrived. In total, we'd lost four: Porter, Lee, Finch, and Lydia. If we included our Grifter allies and the researchers, that tally grew. Still no sign of Durgan, his children, or Helix. I squeezed my hands, scanned the chaos of the room, and didn't exhale until I saw Durgan limping from the clutter, supported by Durgson and Ly, cradling a wailing Tam against his chest.

I bolted upright. *My harsk,* I found myself saying.

He saw me and smiled.

When they neared, the Grifters either bowed or hurried to help. Tam wriggled loose from Durgan and ran straight to Agent Porter, where he threw himself across the agent's chest and wailed harder. Keswick gave Cassidy a doubtful look, but she let Tam soil Porter's shirt and didn't voice a single begrudging remark.

Durgan, performing a visual sweep of the fallen, stopped on Lydia. At once, he motioned the attentive Grifters out of his path. Ethan, who surely hadn't blinked since seeing her, stayed equally unresponsive when Durgan clapped him on the shoulder and knelt. He lay his other hand on Lydia's forehead and murmured something—in Swedish, I realized now. The Grifters responded in kind. Whatever it meant made James' eyes water.

Ethan trembled. With Durgan's fingers still on his shoulder, he dropped his chin and let himself cry.

We made an odd mix: Grifters and metas; Whitewash and the MTA; telepaths, proteans, and clones. Plenty of us barely knew one another. One of us knew only a Tacemus.

Jimmy kept to the outskirts of the circle, towering behind One. He observed passively. This was *his* victory, *his* team. Yet he shared none of our triumph.

"They died well."

Everyone looked up as Agent Walker completed the circle. "This is how they wanted to go," he continued. "Fighting corruption. And they've done it. We won today." He eyed me and motioned for me to rise.

I did so wearily. Would he make me recount that moment on the lake?

"To Kepler," Walker said, "we owe our gratitude."

I shook my head, trying not to notice Jimmy but finding him anyway. Not that my words would mean anything to him. "I didn't do it," I said. "Banks did. He freed them. And he did it for One, the reason Whitewash exists in the first place. So thank One. And Helix, for linking them. And Durgan, for teaching me more than he realized. And his Grifters, for allying with us, and the cadets for making the tough call to leave the MTA."

"Thank Porter too," Cassidy said, regaining her usual glower.

"And Arthur, of course," Dom piped up. "I can't say for certain he ever *did* realize we were in battle, but I'm sure his efforts were valiant."

"And my endearingly anxious Lee." Dr. Saini fussed with the nonexistent creases in Dr. Lee's shirt.

"I'm sure Kepler was including them in her lengthy—" Walker began, but commotion from the dilapidated area interrupted him and made everyone turn.

Helix dragged Chron across the rubble. He appeared semiconscious; his head lolled and jerked. She threw him beside Walker. "He can now be punished for his crimes," she said, "that justice may be paid." She tremored, from her limbs to her words, yet her foot pressed firmly on her brother's back, pinning him.

Chron lifted his head. When he saw every salvaged weapon aimed at him and the plain fact that he was outnumbered, his lips twisted.

"*I* will execute him, Father," Durgson said. He stomped forward, reaching for his belt as if expecting a sword. His fingers scrabbled at air, and he faltered.

"Here." Agent Cassidy tossed her staff.

Durgson caught it. After a brief inspection, he evidently found the weapon acceptable. With a nod, he began again, but Durgan pulled him back.

"Chron will be tried," Durgan said, "as is custom."

The Grifters muttered their protests. One sweeping look from Durgan and they silenced—even Durgson, who clenched Cassidy's staff but stayed put.

"I know what my fate will be." Chron, successfully propping himself up despite Helix's forceful pressure, wore an unnerving expression. A strange mix of hatred and triumph, it pulsed with strength. "Do not delay."

Durgan strode through a crowd that parted for him. Even the metas did. When he settled before Chron, I thought the latter might at least avert his glance. But Chron stared boldly back, still with that eerie glitter.

"This postponement is a mercy, Chron," Durgan said quietly. "Let it be worthwhile. For there is a fate far worse than death."

Chron bared his teeth. Blood and grime stained them. It was enough to unwind anyone, but Durgan merely turned away, his air so calm he seemed to have forgotten who lay behind him.

Walker cast the blackest eyes on Chron and, in a deft motion, unholstered his stun gun and fired. Chron smacked his chin as he collapsed. Only then did everyone seem to remember how to breathe.

"Any resources you need, Durgan: they're yours," Walker said.

Durgan bowed. "I thank you."

Perhaps eager to forget the uncomfortable tension Chron had brought with him, people began chatting, doling out ideas. We had to figure out where to stow Chron's surviving Grifters, still held unconscious by the stunner's power. Where would Whitewash go? Durgan's Grifters?

Those questions were for Walker. I had somewhere to be.

I searched past the bedlam for One. He'd had the same idea; our eyes met in sync. *Are you ready to see the Tacemus?* I asked.

One smiled. *I have been waiting for eighteen years.*

THE TACEMUS' CALIFORNIA CONFINEMENT was the size of a football stadium because it had once been one. Shielding the aerial view of the field was a black tarp, a makeshift roof to hide whoever hid beneath. It lay uncomfortably close to civilian life. We had to fly through downtown to access it.

Walker had understood why One and I wanted to leave as quickly as possible, but he refused Ethan the same leniency. The disapproval made no difference to Ethan, who promptly gave his first disobedient answer. Dr. Saini solved the impending disagreement by reminding Ethan that he still had a bullet lodged in his cornea. He might've telekinetically slowed the shot, but any sudden movements and the bullet could finish the job.

"You're not going anywhere until I remove it," she'd said, and Ethan had reluctantly stayed behind.

Factories billowing fumes pumped on one side of the stadium. Shanty buildings and a river bordered its entrance. The aircraft's autopilot set us in a harrowing landing near the riverside.

One led. Just him and me. It felt wrong, leaving Jimmy behind, but Walker wasn't about to set Whitewash's former enemy loose, regardless of his evident neutrality. Jimmy had disliked that order as much as Ethan had his. He couldn't remember Walker—why should he obey him? Only One's urging had convinced him to listen. We would witness the result of Jimmy's sacrifice without him. It seemed hardly fair. He'd fought for this with everything he'd had.

Trepidation accompanied us to the entrance. When One had realized he was an individual person, the realization had jarred him. These Tacemus had endured hours of confusion; we couldn't predict how they'd react to us.

A lengthy tunnel of a foyer barred us from immediate access to the Tacemus, but confusion had a noise, and theirs was voluminous. They were *speaking*.

One and I gaped at each other. "He... he gave them their voices back," I whispered.

We followed the clamor until the hallway widened into the stadium's mouth. Concrete lay where a hundred yards of grass should've been. Covering every inch, matching in clothes and baldness, Tacemus pressed against one another. For a moment, One and I stood unnoticed and watched their frantic discussions.

Their ages varied between juvenile and wrinkling, all variety of Tacemus interrupted from every stage of life. Outside Eugene's memory, I'd never seen Tacemus so young—and *no* one in existence had seen a group of them so animated.

An adolescent Tacemus, fourteen at the oldest, noticed us first. His gaze grew, and he prodded those nearest. There was a strange thrill in seeing them turn toward us individually. No longer did they act in unison. Each bore his own shock.

The news of our arrival took time to diffuse, but eventually the stadium quieted into shuffling and the painfully loud silence of expectation.

The young observer stepped from the rest, approaching us in desperate confusion. "What," he said timidly, "what are we?"

I had no clue how to address such a vast question. Exhaustion plucked at my bones. When I cycled through answers, the fatigue grew. Right now, more than food, a shower, or even Ethan, I craved sleep. It would come when it did. For a moment longer, I had to be the solution.

I started forward. One caught my elbow.

No, Ella, he said. Earlier, shadows had darkened his face. Those were gone, storm clouds passing by. Light, like a budding flame, caught his eyes. He squeezed my arm and grew a small smile. *You have done your part,* he said. *It's time to rest.*

Automatic protests brushed my lips. Exhaustion won out. I closed my mouth and nodded.

One stepped into the crowd. He looked around at the Tacemus and spoke the answer they'd never known—the one meant for them, not me. I couldn't hear it, but a telepath had other ways of listening.

Your name is Emmett, he told the young boy. *And you are free.*

CHAPTER THIRTY-SEVEN

FOUR MONTHS LATER

COLD AIR PASSED IN and out of my mouth. Running in the dark meant no passersby, not that many civilians trudged around the muck that divided the stadium from the rest of the city's industrial area. More than anything, it was habit. Metas woke at 0430 and ran until 0700. Not every tradition had to die.

I leaped over an overturned barrel yet to sink into the mud. When I landed, my feet slipped. An easy recovery for a meta, but sometimes I liked forgetting my genes. My bottom smacked the ground first, and my elbows went inches in slimy earth.

I fell in the mud again, I told Kara, then wished I could retract it. *Whoops, did I wake you?*

It's Tuesday, El, she thought.

No way.

Yes way.

Oh. I pushed off the mud and said, *Then I'm guessing you're about to drop Kyle off.*

Your guess doesn't count, cheater.

I didn't cheat!

Liar, too.

We argued until she shooed me out of her head.

Over the past four months, Walker had allowed my leave only twice. Once had been to bring Kara to Briarwood. I'd been wary about reuniting Kara with her ailing dad and bully of a brother. However, when Kyle Watson opened the front door, I knew things would be different. For starters, he'd combed his hair. Secondly, I'd noticed the medical logo on the car parked in the driveway. Kyle had picked up Kara's duties and taken care of their dad. The Watson family was no longer broken; just fractured, and those cracks could mend.

My second time leaving had been for a more unpleasant reunion. I'd dreaded the mission. Since realizing the truth about Jimmy's origins, I'd figured the day would come.

George Wheeler, his name as fake as the DNA stored in his MTA file, seemed annoyed by the interruption. His eyes rolled the duration of our two-minute interaction. Hazel eyes, though he wore his hair short, keeping the waves at bay. The buzzed head made him appear older than twelve, but he still reminded me of the Jimmy who'd curled beside me in a playground tunnel and told me I could fear spiders if I wanted to.

The next visit before my return to California took me to a primary school. Traditors proved kinder than most metas. Jacob Corrigan's traditor held his hand as I crouched before him and tried to smile. Tried to look friendly, though my jaw trembled and none of my words came out right. He had a baby face and a mop of hair and teeth too big for his mouth. Jacob was sweeter than George. He beamed when I patted his head and told his traditor he was cleared to return to class.

Both boys had no segregated stacks nor warning signs in their minds. They were ordinary metas and nothing more. I'd passed the message along to Walker. Eugene Andrews' three remaining clones were free of his contamination.

Sunrise gleamed a soft orange by the time I returned to the stadium. Somedays, it felt like a prison. At least I had company — though it was the company that made me feel confined. The Tacemus had plenty to bombard me with, now that they had the freedom to ask. One could only rescue me so much.

The lock disengaged. I passed from winter breeze to the equally cool hug of air conditioning. In the center of the entryway, I stooped over and caught my breath.

"I trained you to be more observant than this," someone said.

My heart kicked this way and that, yelling at me to turn around, but I savored the excitement. Slowly, I straightened, passed a casual hand through my ponytail, then turned. Leaning against the wall, content as if he'd lean all day if duty called for it, Ethan grinned at me.

"You're supposed to be in Rochester," I said.

"No, I'm supposed to be here. Agent Walker needed someone to pick you up." Black hair tickled one eyebrow. The other was obscured. Dr. Saini had fashioned him with a metal patch that fit over the socket. Electric blue streaks, the MTA's color for all things tech, accented the silver. He'd have a permanent reminder of his identity.

He quit his wall perch and stopped before me, frowning. "You're covered in mud."

"Yeah, I tripped."

"What do you mean, you tripped?"

"It means to fall over. Stumble. You should read a dictionary, Kelly."

His eye rolled, either over the tease or the reminder. He was still getting used to the name.

"Are you not going to hug me until I shower?" I said.

"Correct." He indicated his outfit, and I finally registered the slacks and collared shirt. The eye patch had been far more distracting.

"Really?" I said. "Months without seeing each other, and you can't—oh, fine. Be right back." I hurried toward the exit.

He snagged my arm before I got too far, making sure I ran into him and not the doorway. I was sweaty and muddy, but he held me anyway.

"I—" he started.

"Me too," I whispered.

"Missed you." Ethan touched a stray lock of my hair, curling the ends around his thumb. "Stop interrupting me."

"It's a bad habit." I tentatively raised my fingers. "Can I touch it?"

"Why does everyone keep asking me that?"

"Because it looks cool. Do you let them?"

"No. Only you." Smiling, he moved my fingers onto the smooth, warm bits of metal. It wasn't his freckle, but it would do. "*Now* you can change," he said, inching me toward the door. "Don't forget—"

"Dress clothes, I know. By the way." I appraised the smears on his formerly white shirt.

"There's mud on my clothes," he said.

"Worth it?"

"That depends on how much mud."

When I frowned, he laughed and pushed me through the doorway.

In the corner of the ground floor, sectioned off from the rest of the Tacemus, I had my own room. That rarely meant privacy.

"In a second, Emmett," I said, slipping around the young Tacemus barring my door. Only he had kept the original name, though I didn't have to scan the nametag to guess his identity. It was after 0700; Emmett always wanted to know how many birds I'd seen on my morning run.

"But, Ella," he called after me.

I raced to the bathroom. *Four.*

Thanks, he thought.

Once cleaned, I inspected the solitary hanger in my closet, holding an outfit I'd never worn. The dark skirt was stiffly pressed; the white shirt looked neater tucked in. I fidgeted before the mirror, trying not to scrutinize the taped-on picture, but it had a habit of catching my eye. Walker had sent it, along with a note and return envelope addressed to him.

"Found this among his possessions. Return the favor."

He didn't ask how the picture existed. Outside of One, Whitewash had never learned that Jimmy had struck up a friendship with Kara and me. Walker wouldn't know what to make of an image of the three of us. No one would but me, the only person who remembered posing for Kara's camera, Jimmy sandwiched between us, agreeing to smile only at Kara's insistence. This must've been the only physical evidence that our trio ever existed.

Walker knew a thing or two about unexplainable pictures.

One and Emmett waited outside my door. "You're still not coming, right?" I asked One, adjusting my shoe.

Yes, I will stay here. His expression glinted with something close to eagerness, the same since he'd returned from *his* meeting with Walker yesterday. He'd refused to answer any questions then, and he wouldn't now, prodding me out of my room. *Hurry,* he said, gently maneuvering Emmett out of my path.

"But I want to go!" Emmett wriggled away from One and pulled at my arm.

"You know how it is, Emmett," I said. "You can all leave the stadium after Walker's speech. And," I added, unhinging his grasp, "once you're ready."

Anger cast shadows over his young expression. "I don't like rules," he said.

"I know. But they're helpful. Do you want me in your head all the time?"

"No."

"And do I want you to take my memories whenever you're annoyed with me?"

His shoulders slumped; shame booted out the anger. "I wasn't going to," he mumbled.

"Well, that's a relief. I'm on a schedule." I smiled, catching One's eye. His slight head shake revealed his concern. I worried about Emmett too—

about all of them. The Tacemus were no longer blissfully obedient, and they disliked the isolation as much as I did. Sometimes, I had to wear earplugs; memory-wiping didn't work unless heard. But the rebellions were few and the Tacemus willing learners. Just because they *could* manipulate didn't mean they had to. The ability they were born with could only define their actions if they allowed it. If Jimmy could defeat Eugene, the Tacemus could defeat the itch to wipe memories. They just needed to ask for help.

"I'll bring you back something," I said. "How about that?"

Emmett's head shot up, once again an eager boy. "What will you bring?"

"It'll be a surprise." I scooted around them and made for the foyer. "See you guys tonight."

"Bye, Ella!" Emmett called.

Perhaps not tonight, One said.

I doubt Walker will let me be gone that long.

Remember. Rules are helpful.

Touché.

Tacemus appeared out of nowhere to greet me good morning, comment about the day, ask about the upcoming meeting. It took five minutes to bypass them all. Besides being my job to teach them, I did enjoy helping the Tacemus, but sometimes the constant contact left me weary. After a final nod and answer, I ducked into the foyer and pulled the door shut, exhaling. Ethan stood where I'd left him.

"Hi," I said.

He grinned.

ONCE ETHAN CONFIGURED THE autopilot of the small aircraft, he spent the next half hour on the phone with Durgan. The Grifter Management Task Force worked nearly as around the clock as Tacemus Rehabilitation.

Walker had commissioned dozens of teams to force the violent Grifters into hiding. Though word spread of Chron's execution, his rampaging followers—the ones not already detained—only grew angrier. In the end, diplomacy had been the MTA's ally, though not as much as Durgan and Helix. They alone convinced the Grifters to listen, by promising them a security they'd never known. Durgan had passed their idea to Ethan, and he'd passed it to Walker, who spent a day deliberating before finally deciding it seemed the most feasible option. Besides, we owed it to the Grifters after harassing them unnecessarily for centuries.

After years of living in the wild, Grifters would be given MTA housing. We owned countless safe houses and facilities around the country. And one day, the academy buildings themselves would be unoccupied, after we reunited metas with their families. Grifters could live in comfort, and we'd continue to maintain the buildings' mechanics and secrecy. Concealing Grifters — that was what we were best at.

Even after the Grifters had taken to their former shadows, the damage was done. They'd broken the veil between our world and the civilian scene, and no one could shield it again. Supposing we'd wanted to use the Tacemus as clean-up crew, too many phone cameras had caught video footage of the highway attack. Someone needed to meet with civilian world leaders and explain what Grifters were and how they existed. That announcement would take place in a few short hours, and all of Whitewash would be present for it.

No, not all. Some had died. And one had sacrificed his existence to save those who couldn't speak for themselves.

I swallowed, hating the ache for returning. True, it always did, but not normally during daylight hours. In that abandoned football stadium in southern California, I had plenty to keep me busy. At night, the long-suppressed feelings arose. It hurt to wonder about Jimmy. Walker wouldn't let me visit him. My duties rested with the Tacemus, not Jimmy's rehabilitation. Besides, what good would it do either of us? He had no idea who I was. He barely understood himself. A slate wiped clean, he'd awoken into the same confusion as the Tacemus, in a body he didn't recognize with a brain he didn't know. Even if Helix had made herself available, One and I were likely the only ones willing to plug our minds into his, and Walker needed us in California for the *other* job no one else wanted. Any mind-linking was on hold, for who liked Jimmy enough to grant him free access to their entire brain? Kara had, once, but those memories were gone.

His rehabilitation would take longer than the Tacemus'. They, at least, had solidarity in one another. They had One and me. Jimmy had MTA scientists who, in the grand scheme of the MTA's overhaul, couldn't prioritize the therapy of one random meta. Because he was random now, just as insignificant as George Wheeler and Jacob Corrigan.

When not dwelling on Jimmy, the ache steered me toward Thomas and Helen Kepler and the forgotten life they'd given me. They seemed like characters from a novel I'd read as a kid. They slipped from me, and I thought of them less often than I should have. They were trenches in my chest that I couldn't fill—would never fill, though I did have Helix's assurance that, when things settled, she would keep her promise. That day seemed a million years off, so I stayed busy to keep the pain at bay. Honestly, I would have buckled without One. I supposed that happens when you grow up with someone: you tend to mold each other, whether you remember it or not. But I remembered everything now. Every memory One had taken, I'd read them all. I was finally whole. *Hela.*

"You all right?"

I started. Stretched over the center console of the cockpit, Ethan's hand rested on my wrist. On the red yarn I'd been fidgeting with.

"I'm—" I cleared my throat. "Fine. Really."

He thumbed the entwined bracelets, then withdrew his hand and passed it through his hair. An agitated gesture, manifested further by a sigh. I wasn't the only one struggling. Though we rarely discussed Lydia, he thought of her often.

This called for a distraction. Most days, we both needed it.

"Tonight I can badger Walker about your idea," I said. "He can't hang up on me in person."

"Why would your badgering be any more effective than mine?"

"Because I know things about him."

"You expect me to believe that you're capable of blackmailing?"

"Okay, yeah. I'm out of ideas."

Ethan smiled. Then, his phone beeped with probably yet another important message. He set to answering it.

When *not* swallowed by duties, Ethan spent his spare time trying to convince Walker to let him organize a legitimate, public school. Since the MTA was no longer in the practice of kidnapping kids, every future meta would grow up clueless to their potential—until they started breaking furniture and making things float. Those metas deserved a shot at learning how to control their abilities.

Walker dismissed Ethan each time he so much as mentioned the word "train." As commander, Walker was understandably too busy with present worries to start planning for future ones. Margaret Perry might've had something to do with it, too. Walker had joined Whitewash to keep metas with their families, not continue dividing them.

Finished with his phone, Ethan pocketed it, looked my direction, drew his phone back out, pocketed it *again*, then started drumming his fingers on the console.

I frowned. "You're fidgeting."

"Don't read me," he said quickly.

"Well, now I just *want* to read you."

His mouth twitched. "All right, then. Go ahead."

That was a taunt. I knew better than to play along.

"Well?" he said.

"You'll never know if I did."

"I already know you didn't, and won't."

"You're—"

"Annoying? I know that, too."

I clamped my mouth shut. Ethan summoned his grid off the dashboard and settled in his seat with the air of one having nothing better to do.

"Stop looking so smug," I said. "You're as bad as Vires."

"Khalil, you mean."

I snatched the headphones from their hook and dunked them over my ears.

We drifted through the clouds in a comfortable quiet. My finger started an automatic path toward Jimmy's bracelet. I sat on my hand, reminding myself not to dwell.

"I've spoken to Agent Walker about the distance between us," Ethan said in a level volume, despite my headphones and the overall buzz from flying. "He offered a solution. Evidently, he and Dr. Saini ran into the same issue, so they—"

I yanked the headphones off. "Are you asking what I think you're asking?"

"I haven't asked you anything. Yet. If you'd—"

"Ethan Kelly! I can't believe—"

"Ella." He lay his fingers on my mouth. "Stop interrupting, and let me talk."

I tossed the headphones aside—he caught them—and hugged him as well as I could from my chair. The console made for an annoying wedge between us, digging into my stomach. "Okay, go," I whispered.

He took his time with returning the headphones to their proper place and made certain to appear as calm as possible. I registered the stubborn wrinkles that meant he had a point to prove.

"And now you're not going to ask," I said, "just to be annoying."

Another wrinkle formed. "Ella, will you mar—"

"Yes," I said, unable to resist one last obnoxious interruption. I really was a horrible meta.

Ethan tried for an annoyed face, but his grin showed through. "It's going to be a challenge," he said, "loving you forever."

"But you like challenges."

"Correct." And he kissed me.

THE AIRCRAFT HANGAR PUT our Virginia one to shame. This could've accommodated the hangar itself, plus our entire base.

Ethan helped me out of my seat, smiling as he took my hand. However, as we exchanged the cockpit for the cramped cabin, he began fidgeting again. His motions of unlocking the exit hatch carried a jittery hurriedness.

"What now?" I said.

"Don't read me."

"Fine."

Honesty would drive him to spill eventually.

The door hissed open. He edged me forward and let me descend first. I straightened my skirt, absorbing the far-away rafters above and the vast echo of concrete floors. I took in more planes, motorcycles, some SUVs, and didn't see anyone until they stepped into view.

My heart leaped.

"Hi!" Kara said, waving and beaming. Surrounding her stood James, Bridget, McFarland, and Vires—or, whatever their names were now.

"Kar!" I rushed down the ramp. "How are you here?"

"She was here when we arrived," James said. He bounced on the balls of his feet, wearing the dress attire far more comfortably than Vires.

"And," Vires said, pulling at his collar, "for some inane reason, she made us stand here and wait for you."

"But...." I clutched Kara's elbows. She'd gained weight in her cheeks, rosy as ever, and her curls had found their volume again. Her extra giddy grin likely had to do with Bridget; tendrils of elation spiked my pulse. "You didn't say anything this morning!" I said.

"It's called a surprise," she said. "Did Ethan ruin it?"

"Of course not," he said.

"He kept telling me not to read him," I added.

"Ah," Kara said. She and Ethan shared an oddly cryptic glance.

"We should go." McFarland was frowning at her watch. "We'll be late. What happened to your shirt, Kelly?"

McFarland took the wheel of a passenger van. Not everyone had stayed in touch, so we—mainly Vires—wanted to discuss fresh intel and compare—again, mainly Vires—workloads to determine who had the toughest job. While Ethan, Vires, and McFarland dealt with the Grifters, James and Bridget worked in Meta Reassignment, the third task force Walker created. Their duties might've kept them out of physical danger, but no one, not even Vires, could pretend they had an easy job. How did one prepare every oblivious meta for the truth of their origins? Their job required delicacy and tact. Bridget's ability surely came in handy, helping the metas keep calm while Meta Reassignment dropped the bombshell.

Conversation shifted to Walker's speech next. Once he explained our purpose, the MTA couldn't deny its metas' origins. Hundreds of families were about to get a dose of horror. All at once, my stomach churned with it. We grew edgy.

"Sorry," Bridget said, burning red. "I can tell, now, whenever I project."

We released a collective sigh when the tension drifted out the vehicle.

"I keep telling her not to feel bad," James said, ruffling her hair. "She's gotten much better at controlling it. Right, Keane?"

"A little." She peeked at Ethan for some reason, which would've drawn my curiosity, but a tingle nudged my thoughts elsewhere.

"Your last name is Keane?" I said.

She nodded.

Keane. Bridget Keane. Why did that sound so significant?

"Seems a lot of us share last names beginning with 'K,'" James said.

"Excluding James Winston Thorpe, the Fourth," Vires said, "a name I'm tired of hearing."

"It isn't my fault I—"

"Mae Keane is her mom!" I gaped at Ethan and saw the comprehension dawn. "We met your mother when we were at SPO-10!" I said to Bridget. "You look just like her!" When the next wallop struck me, I got so excited I sprung to my feet and hopped. "Your coin! She gave it to me! And I gave it to you!" Then, because Vires was staring at me like I was insane, I told them of Mae's warmth as she cheered me up, then gave me a round trinket, painted like the sun, to hold whenever fear struck. Her husband employed the same tactic when his vertigo hit, a fear he'd passed along to Bridget.

Afterward, it wasn't only my emotion spilling over; Bridget was projecting the full force of her joy, strong enough to take out any birds overhead. She sat glowing a golden honey, freckles swarmed by tears.

Vires cleared his throat. "Keane, you're projecting." He looked ready to bite his cheek in half, but the effort didn't remove the moisture from his eyes.

McFarland parked outside an impressively white building in downtown D.C. The MTA alone operated out of this facility; no worries about running into civilians.

Glossy tile stretched across the ground floor, a vast room empty of all but the MTA's logo and two people. Agents Cassidy and Keswick waved us toward an elevator, Cassidy with a critique on Ethan's shirt and a pointed gesture toward the bathroom. She prohibited him from joining us until his clothes were clean. I was starting to feel guilty.

"Those stains look suspiciously like dirt," Kara whispered, "as if he got very close to someone who tripped in the mud."

"You *tripped*?" Vires, head nearly smacking the elevator ceiling, gawked at me.

"First of all, it was intentional," I said. "Second of all, stop eavesdropping."

"Why would one intentionally trip? In filth, no less."

"Because I wanted to, Vires."

"Khalil," James said.

"*Thorpe*," Vires shot.

"Keane," Kara said, grinning.

"Jordan," Bridget said, pointing to McFarland with a giggle.

McFarland raised her brows. "Out of the elevator, Thorpe. And stop glaring, Khalil, unless you want wrinkles."

"She's worse than Kelly ever was," James whispered to me as we tread onto the hallway carpet.

Behind us, Vires badgered McFarland about whether or not he had wrinkles.

On the highest floor, where an oblong window overlooked the sprawl of buildings, busy streets, and hurrying pedestrians, members of Whitewash congregated in a conference room. Had this been at the academy, Tacemus would've manned the buffet tables. Instead, those crowding the food served themselves, Dom Bist wearing Arthur Finch's headphones around his neck and nodding to Hina Akamu over a steaming mug.

Atop a long table waited the projector which, shortly, would display Walker's pre-recorded speech, aired on the single civilian news channel we trusted. Fortunately, he hadn't written the speech. That would've roughly resembled "The MTA fights Grifters, and all metas were abducted by their parents. Any further questions can be directed to Amy Lane."

In the end, the MTA would stake its claim using words. Not fabrications or illusions. Not the manipulations of a protean. Not even with strength of arm or weapon. Metahumans had come into the world through lies, but when the truth finally demanded its rights, the MTA would do what it had always done: accept the challenge.

The room gradually filled, and the cadets dispersed among those in their respective task forces. That left Kara and me alone to catch up, though she grew oddly discomfited once the cadets walked away.

"What's wrong?" I said.

"Nothing," she said quickly, despite her twisting fingers and encroaching flush. "Don't read me," she added.

"You too? What's with you and Ethan today?"

"Ethan? What about Ethan? What did he say?"

I crossed my arms. "I'm very tempted—"

"Don't!" She flung her hands over my mouth, wide-eyed.

You realize I don't read minds with my mouth, I said.

"Oh. That's true." A sheepish grin overtook the flush as she lowered her arms.

I scooted closer and murmured, "Is this about the *thing* he asked me?"

"Wait. What did he ask you?" Kara gasped and squeezed my elbow. "Did he pro—"

"Good afternoon, girls," Dr. Saini, bearing a polite smile with a hint of apology, called as she neared. "I know I'm interrupting, but I don't see Kelly anywhere, and I need to speak with him."

"I'll show you," Kara said—more like yelped. With all the air of relief, she stepped away from me.

"He's just in the bathroom," I said. "He'll be right up."

"No matter," Saini said. "I'd like to speak with Kara, too." She motioned Kara toward the exit, and Kara took full advantage of the opportunity to flee, nearly beating Saini to the door.

I watched them leave with a frown that tilted upward when Agent Walker appeared in the doorway.

"Agent Walker," Saini said, nodding.

"Dr. Saini," he said, nodding back.

The two passed by each other with no other comment. When Walker caught my grin, he glowered. I hurriedly resumed my frown.

I tried to imagine any reason Saini would need a private word with Kara. Could it have to do with her family?

One? I said.

His thoughts sounded terse. *You are supposed to be with your friends. Spend time with them.*

I will. But have you heard anything bad about Kara's family?

If he could have sighed in his mind, he would have. *No. You are unnecessarily worrying again.*

It's hard not to.

You must try, Ella.

I nodded. We had this conversation about once a week, when the Tacemus were through with their lessons and I found the freedom to think. To wonder. And to worry.

Contentment was fragile, easily fractured, and not in the habit of lingering. Being a telepath compounded the anxiety. Bridget could project outward, but I drew everything in. I absorbed the Tacemus' worry over their unnerving new identities; Ethan's worry over his school idea; Kara's worry that Kyle would revert to his former self, despite every visible proof that he'd changed for the better; One's worry that the Tacemus would forever struggle to adapt—and my worry that I teetered one unpleasant memory away from falling apart.

A fingernail got caught on the yarn before I realized I'd begun fiddling. Sighing, I thrust my hands under my armpits. People-watching always made a good distraction, so I stared. Everyone in the room mingled while I stood in one corner. Alone.

Suddenly, I felt tiny. Had I complained that the Tacemus never gave me peace? I would've teleported back to California if I could've.

I took a step, determined to converse with the first person I encountered. Based on proximity, that would be Amy Lane. She was shy in conversations, meaning I'd have to think of an interesting topic now or risk answering questions about myself.

A familiar figure nudged my peripheral. I switched trajectories and nearly sprinted to Ethan, who stuck to the edge of the room in his journey my way. Probably hoping to avoid comments about his shirt.

"It looks better," I said, indicating the water stains that were a step above mud streaks.

"Repeat? Oh." More noticeable than a damp shirt, Ethan's fitful mood prevented him from meeting my eyes. "Come with me," he said, snatching my hand.

Panic put a bubble in my throat. *What's wrong?* I said. *Is it Kara? What did Saini want?*

"Don't read me."

Stop saying that! It makes it worse.

"I'm sorry. You'll see in a moment." He steered me into the lobby area outside the conference room. Kara, doing a jig in place, shuffled between a couch and potted plant. Their jittery anticipation made my worries multiply.

"Stop," I said, tugging Ethan to a halt. The waiting area was as cozy as the MTA could manage, with seating that looked comfortable, a few decorations, and a lamp that didn't glare with fluorescent lighting. Despite that, I felt nauseated. "What's going on?"

When Ethan set his hands on my shoulders, like *I* was the bomb he needed to disable, my teeth clenched. "Dr. Saini had the idea that Bridget's ability could provide an empathic stimulus for Helix. She thought their abilities could co-function, creating potential for memories to settle when Helix mind-links. But she needed a subject."

"So I volunteered," Kara said. She settled beside Ethan, nervous energy giving way to a soft smile. "Helix linked One and me yesterday, with Bridget there. I remember Jimmy now."

"And I remember the events from SPO-10," Ethan said.

I lost the ability to blink. To breathe. To think about anything but the answer Ethan hadn't given.

Fortunately, he knew how to read me too. Smiling, he brushed my cheek and murmured, "This means your parents' memories can be fully restored."

Everything previously balanced on tenterhooks crumbled. For a moment, I held on to that pit in my gut, the one I'd accepted as my permanent second shadow. Then, with a cough, I let it go. Told it to leave. Commanded it with every assurance that it would obey.

Ethan and Kara slipped their arms around me at the same time. We formed an awkward hug. I couldn't decide who to lean against, so my tears never got the chance to smudge anyone's shirt.

"We didn't tell you our plan ahead of time because we needed to know it would work," Ethan said. "We didn't want to give you false hope."

I nodded. *Thank you.*

"El...." Kara said. Her head lifted; she and Ethan shared their cryptic glance. "Helix also linked us with Jimmy."

My pulse skipped. They'd seen Jimmy? How was he? I nearly dove into Kara's head to find the answer. "You've... you've...." My mouth went dry. Jimmy had been so sure no one would be willing to loan him free access to their thoughts. "You mean," I whispered, turning to Ethan, "you let him in your head? You don't even like him."

"But I like you," he said, and my heart flopped.

"Jimmy's not exactly his old self," Kara said.

"But when you link with him," Ethan added, "and he sees his life through your point of—"

A door slammed. Kara jumped, but Ethan peered over my shoulder and frowned. "I told you to wait," he said.

"You were taking too long."

Everything in the room, from the lamp to those encroaching footsteps, seemed to flicker. Caught in time. Stretched out and humming and blurring all at once. Because I could recognize that voice anywhere, though the voice itself had failed to stop everything in its tracks. After all, I'd heard it in memories centuries old and from someone I never wanted to meet again. The tone—*that* was what I recognized. In just five words, he had bled through, that impatient and annoyed Jimmy.

When he strode into view, he could've been a giant for all the space he took up. He wore leisure pants and the standard white shirt, evidence that he hadn't earned back his old spot on Whitewash's team. I had to dissect his clothing; meeting his eyes felt too enormous. Who would I find in them—Banks? Jimmy 2.0? A half-Ethan, half-Kara mixture?

Ethan nudged me forward. "Banks wanted to officially meet you."

"To thank you," Jimmy said. "Ethan was adamant that I learn gratitude before anything else."

My throat burned, but swallowing proved impossible. He'd called him *Ethan*. He wanted to thank me. This was too foreign. Not Jimmy.

His head turned. "Why is she crying?" he asked Kara.

"Because you didn't keep to protocol," Ethan said.

"I doubt it. She's not as obsessive as you are. But fine. I'll leave." He moved.

"Banks." Ethan disrupted Jimmy's exit by a grip of the latter's shoulder. He steered Jimmy closer to me, and Jimmy let him. "Why don't you introduce yourself?" Ethan said, though not in his stern voice. He sounded like a patient teacher giving advice to his student.

"Okay," Jimmy said. He stuck out a hand.

The three of them waited. Staring. It would be rude to ignore him. Besides, I'd made a promise. It just hadn't panned out the way I'd meant it to. Nothing ever did.

I looked up. There, hair still tousled more than MTA regulation, a quieter shade of Jimmy peered down at me. He looked exactly as he should have, not having developed a random mole or third eye over the months. Nothing about his appearance sounded any alarm bells, but I couldn't bring myself to smile.

"Ethan calls me Banks," Jimmy said.

We'd done this act before—the forced introduction. I'd always initiated it, and he'd always found it childish.

Then, as his hand continued to hover, I observed him more closely. I saw what stirred behind the awkward discomfort. Jimmy thought this was stupid. Somehow, I knew he'd drop his hand if I didn't accept it within the next five seconds. He'd already waited longer than necessary. For me. Because, stupid and cheesy though this was, he wanted to try.

I touched his hand. Sweatier than mine. Neither of us shook. It must've looked ridiculous.

"Hi, Banks," I said.

His fingers twitched. The slightest sigh escaped him. Was he annoyed? I searched again. Another layer—the mask everyone donned when first meeting a stranger—shed away, revealing a hint of something familiar.

My heart thumped, because sometimes hope made noise.

Jimmy noticed. The corner of his mouth lifted with a smirk. "Ignore what Ethan says." He gripped my hand and shook. "I prefer Jimmy."

THE END

ACKNOWLEDGEMENTS

I never thought I'd write a book in which the characters fail at the critical moment. It certainly wasn't my goal when I started this draft. *The Anamnesis* was meant to be perfect and all my characters successful. The more I forced that impossible perfection, the more this story fell apart, until—finally—I realized what my characters were trying to tell me.

I am Ella, convinced everything's my problem to fix.

I am Jimmy, not a fan of asking for help.

I am Ethan, taking the world far too seriously and not sure what it means to lighten up.

This is their story, but it's mine too. At least, it was. Then, God reminded me that *He* shall have His way in perpetuity, and I had to swallow my Vires ego and recognize that I'm too weak to do much of anything.

It hurt. At first.

I resisted. A lot.

In the end... well, you're reading this, aren't you?

Now onto thanks. First in line is my family: Dad, who first introduced me to sci-fi through Dean Koontz books and countless re-watches of *Star Wars*; Mom, the first author I knew, always telling me stories as she brushed my hair at night; my three older siblings, who made sure their baby sister had plenty of reading fodder for her imagination.

Annie, the second person to read those heinous early drafts of *The Trace*, and the reason my story wound up having nothing to do with soccer. You're my Kara.

Erica, who not only coined #*Ethella* but read every variation of this book—including the version where Jimmy dies. Thank you for helping me devise a way in which my dear Jimmy gets a happy ending.

Baj, who daily teaches me that, at the end of the day, it's just a book. You're the PB to my jelly; my soul sista and INF counterpart.

Ash and Han, for unlimited fangirling, beta reading, translating (Ash), brainstorming, nazguling (Han), hashtag-crafting, and the reason I decided Vires and McFarland should probably love each other already. #*Virand4ever*.

Darren, the editor who taught me all the things I thought I knew about grammar and made my writing stronger these past three books.

Thanks for readjusting every awkward sentence and answering every random email. Oh, and for making my action scenes so much better.

My alpha & beta team: Becci (best narrator + name ever); Cora (cat-lady friend for life); Daphne (every word out of your mouth touches my soul); Kelly (when we meet, there will be hugs and confetti); Lauren (who is unfazed by reading obstacles like pregnancy, labor, and delivery); & Vida (maybe one day we'll paddleboard and read simultaneously).

My IG street team: Abby, Breny, Emily, Hope, Lilah, Sara—you all rock! Thanks for all the sharing, love, and support.

Every #Whitewash fan... I can't even. How did I get so lucky? I hope this book answers all your questions ("Are the Grifters the result of scientific experiments?"), satisfied all your requests ("That Ethella ship *will* sail, right?"), and brings you a bit of hope when you feel like you're doing everything wrong. Ella fails a bunch. I do so even more, with masterful precision. We're all weak in this world. And *it's okay*.

Nathan: my patient, selfless, logical, calm, generous husband, who dealt with every shade of my ups and downs. I really don't know how to emphasize to the world how wonderful you are—way better than Ethan, whom everyone assumes I crafted after you. Little do they know Ethan is me. (Though he does harness your rule-followy ways, so thanks for the inspiration.) These books never would've been written without your encouragement; and while you must be rejoicing over the fact that I'll never interrupt you again with outbursts of "I JUST REALIZED MY BOOKS ARE GARBAGE AND SHOULD BE DESTROYED," don't get too comfortable with the silence. I'll need you for my next book. And, you know, for the rest of my life.

Lastly, firstly, and always: I must acknowledge my Creator. How I regret every moment in which I did not have You on my mind. This process sure would've gone a lot smoother had I remembered You more often. Yet You never failed me, though I let You down plenty. I hope to thank You for an eternity.

Or, as they say, *saecula saeculorum*.

ABOUT THE AUTHOR

After her stick figure comic series "The Adventures of The Unstoppable" failed to garner any fans, Adelaide Thorne accepted that drawing would never be her superpower. She also accepted that she was not, after all, The Unstoppable. Twelve-year-old Adelaide never forgot the thrill of adventure, however, and the mystery of heroes, powers, and a bad guy who maybe is only bad because he feels stuck. Or maybe he's just bad, and that's interesting, too.

Adelaide's writing has taken her around the worlds of her brain, and also around a lot of restaurants. After years of being the pickiest eater in the South, she somehow got a stint as a city blogger and food columnist, which taught her that people are too obsessed with queso and not excited enough about chicken noodle soup. She's since said goodbye to journalistic writing and hello to creative writing, which is, after all, what she's always done.

She currently lives in Florida, where she complains about the humidity but never makes any plans to move.

Please visit her at:
www.AdelaideThorne.com
Instagram: adelaidethorne

Stay part of the Whitewashed universe and get exclusive access to Adelaide Thorne's *Project Anamnesis* series — a collection of never-before-seen stories from the perspectives of characters we love and love to hate. Sign up for Adelaide's newsletter for all bonus content, including giveaways, sneak peeks, and more!
AdelaideThorne.com/newsletter

More from Evolved Publishing

We offer great books across multiple genres, featuring high-quality editing (which we believe is second-to-none) and fantastic covers.

As a hybrid small press, your support as loyal readers is so important to us, and we have strived, with tireless dedication and sheer determination, to deliver on the promise of our motto:
QUALITY IS PRIORITY #1!

Please check out all of our great books,
which you can find at this link:
www.EvolvedPub.com/Catalog/

Thank you!

CPSIA information can be obtained
at www.ICGtesting.com
Printed in the USA
JSHW011741021219
2719JS00005B/13